Transmission

By the Same Author

The Impressionist

Transmission

HARI KUNZRU

HAMISH HAMILTON
an imprint of
PENGUIN BOOKS

HAMISH HAMILTON

Published by the Penguin Group
Penguin Books Ltd, 80 Strand, London WC2R 0RL, England
Penguin Group (USA) Inc., 375 Hudson Street, New York, New York 10014, USA
Penguin Books Australia Ltd, 250 Camberwell Road,
Camberwell, Victoria 3124, Australia
Penguin Books Canada Ltd, 10 Alcorn Avenue, Toronto, Ontario, Canada M4V 3B2
Penguin Books India (P) Ltd, 11 Community Centre,
Panchsheel Park, New Delhi – 110 017, India
Penguin Books (NZ) Ltd, Cnr Rosedale and Airborne Roads,
Albany, Auckland, New Zealand
Penguin Books (South Africa) (Pty) Ltd, 24 Sturdee Avenue,
Rosebank 2196, South Africa

Penguin Books Ltd, Registered Offices: 80 Strand, London WC2R 0RL, England

www.penguin.com

First published 2004
2

Set in Monotype Dante by Palimpsest Book Production Limited, Polmont, Stirlingshire
Printed in Great Britain by Clays Ltd, St Ives plc

A CIP catalogue record for this book is available from the British Library

HB ISBN 0-241-14170-2
TPB ISBN 0-241-14268-7

It’s for the Fran

Signal

It was a simple message.

Hi. I saw this and thought of you.

Maybe you got a copy in your inbox, sent from an address you didn't recognize: an innocuous two-line email with an attachment.

`leela.exe`

Maybe you obeyed the instruction to

check it out!

and there she was: Leela Zahir, dancing in jerky quicktime in a pop-up window on your screen. Even at that size you could see she was beautiful, this little pixelated dancer, smiling as the subject line promised, a radiant 21-year-old smile

just for you

That smile. The start of all your problems.

It's not as if you had asked for Leela to come and break your heart. There you were, doing whatever you normally do online: filling in form fields, downloading porn, *interacting*, when suddenly up she flounced and everything went to pieces. For a moment, even in the midst of your panic, you probably felt special. Which was Leela's talent. Making you believe it was all *just for you*.

But there were others. How many did she infect? Thousands? Tens, hundreds of thousands? Impossible to count. Experts have estimated her damage to global business at almost 50 billion US dollars, mostly in human and machine downtime, but financial calculation doesn't capture the chaos of those days. During Leela's brief period of misrule, normality was completely overturned. Lines of idle brokers chewed their nails in front of frozen screens. Network nodes winked out of existence like so many extinguished stars. For a few weeks she danced her way around the world, and disaster, like an overweight suburbanite in front of a workout video, followed every step.

Of course the whole thing made her famous, beyond even her mother's wildest imaginings. Leela was already a rising star, India's new dream girl, shinnying up the greasy lingam of the Mumbai film world like the child in the conjurer's rope trick. But while Leela's mother had thought through most eventualities, she hadn't factored the march of technology into her daughter's career plan. Mrs Zahir was decidedly not a technical person.

And so Leela found herself bewitched – the girl with the red shoes, cursed to dance on until her feet bled or the screen froze in messy blooms of ASCII text. Yet despite what her mother may have thought, she was a surface effect. The real action was taking place in the guts of the code: a cascade of operations, of iterations and deletions, an invisible contagion of ones and zeros. Leela played holi and her clinging sari diverted attention from the machinery at work under her skin.

A chain of cause and effect? Nothing so simple in Leela's summer. It was a time of topological curiosities, loops and knots, never-ending strips of action and inside-out bottles of reaction so thoroughly confused that identifying a point of origin became almost impossible.

Morning through venetian blinds.

A cinema crowd watches a tear roll down a giant face.

The beep of an alarm. Groans and slow disengagement of limbs.

She shuts down her machine and

They sit together in a taxi

A curvature. A stoop.

swivels her chair towards the window and

Someone in the stalls makes loud kissing noises

poor posture

between the two of them a five-inch gap

she takes another bite of her sandwich

laughter

the posture of a young man standing outside a New Delhi office tower.

An arbitrary leap into the system.

Round-shouldered, he stands for a moment and pokes a finger inside the collar of his new polycotton shirt. It is too tight.

Around him Connaught Place seethed with life. Office workers, foreign backpackers, messengers and lunching ladies all elbowed past the beggars, dodging traffic and running in and out of Palika Bazaar like contestants in a demented game. For a moment Arjun Mehta, consumed by hesitation, was the only stationary figure in the crowd. He was visible from a distance, a skinny flagpole of a boy, hunching himself up to lose a few conspicuous inches before making his entrance. The face fluttering on top wore an expression of mild confusion, partly obscured by metal-framed glasses whose lenses were blurred with fingerprints. Attempting to assert its authority over his top lip was a downy moustache. As he fiddled with his collar, it twitched nervously, a small mammal startled in a clearing.

Finally, feeling himself as small as he would ever get, he clutched his folder of diplomas to his chest, stated his business to the chowkidar, and was waved up the steps into the air-conditioned cool of the office lobby.

Marble under his feet. The traffic noise suddenly muffled.

Behind the front desk sat a receptionist. Above her a row of clocks, relic of the optimistic 1960s, displayed the time in key world cities. New Delhi seemed to be only two hours ahead of New York, and one behind Tokyo. Automatically Arjun found himself calculating the shrinkage in the world implied by this error, but, lacking even a best estimate for certain of the variables, his thoughts trailed away. For a moment or two the image hung around ominously in his brain – the globe contracting like a deflating beach ball.

It was punctured by a cleaner pushing a mop over his toes. He frowned at the man, who stared unapologetically back as he continued his progress across the lobby. At the desk the receptionist directed him to a bank of elevators. Stepping out at the eighth floor, he walked up and down a corridor searching, with rising panic, for Office Suite E. Just as he was beginning to think he had been given an incorrect address, he came to a door with a handwritten sign taped over the nameplate: INTERVIEWS HERE. He knocked, received no reply, knocked again, then shuffled about for a while wondering what to do. The shuffling did not seem to help, so he kneeled down and polished his smudged shoes with his handkerchief.

'Excuse me please?'

He looked up at a prim young woman in a peach-coloured salwar-kameez.

'Yes?'

'Would you mind moving out of the way?'

'Sorry.'

She brushed past him and unceremoniously pulled the door open to reveal a waiting room filled with nervous young people, sitting on orange plastic chairs with the peculiar self-isolating stiffness interview candidates share with criminal defendants and people in STD-clinic reception areas. The woman swept in and announced herself to a clerk, who checked her name on a list and assigned her a number. Consumed by his own inadequacy, Arjun followed.

The candidates squirmed. They coughed and played with their hands. They pretended to flick through magazines and made elaborate attempts to avoid eye contact with one another. All the seats were occupied, so Arjun picked a spot near a window and stood there, shifting his weight from foot to foot and trying to reboot himself in positive mode. *Listen, Mehta. You don't know how many positions Databodies has open. Perhaps there are several. The Americans have a skills shortage. They want as many programmers as they can get.* But such a number of applicants? There were at least fifty people in the room.

The air-conditioning system grumbled, failing to counter the heat gain from the mass of sweating job-hungry flesh. Candidates fanned themselves with filled-out forms. Chairs squeaked under moist buttocks. There were three interview rooms in simultaneous operation; and, as people were called in and others arrived, the scene around Arjun changed like a time-lapse photograph of some uncertain natural process, neither generation nor decay. Whenever a seat became free he willed someone else to take it, the illogical hope growing inside his chest that by staying very still and quiet he could preserve himself, would not have to pass through any of the three frosted-glass doors.

'Mehta A. K.?'

He stared hard out of the window.

'Mehta A. K.?'

It was no use. The woman with the list was speaking to him. Weakly he put up his hand and allowed her to show him into an office, where she indicated a seat in front of a pine-veneer desk. On the far side, legs ostentatiously crossed, lounged a man who appeared to be less a human being than a communications medium, a channel for the transmission of consumer lifestyle messages. From his gelled hair to his lightly burnished penny loafers, every particular of his appearance carried a set of aspirational associations, some explicit (the branding on his tennis shirt, his belt buckle, the side arms of the UV sun goggles perched on his head), some implicit (the heft of his Swiss watch, the *Swissness* of that watch) and some no more than hints, wafts of mediated yearning written in the scent of his scruffing lotion, the warp and weft of his khaki slacks.

Arjun tugged at his collar.

'Sunny Srinivasan,' said the channel, leaning over the desk and shaking hands. 'So how are you today?'

Sunny Srinivasan's features were regular and well defined. He had the polite yet aggressive air of a man who enjoys competitive racket sports. When he spoke, his words rang out with decisiveness and verve, his dragged vowels and rolling consonants returning the listener to the source of all his other signs of affluence: *Amrika*. Residence of the Non-Resident Indian.

'Arjun Mehta,' said Arjun, immediately kicking himself for forgetting the transatlantic mode of address. 'I mean, nice day. I'm having a nice day.'

Sunny Srinivasan opened his mouth, unhooding a smile like a

dentally powered searchlight. 'I'm glad to hear that, Arjun. Everyone should have a nice day – every day.'

Arjun nodded gravely, shrinking a little further in his chair. The careers counsellor at NOIT had more than once told him he lacked positivity. Sunny Srinivasan, by contrast, exuded the stuff. Here was a fellow who had patently experienced an unbroken progression of nice days, stretching back into the mists of what had probably been a very nice childhood. As Sunny reached out his hand to relieve him of his documents, Arjun marvelled at his skin. Every section of the man not covered with luxury cotton casual wear seemed to glow with ostentatious life, as if some kind of optical membrane had been inserted under the epidermis. He glanced down at his own arms and hands, ordinary and unremarkable. They looked like the 'before' illustration in a cosmetics advertisement.

As Arjun considered skincare, Sunny flicked through his certificates, holding one or two up to the light. 'So,' he concluded, 'it all looks *most* excellent. What I need to know from you now is how much you're bullshitting.'

'Bull –? What do you mean?'

'Well, Arjun K. Mehta, educated to B.Sc. standard at North Okhla Institute of Technology, on paper your qualifications look good. Not great, but good. The question is, are they real?'

'Entirely. One hundred per cent.'

'Glad to hear it. Half the losers out there in the waiting room bought their diplomas in the bazaar. Another quarter have completed some two-bit nightschool computer course and faked it up to look like a college education. But you, Arjun, you're telling me you're the real deal. Right?'

'Absolutely. Real deal. Thumbs up. As I said on my application, I can provide references. I am skilled in all major areas – networking, database –'

'Let me stop you there.' Sunny held up his smooth, lipid-nourished hands. 'You don't need to wow me with all that. I'll tell you a secret, Arjun: I don't know the difference between SQL and HTML. And I don't care. To me it's all letters. What I care about is butts, good properly qualified desi butts sitting on good American office chairs, earning good consultancy dollars for Databodies and for me. Understand?'

'Absolutely,' murmured Arjun. Sunny Srinivasan was appearing more impressive by the minute.

Sunny leaned back in his chair and clasped his hands behind his head. 'So what I'm going to do is this,' he announced, as if the thought were the product of long rumination. 'I'm going to take your application, get you checked out by my people, and, if you're telling the truth, I'm going to send you to America and start making you rich.'

Arjun could not believe it. 'Just like that?'

'Just like that, Arjun. When you're a Databodies IT consultant, things happen. Your life starts moving forward. You start to become who you always dreamed of becoming. That's our mission, Arjun. To help people become their dreams. That's what we stand for.'

'And you can guarantee me a job in America?'

'Boy, good programmers like you are gold dust over there. Everyone knows American college students are only interested in cannabis and skateboarding, right? You leave it with me. If you're telling the truth, you're going to be raking in the dollars just as soon as we can get you on a flight.'

Arjun could barely contain his gratitude. He reached across the desk and clasped Srinivasan's hand. 'Thank you, sir! Thank you! Have a nice day!'

'No, thank *you*, Arjun. Good to have you aboard.'

Several thousand miles away, in a picturesque yet accessible area of the Masai Mara game reserve, India's dreamgirl clutched the rim of the basket as she felt the balloon break contact with the earth. The propane burner roared, and, as instructed by the director, the pilot crouched down by her feet to keep out of shot. There was a sickening lurch, the wind blew her hair across her face, and she tried to keep smiling at the glass disc of the camera lens as it receded fifty, eighty, a hundred feet below her. Soon the crew and all their mess of lights and cables were lost, one more dark patch mottling the savannah. When she felt it was safe to stop smiling, she relaxed her face muscles and asked for a drink of water.

*

Arjun Mehta walked back out on to Janpath, grinning at the drivers leaning against their cars at the taxi stand. Amrika! Becoming his dreams! More than any other memory of the meeting, even that of Sunny's sunglasses, this phrase stuck in his mind. His current favourite daydream was set in a mall, a cavern of bright glass through which a near-future version of himself was travelling at speed up a broad black escalator. Dressed in a button-down shirt and a baseball cap with the logo of a major software corporation embroidered on the peak, Future-Arjun was holding hands with a young woman who looked not unlike Kajol, his current filmi crush. As Kajol smiled at him, the compact headphones in his ears transmitted another upbeat love song, just one in the never-ending library of new music stored in the tiny MP3 player at his belt.

As the bus trundled over the Yamuna Bridge, past the huge shoreline slum seeping its refuse into the river, he ran several variations of this basic fantasy, tweaking details of dress and location, identity of companion and soundtrack. The roar of public carriers receded into the background. Lost in his inner retail space, he stared blankly out of the window, his eyes barely registering the low roofs of patchworked thatch and blue polythene by the roadside, the ragged children, standing under the tangle of illegally strung power-lines. High in the sky overhead was the vapour trail of a jet, a commercial flight crossing Indian airspace en route to Singapore. In its first-class compartment sat another traveller, rather more comfortably than Arjun, who was squashed against the damp shoulder of a man in a polyester shirt. Did Guy Swift sense some occult connection with the boy on the bus 30,000 feet below? Did he perhaps feel a tug, a premonition, the kind of unexplained phenomenon which has as its correlative a shiver or a raising of the hairs on neck or arms? No. Nothing. He was playing Tetris on the armrest games console.

He had just beaten his high score.

Guy Swift, thirty-three years old, UK citizen, paper millionaire and proud holder of platinum status on three different frequent-flyer programmes. Guy Swift, twice Young British Market Visionary of the Year and holder of several Eurobrand achievement awards. Guy

Swift, charter member of a Soho club, a man genetically gifted with height, regular features, sandy-blond hair which tousled attractively, relatively inactive sweat glands, clear skin and a cast-iron credit rating. For two years he had lived with the reputedly unattainable Gabriella Caro, voted the most fanciable girl in her class every year of her studies at the International School of Fine Art and Cuisine in Lausanne. He had the number of the door-picker at the Chang Bar on his speed dial. You would have thought he was untouchable.

Guy's seat had eight different parameters, all of which could be adjusted for his comfort and well-being. The airline had provided a pouch of toiletries, a sleeping mask and a pair of disposable slippers embroidered with their new logo. He rifled through the pouch, ignoring everything but the slippers, which he turned over and over in his hands. A recent trend report had hinted that the airline was about to break the taboo on yellow-accented greens in the cabin. But the slippers and accompanying items were still presented in the conservative blue colourway. Was this, he wondered, a failure of nerve?

'More champagne, sir? A drink of water?'

He took a glass from the smiling female attendant, unself-consciously bathing in the soft-porn ambience of the moment. Mentally he noted the experience as a credit on the airline's emotional balance sheet. He enjoyed the attendant's android charm, the way this disciplined female body reminded him that it was just a tool, the uniformed probe-head of the large corporate machine in which he was enmeshed. He (or rather his company) was paying this machine to administer a calculated series of pleasures and sensations. Respectful of its efforts, he had for the last four hours been sitting as immobile as a hospital patient, relishing them one by one. The heft of china and glass, the frogspawn dampness of a miniature pot of eyegel.

The flight was well into its nocturnal phase. The cabin lights had been dimmed. His fellow passengers had put aside their complimentary copies of the *Wall Street Journal* and settled into various states of trance. They fell within the standard demographic, these first-class people, balding business pates anaesthetized by meetings and conference-centre hospitality, glossy retirees occupying the stewards with long lists of requests. He settled a pair of headphones into his ears and pressed play on his current favourite personal soundtrack, a mix by DJ Zizi, the resident at Ibiza superclub Ataxia. Zizi, who bestrode the Uplifting Ambient scene like a tight-t-shirted colossus, had chosen to call his mix 'Darker Shade of Chill'. It was, Guy thought, a good name, because although dark, the music was still chill. Breaking surf, feminine moaning and fragmented strings were countered by foghorns and echoing piano. DJ Zizi was comfortingly committed to the centre ground.

The music trickled into Guy's brain, slowly clearing his mental space like an elderly janitor stacking up chairs. He had a sense of angelic contentment. Here he was, existent, airborne, bringing the message of himself from one point on the earth's surface to another. Switching his laptop on, he tried in a half-hearted way to compose a mail to Gabriella, but, confronted by the blank white screen, he could think of nothing to say.

Some way below him, in one of the newer sectors of the North Okhla Industrial Development Area (acronymically known as Noida), there was more to communicate. Horn Please. Bye Bye Baby. Maha Lotto. Dental Clinic. Everyone wanted everyone's attention, and they wanted it now, from the State Bank of India to the roadside proprietor of Bobby's Juice Corner. No. 1 in affordability. Inconvenience Regretted. Lane Driving is Sane Driving. Sunny Honey. Suitings Shirtings. All the action of Noida fizzed through Arjun's sensorium without leaving a trace. Love's Dream. Horn Please. *Aishwarya Rai, on a schooner, whatever that is, some kind of boat, in Sydney Harbour. Or Venice. On a schooner in Venice . . .*

Horn *please*?

Despite his father's frequently vocalized suspicions, Arjun felt he was in no danger of confusing his daydreams with reality. His desires expressed themselves as images of a world which appreciated the importance of the principles of prediction and control. Reality was Noida. The gap was too great.

The promotional literature called it the 'new industrial fairyland of the nation'. In the mid seventies the Uttar Pradesh state authorities had realized that the area on the east bank of the River Yamuna was rapidly becoming a de facto suburb of Delhi. Farmland was giving way to a chaotic sprawl of factories and shanties. The government started a programme of compulsory land purchases, and, amid corruption and speculation, the displacement of many people and the enrichment of a few beyond their wildest dreams, they zoned a huge grid which promptly exploded with life, generating a city of half a million people in less than twenty years. Shopping malls, multiplexes, temples and stadia jostled for position with hectare upon hectare of new twenty-storey blocks, built in every imaginable variant of discreet low-cost modernism.

The bus dropped him on the corner, and he picked his way through building rubble and piles of unlaid sewer pipe to the gates of the BigCorp Industries Housing Enclave, soon to be renamed H. D. Kaul Colony, after the company's managing director. Greeting the chowkidar, who was hunched over a transistor radio following the cricket, he made his way across the parched lawn into the stone-clad body of Tower No. 4, Gleneagle House. No. 18 Gleneagle House was Mr Mehta senior's greatest source of personal pride, the chief perk of his Move. The leap from government service (whose values had been so eroded over the years) to the private sector had paid off. The Mehtas were no longer the family of a small-town administrator but modern people, participants in the great Indian boom. The apartment was proof. It stood for The World, with which his son appeared to be disastrously out of touch.

In real life, Arjun just stared at his feet when his father lectured him. In his head he issued fluent rebuttals. In many respects his daydreams were superior to Noida. Noida was upheaval. A properly organized daydream had formal coherence. It could respond to commands, reconfiguring itself according to well-understood operations. Outcomes could be built in as required. Obviously the preferable choice.

But dreaming was penalized. If you ignored the world, it tended to ignore you back. Though he held several class prizes and was once a runner-up in a national computer problem-solving competition, Arjun's certified honours were not as impressive as they ought to have been. He had scored badly in the IIT entrance exams, a failure which his disappointed teachers put down to 'lack of focus' but more accurately was due to focal misdirection, the star comp. sci. pupil having got obsessed during the crucial revision period with constructing a database of his all-time favourite films of the 1970s, searchable by name, cast, director, box office takings and personal critical ranking. As a consequence of his passion for cinema, his (entirely genuine, non-bazaar-bought) higher education had been conducted not at one of the prestigious Indian Institutes of Technology but at North Okhla, a middle-ranking school which had the compensatory advantage, felt more keenly by his mother than by Arjun himself, of allowing him to live at home while he studied.

He was still at home two years after graduation.

'Mummy? Mummy?' He bounded into the hall, almost knocking over Malini the maid, who was carrying a glass of tea.

'Oh, sorry, Malini. Ma, are you there?'

'Yes, Beta. Come through. I'm only resting.'

He flung open the door to his mother's bedroom and gave her the news.

'Mummy, I'm going to America!'

He might as well have said *prison* or *be trampled by horses*. Letting out a groan, she buried her head in her hands and burst into tears.

It was to be expected. As an Indian mother, Mrs Mehta's prime directive was to ensure that her first-born son was never more than ten feet away from a source of clean clothes, second helpings and moral guidance. She expected to have to release her child eventually, but only into the hands of another woman, whose family tree had been thoroughly vetted and whose housekeeping could be easily monitored from the vantage point of a chair in the living room of No. 18 Gleneagle House, into which the girl would naturally move. America, unhandily located several thousand miles away, was known to be populated by females who would never dream of starching a collar, and whose well-documented predilection for exposing flesh, drinking alcohol and feeding ground beef to unwitting Hindu boys was nothing short of an international scandal. Hardly the place for her beta, her unmarried 23-year-old baby.

Arjun, who felt he did not really understand emotions as well as he might, made the gestures you make when you are trying to comfort someone. Disconcertingly, when his father came back from the office he started to cry as well. 'My son,' sobbed Mr Mehta, 'America? Oh, my son.' Even Malini was at it. At least Priti, his younger sister, seemed unmoved. She was hopping up and down behind her father's shoulder with impatience. 'What about my news? Is no one even vaguely interested in what happened to me today?'

For a long time Mr Mehta had been unable to feel altogether optimistic about his son. Something about the boy emanated muddle, and if thirty-five years of line management had taught him anything, it was that muddle is prejudicial to career success. News of a job in America was most affecting. His joy was augmented by the thought that finally he had got one back on his brother-in-law. Arvind, the sala in question, was the owner of an aggregates firm, with a contract to supply gravel to the Gujarat State government. He and his preening wife lived in what could only be described as a mansion in one of Ahmadabad's most exclusive colonies. They had dedicated a statue at a local mandir; there was a photo of them standing next to it, with some sadhus and a minister. Their unappealing son Hitesh had for some years been employed by an artificial-flavourings company near Boston. For as long as Mr Mehta could remember it had been Hitesh this, Hitesh that. Hits is topping fifty k. Hits is team-leading a push for a new minty-fresh aroma. And all the while his own fool of a boy never seemed able to keep his head out of filmi magazines. But now Amrika! God be praised!

Of all the Mehtas, the one with the best excuse for crying was Priti. She loved Arjun dearly. It was good he had finally stopped being such an idiot, but her parents were only going bananas over him because he was a boy. Why should he get chucked on the cheek for every fart and belch, while she made her way in the world with the bare minimum of encouragement? Since she had passed her communications degree, all her parents appeared to want was to marry her off to the first all-four-limbs-possessing boy who wandered through the door.

As it happened, Arjun was not the only one to have a new job. But did anyone care? Did anyone even notice? Finally, after her parents had phoned almost everyone they knew with her brother's news and her father had put the receiver down at the end of a particularly gratifying call to Ahmadabad, she got to tell them.

'What do you mean you've never heard of DilliTel? They're only the most dynamic call centre in the city!'

She explained the New South Wales connection, how she would be 'in the hot seat', providing service and support to customers of one of Australia's biggest power companies. Her mother asked why she needed a job at all. Wouldn't she rather stay at home? Her father frowned over his spectacles, grappling ineptly with the fundamentals of modern telecoms.

'What?' he asked. 'You mean they call on the telephone here, all the way from Australia?'

'Exactly. These big companies find it cost-effective.'

'Cost-effective? It must be like throwing money down the drain!'

'Daddy, they buy capacity. The customers don't pay. They don't even know they are calling abroad. It's such a great job, Daddy. I'll receive training in Australian language and culture. We all have to be proficient in vernacular slang and accent, and keep day-to-day items of trivia at our fingertips.'

'Trivia?'

'Sporting scores. Weather. The names of TV celebrities. It adds value by helping build customer trust and empathy. As operators, we even have to take on new Australian identities. A nom de guerre, the manager calls it. What do you think of Hayley?'

'Namda-what?' spluttered Mr Mehta. 'Now look here, young lady, what all is wrong with your own good name?'

Her mother nodded in agreement. 'Beti, I don't like the sound of this at all. It doesn't seem decent. Why can't you tell these Australian fellows to call you Priti or, better still, Miss Mehta? That would be so much *nicer*.'

Priti had been trying her best. The tears would not stay in any longer.

'I don't believe it. I do something good and you throw it in my face. I hate you! I hate all of you!'

'Don't you talk to your father like that,' snapped Mrs Mehta, but she was chastising her daughter's departing back.

Mr Mehta looked towards God and the ceiling. 'This is what comes of too many TV channels. MTV, lady fashion TV, this, that and what all TV. No daughter would have spoken to her father in such a way when we were having Doordarshan only.'

'She's turning into one of these cosmopolitan girls,' said his wife. 'I think we should find a boy for her sooner rather than later.'

Mrs Mehta went off to poke a ladle into Malini's dal. Mr Mehta turned back to the business section of the *Times of India*. Arjun quietly slipped into the corridor and knocked on his sister's door. When Priti did not reply, he turned the handle and went in. She was lying on her bed, her face buried in a pile of pillows. He perched beside her, trying to devise a strategy to cheer her up.

'There there,' he said, and patted her shoulder. A muffled voice told him to go away. Obediently he stood up and was about to leave when the voice changed its mind. Priti's face was red and there was a string of snot hanging from her nose.

'Well done, Bro,' she said.

'Well done, Sis,' he replied. She swung her legs off the bed and for a long time they sat together in silence. At the beginning this was comfortable, but questions were preying on Arjun's mind, and finally he felt compelled to speak.

'Do you think you'll have to acquire facts about surfing or is it restricted to team sports?'

Priti looked at him. It was the kind of look which usually meant he was wearing mismatching clothes.

According to *Guy Swift: The Mission*, a summary of aims and ideals which its author had sometimes found occasion to distribute as an A5 spiral-bound document, 'The future is happening today, and in today's fast-moving future the worst place to do business is the past. I strive to add value by surfing the wave of innovation. I will succeed.' He had always liked the Skywalkeresque note of the last sentence, and the Force had indeed been with *Guy Swift: The Mission*. As a written text it had helped its author win contracts and assert his authority with new clients. As a seminar it had once even led to sex, with a McKinsey analyst who had a thing about PowerPoint presentations. In three short years Guy had grown *Tomorrow** into an agency with an international profile. *GS:TM* had undoubtedly played a role in that success.

*Tomorrow** was, he liked to say, different from other agencies. It produced results.

Results*

In a glittering career Guy had raised awareness, communicated vision, evoked tangible product experiences and taken managers on inspirational visual journeys. He had reinforced leading positions and project-managed the generation of innovative retail presences. His repositioning strategies reflected the breadth and prestige of large portfolios. His communication facilitation stood out from the crowd. Engaging and impactful, for some years he had also been consistently cohesive, integrated and effective over a spread spectrum.

At the heart of *GS:TM* lay a philosophy (or, as Guy preferred to put it, a 'way') he had synthesized from a study of the great marketing masters. He called it *TBM*, which stood for Total Brand Mutability. During his twenties he had dabbled in the youth sector, helping the agency he worked for to develop the well-known CAR triangle, whose three corners are Cool, Attitude and Revolution. Having helped to sell an unknown quantity of sporting footwear, alcopops, games consoles and snowboarding holidays to CAR-starved under-thirties in Britain and Continental Europe, he had experienced what he described as a personal epiphany, the realization at a full-moon party in Thailand that his future lay in the science of 'deep branding', the great quest to harness what in *GS:TM* he termed the 'emotional magma that wells from the core of planet brand'. 'Humans are social,' he would remind his clients in pitch meetings. 'We need relationships. A brand is the perfect way to come together. Human input creates awareness and mines the brand for emotion. In a real way, the more we love it, the more powerful it gets.'

For Guy, love was the message. Love the brand and stay ahead of the curve. Much of *GS:TM* was devoted to the nature of the curve and the crucial importance of adopting a forward position in relation to it. Even so, the document's 800 bullet-pointed words and Hokusai Wave intro-graphic left much unsaid about Guy Swift's personal relationship with the future. In certain places – on moving walkways, at trade shows, in car showrooms – he felt it was physically connected to him, as if through some unexplained mechanism futurity was feeding back into his body: an alien fibrillation, a flutter of potential. Heading, say, towards the Senator Lounge at Schiphol Airport, he would feel it coming on, a chemical lift that would grow as he checked in, blossoming into full presence as he stepped through the dimensional portal of the metal-detector into the magical zone of TV monitors and international-marque goods. Surrounded by people on their way to other places, he would feel cocooned in the even light and neutral colours of a present that seemed to be declaring its own provisionality, its status as non-destination space. Then it was a time to grab things: a bottle of Absolut Citron, an open-face prawn sandwich, a magazine. Like the objects buried with ancient kings, these items had only a temporary purpose: to help him get from where he was to where he was going, to ease his transition into the next world.

When, like Guy, you put yourself ahead of the curve, you live in the future. Literally. How else are you to understand it? It is as if you have become subject to a freak physical effect, a blurring which stretches you out beyond the trivial temporality of the unpersonalized masses of the earth. Unlike the package tourists, the high-street shoppers and all the other yearners and strivers, your existence is extreme. The thrills are tremendous, but they come at a price. When Guy slept, he dreamed of tall buildings. He knew that the tiniest lapse of concentration, the smallest failure of response, could send him tumbling down towards the place of discount clothing outlets, woodchip wallpaper and economy chicken pieces. Sometimes at night his twitching took on a regular myoclonic rhythm, a constant cycle of fall and recovery. Boom and bust.

Over the years Arjun had given a lot of thought to Silicon Valley. As a prime daydream-location, it had gradually been elaborated into a lost world, a hidden ravine lined with fibre optics and RadioShacks, where surfer girls accompanied you to films viewable on day of international release and the number of available flavours *N* was always *n*+1, where *n* was the total when you last looked at the menu. *The Valley*: so exciting that, like Lara Croft, you had to rappel down a cliff-face to get in. One up. Player Mehta, proceed.

The first obstacle was the visa application process. He spent days gathering supporting documentation, days sitting for portrait photos and filling in forms, then more days at the American Embassy, submitting the whole bundle in a formal-looking brown envelope. At the embassy he stood in line, part of a jostling crowd of applicants kept in order by a pair of uniformed guards. In every eye there was the same determined blankness, a thousand-yard stare directed at H1B migrant status, at a dollar-denominated future.

Next he had to face the wrath of Khan. Since graduation, Arjun had been employed on a part-time basis by Indus Fancy Products Pvt, a firm owned by the brother of one of his college professors. To Mr Khan, the discovery that his employee preferred America to the export of a wide range of marble and onyx handicrafts was a frank betrayal. 'There is the matter,' he growled, wagging a bony finger in Arjun's face, 'of loyalty. And the matter of patriotism. Who has trained you to do this work? India! Who has provided the schools? What do you think it means for you to take yourself abroad, instead of using your talents for the good of the nation?'

Arjun replied (silently) that if India had wanted him for something it would probably have asked. Aloud he mumbled that he wanted to earn more money. Mr Khan's pockmarked face turned an unnerving purple, and he embarked on a speech which commenced as a taxonomy of those who rejected the nurturing breast of Mother India (the *ingrate*, the *coward*, etc.), then broadened to touch on Pandit Nehru, hydroelectric power, the Bandung Conference of 1955 and the insemination by one another of apes, pigs and dogs. When he began to shout, Arjun beat a retreat, watched by a startled group of clerks.

His mother was behaving erratically. She was (according to Priti) attempting to stave off anxiety by shopping. Whatever the cause, she insisted Arjun trail round after her as she bought the sweaters, scarves, hats and ayurvedic medications that would be necessary if her boy's delicate constitution were to withstand the American climate. Occasionally, in the face of some violently patterned piece of knitwear, he would try to introduce the possibility that his baggage allowance would be very small, or suggest that California might not be as cold as she thought. She dismissed such notions out of hand.

In the evenings Mrs Mehta's twin preoccupations were sewing on name tags and the problem of Priti. As she sat with her work-box, she fretted that paid employment would expose her daughter to undesirable influences and dent her marriage prospects. Mr Mehta was inclined to agree, until he realized how much Priti would be earning. Abruptly he started to incorporate the notion of a call centre into his image of himself as a modern man. 'My dear,' he told his wife, 'it is all a question of the presently booming service sector. What training could be more appropriate for a girl?' In this way the matter was settled. Quietly, without fanfare, Priti started to make the daily commute to DilliTel.

As the day of his departure approached, Arjun spent an increasing amount of time in the bathroom, the only room in the house with a lockable door. Its white-tiled dampness had a soothing and womb-like quality. One day he was in there, sitting on the toilet reading a paper on genetic algorithms, when there was a commotion in the living room. He emerged to find that his brand-new passport had been returned, with its American-eagle visa stamp on the clean first page. 'Sweet as!' said Priti, in her new servicing-Australians accent. Then, a little wistfully, 'Nice one, Bro.'

Despite repeated phone calls, Databodies was unable to tell him where he would be working, or where exactly they had arranged for him to stay during his first weeks in America. One morning they simply sent a peon to his home with a plane ticket: one-way to San Francisco, travelling via Singapore. A note explained that he would be met at SFO by a company representative.

'Sfo?' murmured Mrs Mehta suspiciously. 'This sounds more Russian than American.'

On his last evening Arjun went to the underground bazaar near his home, to make some final travel preparations. Even late at night the bazaar was a bustling place, where tape decks blared movie songs and hard white light washed out the colours from stalls selling polythene-wrapped shirts, cooking utensils, office supplies and electronics. On the lower level, next door to a wedding emporium, was Gabbar Singh's Internet Shack, a room with peeling walls and half a dozen PCs crammed on to a pair of trestle tables. Its only decoration was a poster of Amjad Khan, leering down threateningly against a background of leaping flames. The manager, Aamir, a skinny Muslim boy a couple of years older than Arjun, was proud of the gangster style of his establishment, which he fostered by leaning intimidatingly against the wall outside, smoking bidis and wearing dark glasses. There was usually a free terminal.

That night Gabbar Singh's was completely empty. Seeing Arjun, Aamir put down his new 'torso tiger' chest exerciser and gave his usual greeting, cocking his fingers into fake pistols and firing a volley of imaginary shots. Then, formalities over, he slapped his friend on the back and slipped smoothly into a sales pitch for his latest CD-ROM production.

'So what are you calling it this time?' Arjun asked, sitting down on one of Aamir's wobbly chairs and opening up a terminal window on the screen in front of him.

'*Too Too Sexy 2*.'

'So it's a sequel to *Too Too Sexy*?'

'Achcha! Hot as hell, I'm telling you. The theme is blondes.'

'The theme is always blondes, Aamir.'

'Thank God for full creative control. So, bhai, you will take a copy?'

'Talk to me later, OK? I have things to do.'

Aamir looked disgruntled. 'Whatever you say, boss. Just remember, eight hundred plus lovely ladies on single disk is once-only-in-lifetime opportunity. Don't turn up your nose.'

Arjun nodded and started to type commands at the prompt. He used to wonder how Gabbar Singh's stayed in business, until Aamir revealed his sidelines. The disks, compilations of downloaded pornographic JPEGs, were only one of several revenue streams. He also pirated software, retailed second-hand hardware, and hired himself out as an occasional web designer, computer tutor, wedding videographer and (so his business card claimed) 'superstar movie hero / villain'. Rebuffed for now, he dragged a chair into the store doorway and sat reading the film gossip in *Cinéblitz*, singing along tunelessly to the Hindu religious songs pumping out of the wedding store.

Meanwhile, using a password he should not have known and a user name assigned to someone else, Arjun logged on to the network of NOIT, an institution which mistakenly believed it rescinded all access to students when they graduated. The discovery that Arjun had an active account would surprise the network administrator, Dr Sethi, who was under the impression he was very careful about such things. Tell the doctor that an ex student possessed full root privileges, the power to alter or delete data and the ability (among other things) to monitor every other user's activity, and he would have dismissed you as a fantasist.

Yet Arjun could do all this and more. He had enjoyed unimpeded access to Dr Sethi's beloved system since his very first term at NOIT.

No one had ever noticed Arjun's unauthorized presence, since he had always taken care to conceal it, especially when making his own alterations to the configuration of the network. If so inclined, he could have wreaked havoc at any time, but havoc had never been on his agenda. Why destroy something so interesting when you could be creative instead? That night, as usual, he bypassed the directories containing the college accounts, the Principal's private correspondence, the staff payroll information, next term's examination papers and Dr Sethi's private archive of bodybuilding pictures. Instead he accessed an innocuous-looking subdirectory, one that the doctor had probably never noticed or, if he had, no doubt believed was full of old log files or other uninteresting artefacts of his system software. Arjun chose a small executable from this subdirectory and ran it. The little program generated a second log-in screen at which he typed a second password, thus gaining entry to his own private area of the network, a zone which over the years he had gradually partitioned off and screened from other eyes.

A secret garden. A laboratory.

He allowed himself a quick peek at one of his projects, then got down to the tedious business of backing up, selecting files and copying them to his local drive, a process which, over Gabbar Singh's patchy connection, took the best part of an hour. While the blue bar inched across the screen he wandered upstairs and drank a sweet milky coffee at a dhaba facing the main road. It was raining. The traffic, as usual, was relentless, the low rumble of public carriers blending with the clatter of taxis and the angry buzz of auto rickshaws into a full-spectrum roar that never diminished, even this late at night. Small boys ran after the buses, selling corn and peanuts. Soaked cyclists pedalled past with plastic sheeting over their heads. For a while he joined the crowd participating in the aftermath of a traffic accident. A two-wheeler lay on its side, and various people were arguing with the driver of the white minivan which had knocked it over. The shaken scooter driver sat on the kerb a little way off, pressing a handkerchief to his head and staring blankly at an opportunistic stallholder who was trying to sell him a helmet.

Arjun headed back underground to Gabbar Singh's, where he used Aamir's cherished rewriter to burn a couple of CDs. All his best toys were now etched on to the little silvered disks, ready to travel in solid state to America. Next he cleaned up: he deleted his data from Aamir's machine and before exiting the NOIT system ran a script that erased all traces of his session from the school's logs. Behind the walls of his secret garden, which existed not so much apart from as *in between* the legitimate areas of the college network, his various experiments were still running their course, stealing spare processor cycles from idle machines, storing themselves in tiny splinters on dozens of different hard disks. Together these fragments formed an interstitial world, a discreet virtuality that could efficiently mask its existence from the students and teachers doing their online business round about it. It was a world which could look after itself for a while, until its creator had time to check on it properly. Until he was successfully installed in California.

Arjun packed the disks into his old purple backpack. He was about to walk out of the door when he remembered something.

'By the way, Aamir, I won't see you for a time.'

'Bhai?'

'I'm going to America.'

'No, you don't say! For holiday?'

'No, for work. I'm going to be an engineer in Silicon Valley.'

Aamir shook his head in disbelief. 'So you're going to do it?'

'I am.'

'Just like you said.' Aamir looked impressed, but, as he thought through the matter, his face clouded. 'I am happy,' he said, holding up his hands. 'Yes, I am happy. But what I am saying is that really you should go to Hollywood. That's where the action is.'

'Not any more, Aamir.'

'Arré, not in Hollywood? Pagal! What will you rather run your fingers over, computer keyboard or Cameron Diaz? Bhai, you are hundred per cent sure you don't need some hot pictures? Loneliness is a terrible burden.'

'No, Aamir. They have real girls there, remember.'

'Achcha . . .'

Leaving Aamir shaking his head at all the out-of-reach blondeness in the world, Arjun hurried out of the bazaar into the rain.

The next day Mrs Mehta woke early, and after a light breakfast spent her morning squeezing name-tagged woollens into a pair of new vinyl suitcases, already bursting with packages of sweets, nuts, homoeopathic remedies and soft fruit. Arjun stayed in bed for as long as possible, then fiddled around desultorily with batteries and toothbrushes. Finally, unable to bear his mother's frenetic preparations, he locked himself in the bathroom. Only when it got too dark to see without switching on the light did he come out again.

The last supper was an ordeal. Various relatives were present, all in a state of high excitement, but Arjun was so nervous he could barely bring himself to eat. This upset his mother, who took it out on Priti, telling her off for toying with her food and for saying it would taste better *on-the-barbie*, an Australian style of tandoori cooking. Only Mr Mehta was straightforwardly happy, marshalling helpings of rice and dal into his mouth with the air of a man for whom mealtimes had recently revealed themselves in a very positive light: as a celebration of family life, an expression of the joy of producing and managing successful and in-their-turn-productive children, not worthless after all, who would soon be providing for one during a prosperous old age.

Finally it was time to leave for the airport. Uncle Bharat took photos and Cousin Ramesh panned a video camera across the scene as Mrs Mehta performed aarti to bless the traveller, placing a lamp on a brass tray and circling it high and low in front of Arjun as if he were a statue of God. Saying a prayer for his safety and swift return, she fed him sugar and placed a red tilak mark on his forehead with her thumb. Then, sniffling a little, she slipped a garland of marigolds round his neck. Arjun dipped down impatiently to touch her feet, then those of his father.

'Can we go now, Ma?' he pleaded.

'Beta, the plane will not fly off without you.'

'Ma, actually it will.'

'Don't be so silly.'

Though his flight was not scheduled to depart until three in the morning, a total of eleven people were staying up to see him off. After a delay which he experienced as several millennia in duration, a convoy was finally assembled, engines running, outside the gates of the enclave. Mr Mehta settled himself in the driver's seat of the family Ambassador. The suspension groaned with the weight of people and luggage, the chowkidar saluted, and he swung the car imperiously into the road, forcing a cycle rickshaw to swerve and a bus-driver to stamp hard on his vehicle's worn brakes. Two other cars followed behind.

The convoy sailed through the unlit Noida streets and Arjun rested his cheek against the cool glass of the window. On the other side the night was damp and broken, an underworld strafed by truck headlights and mottled by the orange glow of bustee cooking fires. The traffic was heavy, and it took an hour to reach the airport. With their billboards promising denim and sports shoes, the clothing outlets on the approach road beckoned like a premonition of the American future. The Mehta party shouldered its way through the crush of touts and drivers outside the terminal, and all eleven relatives joined a long queue. At the check-in desks airline employees handed out customs forms as red-uniformed porters manhandled luggage on to the conveyor belt and wildly overladen Indian families pushed trolleys against the ankles of disoriented foreigners, all dressed in the same characteristic mélange of factory-made handicrafts, religious paraphernalia and hiking gear.

Little by little the line inched forward. As they neared the front, Mrs Mehta started to sob in earnest, comforted by her next-door neighbour and digitally recorded by Ramesh for posterity. Arjun handed over his documents, explaining that despite appearances he was travelling alone. He felt proud that in the eyes of his family he was finally doing something worth while. In a film the scene would be accompanied by music, and he would lead a crowd of long-haul passengers in a dance routine.

His father put his hands on his shoulders. 'Son, we know you are going to be a great success. Don't disappoint us.'

'I'll do my best, Babaji.'

Priti tugged at his sleeve. 'Come back a millionaire, Bro!' Relatives clustered round to add their good wishes. Mrs Mehta's wailing rose in pitch. 'God bless you, Beta!' she cried. 'God bless you!' Consumed with impatience, Arjun hardly took in what they were saying. Quickly, he took his boarding pass and hurried towards passport control. As soon as he was out of sight, he headed for the toilet, where he stuffed the garland into his bag and washed the paste from his forehead.

The engines roared like a distant sports crowd as the damp polymer smell of microwaved food slowly permeated the fug of the cabin. It was Arjun's first time on a plane, and from the moment he sensed his body being lifted clear of the ground, he had been in the throes of a near-religious rapture. First there were the city lights, spread out like wedding decorations below the line of the wing. Then came the more intimate satisfactions of a refreshing towelette and a wrapper containing a toothbrush, a tube of toothpaste and a black nylon sleeping mask. As soon as the seatbelt signs were switched off, he made a pilgrimage to the toilet, where he discovered the existence of paper seat-covers and spent a considerable period of time examining the sanitary-towel disposal unit and the automated vacuum flush. Eventually there was a knock on the door and a mellifluous stewardess voice asked if he was all right. He confirmed that he was fine, thank you, and carried on with his researches. When he finally emerged, he was surprised to find a cluster of jaded-looking people gathered in the corridor.

Now, with the sleeping mask perched on the top of his head and the sponge covers of a set of headphones clamped over his ears, he was engaged in an appreciation of the ergonomic rigour of his meal tray. The way the tub of fruit juice sat inside the coffee cup, the geometric abstraction of the nameless pink dessert, even the segmentation of the tray itself – all seemed to have been designed with his lifestyle preferences in mind. Certain items, such as the plastic ring which clipped the napkin to the cutlery, were particularly absorbing. Even the doughy and compacted quality of the food, so at odds with its description in the in-flight magazine, had its own uniquely aerospatial charm.

Pressing the stewardess button for a second refill of coffee, he played with the armrest controls and discovered that *Naughty Naughty, Lovely Lovely* was about to start on the in-flight Hindi channel. *N2L2* was a big hit, and, though he had already seen it seven times, he sat back joyfully to watch it again. More than joyfully. Were he not a committed scientific rationalist, he would have taken it as a sign, a *blessing on his endeavour*, that this film was the airline's entertainment choice. After all, *N2L2*, winner of eight *Filmfare* awards and the first Rocky Prasad picture to star newcomer Leela Zahir, was the reason he came to be on the plane in the first place.

Not everyone would make a major life decision on the basis of a movie. To make any kind of decision at all on the basis of *Naughty Naughty, Lovely Lovely*, an entertainment so light as to be almost gaseous, is the mark of a true devotee of popular cinema. Arjun was such a devotee, one of the hordes who queued for tickets during *N2L2*'s first weekend of release, grossing it ten crore rupees and making it one of the biggest openers in Indian cinema history. He had been expecting a lot (he had always liked Rocky Prasad's work), but, sitting in the stalls of the Aakash Cineplex, he found more than he imagined possible: the film was nothing less than a call to change his life. In its hero he found a role model even more potent than the great Amitabh Bachchan, whose gangly form had dominated his teenage years. So, as the great jet engines pushed him on towards California, he toggled the volume and adjusted the spongy earphone covers with a kind of reverence, the attitude of a man about to commune with his innermost hopes and dreams.

N2L2 is a love story. Its hero, Dilip, is a home-loving boy. Despite his good looks and college education, he is content to laze around on his father's farm, set amid the picturesque yellow mustard fields of the Punjab. He does little except lie about in these fields, watching clouds, chewing on stalks of grass and flirting with the troupes of attractive peasant girls who trip gaily back and forth carrying water jars and large squares of coloured silk. Dilip sings about the clouds, the girls, and his general sense of well-being, which is immediately disturbed by the arrival of Aparna, a beauty from London, back in the old country to visit her relatives.

Aparna (played by Leela Zahir) is everything Dilip is not. Though she has traditional values, as we witness in a montage of winsome roti cookery, demure prayers and well-manicured hands pressing the feet of aged relatives, she is also a thrusting investment banker, driven to career success by a wish to avenge her father's ruin in a long-running law suit. In an amusing mistaken-identity scene, Dilip speaks to her roguishly, thinking that the pair of dark eyes behind the veil (she is traditionally and demurely dressed) must belong to some village girl, temporarily without silk square or water vessel. He is taken aback by her college-educated retorts, and falls instantly in love.

Despite Dilip's attempts to impress Aparna by riding a horse very fast, standing on his hands and boxing the ears of a group of eve-teasers in the marketplace, she remains unmoved, singing to him that the man who wins her heart must have more than a distinguished nose, flat abs and a happy-go-lucky manner; he must also command the respect of his fellow citizens and hold down a highly paid job in commerce or industry. Dilip is confused, until he spies Aparna and her uncle praying before a picture of her dead father. Eavesdropping on their conversation, he learns of the law suit, and of the patently very evil Christo, a well-connected London financier and underworld don who drove the dead man to alcoholic collapse.

That evening Dilip spots Christo on CNN World Business Report and realizes that the key to his beloved's heart lies in acquiring NRI status. He vows to change his life, and become the man Aparna wants him to be. Bidding farewell to his father, he sings that he will tarry among clouds and mustard fields no more, but will go forth to seek his destiny in the international capital markets. When Aparna flies back to London, he follows her, pausing briefly at Heathrow to rescue the stolen luggage of a European bigshot, before heading into the city centre. There he encounters a series of snooty British types who sing to him of his country manners and woeful desi ignorance, as he searches for a cheap hotel in the vicinity of Buckingham Palace.

Sidetracked by the delights of tourism, Dilip visits Madame Tussaud's and Covent Garden, then foolishly exhausts his meagre funds by taking repeated rides on the London Eye. He is sitting at a table in the Hard Rock Café, facing the chilling realization that he will be unable to pay for his chicken burger combo, when he bumps into his friend the grateful Eurobigshot, who reveals that he heads the biggest investment bank in the City and would like to offer Dilip a job. Dilip agrees, Bigshot settles his bill, and our hero moves from his sleazy Buckingham Palace dive into a riverfront apartment with a view of Big Ben.

Dilip discovers that a childhood of haggling in the Jalandhar Market has given him an aptitude for finance, and in no time at all he is vastly wealthy. Spurning the advances of Bigshot's beautiful daughter, he decides the time has come to make himself known to Aparna, who has been passing the time in a montage of demure praying and chewing a pencil at her desk. As a boring meeting comes to a climax, Dilip strides in, buys the company and sings to Aparna of his undying love. She is bowled over and agrees to be his, subject to her uncle's blessing. They go walking by the Thames, on the white cliffs of Dover, on the battlements of Windsor Castle and briefly in the Swiss Alps, wearing a variety of outfits and describing the life they will lead together once they are united in marriage.

Everything is joyous. It is holi, so Dilip and Aparna run through Piccadilly, throwing coloured dye at each other and annoying policemen. In a fantasy sequence, the action switches to the Punjab, and Aparna (whose modern London clothes have been swapped for a traditional wet sari) sings that Dilip has won her heart through his bravery, decisiveness and diversified investment portfolio. Evil Christo chooses this moment to kidnap Aparna, whom he intends to make his wife. His henchmen beat up Dilip, leaving him for dead among the pigeons in Trafalgar Square. As Dilip's prone body is pecked by hungry birds, the villains take Aparna to the gang's underground hideout beneath Brighton Pavilion. Luckily Dilip is helped by an old pigeon-feed vendor who was himself ruined by Christo many years ago. Mr Vilson, the vendor, leads Dilip to the underground hideout, where together they spray a high-pressure hose over the gang, washing them all into the English Channel. The police arrive, arrest the evil boss and take him off to prison. Aparna's uncle and Dilip's father (who are passing through Brighton on their way to Chandigarh) bless the union. Dilip and Aparna garland each other, singing the title song:

Something naughty
Can be lovely
Something lovely
Can be naughty
Naughty naughty
Lovely lovely
Love!

As the end credits rolled over a dissolve of a queue of relatives feeding the happy couple sweetened rice, Arjun experienced the same sense of potential that had struck him so forcefully on his first seven viewings. As he had argued to Aamir over frequent coffees at the Internet Shack, *Dilip was him*. It was as simple as that. He was a dreamer. He had been idling his time away. If he wanted to live in reality, instead of in his imagination, it was time for a change. How could he not see this movie as a parable?

The rest of the flight passed in a haze, interrupted only by a jetlagged stumble through the duty-free zone at Singapore Airport. Finally, after what seemed like several days' travel, Arjun found himself descending through a thick fog towards San Francisco Airport. He stowed his tray table, put his seatback in the upright position and carefully packed his complimentary sleep-socks into a side pocket of his carry-on bag. The throb in his depressurizing ears seemed to be sending him a message: *It is time, it is time.*

A figure, a walking man, trudging along the margin of a wide California highway. One foot in front of the other, each pace bringing him a little closer to the point, marked with a low concrete barrier, where the Taco Bell lot ended and the Staples lot began. Beyond Staples was a Wal-Mart and beyond that a road junction. Beyond the junction, perhaps three blocks or thirty more minutes' walk away, was a mini-mall with a Thai take-out, a dry-cleaner and the convenience store which was the pedestrian's intended destination.

Anyone on foot in suburban California is one of four things: poor, foreign, mentally ill or jogging. This person, whose thin frame was almost lost inside a grubby Oakland Raiders shirt, was moving too slowly to be a jogger. He appeared edgy, dispossessed. Defeat radiated from him like sweat. If the soccer moms zipping by in their SUVs registered him at all, it was as a blur of dark skin, a minor danger signal flashing past on their periphery. To the walking man, the soccer moms were more cosmological than human, gleaming projectiles that dopplered past him in a rush of noise and dioxins, as alien and indifferent as stars.

He stopped for a moment, squinting into the harsh sunlight at the way ahead. The cracked concrete lots expired in a grudging ribbon of public space, a not-quite-sidewalk that stretched away from him in a glitter of shattered windshield glass. At the Taco–Staples border he paused again, this time to fumble with his Walkman, a low-status hunk of black plastic attached to headphones with dirty foam pads: homeless audio, the type of machine the socially excluded keep on loud to drown out the voices. He replaced the batteries, untwisted the headphone flex and carried on.

*

It was July, and Arjun had been in the States for a year, a year of repeating this walk, or walks like it. To the store, wherever the store happened to be. Back from the store. To the bus-stop. Back. Long intervals, standing in skeletal vandalized shelters. Wind and silence. The California of the non-driver.

At first it had been because he did not feel confident, settled enough. Then it was because he was never in one place. More recently, now that he was desperate, now that the sense of being diminished by this environment had become a suspicion of *actual physical shrinkage*, it was because he no longer had the money for driving lessons.

Living his dreams was proving hard.

In retrospect, the signs were there at the start. When Sherry collected him from the airport, he had been too busy looking out of the car window to spot her fixed grin of distaste. With her business card (*Sherry L. Parks, Databodies Personnel Liaison Manager*) clutched in his hand, he had sat in sublime passenger-seat contentment, counting off his first McDonalds, his first stop sign, his first highway patrol car. Even when they clattered his cases through the screen door and stepped into the house, he had been too blinkered by his expectations to notice, *really* notice the glum faces of the men in the living room, sitting silently around a fuzzy portable TV.

'Hello, Vee-jay, hello, Sah-leem, hello, Row-heet,' twittered Sherry, her mouth stretched into what Arjun would later hear the others call her 'Mother Teresa among the lepers' smile. No one responded. He felt embarrassed and looked down at the floor. Objects on the patterned carpet: empty soda bottles, socks, chappals, O'Reilly technical manuals, convenience-food packaging. The one with the bushy moustache had a dirty plate balanced precariously on the arm of his chair. He ashed his cigarette on to it, then leaned forward and held out a hand.

'Welcome to the bench, bhai.'

The bench. Waiting to play. For about three days, being on the bench was cool. At least when Arjun used his new calling card to talk to his family, it sounded cool. *On the bench*. As if he had been assimilated into the quasi-military culture of American sports, and was living a life of high-fives and huddles, time-outs, play-offs, spit-balls. When Sherry drove him into the city for his induction, he made her stop off at a Foot Locker, where he bought the Raiders shirt, so as to feel even more *on the bench*.

Linguistic glamour. Examples: when he watched TV, it was 'tube', when he thought of his parents, he didn't think of them as his parents, but as 'the folks back home'. The others did it too: little experiments with slang, tentative new accents. You spoke from the TV couch to whoever was trailing telephone flex down the stairs, coming back after a family call.

How are the folks back home?

And they replied: *A-OK, man. They're good.*

The folks. The bench. Man, good.

Good. Until the second day, when Arjun asked where he would be working and was told that the job Databodies had guaranteed him was not in fact guaranteed at all. He would have to interview by phone with potential clients. Until at his induction meeting he shook the hand of a man who seemed like a clone of Sunny Srinivasan, except seedier, sharper, less seductive, a man who turned out to be Sunny's brother-in-law and who coldly informed him that until he successfully secured a post, Databodies would pay him a grand total of $500 a month, half of which would be taken back as rent for the house-share. Arjun reminded him of the $50,000 a year his contract guaranteed. Sunny's brother-in-law shrugged. If you don't like it, he said, you can always go back home. You'll owe us for your visa and ticket, and we'll have to charge you an administrative fee for the inconvenience. Ten thousand should cover it. Rupees? No, bhai, *dollars*.

Arjun did some calculations. It quickly became obvious that (after he deducted his outgoings) every day he spent on the bench he would be losing money. He did not have many savings. There was only so long he could last. Still, he did not despair. He was a qualified IT consultant, and even though the terms of his visa meant he had to stay with Databodies or leave the country, there would be work soon enough. After all, American companies were desperate for people like him.

Weren't they? Salim, the chain-smoker, found this so funny he made Arjun repeat it three times. He had already been on the bench ten weeks. Rohit, twelve.

'Don't you ever read the business pages?'

As a matter of fact Arjun didn't. When they told him he actually laughed; it seemed so absurd. America was booming. This was known (in India, at least) to be a permanent condition, a fact about the country like its fifty states, 19,924 km of coastline and 12,248 km of land borders. Furthermore, as if their old economy weren't booming enough for them, they had declared a new one. Double-boom. The idea that not one but two economies could shudder to a halt was inconceivable. Yet there it was: market correction, cyclical downturn, crash. Not an atmosphere in which to learn a new and difficult skill, like driving a car.

All he could do was to wait for a call. In the meantime he set out to discover America via regular ten-block walks to the store. The new specificities were absorbing. The bass pumping out of lowrider cars was an inversion of India's screaming treble. Grown men wore short pants like children. Behind the 7-Eleven, feral-looking kids, surely the poor, rode battered skateboards, kicking them up against kerbs and railings to go airborne in flurries of baggy cotton. Not for American shoppers the bustle and haggling of the marketplace. Inside a sepulchral Safeway the air-conditioning played icy breath on his neck as he padded down aisles where the produce was lit like a film set and sprinklers sprayed cricket-ball-sized tomatoes with a fine mist of water. In every parking lot men and women dressed in pastel lycras and cottons pushed staggering cubic volumes of merchandise towards their cars – and what cars! Mythical chariots gleaming with window tint and metallic paint, vehicles built to transport whole clans, entire communities, from one place to another. The first time he saw an RV he actually forgot to breathe. There it was, forty feet of elephantine home-from-home airbrushed with a rock-opera design of white horses in a forest glade, passing by with the immensity and slowness of a science-fiction mothership. This vision had a brace of trailbikes on the back and a bearded man at the wheel, a man who Arjun could only imagine was possessed by some blood-memory of covered-wagon times, prisoner of an obsessive urge to migrate, to set up further on down the road.

Though for a while he believed nothing could be more magical than the casual mastery of a Californian turning out of a Starbucks parking lot (the slumped tensionless driving style, one hand lazily swinging the wheel as the other administered hits of latte), he discovered that anything can become mundane. Fire hydrants, billboards, even the enamelled blue sky: all had shelf lives. One by one they expired.

Last to lose its aura was the TV, which was somehow more compelling than the world outside. The four benched consultants spent whole days in front of it, eating chips and salsa and trying to ignore their creeping panic. Most mornings one of them would have an interview, a tense half-hour hunched over the phone upstairs with the others trying not to listen, turning the *tube* up high, half hoping and half fearing that the interviewee would come back down hired. Usually as soon as the client found out he was talking to a foreign national on a temporary visa, the conversation was terminated. Victoria warned Diego she was on to him. Belle learned the truth about Jan's pregnancy. Jerry goaded plus-sized women to fight with their love-cheat partners and Arjun spoke to three, five, seven companies. None of them wanted to employ him.

As he became more attuned to American language and economics, he realized he was living in a 'low-income area'. In his bedroom the drone of traffic from Highway 101 was a constant presence. On the corner, listless young black and Latino men played bass-heavy music and leaned into car windows to have short conversations with the drivers. A hydrocarbon stink lay heavy in the air, and during the night the traffic hum was accompanied by police sirens and cracking sounds which, Vijay announced authoritatively, were gunshots. The idea of American poverty, especially a poverty which did not exclude cars, refrigerators, cable TV or obesity, was a new and disturbing paradox, a hint that something ungovernable and threatening lurked beneath the reflective surface of California. Arjun spent as little time as possible outside the house, convinced by his scrutiny of cable news channels that he would be putting himself in danger. Even unarmed, he found Americans physically intimidating. When he went to 'middle-class' areas (*middle class* being, he had discovered, an American word for *white*) he felt overwhelmed. Used to a world where everyone looked more or less like him, he found it took nerve to move through crowds in which everyone was so tall and heavy, so *meaty*.

During this time, the only direct contact they had with Databodies was through Sherry. She would park her Chevy Suburban on the street outside, arm the alarm, look around nervously and scuttle into their smell of dirty laundry and cooking oil, mispronouncing their names and bringing another set of administrative paperwork for them to sign. Everything about her seemed insufferably smug: her big hair, her gold S-H-E-R-R-Y necklace, her matching pink lipgloss and nail varnish, even the album of family pictures she carried in her purse. Her very averageness seemed arrogant, the bland superiority of a person whose access to the US labour market was a birthright.

They could have forgiven Sherry her choice of accessories had she not exuded such contempt for them. 'How *unusual*,' she would say, confronted with some unpalatable desi tic like Rohit chewing paan parag or Vijay singing along to bhajans. At least once a visit she would mention that her husband Bryan was having business difficulties, the subtext being that this was the only reason she would demean herself by pandering to their personal needs. 'When she looks at us,' Salim complained, watching out of the window as she started her car, 'she sees a bunch of starving coolies. The bitch thinks she's doing us a favour just by coming here. She might as well have "gift of the people of the United States of America" stencilled on her butt.'

But they had to be nice to Sherry. She was their only source of information, their sole reference point in the vast flat sprawl of the valley. And, though they didn't like to admit it, her visits were, next to the afternoon *Baywatch* reruns, the highlight of their empty weeks.

Arjun would sit on the phone to India, horribly aware of the cost. The family would want to know everything, but somehow their questions only pushed them further away from him. Where is the mandir, asked his mother. Are you drinking bottled water? Are you cold? His father wanted to know about the 'corporate culture' of his workplace. It was impossible to tell the truth. 'Yeah,

Sis, Oracle is great. The work is very challenging. No, I didn't spot anyone yet. Yes, if I see him I'll get his autograph. No, not at all, I'm just kind of wiped out, that's all.'

Finally, just when he could bear his state of suspended animation no more, something gave. Within the space of three days Salim and Rohit were placed with companies, one in Los Altos, the other in Menlo Park. In the little house off 101, there was Johnnie Walker and Häagen-Dazs. Two days later it was Arjun's turn. The employer was a fish processor based somewhere called Portland, Maine. They needed someone to modify a database. They wanted him to start Monday. That, he told them, was no problem.

Until he saw the ticket and realized he was flying via Chicago, he thought 'main' must be like 'central' or 'downtown', and meant that the job was based in the business district of the city in Oregon. But Databodies had subcontracted his services to a bodyshop on the East Coast. Both sets of middlemen would be taking a percentage. He didn't bother arguing.

As he packed his sweaters, he was uncomfortably aware of the TV booming out from downstairs: Vijay, the last man, mournfully watching a cookery show. Arjun had not known what to say.

'I'm moving,' he told his father on the phone.

'You are being promoted already?' Mr Mehta's voice was thick with pride.

'Yes,' he heard himself say. 'I'm heading up a software development team in Portland. Troubleshooting.'

'Troubleshooting? My boy. Wait a moment while I tell your mother.'

Eventually his mother stopped sobbing and passed the receiver to Priti, who squealed and made a static sound with her mouth that he guessed was supposed to be a crowd applauding. He had wanted to be honest with her, but she seemed so entranced by her image of his American life that in phone call after phone call he had never had the heart. She was so happy for him that he had even made up a few things to please her. Keanu Reeves in a Pizza Hut. An earth tremor. Crazy golf. She asked him about the job, and he said it would be 'an exciting challenge', hearing the hollow sound of his voice as he said the words. Then she asked for his 'other news', and he was suddenly racked by a profound homesickness, wanting so much to be back in India that he could not speak and had to end the call. Ten minutes went by before it occurred to him that throughout their conversation she had spoken with a perfect Australian accent.

As he changed planes at O'Hare, striding from one gate to the next, he felt his dreams were finally coinciding with reality. In Portland he was put up in a Super 8 Motel, where he briefly luxuriated in clean towels, MTV, packets of non-dairy creamer and, most of all, the snow. Surreptitiously he crept outside to the parking lot and scooped a little up in his hands. His first snow. It was more or less as he had imagined, apart from the sounds: the crunch as you walked on it, the squeak when you compacted it in your fist. He took some inside, thinking he would call Priti and get her to listen, but by the time he got to the phone it had melted.

BSC Seafood had a hangar-like plant on the pier next to the Fish Exchange. Inside lines of workers filleted, buttered, breaded, stuffed, packaged and wrapped sea creatures of every kind, slinging hundred-pound airfreight boxes of flatfish into waiting trucks and manhandling blocks of cod towards the machines which would saw them into sticks. Arjun was taken on a brief tour of the facility by the CFO, who told him they were starting up a line of roe products, needed some more fields in the inventory database and had chosen Arjun because 'your boss said you came cheap'. The job was so trivial that he had to use his imagination to stretch it out to two weeks. He took long breaks, locked in the bathroom with a UNIX manual or standing on a gangway peeking down at the factory floor, an underworld peopled by wraiths in rubber boots and overalls. After three weeks he had to admit to his supervisor that the project was finished. A week later he was back on the West Coast, on the bench.

From: arjunm@netulator.com
To: lovegod2000@singhshack.com
Subject: RE: small pants?

hello aamir thankyou for your message how are you yes i am all american now even eating beef pork products that is between you and me someone just gave bacon cheeseburger this is how it starts things ok here yes lots of girls wear short pants yes it is nice no have not spoken to many yet or seen p anderson or bv slayer busy got to go – arjunm

His first anniversary in the US found him sharing a ramshackle house in Daly City with a pair of indistinguishable Tamil Java programmers he privately nicknamed Ram and Shyam. The area was, if anything, lower income than the last. The lot backed on to an electricity substation with a giant humming transformer. His neighbours were a clan of enormous Samoans, who were coated in blue-black tattoos and spent their days fixing their cars and having loud explosive arguments. The Samoans had many enormous Samoan friends, who owned an indeterminate number of enormous dogs that lay slavering on the sidewalk outside his door in a litter of oily engine parts, forty-ounce beer bottles and shit.

No one ever messed with him, not even the dogs, but his over-stressed imagination produced scenes of unimaginable violence, like WWF wrestling filtered through the dark side of the National Geographic Channel. He was having trouble sleeping. He had developed eczema on his hands. He knew every plot line in *The Young and the Restless* and was becoming cynical about his employer's business model. Databodies charged the companies he worked for twice, even three times what they paid him, and still deducted money from his pay for rent, legal and administrative fees. He had made no money, gained nothing at all since coming to America except a new and harder picture of the world.

So see the walking man, going to the store again. Instant coffee. Breakfast cereal. Plastic-wrapped bread, 10 per cent polystyrene, 90 per cent air. See the man trudge along the margin of a wide road, a man who suspects either that he is shrinking or that this landscape is actually expanding in front of him, stretching itself out ahead of his weary feet. He has worked for only three and a half months out of twelve. He has been given credit and had it withdrawn. He knows what lies above him, the sublime mobility of those who travel without ever touching the ground. He has glimpsed what lies below, the other mobility, the forced motion of the shopping-cart pushers, the collectors of cardboard boxes. At least in India the street people can lie down for a while before being moved on.

In honour of the balloon scene, the party planners had proposed the theme 'floating on air'. Thousands of silver helium bubbles hovered in nets above the heads of the guests, who were served drinks and chaat by waiters dressed as 'ethereal spirits', a look heavily reliant on silver lamé. The DJ mixed the obvious songs ('Up, Up and Away', 'Summer Breeze') into selections from the film's soundtrack, ignored by a crowd of Mumbai film people too intent on networking to do anything as socially unproductive as dance.

Leela Zahir, it was noted, arrived on the arm of Naveed Iqbal. The corpulent producer waved and made namaste to his acquaintances, apparently oblivious to the furious stares of the Thakkar camp. *Kiss Me, Tickle Me* was Manoj Thakkar's film. Leela was supposed, for tonight at least, to be Thakkar's star. Still, no one wished to cause a scene with Iqbal, not with the friends he had. Leela's glamorous mother, Faiza, followed behind, escorted by Big Gun Number One himself, Rajiv Rana. Between them, the two women must have been wearing ten lakh rupees of jewellery. The new alignment of forces was hurriedly analysed by the party guests. What did it mean? What promises had been made?

Leela smiled her way into the room, and more than one person experienced a momentary suspension of their cynicism. She had something otherworldly about her, an unmannered, almost involuntary beauty that silenced catty remarks and deflected leering gazes chastely to the floor. She was India's girl-next-door, and at the same time her newest goddess. In the background, unobserved, hotel staff were crowding the doorways, porters and doormen and gardeners and maids peering across the room, feasting on the crumbs of her presence like uniformed mice.

Leeladevi. Protect us, grant us a boon . . .

The lucky waiter who carried away her empty glass wrapped it carefully in a cloth and hid it in the kitchen. After his shift he sat on the bus, gripping the package on his lap, conscious of bringing home to his wife and children a treasure, a sliver of goodness to set against the evils of the world.

What does a walking man dream of?

OK, now turn the wheel. That's right – no – other direction, you were OK the first time. There you go. Check for traffic. Mirror. Signal. Now move off slowly . . .

He dreams of powered motion.

As a gap opened up between kerb and rim, the wheels of Chris's Honda Civic performed a single complete revolution, then a second. Driver and passenger sensed an infinitesimal gain in speed. As the car started to travel down the road *under his control*, the driver experienced a strong and unexpected set of emotions. Components: relief/fear/elation/melancholic recognition of past stasis. Result: a pang so strong he found himself fighting back tears.

Two minutes into his first driving lesson Arjun stamped on the brake (unwittingly executing his first emergency stop) and rubbed his knuckles roughly across his eyes.

Christine leaned over and pulled on the parking brake. The car gently stalled.

'Arjun, honey, are you OK?'

'Yes, yes. Of course.' He hunched into the driver's seat, gruff and embarrassed. Somehow when he was with Chris, these moments, these *emotional* moments, seemed to occur. They were very awkward. He tried to pull himself together, announcing like a commander encouraging his troops to go over the top, 'We must start the engine again.'

'It's OK, Arjun. There's no one coming.'

'It's OK?'

'It's OK.'

He grinned with relief, the sudden clouds-vanishing grin which Chris secretly thought was cute.

'Ready to try again?' she asked.

He nodded.

Only song lyrics have a purchase on such reversals of fortune. What a difference a day, etc. Lyrics also teach (joy/pain, sunshine/rain) that you can only know how good *up* feels when you have tasted *down*.

Up in this instance looked like the municipality of Redmond, Washington. Tall trees, sunlight glittering on the blue-green waters of Lake Sammamish. Biotech and mountain bikes. Neat landscaping and plenty of designated parking. A place dedicated to the healthy alternation of work and play. Software and jet skis. Aerospace and hiking trails. And for Arjun an American life. It had come, boxed and shrinkwrapped, thanks to the final interview, the one after which he knew he would snap, would not stay to breathe another lungful of hydrocarbon-laced valley air but would take the first plane back to New Delhi to breathe the comforting hydrocarbons of home. And instead Virugenix hired him. *Virugenix*. And not just any job, but a position in the holy of holies, home of the Ghostbusters, the Cyrus J. Greene Labs.

Home was now a third-floor studio in Berry Acres, a new development enclosed by high decorative ironwork gates that opened in response to a magnetic swipe card. His window in Bilberry Nook (Unit 12, located for him by the efficient Virugenix personnel division) looked out on a row of identical wooden-fronted buildings, all painted shades of grey and white. On a clear day he could also see the mist-shrouded peaks of the Cascade Mountains, hanging above the roofs like a dream of Kashmir. It was, as he told Priti, the most beautiful place he could imagine, as far away from the dust and bustle of Noida as the moon.

Some things, however, do not change. Arjun's apartment was several degrees warmer than anywhere else in Bilberry Nook and from behind its closed door came a low threatening hum, like a wasps' nest. The sound emanated from a quantity of elderly computer equipment which he had begged, borrowed and networked together in an insanely complex configuration that left space only for a futon and a wobbly operator's chair, nestling among a fantastical snake-pit of cabling. Backless tower cases bristled with connectors, each resource allocated, each slot stuffed with network cards, SIMMs, removable drives and various warranty-invalidating home-made devices which gave the whole mess a dubious about-to-blow look. Here and there he had attempted to impose order on the chaos, mostly with duct tape. Intractable ganglia of wire had been plastered to the walls, the skirting, the underside of the home-made desk. On the remaining horizontal surfaces were stacks of storage media, almost all computer-related, except for a vertical tower of VHS tapes which reached almost to the ceiling. In one corner, a grudging afterthought, were a couple of IKEA storage cartons containing his clothes, mostly promotional t-shirts bearing the logos of software companies. The only concession to decoration, indeed to RL lifestyle of any kind, were the posters on the wall above the bed. To the left was Amitabh Bachchan in a still from *Zanjeer*, frozen in a posture so action-packed that it threatened to split his pants. Beside him was a sulkily pouting Leela Zahir, playing the role of wayward Mumbai co-ed Mini in *You'll Have to Ask My Parents*.

Every weekday morning Arjun woke up in the midst of his chaos and grinned at the evergreen framed in his window. The tree presumably had a name (was it a *fir* or a *pine*?), though he did not know it. It looked like one of the trees that you could make appear with a mouse click and a little noise when playing SimCity. In fact, if he was honest, most of the Puget Sound area looked like that: perfect, glossily pleasing, somehow *placed*. Then he put on the cleanest of his t-shirts and took the bus downtown, past the Sim marina and the Sim park and the mall full of Sims shopping at the drugstore and drinking tea at the British Pantry. Redmond was a town with nice graphics and an intuitive user interface. His kind of town.

After his bus-ride he would buy a large-sized latte at Starbucks, add three packets of sugar, stir with the plastic stirrer (the ritual of picking up and choosing these items from the stand of assorted lids and cardboard sleeves was very satisfying), then transfer the whole lot to his own insulated plastic beaker for the two-block walk to the Virugenix campus, a cluster of low glass-clad buildings set in meticulously landscaped grounds.

In those days everyone knew Virugenix, the global computer-security specialist. Most computer users had Virugenix software somewhere on their machines, running a firewall or scanning their hard drive for malicious code. Their Splat! product suite was an industry standard. Though they had offices in twelve US cities and sales presences in many other countries around the world, Redmond was the site of their research and development operation, the prestigious Greene Labs. To Arjun r & d was *it*, the alpha and omega. Everything else about a software company was peripheral, more or less just *selling*.

Miraculously, or so it seemed to him, the anti-virus team had an opening for an assistant tester. Though it was not a position for a fully fledged virus analyst, it was the next best thing: checking that the daily batch of new definitions picked up what they were supposed to, and testing the patches the AV team produced to fix the damage. He would be working with the kind of code he loved most. Within two weeks of his interview, he had said goodbye to Ram, Shyam, the Samoans, dogshit, California and daytime TV, and moved to Washington State.

At the campus gate he would smile and show his ID card to security, who waved him through to the well-signed path that led to the Michelangelo Building. The AV group occupied the top floor of Michelangelo, and he had to swipe his pass twice to access the test lab. Whenever he entered and left the secure area, his bag was checked for storage media. As numerous laminated signs in the corridor pointed out, if a disk went into the AV lab it did not come out again.

Arjun liked the security procedures. It felt good to show his pass with its code numbers and little colour headshot, and he was excited by the rumour that Virugenix was about to install an iris scanner. Biometrics were neat. The security controls seemed to underscore his elite status, to confirm that his daily routine had drama and importance. He sometimes imagined film plots in which he (played by Shah Rukh Khan) worked against the clock to outwit evil Pakistani virus writers who were holding Leela Zahir hostage. *If*

. . . I . . . can . . . just . . . figure . . . this . . . encryption . . . algorithm . . . out . . . But mostly he was too busy for daydreaming. From the time he fired up his terminal to look through the first batch of new test files until the time he powered down at night, he was deep in the netherworld of malicious code, one of the good guys, the white hats, dedicated to keeping you safe in your digital bed.

The top floor of the Michelangelo Building was just one of the nodes on what Virugenix grandly called its Global Security Perimeter. After the big email attachment scares of the late nineties, the company had decided to offer its jittery corporate clients a 24-hour service. They opened satellite labs in Japan, Finland and on the East Coast, so that whenever a new threat was identified, an analyst somewhere in the world was awake and on hand to assess it. The GSP nodes were linked by two entirely separate networks: one for ordinary corporate traffic, the other for the transmission of code samples and other potentially infectious material. This second network of computers was known to the analysts as the Petri dish. It was the place where they watched things grow.

As the morning wore on, Arjun's first latte would be followed by several more, made at the gleaming coffee-station in the employee kitchen. Virugenix also provided a refrigerated cabinet of complimentary sodas, and some time around noon he tended to make the switch from coffee to cola. He had decorated his workspace, a standard six-by-six grey cubicle, with a mixture of family and film pictures. Priti grinning at her college graduation. Hrithik Roshan in a tight t-shirt. The cubicle was part of a cluster abutting an area walled off from the rest of the office by clear plexiglas panels. This room contained several racks of ordinary household PCs, a whiteboard and three large plasma displays. It required high-level clearance to enter, and the analysts nicknamed it 'the hot zone'. The racked machines were the dirtiest part of the Petri dish, an isolated sub-net on which infections were induced to spread. Once or twice a day a gaggle of senior researchers gathered round the screens, watching some new digital creature overwrite sectors of a disk or hunt for somewhere to migrate. Arjun watched surreptitiously (an activity which involved poking his head over the top of the cubicle like a meerkat) as arguments broke out, theories were outlined, and dry markers brandished in passionate defence and refutation, all in other-side-of-the-glass dumbshow. He wished he could be part of these conversations, but underneath the informal surface of the AV group there was a clear hierarchy. He had neither the clearance nor the status to join in when the Ghostbusters were at work.

The movie nickname came from a 1998 *Wired* feature. Under the headline 'Who Ya Gonna Call?' the magazine ran a double-page photo, taken from a low angle, of Virugenix's senior anti-virus team, arms folded, stony-faced, wearing Oakley wraparounds and grey quasi-Trekkie jumpsuits. It was grudgingly agreed by their peers that the picture almost made them look cool. Or if not cool then at least functionally socialized. The article painted Virugenix as a new-economy success story, and its employees as heroic defenders manning the walls of the internet against the viral dark hordes. Naturally the team loved it, producing 'Ghostbusters' tees, sweatshirts and caps for themselves, strutting around and generally lording it over everyone else in the company.

By the time of Arjun's arrival the Ghostbusters were still lording it, though many of the individuals featured in the picture had moved on. In Michelangelo there were fifteen, all men, assisted by a similar number of support staff. The oldest was the team leader, Darryl Gant, who Arjun reckoned to be in his fifties. 'Uncle' Darryl had a bushy grey-flecked beard and was the only person to have his own office, a workspace packed with waste paper, technical manuals and his extensive collection of NASA memorabilia. Inside this cocoon-like box he made whooshing noises at a 1:288 model Space Shuttle, disassembled code samples and tried as far as possible to avoid face-to-face contact with his employees. The youngest Ghostbuster was 21-year-old Clay. A native of Marin County, he was an object of special wonder for Arjun, who had yet to come to terms with the Virugenix corporate culture. While Arjun tended to wear his blue blazer to work, Clay slouched about the office in shorts and Birkenstock sandals, his blond dreadlocks tied up in a strange hairy pineapple on top of his head like a Hindu mendicant. As far as Arjun could tell, Clay was not religious or even particularly ascetic, except when it came to toxins, which were apparently to be found everywhere in their workspace. On days when he judged the toxin count particularly high, he would wear a face mask and a pair of surgical gloves. He seemed to be Darryl's special protégé, and the two of them were the analysts most regularly to be seen wearing the blue Ghostbusters splash-tops that were the latest badge of gang membership.

Clay occasionally came to talk to Arjun, leaning over the cubicle partition and telling war stories about a vacation he took in Goa, where he met a noted spiritual leader on Anjuna Beach and played host to an intestinal parasite with an unusual and picturesque lifecycle. Clay would usually slide into reminiscing about Inge, a Danish girl he met at an ashtanga yoga ashram. Sometimes, drinking smoothies through a sterilized straw, he would recount his epic fight with a person called 'the ear-cleaning dude', who attacked him with sharp instruments and had to be given money to go away.

Apart from Clay, most of the AV team were not particularly gregarious creatures. People did their thing and other people left them to get on with it. No one took much notice of Shiro's habit of flapping his arms violently every few minutes or Donny's refusal to allow purple objects into his field of vision. Everyone left their phones on voicemail and most wore headsets while they worked, creating a private sonic space that was, according to custom, violated only in an emergency. Interaction was via email, even if the participants occupied neighbouring cubicles. This made sense to Arjun. Personal space is valuable. The ability to prioritize one's communications is valuable. Interrupting someone to talk to them is a way of pushing your query to the top of their stack. It overrides someone's access controls and objectively lessens their functionality, which was as close to an engineering definition of rudeness as he felt he was ever likely to come.

Away from the top floor Arjun's social life was limited. This was not a problem, since out of the office he was fully occupied with the various novelties of Redmond life (bus timetables, local government regulations, tree names) and the construction and maintenance of his home-computer network. In the cafeteria, like many of his colleagues, he tended to eat alone. A lot of people in the AV team shunned the communal areas of the campus altogether, finding them threatening and unpredictable. Though Arjun followed the workaholic Virugenix ethos (unofficial company motto: '*Sometimes it is noble to sleep in the crawlspace of your desk*') in his rare moments away from his cubicle he sometimes craved conversation. He tentatively struck up nodding acquaintanceships with a Bengali who worked on firewalls and a Dilliwallah who did something or other for the diagnostics product team. He even took up an invitation to dinner with the Dilliwallah's family, but, though he took the precaution of preparing a list of conversation topics, the evening was not a success.

What in-house socializing did exist was largely conducted through the circulation of entertaining data sets. The *joke*, in its classic office form, was popular.

Q. How many programmers does it take to change a light bulb?
A. None. It's a hardware problem.

Unfortunately jokes seemed to cause confusion for some staff members, often provoking detailed (and even angry) dissections of their semantics. A safer mode was the *questionnaire*. Something about multiple-choice tests chimed with the r 'n' d personality, and formatted quizzes were sent round at the rate of several a day, asking the respondents to assess their knowledge of *Angel*, their 'nerditude quotient', their sexual performance. Week by week, Arjun learned more about himself. His dungeons and dragons alignment turned out to be Lawful Good. His penis was of average size. He was not a secret Mac user, though his lack of familiarity with sex toys and his inability to recall an occasion when he dressed up in leather or rubber clothing to please his man rated him 'an old-fashioned gal'. Twelve lattes and nine Cokes a day also bracketed him a 'high-level caffeine addict'. Worried, he sent an email to a support group, who mailed back suggesting he drank fewer caffeinated beverages.

One questionnaire generated more traffic on the Virugenix intranet than all the others. Under the heading 'How Asperger's are You?' it asked the respondent to consider such issues as:

Do you meet people's eyes when you talk to them?
Do you find it difficult to develop or maintain relationships?
Does ambiguity confuse you?
Do people accuse you of failing to share their interests?
Do others get angry or upset at you for reasons which appear illogical?
Do you have any inflexible routines or habits?
Do you excel at detailed logical tasks?
Do you have to remember to modulate your voice when speaking?
Do you have difficulty decoding social behaviour?
Do you have an encompassing obsession with one or more specific and restricted activities?
Do people tell you your technical preoccupation with parts of objects is abnormal or unusual?
Are small personal rituals important to you?
Do you have any repetitive motor mannerisms (tics, gestures, rocking, etc.)?
Are you or have you ever been employed as an engineer?

Asperger's Syndrome was a bad thing, a *disease*. Yet, as he filled in his answers, Arjun realized that this profile fitted the majority of people in the AV group, possibly including himself. He was obsessive. He liked repetition. He hated ambiguity. Change could be a problem. Was he ill?

Others evidently harboured similar suspicions, and for several days a stream of messages flowed around the intranet. To his surprise Arjun discovered that at Virugenix (unlike most workplaces, where being diagnosed with a neurological disorder might be a cause for concern), Asperger's was a badge of honour. Emails pointed out that mild AS is associated with extremely high IQ scores, that AS sufferers are often brilliant programmers, and that Bill Gates (who rocked back and forth, spoke in a monotone, was obsessed with technical detail and happened to be a billionaire) was proof that high-function autists were superior to the common herd. Someone mailed to say that he had always suspected 'people like us' were wired differently to 'people like them'. Gradually a competition developed, as people tried to prove that their own special cocktail of dysfunctional personality traits was casually connected to professional brilliance.

To: avgroup@virugenix.com
From: darrylg@virugenix.com
Subject: I WIN FOOLS

FACT: If I did not have sound and visual reminders programmed into my PDA, I would forget to change my clothes EVER.
FACT: I can recite pi to ninety-seven decimal places and know the exact times of sunrise and sunset at seven named locations in the continental United States FOR EVERY DAY OF THE YEAR . . .

Arjun suspected that Darryl's email disqualified him, since boasting was excluded by a clause in the American Psychiatric Association's definition of Asperger's, which mentioned a 'lack of spontaneous seeking to share enjoyment, interests or achievements with other people'. He tried to assess his own situation. He was clearly less symptomatic than some of his workmates: Shiro, for example, never spoke and his only discernible enthusiasm was for a certain series of telephone switches used by Pacific Bell in the early 1970s. He, on the other hand, knew not to stand too close to people and responded to body language with his own appropriate body language. But did he do so naturally, or was it a learned response? At what point should one consider oneself abnormal? The question started to preoccupy him (was that itself a symptom?), so finally he emailed the person who had first sent out the mail, and asked for advice.

To: chriss@virugenix.com
From: arjunm@virugenix.com

hello chris girl or boy i am wondering about your quiz . . .

A response came back that afternoon.

To: arjunm@virugenix.com
From: chriss@virugenix.com

2 x chromosomes. How do you feel about team sports?. . .

She had been roped into a softball game over at the Microsoft campus. If he wanted to talk to her, she would be there on the sports field after work. He would recognize her easily enough.

I'll be the one with most visible tattooing.

As befitted the demesne of the reigning power in Redmond, the Microsoft campus sat on top of a hill. Arjun could walk there from Berry Acres in ten minutes, and he had hovered outside the entrance once or twice, but his meeting with *chriss* was the first time he had gone any further. The MS perimeter enclosed almost 300 acres of terrain, landscaped around discreet buildings that for some inexplicable Gatesian reason were all named after famous golf courses. The structures were functional glass-clad boxes, with few architectural quirks or tics. Security cameras perched proudly on their roofs, and they were linked by marked fitness trails, colour-keyed according to length and difficulty. New cars sat in the parking lots. Young people in conservative casual clothing walked along the paths or waited for company shuttle buses. At the centre of the complex was a large playing field, used by staff, their guests and local freeloaders for every kind of activity from five-a-side soccer to interdepartmental croquet tournaments.

The softball game was not hard to find. Arjun just followed the sound of whooping and cheering. When he reached the diamond he found to his surprise that there were very few spectators. The noise was generated by the players, who were positively reinforcing each other with a vigour peculiar to corporate employees engaged in an organized bonding exercise. One team even had yellow polo shirts with *Go Sales!* printed on the back. At the side of the field, an impressive buffet table had been set up, laden with soft drinks and finger food to stimulate post-game networking. Despite the yelling, no one appeared to be taking the game very seriously.

As Arjun walked up, he spotted her: a slight young woman in grass-stained denim cut-offs and a sleeveless black t-shirt with *iloveyou.vbs* written in white across the front. Her brown hair was tied up in a scarf, and from biceps to wrist her left arm was covered in a blue-black coil of intricate tattooing. Against the backdrop of khakis and polo shirts she stood out. Hesitantly he held up a hand. She beckoned him over.

'Arjun, huh? Chris. Good thing you made it. We're one short.' She handed him an aluminium bat. 'You're up next.'

Off the bench. On the team. Chris's first gift to him.

That afternoon Arjun surprised himself, making contact with the ball more often than not and sending sedentary yellow-shirted salesfolk huffing and puffing into the outfield. His success modified his natural contempt for softball, which he considered basically an attention-deficit version of cricket, a sort of child's bat-and-ball game with no real tactical complexity. Naturally he kept this opinion to himself; it was fun to be congratulated on his play, especially by someone as unusual as Christine Schnorr.

She was not beautiful exactly, or even inexactly. Her face was lopsided, as if it had drifted down to the left, and her right eye wandered intermittently when she was talking, lending her expression an uncannily divided quality, as if she were concentrating simultaneously on him and on some object in the middle distance. At twenty-nine, she was older than Arjun, and he got a sense that she had seen more of the world than him. Since Arjun had seen relatively little of the world, he reasoned that many people (particularly in an affluent country with a developed tourist industry) would statistically come into this category, were the idiom to be understood in a strictly geographical sense. But there was something less definable, something extra-geographical about her confidence, a restrained energy that seemed to come from knowing things he did not. He liked it.

Christine worked for the firewall group, and her preferred mode of social interaction was the *interrogation*. As the game dissolved into chat and buffet-grazing, she started to question him. Had Arjun any brothers and sisters? Where *exactly* in India? What social class would he say his parents belonged to? His answers appeared to form a satisfactory constellation of data points, and she nodded encouragingly, as if he had confirmed a hypothesis or made progress in some unstated experimental task. She appeared to have forgotten that the purpose of the meeting was for him to ask her something, rather than the other way around. He took a deep breath.

'I'm worried, Christine.'

'Chris. Why do you say that?'

'Oh, sorry. I'm worried, Chris. This Asperger's condition. I –'

'Plot or detail?'

'Pardon?'

'When you go to see a movie, what do you remember? The story, or weird stuff like the number the hero dials to call his mom?'

Arjun thought for a moment. 'The story.'

'I wouldn't worry too much. You're doing a lot better than most of us. Anyway, you seem functional to me, on the surface at least. Would you say you were functional?'

This was a harder one. He hesitated. She threw up her hands.

'OK, OK. Existential question. Uncomputable. You know, I'm kind of beginning to regret sending that thing round. Don't get me wrong, Arjun, you seem like a nice guy and all, but some of the email I've been getting – Jesus, it's a can of worms.'

'So you think I'm all right? Though I'm also correct in saying you're not medically qualified?'

'Medically qualified? Dude, lighten up. I just pulled it off some website. Anyway, what're you so worried about? Who's to say what's normal and what's not? You're happy, no?'

'Yes.'

'Well,' she said with an air of finality, 'then shut the fuck up.'

He looked shocked. She started to laugh. After a moment, he laughed too.

Chris's decision to take the dorky Indian guy under her wing had no rational basis. Sure, the Asperger's thing slayed her. While every other macho idiot in AV was trying to prove how interesting he was, here was this sweet sincere guy, just worried about his health. His literalism (actually he was kind of literal – maybe he *was* Asperger's) was cute. It was also a form of directness, and for Chris directness was a good thing. And though he dressed even worse than most computer guys and had a wispy moustache on his top lip, he was not totally unpresentable. He was tall, for example, and had nice skin. There was something else too: a hiddenness. He acted like he had something important going on, that on some frequency of his life beyond the visible spectrum there was great excitement. When she went to the movies, Christine tended to concentrate on detail rather than on plot, but she did enjoy a mystery. She also enjoyed tinkering with people, taking them apart and putting them back together. So as they walked back to the parking lot after the game, Chris made two decisions: to hang out with Arjun and find out his secret, and to really truly try to give up this whole AS/non-AS game, which was beginning to screw with her head. It was getting as bad as the previous year, when everyone at Virugenix had fixated on a system for classifying your personality type according to your preference for early or late Beatles.

A group of them drove downtown, and she and Arjun wound up in a bar sharing a pitcher of bad margaritas with some of her Microsoft friends. The conversation circled round the usual stuff: apartments, jobs, where people were going on vacation. She gave Arjun the executive summary of her life (family in New Jersey, college years at Stanford, always wanted to be a programmer, weird for a girl, but there you go) and found out some surface information about him.

He was, as she suspected, on one of those slave visas, being paid a fraction of what it would cost Darryl to hire an American engineer. She dropped in what an asshole she thought Darryl was, with his bits of moon rock and his I-was-in-*Wired* Ghostbuster bullshit. Arjun seemed really uncomfortable, as if he didn't want to say bad things about his boss. He seemed to miss his family, especially his kid sister. He had a picture of her in his wallet. His *sister*. Chris was not given to fits of girlie emotion, but the only available term for that was *sweet*. When she asked what he did when he wasn't working, he hedged, saying something about personal projects. When ten thirty rolled around, he looked at his watch and announced he had to go.

'Up early tomorrow?'

'I suppose so. I have things to do.'

'Where's your car? Did you leave it at Microsoft?'

'No. I don't have a car. I'll walk home.'

Out it came, bit by bit. He didn't drive? Chris was actually shocked, wondered for one dumb moment whether this was a sort of Hindu religious thing, like orthodox Jews not being able to tear toilet paper on the sabbath.

'It must be hard for you.'

'It's OK. I like to walk. It gives me time to think.'

'How about a bike?' suggested one of the other guys.

Arjun nodded uncertainly. Chris found one of those third-margarita sentences forming on her lips.

'I'll teach you.'

'What?'

'To drive. If you want, I'll teach you. I'm a good teacher. I have strong interpersonal skills.'

His face crumpled into a huge grin. 'Really?' he said. 'You mean it?'

'Sure.'

'Great. That's so – so great. Fantastic! You know, Chris, you really are a very nice person.'

Out of anyone else's mouth that would have been ironic.

He ended up getting a ride from one of the Microsoft guys, who lived near Berry Acres. Chris finished margarita número cuatro and wondered what she had gotten herself into.

'OK, now turn the wheel. That's right – no – other direction, you were OK the first time. There you go. Check for traffic. Mirror. Signal. Now move off slowly . . .'

Teaching Arjun to drive turned out to be – well, not the *lowest* stress activity Chris had ever undertaken. More than once she said a prayer for the Honda's mirrors, and the front bumper lost a low-intensity conflict with a wooden planter in the Virugenix parking lot.

'Slow down, Arjun. Brake . . . brake!'

The car was a piece of crap anyway, so Chris could be reasonably zen about the damage. From her point of view the first lesson was a qualified success, apart from the weird moment when Arjun burst into tears. Two or three sessions in, he could more or less propel the car forwards and backwards, understood the basic rules of the road and even seemed intermittently aware of other road users. After an hour of white-knuckle 15-m.p.h. progress round Redmond, Chris tended to need a drink, which was how the two of them came to be regulars at Jimmy's Brewhouse, a snug little place with a neon Budweiser sign in the window and a selection of microbrew ales which Arjun was working through in strict alphabetical order.

Chris liked him. When he drank, his shyness evaporated and he became animated, waving his arms and laughing. He talked a lot about his extended family, which seemed to have more members than American Express, and he had a habit of comparing events in his life with scenes in Indian movies. Since Chris had never been to an Indian movie, the parallels were mostly lost on her, but it became clear that at least some of his hidden life was spent in a swashbuckling world of passionate love affairs, family feuds, epic struggles and big MGM-style production numbers.

'You're not gay, are you?' she theorized one night, after one too many pints of Jimmy's Big Bear Porter. Seeing his crestfallen face, she backtracked hurriedly. 'Forget I said that.' Later she caught herself flirting, wagging a finger and giving him arch smiles. 'You know,' she heard herself say, 'you should shave off that moustache. You'd look much better without it.'

'Really?' he said. 'You think so?'

The next day at work the moustache had gone. Despite the warning bells ringing in her head, Chris decided she was pleased. He did look better.

Another night at Jimmy's, they worked a little too far through the alphabet. By the time she found herself staring down into a half-drunk glass of Sammamish Steam Ale, Chris was reconciled to leaving the car on the street and getting up early to pick it up before it got a ticket. Arjun was propped up on his elbows, staring at her tattoos. 'They're intense,' he said in that odd in-between accent of his – American vowels caught between treacly Indian consonants.

'It's a tribal design,' she told him.

'Of which tribe?'

'I don't think it's *from* anywhere, Arjun. It's more of a generic thing. Just generically tribal.'

He considered that for a moment.

'Didn't your parents mind?'

'They didn't really have a say. I wanted to do it, so I did. End of story.'

'But why?'

'Why? It was something I wanted. Nic and I both got tattooed around the same time, at this place in San Francisco. The scene is really big here, Arjun. It's a kind of a ritual act. You guys do it in India, right, the holy men or whoever . . .'

She trailed off. Arjun was not listening. His eyes looked glazed.

'Who's Nic?' he asked.

'I've told you about Nic,' she said, but realized she hadn't, not really.

He nodded, jutting out his bottom lip in a sagacious expression. 'I think I need to go home.' As he tried to stand up, he knocked his chair backwards on to the floor and staggered into the table. Beer spread across the wood-effect surface. One or two of Jimmy's patrons turned round from the bar to watch.

Chris grabbed on to his arm. 'Hold on there, partner. Let's just take it one step at a time.'

There was no way he was going to make it back to Berry Acres so Chris took a blurry executive decision and steered him in the direction of her place. Nicolai wasn't home, and she deposited Arjun on the couch in her living room while she searched out some extra bedding and drank several glasses of water, hoping to stave off the worst of the hangover which was already bearing down on her like a truck. When she went back in to check on him, he had passed out. She arranged him lengthwise, removed the sneakers from the feet dangling over the end of the couch and laid a quilt over the top like a shroud. Then she went to bed.

When Nic tumbled through the door an hour later, loaded and horny after a night out with his buddies, he made so much noise that Chris was sure Arjun would wake up. Even when the two of them went at it like teenagers, Nic yelling incomprehensible Bulgarian sexy stuff and taking her hand away from his mouth every time she tried to shut him up, there was no sound from the next room. Arjun was probably down for the count.

Unfortunately not, though he had no memory of arriving in the dark place. His head was spinning, his mouth was parched, and somewhere off to his left someone was shouting. He listened, trying to gather his consciousness into one portable bundle. There is something about the sound of other people having sex which clears the head, and little by little he was drawn through the wall towards the noises, gradually discerning ragged breathing, muffled groans and unmistakably Chris-like giggles beneath the repetitive beat of the thumping headboard. There is also something about the sound of sex which, if you are lying on a lumpy couch with the beginnings of a hangover and your feet sticking out from under a strange-smelling quilt, can induce feelings of melancholy. For a few moments Arjun contemplated the world's colder and lonelier aspects, then blacked out into a turbulent alcoholic void.

Guy was sitting next to Gabriella in a booth at Sake-Souk, a newly opened Mayfair restaurant. Whenever a waiter came by, he was witty and she dispensed one of her vivid smiles, but as soon as they felt they were not being observed they lapsed into uneasy silence, chewing their way through the chef's Japanese–Lebanese fusion food as if oblivious to its trendsetting collisions of taste and presentation.

Guy watched the evening traffic through the restaurant's front window, the yellow lights of taxis, the sleek European cars delivering their occupants to places of discreet entertainment. He was thinking about money, its generation and decay. Specifically about his money, which was unaccountably refusing to regenerate at the required rate. He was a man with overheads. He glanced back at Gabriella, who was pushing an aubergine and chickpea dragonroll around her plate and staring inscrutably at a point behind his shoulder. She looked beautiful. Her hair and eyes and nose and teeth. He put a hand down on the banquette, next to her thigh. He had not mentioned his money troubles; Gabriella could sense neediness and did not tolerate it very well. He wanted to touch her, but it felt unwise. Gaby could do this, generate invisible armour for herself.

Realizing she was being watched, Gabriella smiled and ran a self-conscious hand through her long brown hair. Guy smiled back, trying to feel reassured. She really was the best-looking girl in the restaurant. When he first saw her at the Film Fund party, he had hoped she would be the one, by which he meant the one who would become the centre of his life, or at least would be located at the centre of the several intersecting value circles which he visualized as defining his life. He risked slipping a hand on to her lap, sliding his palm over the sheer surface of her skirt. She put a hand over it and patted. He was not sure how to interpret this.

Gabriella was too caught up in her own reflections to notice Guy's anxiety. She had got lost in the restaurant's dark wood and white linen interior, a world in which space occurred in discrete platonic units, boxes of vacancy. She watched Guy take a bite of his hamachi kebab, making that irritating clicking sound with his teeth. Across the room a man was staring at her. She did not feel hungry.

When people were looking for a comparison for Gabriella, they usually went for Audrey Hepburn. She had the same high cheekbones and air of aristocratic startledness, of having been marooned wherever you encountered her, a refugee from a better, gentler place. But, unlike Hepburn, there was a rough edge, a raggedness of chewed nails and cigarette smoke which gave her an air of potential promiscuity that Guy (among many others) found irresistible. Gabriella knew this. She had learned about irresistibility aged twelve, when a friend of her mother tried to kiss her at the zoo. In the reptile house.

A multiplication of boxes. Nothing but trouble, really.

The previous night she had stayed up late with Sophie, her friend from the Sussex boarding school where she had spent an unhappy year trying to do A-levels. Gaby had had a bad time because of food and boys and being foreign. Sophie had had a bad time because of food and no boys. They sat opposite each other on the tropical hardwood floor of Guy's flat, comfortably occupying their old roles: Sophie watching Gaby do something, in this case chopping out lines of coke on a framed photograph of herself and Guy diving in the Red Sea. 'You look so happy in that picture,' she said. Sophie said things like that. You have such nice eyes. That is such a pretty dress. It was one of the things which made them friends.

Gaby looked down at the two people in the photograph, at their salty hair and the masks perched on top of their heads, and tried to remember what the one who was her had felt. Careful to keep her hair out of the way, she did a line and from between pinched nostrils told Sophie, 'He's being such an idiot at the moment.'

Sophie was always eager to hear dirt about Guy, who misheard what she said and looked over her shoulder at parties. She rolled her eyes sympathetically and waited for more. Gaby passed her the rolled-up note.

Guy had put the picture up. It was evidence: that they were together and this was their place, that because of shared memories as demonstrated in Exhibit A they also had a future. For her part, Gaby mistrusted snapshots. She possessed very few of her own, perhaps a dozen recorded instants of time which she could not fit together to make a pattern, let alone a life. Herself, five years old on the gangplank of a yacht in Greece, holding the hand of the captain. As a baby on a rug in the apartment in Vienna. Spindly angry thirteen by a hotel pool in Singapore. There was one of her parents getting married, an ostentatious eight-by-ten which had run in a magazine. They wore the flamboyant hats and collars and scarves of 1971 and were surrounded by people. To Gaby it looked no more or less than it was. Financier marries fashion model, turn to page 86. There was one of her sister too, squinting into the camera somewhere hot and dry.

She had always been in motion, even when they were all together. Money moved her. First it was her father's; later it belonged to her mother's boyfriends. It took her to various places in which had existed various versions of herself, each furnished with a nanny and a school and an address to memorize and another set of little girls to invite to a birthday party in an expensive restaurant where there was always a clown and no one laughed. There was only one constant: sooner or later everyone and everything was left behind.

By the time she was sixteen her father was a man she met in hotels and her mother was thinking of marrying again, so on a whim she asked to go to boarding school. An English girls' school like the ones in books. At the time everyone thought it was the perfect solution. After it didn't work out there was Lausanne and Paris and her own modelling and a Brazilian photographer boyfriend and too many drugs, but weirdly it was her sister, the self-sufficient one who shouted at her mother about guilt and responsibility, who took the overdose. Caroline's movement had mostly been across Asia. Beaches and ashrams. Jewellery-making.

Towards the end it accelerated, took on the quality of flight. By then she was back in Europe and always part of a group, as if she needed people as ballast, numbers to hold her down. Political and religious groups. Self-actualization. Healing. There were retreats and communes. Fasting and chanting. Then sleeping pills on the bathroom floor of a farmhouse in, where was it, Andalusia? It had been hard to find out exactly why she had gone there. Like so many events in Gaby's life, Caroline's death made no particular sense. It was just a thing.

Her parents spent the funeral politely convincing each other the death was accidental, though Gaby knew how the money had hounded Caroline, how she hated it for making her life into a game. Watching the two of them edit the story to suit themselves made them so terrible in her eyes that she left Firenze that afternoon and for good measure left Paris and the photographer too and somehow London was where she ended up.

Sophie chattered, taking gulps of Chardonnay and rubbing her nose with her fingers. 'I don't know why you stay with him. Of course he's rich and everything. Or at least he seems rich. You can't tell with men these days. One minute they are, then you discover they're not.'

Gaby looked at her with a twinge of distaste. Underneath its crown of expensively streaked hair her face was flushed with wine and cocaine. Pink patches mottled her neck and cheeks, giving her the appearance of a side of marbled beef. She had, Gaby reflected, got bigger since school. Now a size eighteen with a pure maths degree, she combined high earnings as a telecoms analyst with a bleak and hostile view of men. In her Fulham townhouse there was a walk-in closet filled with shoes, tiny pointy confections of silk and leather which cost hundreds of pounds a pair and made her feet hurt. Gaby looked at the twin plasters on her friend's bare heels. Poor Sophie, with her dreams of daintiness.

She got up and slid the door open on to the balcony. Sophie followed, and they looked over the river, at the costume-drama ripple and glint of Chelsea reflected in the water.

'It's a good view,' Sophie snorted. 'But is that enough? I mean, what else is Mr Swift bringing to the table?'

*

So Gabriella sat in Sake-Souk listening to Guy chewing his main course and thinking about what he was bringing to the table and eventually found herself staring back at the man on the other side of the room. He looked familiar, an actor maybe.

Guy followed her eyeline. 'Do you know him?' he asked suspiciously.

'I don't think so.'

Guy took a moment to revel in her voice, the way her beautiful mouth turned *th* into *f*, her bored elongated *i*. He heard in it the generic European female tone of techno records, a voice made to say, 'Oh baby, you make me feel so good.' The untapped erotics of Gaby's accent diverted him from the problem of the man at the far end of the restaurant, and he forgot the icy look he was about to flash him and instead made an attempt to bridge the gap which had opened up during dinner.

'Sweetie, I thought maybe we could try out Thailand this summer.'

'Try it out? Why? Do you want to buy it?'

She was looking at him with an expression of unfathomable scorn. He began to think he had said something wrong. Gaby was a great girl but she did have her moods.

When Chris's alarm went in the morning, she stumbled out of the bedroom to find the couch vacant and the spare quilt neatly folded up on top. A note was propped up on the coffee table thanking her without punctuation or capital letters for a nice evening, and as Nicolai groaned and called out plaintively for coffee a momentary stab of unease penetrated her nausea. Did she do something last night? Later, from her desk at Virugenix, she sent Arjun mail. He did not reply. That week she was swamped by work, and the silence lengthened into several days, a weekend. The following Monday she spotted him in the cafeteria and went over to say hi. He said hi back and carried on eating. She asked if he still wanted to go on with the lessons. She meant it as a joke. He nodded hesitantly but wouldn't make eye contact, shuffling his feet under the Formica table as if he couldn't wait for her to go away.

'Arjun, did I piss you off the other day?'

'Pardon? Oh, no, not at all.'

'So why are you acting like this?'

'Like what?'

'You know what I mean.'

He grimaced and shrugged his shoulders petulantly. 'I'm not pissed off; I'm very happy. Yes, let's have a driving lesson. Email me, OK?'

'Come on, don't be an asshole. Was it Nicolai?'

'Who?'

'I told you I lived with someone.'

'No, you didn't.' There was a long uneasy pause, as he struggled for words. 'Well you did, but I thought you just meant – that is – you didn't tell me you were married.'

'Not married, Arjun, just living together. And we – well, it's not like we're exactly traditional – look, why am I even explaining this? All I'm saying is I'm sorry, OK, for whatever it is. I want us to be friends.'

'So do I,' he said.

This was Chris's cue to say great absolutely see you some time and walk off. When they start to get weird on you, it's a prelude to one thing only. Mr Arjun Mehta was turning into trouble. He would have to go somewhere else for driver ed. For some reason what came out of her mouth was 'Good, so why don't we act like friends and hang out for an evening? We could do something – I don't know – we could catch one of your movies.'

Arjun looked confused. 'My movies? You mean Indian movies? You want to see a Hindi movie?'

'Sure.'

He looked surprised.

'Great,' he said uncertainly. 'I'm not sure you'll like it.'

'Why not let me try? How about tomorrow night?'

'Uh, OK.'

Which is how they ended up driving to a mall in Kirkland to see a movie that involved two boys and two girls who took three and a half hours to persuade their parents to let them marry each other in the correct combination. Chris was bored. Was the guy in the see-through organdie shirt really supposed to be cool? He had a mullet, for chrissakes. And how precisely did they make it to the pyramids? Since it was shown without subtitles, Arjun had to whisper the important plot points to her, and while he sat entranced, she drifted in and out of the story, following trains of thought about the reality or otherwise of the older guy's beard, the stones in the mother's necklace, the vaguely *Dynasty* salmon-pink palace where much of the action took place. Finally the nuptials were completed, and the audience spilled out into the muted evening lighting-scheme of the mall. Chris looked around at the young Asian couples and single-sex clusters of teenagers and saw that everyone was animated, smiling. Arjun had the same look. Satisfied. Emotionally replete.

'That,' he said, humming one of the tunes from the film, 'was just too *too* good.'

Chris spotted three other white faces, a man and two women, each half of a couple, each looking as mystified as she felt. Quickly she devoted her attention to rustling up some kind of critical response; Arjun was going to ask her what she thought, and she was going to have to come up with something better than the real-beard-real-rocks-real-palace conundrum or he would be offended. This was supposed to be about the two of them making up, after all.

She was prevented from giving an opinion by one of those sudden and unexpected encounters that can be given a positive spin only by reminding yourself that it would have been worse if you were with your mother. What Tori and the girl-bar crew were doing staggering around at midnight in the Totem Lake Mall was anyone's guess. The first Chris knew about it was when her hair was jerked back and a pierced tongue was rammed down her throat as the centrepiece of a very wet French kiss.

'Hey there, you little piece of chicken,' growled Tori, releasing Chris's face and playfully pinching her nipple. 'How *you* doing?' Six-one in her socks and worked-out some way beyond the call of duty, Tori (the joke went) was born too late. Had she been on the scene before 1989, she could have found work as a monument in an Eastern bloc town square. Ordinarily she was a handful, but tonight, whacked up on this week's c.n.s. stimulant of choice, sweating profusely and surrounded by her adoring biker-jacketed fan club, her name would head any list Chris could compile of people not to introduce to shy heterosexual men from countries with conservative moral codes.

'Who's your buddy?' asked Tori, eyeing Arjun like a particularly dubious fast-food menu item.

'Christ, Tori,' seethed Chris. All around them, the South Asian film fans of Kirkland were reacting to their first lesbian kiss. Tutting parents scooped up their children. Gap-clad teens experienced a sudden broadening of their horizons. Arjun looked as if someone had rewired him, badly. Chris was pissed off. Tori's friends were making eyes at her and sniggering at Arjun. Luckily the crew were on their way to a party, and once Chris had made it clear she wouldn't be tagging along, they headed off in a tramp of engineer boots and ripped cotton. She watched them, relieved that nothing involving more nudity had taken place.

Next she had to deal with Arjun, whose system appeared to have hung.

'You. Bar. Now. We need to talk.'

And so Arjun was led to a Mexican-theme place with a plastic bandito figure outside it where the staff served them even though they were stacking chairs and wiping the tables and there he was made to down two shots of tequila and given a crash course in contemporary American sexual mores. Chris, it seemed, lived and slept with Nicolai, and, though they were not married, this arrangement had been their default setting for the last two years. Though Nicolai could correctly be called Chris's *boyfriend*, the two of them (here was where it got complicated) also slept with other people, on a basis described as open but limited, the limit being defined by the degree of emotional involvement with the outside partner. As Chris explained all this, Arjun experienced a turbulent flow of emotions including (but not limited to) disappointment, jealousy, hope, intrigue, sexual arousal and guilt. Blushing furiously, he tried to bury them all. He put it to Chris (perceptively, he thought) that her limit-definition was unsound, and a less vague system for running her relationship would be to use measurable criteria like time spent away from the partner or the performance of particular sex acts. Chris told him to concentrate on what she was saying. Arjun started to argue that this was precisely what he had been doing, but something in her expression stopped him. He had a question.

'Where is he from?'

'What?'

'Your boyfriend. Which country is he from?'

'Nic's Bulgarian-American. Is that relevant?'

'Ah, it was *Bulgarian*.'

He stared intently at his empty shot glass; even in America it was probably indecent to meet someone's eyes while remembering what they sound like having sex. He was so busy trying to route around this problem that he missed what she said next.

'I beg your pardon?'

No, he had heard right. Some of the people Chris slept with were women, and the tall one with the shaved head was one of them. Chris accepted that because of his culture Arjun might be shocked by this but she hoped he would try to be open-minded. He ought to recognize that it was not as if she owed him this explanation, or anything at all. She just wanted things to be clear.

Arjun was in fact familiar with lesbianism, which was a favourite theme of the CD-ROMs Aamir sold at Gabbar Singh's Internet Shack. Admittedly the physical appearance of these particular lesbians had thrown him, since all the ones in Aamir's pictures had big hair and lacy underwear. But that was only one of a number of problematic areas in Chris's speech. It was difficult to know where to begin. In confusing semantic situations, he had often found it helpful to define terms before proceeding.

'Is there a word for someone like you?'

'Hello? Think before you speak there, buddy.'

'You are a bisexual, yes?'

'You make it sound like a medical condition.'

'Oh, so you think it has a physiological basis?'

For some reason the question seemed to make Chris angry, and she stormed out of the bar. Arjun was careful to leave a tip for the barman before he followed her. Four drinks. One two three four singles, tucked under a glass. He tried to take this mood-swing in his stride. Christine Schnorr was an alien creature (what Indian girl would have such tattoos?), and her unusual operating rules were part of her difference. Some things about her personality were clearly national traits: her hostility to her family, for example. Others, like her anger and this new set of sexual revelations, had some mysterious alternative source.

Apart from Priti and a couple of cousins (aunties didn't count) Arjun had never spent much time with women. He certainly had no idea how to handle an angry one. When he caught up with Chris at the car, she was pacing up and down, twirling her keys threateningly round one finger. Spotting him, she launched into a tirade which echoed through the underground lot.

'I don't fucking believe this, I really don't. What in hell gives you the right to talk to me that way? I don't have to answer to you for anything. Not a damn thing, you understand? Yeah I fucked Tori. So what? I mean, is this Nazi Germany or something? Who are you to call someone sick? What gives you the right to judge people? You know what? Fuck you, Arjun. Fuck! You!'

She pulled open the car door and got in. The engine started with a roar. Arjun's composure began to fall to pieces. His wrongdoing was obviously more serious than he thought. Why would she be like this? What were you supposed to do? Maybe there was a physical technique, a fireman's lift, an angry woman Heimlich Manoeuvre. Chris started to pull out of the parking bay. Desperate to stop her, he ran round to the front of the Honda. As she jerked the car forwards, he ended up sprawled over the hood.

'Why are you so angry?' he mouthed through the windshield. Chris wound down a window.

'Get the fuck off my car!'

'I'm sorry,' he implored. 'Why are you angry with me?'

'Fuck off!'

'But tell me why?'

'Because – because I hate bigoted assholes like you. Just because your religion or whatever says women are your slaves doesn't mean I have to play along. Now will you get off my fucking car or am I going to have to run you down?'

Now Arjun was scared. Never before had he faced the serious threat of violence.

'You mustn't do this!' he shouted. 'I'm not a religious person. I'm a rationalist! Please, Chris!'

Chris leaned her head against the steering wheel. How did she get into this? Splayed across the hood, Arjun looked like a tall, skinny marsupial. A lemur perhaps. Or a sloth. A mall security guard was jogging towards them, speaking into a walkie-talkie. She waved him away.

'It's fine, OK. Don't sweat it.'

Uncertainly, the guard slowed down. She waved again and smiled a sweet good-citizen smile. Then she stuck her head back out of the window.

'Get in.'

Arjun gingerly released his grip on the windshield wipers and slid into the passenger seat. Chris pulled the rest of the way out of the spot and headed for the exit. Arjun decided to trust her. It seemed unlikely she would do anything rash now.

Since the night they got too drunk, Arjun's feelings about Chris had undergone a transition. The sounds that seeped through the partition wall had flayed away a skin of romantic possibility. He understood now that there could never have been true love between them, not as he had pictured it: Radha and Krishna, Devdas and Parvati, Raj and Bobby. Only after the illusion was crushed did he admit to himself he had considered it at all. What would his parents have said? It would have been impossible.

They were on the freeway before he felt it was safe to try to clear things up. 'I'm sorry,' he began, truthfully. 'I've offended you. I don't think you're sick and I have no professional legal experience and I know this is the land of the free and you have full citizenship rights to do whatever you want at any time.'

Chris allowed herself to be slightly mollified. 'That's a start.'

'All I wanted to know is – well, this is all rather new to me. I expect you are taught about it in sexual-education classes. You have to remember I haven't had your experiences.'

Chris narrowed her eyes. 'What do you mean, experiences?'

'Sexual experiences. Of course – I understand the procedure. I'm not entirely ignorant, you know.'

'You understand the procedure?'

'For sex. I've read a lot of things about it. It's important to educate yourself. I've seen pictures too, of course . . .'

'You've read a lot.'

'Yes.'

'But you've done it too.'

The silence stretched out between them, broken only by the rumble of passing cars. Arjun looked at his hands.

'Well, not as such.'

'You mean with another guy. Homosexuality.'

'With anyone.'

'You've never had sex at all?' She picked her words carefully. 'Arjun, are you telling me you're a virgin?'

'There's no need to be crude about it.'

'I'm sorry. But you're how old? Twenty-three?'

He nodded. Chris considered the matter.

'This is a line, right? You think if you say you're a virgin I'm going to feel sorry for you and fuck you.'

Arjun went very quiet. When he spoke again his voice was small and tight. 'Maybe you should just stop the car. I don't like to sit here and be insulted.'

'My God, you're telling the truth.'

'Why would I lie?'

'Why would you lie?'

She decided not to get into that one and carried on driving down the road, thinking to herself, a *virgin*? Oh, brother.

Chris would want it known that her decision to have sex with Arjun should be put down solely and entirely to drugs. Were there a national system of learning from mistakes, the story would be written up and distributed to schoolchildren as a government information leaflet, a true-life illustration of why drugs are bad and the people who take them are stupid.

A few weeks later, on one of Nic's guy Saturday nights, when their apartment was invaded by men with beer and snack-foods and a primal urge to swap Mariners stats, she found herself at the Iron Bar, a vaguely fetishy mixed-gay place in the city, filling in Tori's crowd about that evening at the mall and the world of Arjun Mehta more generally. Arjun, she explained, was actually a sweet guy. He wasn't really misogynist or homophobic, just naive. Get him on the subject of computers and you almost forgot what a freak he was.

Maybe it was cruel to bring up the virgin thing, maybe it made her a bad person, but it was Saturday night and she did it and it got a laugh. I'm telling you he's as fresh as the day he stepped off the plane. You're kidding. How old? Carlos (predictably) said oh give *me* his phone number. Tori (ditto) started talking about strap-ons. In the air hung the consensus idea that it would be somehow *entertaining* to do something about Arjun. The topic cycled back intermittently through the evening. Scenarios were imagined, positions devised. For a while an extended riff on the word *deflower* took hold of the table. Somewhere later down the line Chris did half an E and a line of speed and some time after that, when she had done a couple more lines and was bored with the music at the club but not yet ready to face drunken horny badbreath post-guynight Nic, it started to feel like a good idea to actually go through with it, to take another half a pill and go round to Arjun's place and fuck him.

This, she thought as she slid around in the back seat of a taxi, was going to make a great story. She was getting little fluttery rushes and the idea of being touched seemed really good, and she took sips of bottled water and chewed gum and didn't really think about what she was going to do or say when she got there. He was a guy. She was going round to offer him sex. Lab-rat stuff. What could be more simple? Her serotonin-drenched brain pulled up a sugar-coated version of Arjun, somehow less gawky than *lean*, less sallow than *mahogany-skinned*, a tender young man in more or less matching clothing, ready to be initiated into the art of love.

Standing outside Berry Acres, reality failed to bite. Arjun's voice on the intercom was perplexed, but he buzzed her in, opening the door dressed in a pair of boxer shorts and a t-shirt with *Hi from Seattle!* printed over a picture of the Space Needle. Chris rose above this and dispensed her most seductive grin, which, in her narcotized state, somehow extended itself into a sort of street-corner leer, an expression to match a stained polyester suit.

'Sorry, did I wake you up?'

'No, no, I was working.'

She amped the grin up a little. 'Aintcha gonna invite me in?'

'Sure.'

She had never been inside Arjun's apartment. It looked as if someone had gone dumpster-diving behind an electrical store and left what they didn't want there. Computer equipment was everywhere, coated in a teenage-boy mulch of dirty plates, underwear and paper waste. The whole place smelled strongly of fried chicken. As she stood, swaying slightly, Arjun ran around, kicking a hole in the mess so they could sit down.

'Would you like a cup of coffee?' he asked, hurriedly closing windows on his computer screen.

'That would be a start. What were you doing, checking out porn?'

Arjun looked shocked. 'No.'

'I bet you were.' She stepped over a dismantled tower case and a slew of Indian magazines, and started to clean a cup at the sink. Arjun bobbed up beside her.

'I'll do it,' he said.

'Just want a drink of water.' She stroked his cheek. 'Hello.'

'Um, hello. So not coffee, then?'

Stroking felt good. She carried on.

'What are you doing?' he asked.

'Oh, nothing. Give me a hug.'

'What?'

She drew his arms round her. Obediently he squeezed. The warmth set off more MDMA shivers in her body.

Despite her euphoria, Chris could not ignore the substandard ambience of Arjun's living space. The smell she could live with, but the ceiling light-fitting had a bare high-wattage bulb, which cast hard shadows on the piles of junk and the undecorated walls and particularly on the man she was hugging, making him look disturbingly cadaverous and unmahogany. From somewhere beneath a pile of chemical pillows came the faint sound of an alarm bell ringing. She ignored it and pressed on.

'It's too bright in here. You got any candles?'

'Candles? Why? Are you expecting a blackout?'

She barged around, stumbling over something which felt mushy underfoot. Ignoring it, she switched off the main light and turned the bulb of the desk lamp to the wall.

'There. Much better. Music?'

Arjun, bemused, headed for the computer. The decision was too important to leave to him, so Chris waved him off, sat down and browsed a directory of MP3s. Discarding the Indian film music left her with a limited choice. Arjun hovered at her shoulder. He seemed nervous at having her around his system. As high as she was, she could tell he had it configured to do something unusual. A lot of crummy-looking hard drives had been networked together, and before he switched it off an old fourteen-inch monitor was displaying some kind of constantly updating log. She settled ('N Sync? *Jesus*) for a Moby album: semi-lame but OK. Lush strings and blues samples filtered into the room.

'There,' she said, putting her arms round him. 'That's better.'

Arjun's back muscles tensed under her hands. 'This is all – I mean, it's a – very nice surprise.'

'Yes, it is, isn't it?'

'You seem hot. Have you been taking exercise?'

'No, baby, I came here for that.'

'Really? How come? I don't actually have any equipment or anything.'

She ignored the buzz of his voice and slipped one hand underneath his shirt, drifting away into a world of touch. His back felt smooth, warm. She nuzzled his neck. It was annoying that he was still talking. The important thing right now was to be naked.

'Arjun?'

'Yes?'

'You seem stressed. Would you like a massage?'

'Um – is that why you came? To give me a massage?'

'Maybe.'

'Well, I must say that's very – I wasn't really expecting – but I suppose that would be OK. I was more or less finished with –'

'Arjun?'

'Yes?'

'Shut up. I mean stop talking. You don't need to talk. Lie down and take your shirt off.'

He made some more incoherent protests, but, after clearing the bed of printouts and Pringle tubes, she had him more or less where she wanted him, prone on his stomach with her straddling his hips. She started kneading his narrow back. After a minute or two she took off her top and unhooked her bra. He had his eyes shut and didn't seem to notice. When she slid a hand under the waistband of his shorts, he did notice: his buttocks clenched and his back went rigid. Struggling underneath her, he flipped on to his back, only to be confronted by the crowning artistic achievements of San Francisco's Needle Bob, snaking over her naked torso.

'What are you –' She took his hands and put them on her breasts. 'Oh,' he said. 'Oh.'

Some hours later the grey morning light revealed a scene of devastation. Since Chris's contact lenses were glued to her eyes the world appeared mercifully hazy, but even with the visuals turned down she knew it was bad. Someone had filmed a splatter movie in her mouth. Someone else had administered a spinal tap. She had not slept, at least not in any meaningful sense of the word. Since Arjun stopped talking and started to breathe regularly and noisily through his mouth, she had been less aware of her surroundings at certain times than at others. Did that count? Carefully she lifted up his arm and slipped out of bed. With her first pace she stubbed her toe on something sharp and had to put a hand over her mouth to keep from crying out. The message was clear. It was imperative to leave. This was a bad place with sharp things in it. This was a chicken-smelling place of horror.

She swilled out her mouth with water and hunted for her clothes. Arjun lay on his side, one thin arm outstretched where she had left it. Squashed against the pillow, his face looked childish and undefined. She could not find anything in it, or in the section of shoulder and chest exposed by the turned-down quilt, to remind her why it had been so important to come by at 2 a.m. and have sex with this man. Physically she felt battered but mentally things were worse, her ordinary landscape of thoughts and feelings reduced to a scoured bleakness, a waste land strewn with the shattered remnants of whoever she had been before she got high. It was the traditional moment to swear never to touch ecstasy or coke or alcohol again. It was the feeling that would work on the kids. Don't do it, OK? Don't feel like me.

She gathered her purse and groped for her second shoe among the nameless horrors around the bed. When it had finally been located, she tiptoed out and closed the door, realizing as she stepped into the brutal daylight that she didn't have her shades. Or her car. She stumbled down the driveway and, before buzzing herself out, leaned her cheek for a moment against the cool metal of the security gate. Then, in a halting b-movie-zombie shuffle, she headed in the direction she judged most likely to contain coffee.

Four hours later Arjun opened his eyes into a warm summer Sunday morning. He felt fresh and relaxed, suffused with a sense of the rightness of things. Ordinarily he slept in kurta-pyjama, but this morning he was naked. Unable for the moment to remember why, he turned on his side and spotted the little wrinkled slug of a used condom among the socks and foil trays on his floor. From this point of origin his memory expanded in a rush, bringing with it a sense of frank amazement at what had taken place in his apartment (*in this very bed!*) only a few hours previously.

The detail was too intense to face without embarrassment. The sheer *bodiliness* of it all. Wetness. The smell of skin. He remembered feeling out of control, which in itself seemed indecent. The memory had the confused quality of a dream.

And yet. The things she had done for him. Without help he would probably have never managed it. Now Chris had showed him, solved the uncomputable problem of finding another person to touch and be touched in return. He felt humble, grateful.

But also guilty. He got up and switched on the computer and ate breakfast still naked, listening to a desi talk-radio stream. So who was Chris? She was his *lover*. He was *a man with a lover* or, to use the shortened version, a *man*. This seemed good, though not pure. Masticating a cherry poptart, he found his mind turning to Papaji.

A week or so before he died, Arjun's grandfather, already confined to his sickbed, had indicated that he wished to pass on certain advice to his grandson. Arjun, who was only eight, was not normally allowed into Papaji's room and his mother made a great performance of presenting him to the old man. Arjun was shy. He had liked Papaji, but now the smelly shape in the bed frightened him. Squirming, he was led up close so that the frail figure had only to turn its head to speak. From under the covers a thin arm extended. A quivering hand fluttered over his cheeks and forehead. 'Beta,' came the whisper, 'God bless you. You are a good boy. I want you to remember two things. Always conserve your semen. It is your strength. And –' Arjun never got to hear the second thing because his mother dragged him indignantly out of the room. 'His mind is wandering,' she snapped. 'Go and play.' When he sneaked back in, Papaji was asleep.

Denied half his bequest of ancestral wisdom, Arjun had always given particular weight to the half he had. He had rarely participated in competitive sport, but knew that if he ever did, he would be certain to practise abstinence on the night before a crucial game. He had almost always steered clear of Aamir's dirty pictures and assumed that when the time came, his sexual partner (he never thought in the plural) would be chosen with meticulous care. Continence had always seemed like the proper thing; holding back from the vicious cycle of seminal accumulation and expenditure was the mark of a mature man. Yet now at the first opportunity he had fallen headlong into incontinence. What did that make him?

And what did it make her? He knew what his mother would say.

Set against that were other arguments: the blue snakes coiled around Chris's arm, the sway of her breasts as she ground back and forth over his pubis.

It occurred to him that since Aamir would be jealous, it would be fun to write him an email. He started, then stopped. For the moment he wanted to keep his news to himself. That morning he could not concentrate on his projects and spent most of the time lying on his bed, drawing out the 'afterwards' feeling like wire. It was a clear day and the sunlight filtered through the leaves of the tree outside his window, warming his skin, keeping alive the sense of being touched. Once or twice he dialled Chris's number, but it went straight to voicemail.

Chris spent the afternoon with Nic, huddled on the couch watching eighties teen movies on cable. The scale of the disaster was becoming clear. Though Nic was asking no questions, mired in his own hangover, she could still feel a tautness about him, a clenched thing he got whenever he suspected she had been with someone else. Inquisitions were against the rules, but all the same he was wondering. She snuggled furtively up to him, pulling the quilt tighter around her.

It had been such a mess. Arjun's erection had come and gone: when she first touched it, when she rolled on the condom. As she finally lifted herself up and tucked his penis inside her, the gesture felt (of all things) *motherly*. Instantly she lost her bearings and a grim self-consciousness lit up their struggling like a flare. She rocked back and forward and the drugs made her feel that someone else, not her, was having sex in that bombsite of a room. By shutting her eyes she could block out Arjun's ridiculous slack-jawed expression, but she could still hear his throttled yelps of surprise, feel his tentative hands on her. She looked back down and his face suddenly crumpled like a piece of brown paper. It was over. She felt more or less the same as before, except now there was nowhere else to go, no way to squeeze any further sensation out of her Saturday night, and she didn't feel like a sexual adventurer, just limp and tired, a rag of a girl held up by the drugs like a damp shirt on a clothes hanger, forced to carry on with consciousness when all she wanted to do was throw the off-switch and fade to black.

Even if he had not been preoccupied that Monday morning, Arjun would not have noticed the atmosphere at the labs. To most other people the tension would have been obvious. He dived happily into his testing routines, unfazed by the way the senior analysts kept shutting themselves in the conference room to make phone calls or have hurried conversations. He knew Darryl had been called away to a meeting, but did not spot the doleful way his colleagues were staring at Darryl's office door, at certain tech news and financial websites, at the floor. Concentrated stares. People looking at their future.

He sent mail to Chris, but she didn't respond. Probably busy, he decided. At the end of the day he went home as usual and worked solidly on his projects until one in the morning. Usually he kept a chat client open on his desktop, but that night he wanted to concentrate, which was how he came to miss the storm of Virugenix-related discussion in the AV forums. Before he went to bed, he tried Chris's number again, now concerned that she did not pick up. By Tuesday morning he was probably the only Virugenix employee still unaware that the company had issued a profits warning, the stock price had tanked, and the board had pledged to cut operating costs across all divisions. Everyone else, the whisperers and the starers, knew what that meant.

In times of tech-corporate crisis the normal rules of communication are reversed. Virugenix staffers knew that campus email and phone channels were insecure. Only face-to-face conversations were sure not to be monitored by the company. The cafeteria, usually half empty, was filled with groups of people picking at salads and speaking in lowered voices, people who in some cases had not ventured into a public space for years. Buying a chicken wrap to take back to his desk, Arjun walked past them, preoccupied with thoughts of Chris.

On Wednesday morning, as he cut across the parking lot past a line of people carrying cardboard boxes to their cars, he could think about only one thing: why had she not returned any of his messages?

He swiped his pass to get into the lab. Clay came up behind him and clapped him on the back.

'I just want to say I'm sorry, man. You're a good guy. It's a shame.'

The door catch released with a click.

'What's a shame?'

Clay's eyes widened. 'Well, Darryl wants to see you, and so –' He shrugged. 'You know.' Before Arjun could ask any more questions, Clay dived for cover.

Sure enough, when Arjun switched on his terminal there was a message from Darryl. A formal meeting: 4 p.m. There were several other messages, all asking him to contribute to leaving gifts for people he didn't know. As he watched, another popped into his inbox, from Aamir.

bhai – Saw bad news on cnet U been such superstar an all Im sure it dont affect U see cute girl attached ; – p a

The cute girl had been blocked by the company's filtering software, but Arjun had other things to think about. Bad news? By the time he knocked on Darryl's door, he had read the reports and watched three of his colleagues go into the office and walk out with set expressions. He felt dazed. It was not possible. Not this.

There were two people in there. Darryl and a woman. The woman was not part of the research division. You could tell because she was wearing a suit. The suit was well cut and charcoal-grey and accessorized with a businesslike pearl necklace. The face above it was alert and good-looking, its highly maintained skin framed by a neat blonde bob. The woman smiled at Arjun and looked over at Darryl, expecting him to make an introduction. Darryl did not look as if he would be able to do this. He was curled up into a kind of ball on his office chair, a Ghostbusters cap crammed down low on his head. Beneath it he was staring fixedly at his SETI belt buckle and swivelling himself to and fro by pushing his hands against the top of his desk.

The woman sighed. 'Good afternoon, Mr Mehta,' she said. 'Thanks for your promptitude. My name is Jennifer Johanssen, and I'm a deputy director of personnel here at Virugenix. Head office asked me to come down and facilitate today's employee encounters. Mr Gant here has briefed me on your performance. I know he rates your contribution to the anti-virus research team very highly.' She paused and turned to Darryl, who clawed at his beard and swivelled faster.

The meeting seemed to be taking place a great distance away. Arjun was merely an observer, a scientist monitoring the progress of an experiment on the other side of the glass. Transmitted across the vastness of space, Jennifer Johanssen's voice sounded calming and competent, a moisturizing balm formulated to take away the pain and soreness of the words it uttered. Aamir would like her, thought Arjun. She's his type.

'In your time here,' the aloe vera voice intoned, 'you have added quality and value.' Then it spoke for a while about compassion. The room felt cold. Maybe I'm getting sick, thought Arjun, palpating the glands on the side of his neck. The voice talked about reversals of fortune and minimizing negative outcomes. It talked about the executive team's strong desire to lead by demonstrating fiscal responsibility at all levels. It talked about last in, first out.

It talked about reality.

Then it struck him. This was not his story. This was not his story because this was not how his story went. There had been a mistake.

'There's been a mistake,' he said.

Jennifer Johanssen nodded as if to signify that yes, she could see why he thought so. Then she shook her head as if to signify that no, despite his perception, he was wrong.

'Mr Mehta, I understand how you feel,' she said. She was beautiful, really. You could imagine her participating in outdoor pursuits such as skiing or catamaran sailing. Aspirational pursuits. Pursuits which used expensive specialist equipment.

'Please don't do this to me,' said Arjun.

'I realize that from a human-resource accounting perspective, this could be viewed as a retrograde step for both sides,' said Jennifer Johanssen.

'Please,' said Arjun. 'I'm begging you.'

Darryl moaned softly.

'So I can understand why you may feel we are not making the right move.'

'No, you don't understand. I need this job. This job is all I have.'

'We have looked at the options.'

'Please, if I lose this job I'll have to go back. And I can't go back. Don't you see? I can't go back.'

'I am aware of your visa situation, Mr Mehta, but as I understand it you're still technically employed by Databodies. In reality Virugenix has no obligations to you. It is only because we believe that all our employees, even those on freelance consultancy contracts, should benefit from harmonious termination experiences that my presence here was mandated at all. Mr Mehta, I hold a diploma in severance-scenario planning. I assure you that this encounter has been designed to be as painless for you as possible.'

'Yes,' said Arjun. 'I see. Of course I see. Just don't fire me, OK? I'll do anything. I'll work for less money. I'll do longer hours.'

He was raising his voice. Jennifer Johanssen shifted in her seat. Though she appeared outwardly composed, her eyes were darting towards the door and towards Darryl, who had slipped off his chair and was trying to wedge himself out of sight behind the desk.

'Make him go away,' pleaded Darryl, his voice somewhat muffled. Jennifer Johanssen looked down at him, then back at Arjun, her face bearing the terse expression of a woman who has accepted that she is now on her own.

'What Mr Gant wishes to express is – um, our sincere thanks for your loyal service. And we can offer you two weeks' grace so that you can make whatever preparations you deem necessary for your change in circumstances.'

'You don't mean it,' said Arjun. 'What if things change? What if they get better? You'll need me then.'

'Naturally you'll have to vacate your apartment. I believe the personnel department here at Greene Labs will be liaising with you about that, probably some time later today.'

'But you haven't answered my question. What if things change? What if the downturn suddenly turns up?'

'Mr Mehta, as I understand it there are no indicators of short-term recovery. It's a sector-wide trend. This is what our public-relations team has been trying to underline to investors. It's not just Virugenix, it's across the board. And Mr Mehta, that's the take-home for you too. You shouldn't see this as a sign of personal failure. You're a valuable individual with a lot to offer. It is just that Virugenix can no longer offer you a context for your self-development.'

'But if everything changed, you'd take me back?'

'Of course, Mr Mehta, in a hypothetical situation where we had vacancies for someone of your skill set and background, you would come into consideration.'

'Right,' said Arjun, feeling that he had won some kind of victory. 'OK!'

Jennifer Johanssen nodded. 'Thank you, Mr Mehta, for your understanding.' She craned her neck to look down behind her chair. Only Darryl's legs and feet were visible, a pair of high-top basket-ball shoes poking out from the crawlspace of the desk. She smiled wanly. 'Mr Gant thanks you also.'

As he left the room Arjun's mouth was dry. He took a soda from the chiller cabinet and drank it down in three large gulps. There had been an error. But it was fixable. All he had to do was treat this situation like any other technical challenge. Parse the problem. Find the bug and deal with it. Because this was not how his story went. He was doing well in America. He was a big success.

His head felt as if it were clamped in a vice. They couldn't force him to leave, not like this. What if he could make them see how efficient he was? Then they would change their minds and fire someone else. He sat down at his desk and tried to focus on his monitor. Two weeks? The view from his bedroom window. The mountains floating on a sea of fog. Only two more weeks of those mountains, then back to California. Hard white sun baking the concrete. And what about Chris? He couldn't leave her now. Even after months of working he had no savings. He wouldn't be able to last more than a few weeks on the bench. After that he would have to go back to India.

Then everyone would know the truth.

He blamed the phone. It made it too easy. In the early days, when he had just arrived in the US, he had done it to reassure his parents. They would have been worried if they thought he was having difficulties. And then Priti had been so impressed, so proud of her big brother in America. Aamir also. The thing had taken on a life of its own. *Yes, Maa, I'm doing fine . . .*

The way his mother talked, she had probably told everyone in Noida by now. His story. His version. *Maa, something good happened today . . .* How her son had been on the fast-track to success from the moment he stepped off the plane. How at world-famous Oracle Computers her beta had solved technical problem worrying Larry Ellison for years, but turned down partnership to go to Virugenix and run computer-virus department. How her little boy now socialized with businessmen and politicians. How he had sat next to David Hasselhoff at dinner.

There was no way he could go back to India. He would bring shame on his family.

The air in the office was stifling. His colleagues were pretending not to watch him, peering slyly round their cubicle walls. He had to think. He had to find the bug. At the back of the Michelangelo Building was a wooden deck scattered with white metal cafeteria tables, the type with a hole in the middle for a sunshade to poke through. People came here to eat lunch or hold informal meetings. He swiped himself out of the office and went down into the open air. Sitting at one of the tables, he watched a crow pecking at a plastic yogurt pot, the remains of a lunch which, contrary to policy, had not been cleared away into the receptacle provided.

It was a magnificent crow. Its black button eye glittered with malice. Each feather seemed to be individually present, discrete. He found himself counting them: one, two, five, ten, until he was distracted by the light streaming between the needles of the tall conifers lining the campus perimeter. According to a sign screwed on to the wall by the fire door, *Virugenix has landscaped this zone using native Washington State plants to encourage a land ethic that celebrates our natural heritage*. Yes, he thought. Yes, that's right. Everything seemed precious and perfect, the way things ought to be. The sun marched down correctly through the dense green branches of the trees and the ground sloped away in an ordered mat of native Washington turf grasses. On impulse he stepped off the deck and kneeled down. He ran his hands over the grass. It was fine and soft and thick, like hair. The sunlight was blinding. The world seemed to have dissolved, to be coming to him through a series of prisms. His face was wet. He realized he was crying.

'Are you OK?' The voice was concerned, hesitant. Turning round, Arjun recognized a Singaporean guy who worked on the diagnostics product team. He raised an arm in a weak fine-thanks wave. The Singaporean guy waved too and backed away, still watching. Finally convinced that there was no immediate problem, he turned and went inside. Arjun remained kneeling for a while, smoothing his hands over the grass. Then he got up and returned to his desk.

There were two emails waiting in his inbox.

To: arjunm@virugenix.com
From: darrylg@virugenix.com
Subject: Blame

Blame is MEANINGLESS. You must understand it is NOBODY'S FAULT. Looked at from a cosmological perspective this has VERY LITTLE SIGNIFICANCE. Be aware I have in place COMPREHENSIVE personal security measures. D8rr{l

To: arjunm@virugenix.com
From: chriss@virugenix.com
Subject: are you all right?

Heard the news. So sorry. Meet me after work? Xc

'That bastard.' She meant it. She had always thought Darryl was a shit. 'He couldn't even face you on his own. But it doesn't surprise me. You know how he is with people.'

They were parked by the lake, at the end of a private road belonging to a sailing club. Ahead of them a slipway ran down into the water. A little way out, people who could afford to take Wednesday off were messing about in catamarans. Chris had brought Arjun here because she thought the view might calm him down. She was trying to face up to her responsibilities. He was not making it easy.

'At least I have you,' he said with determination.

'Sure.' She nodded warily. He was not in good shape. His eyes were red. Earlier he had been picking at his clothing and muttering to himself in a fractured mixture of English and what was probably Hindi. Chris was worried. She had been avoiding him all week and was intending to go on doing so for as long as possible, but when she heard he had lost his job, guilt told her she ought to check on him. Karmically speaking, it was the proper thing to do.

He kept talking about going back. She supposed he meant to India, but it wasn't clear. They were trying to make him go back, but it was impossible. He would show Them. He would make Them see sense.

'I think,' she ventured, choosing her words carefully, 'it's kind of a done deal.'

He scowled and said, 'That's not true.' Just that. Final and definite. Which worried her even more.

Since the weekend she had been doing a lot of thinking. Not about Arjun particularly. About her and Nicolai. She and Nic had always tried to be each other's fantasy. That was their bargain, the thing that held them together. No compromises, anything possible, anything permitted. It sometimes made for a strain, especially when other people got involved, but it had always felt like a brave choice. They were making their lives up as they went along, playing by their own rules. And often it worked, which was more than you could say for most people's relationships.

It was just that lately she seemed to be pushing Nic's buttons. He was pissed at her, and he was probably justified. She felt as if she was losing him. Arjun was a symptom, but there had been more significant attachments for her and, she suspected, for him too. A while back she had had a thing with someone which threatened to get serious. Nic knew about it, or at least guessed something was up between her and this other guy, a studio engineer. He said nothing, rode it out.

He was a calm one, Nic, almost too laid-back sometimes, but he had problems and she was supposed to be part of the solution. For a long time she had been kind of shitty to him; now it was time to step up. That's what she had decided. To commit. So when she heard Arjun had been fired, it was, among other things, a relief. That was one more night she would be able to forget about. Arjun would disappear and it would be easier to put things right. It was cold of her; she knew it. She also knew whatever had happened was her fault. She did owe Arjun something. A shoulder. He had been a friend, after all. So she came and scraped him up and put him in her car. She had expected him to be upset, but not like this. He seemed to think he could persuade the company to take him back.

'You'll help me, won't you?' he said.

'Help you do what?'

'You must know people. You could talk to them for me, tell them I can't go.'

'Arjun, that kind of decision takes place way over my head. I'm just a coder. You know that. I realize it's hard, but you'll find another job.'

'You're not listening! I can't! You're my last hope. It's you and me against the world now.'

Chris stared at him in horror. You and me against the world? What movie was that from? 'Arjun, I'm your friend, OK? But there is no you and me. I'm with Nic. You understand that, right?'

'But you came to my place. We – you finally understood, and you came.' He looked at her, almost imploring her. It felt terrible to say what she had to say next.

'I know what happened between us the other night might make you think that, but – it was a mistake. It was my fault. I got high and – well, I shouldn't have done it. It was unfair. I know I've been leading you on.'

He just stared at her. Blank. Uncomprehending.

'I'm a bitch.'

'You're still going to help me, aren't you?'

'Help you do what? There's nothing to do. I can't make them give you your job back.'

'But you have to,' he said. 'It's me and you. We're together. That's how it's supposed to be.'

When you write code you are in control. You construct a world from first principles, drawing up the axioms that govern it, setting in motion the engines of generation and decay. Even in a computer environment designed by someone else you can relax, safe in the knowledge that you are engaged with a system that runs according to potentially knowable rules. From this perspective the real world possesses the paradoxical quality of not feeling real enough. Surely, of all things, reality ought to be transparent, logical. You should be able to unscrew the fascia and view the circuitry inside.

'Chris, why did you have sex with me?'

'I don't know, Arjun. I just did. It was a bad idea.'

'That means you don't love me.'

'Arjun –'

In a world of illusion you have to ask questions. You have to doubt, systematically. Other people may act real. They may behave as if, like you, they are animated by internal processes. But you never know. Some of them are just machines.

'You're supposed to love me.'

'I'm sorry but I don't know what to say to you. It's not supposed to be any way. Things are how they are. This is just how it is.'

Just how it is? Nothing is just how it is. Behind things are explanations. Behind things are the ideas of things and they are what count. He stared at her. Just how it is? Broken automaton.

'I know what you are,' he told her. Then he got out of the car and headed in the direction of the main road. In the distance vehicles whizzed along the highway. Chris was shouting something after him, calling his name.

His feet crunched over gravel. It felt like the floor of a game-world dungeon, shifting, full of traps. Everything was wrong. His life was malfunctioning. He needed a place to stand.

What is more certain than number?

Fifteen sails visible on the water.

Twelve cars parked in the lot by the marina.

Eight windows along the first floor. Eight more above them.

Numbers were the truth of the world, numbers cloaked in materials. Find certainty by counting the things. In decimal. In binary, hexadecimal. How many sixteens of trees in his field of vision? How many around the lake? Streams of numbers came to him, too fast to handle. But he had to try. It all boiled down to your ability to handle complexity.

He trudged home along the side of the road. When he was safe inside his apartment, he locked the door and sat down on his bed, his hands in his lap. Moving was not important. Eating was not important, though somewhere deep down he knew he must be hungry. The important thing was to think. The evening light was soft and yellow. He stared at the tree branches framed in his window. How many needles? *ed ee ef f0 f1 f2 . . .*

For some hours he sat and counted. Around him the light faded. He could not go home, which meant he had to find a way to stay, to make Virugenix keep him on. Parse the problem. Think of a number.

Then it came to him. He scrabbled around in the trash on his floor, squashing a little plastic container of milk with his foot. A squirt of white shot out over the carpet. *Always conserve your semen. It is your strength.* Underneath a pile of papers he found a plate with something growing on it. Wedged behind the desk was the left chappal he had lost. There were letters from his sister, and an Asha Bhosle disc. All useful, but not what he was looking for. Finally he laid his hands on it, a torn copy of last month's *Filmfare* magazine. Yes, there it was. He was right.

Think of a number.

06 13

13th June. The date of Leela Zahir's birthday. Only two days away.

Arjun first saw a computer when he was ten years old. It was a 286PC and it belonged to Cousin Hitesh, whose father, concerned for his son's education, had brought it back from a business trip to America. Hitesh improved himself by playing solitaire and trying to beat his high score on a side-scrolling game which involved bombing villages from a helicopter. Mostly the machine sat grey and untended in Hitesh's bedroom, humming portentously. Arjun's family was staying in Bombay for a week, and, while Hitesh was in the next room watching action movies on the laserdisc, he could spend hours undisturbed, exploring the guts of the extraordinary object. He was thwarted at every turn. *Path not found. Sector not found.* He was asked questions which made no sense.

Abort, Retry, Ignore, Fail?

When he pressed a key and the cryptic pulse of the DOS prompt exploded into graphics, the suspicion was planted in his mind that something inside the machine must be alive.

File creation error.

By the age of thirteen Arjun had long discounted the theory that there were actual living things inside computers. But something mystical persisted, a hint, the presence of a vital spark. A computer booting up is creating itself *ex nihilo*, each stage of activity generating the grounds for the next. A tiny trickle of electricity to a dormant chip allows it to take a roll-call of components, which then participate in a simple exchange of instructions, a setting-out of terms and conditions that generates a more complex exchange, and then another, tier after tier of language coming into being until the display of a holiday photograph or the sweep of a pointer across a spreadsheet become thinkable, their meanings reaching all the way back down into binary simplicity.

Arjun glimpsed a secret in this yes–no logic. Hungry for more computer time, he would beg or steal it where he could: libraries, college labs, the houses of richer or luckier schoolfriends. He particularly loved to run simulations. Anything would do: commercial god-games; cities and armies; a simple world of different-coloured daisies; clusters of digital cells switching each other from red to blue. Watching populations of computer creatures grow and die, he found himself meditating on scale, wondering in a teenage way if his own world was nothing but a stupendous piece of programming, a goldfish-bowl system running for the amusement of other cosmically bored teens.

True or *false*?

Either way this particular system was a problem. He soon found himself in full retreat from it, buffeted by puberty, by the awkwardness of interacting with other people. People were a chasm, an abyss. Their violence, their vagueness, their unknowable motivations and inexplicable changes of mood had been woven into a nightmarish social world. Why would nobody understand? *They were making no sense*. At last laying his hands on his own machine, he became a computing hermit, fleeing into a place where communication was governed by clearly laid-out rules. Logic gates. Truth tables. The world of people could go and rot. He closed his bedroom door on it.

His life might have progressed in any number of directions had he not, one evening, left a floppy disk in the A-drive of his PC. When he started up the following morning, his screen suddenly went blank. He pressed keys. No response. He rebooted. The machine ran slow. He rebooted again. And again. Finally, after an interminable crunch and stutter from inside the case, a message appeared in front of him.

```
u r a pr1z0n7r ov th3 l0rd$ ov m1zr00L
```

He kept shutting down and restarting, but the problem only got worse. His beloved computer had been reduced to a pile of scrap metal. To get it running again, he had to reformat his hard drive, which meant that he lost all his data. Everything. Months of work erased by this catastrophic visitation. He started to research what it was that had happened, and found that he had been hit by a thing with a name, the *Carnival Virus*, a string of code that had hidden itself in an innocuous floppy disk and had used his computer to make copies of itself. Every restart had given birth to another generation. Life.

Information on computer viruses was hard to come by. Even a sketchy impression of where they originated was difficult to form without his own internet connection, and in India at that time, that was an impossibility. By writing off for disks and magazines and making occasional cripplingly expensive calls to foreign bulletin boards, he managed to get hold of a few code samples, which he studied like religious texts. In the privacy of his bedroom he created several simple viruses, careful to keep backups of his data in case (as happened once or twice) he accidentally infected his own machine. He taught himself assembly language, and by his late teens had begun to excel in all sorts of more conventional programming tasks. His parents, who were worried by his reclusiveness, his bad posture, his unwillingness to play sports or bring friends round for tea, began to see an upside to his obsession. Computers were the coming thing, Mr Mehta would remind his colleagues at the firm. My son will be an engineer.

It was only when he went to college, and at last had proper access to the data riches of the net that he was able to properly satisfy his curiosity. He started to burrow into the underground, logging on to chatrooms and IRC channels, navigating with a thrill past the braggarts and hypers, the ranters and flamers and paranoiacs who infested this grey area of the computing culture.

Screw you lamer, don't come running to me when it wipes your hd, i just distributed the thing. Well anyway enjoy doods, cya at my next release . . .

That was the style. If you had knowledge you wore it with arrogance. You put down the pretenders and the fools like a dashing musketeer, a programming dandy. Arjun was shy. Even online, hidden behind the anonymity of a screen name, he lacked confidence. For a long time he just lurked, watching and listening, gleaning information about security flaws, vulnerabilities, techniques, exploits. But in the true underground, the untraceable underground of temporary private channels and download sites with shifting addresses, exchange was everything. If you didn't give, you didn't get.

So, feeling trepid and illicit, *badmAsh* started to appear on virus-exchange boards, offering to trade code for code. To his pleasure and surprise, he found that people wanted what he had, and he soon became popular, respected. It gradually dawned on him that behind the bluster most other traders were not that talented – they were handymen, tinkering with already existing routines. They were not the originators, the architects. *badmAsh* became something of a star.

Further blurring the borderline between life and not-life, the internet had brought computer viruses into their own. When floppy disks were the primary transmission vector, rates of infection were low. Now that files could be sent over phone lines, the number of incidents soared. From his college terminal Arjun watched in fascination as malicious code flared up like a rash on the computing body of the world, causing itching and discomfort to a public educated by science fiction and the Cold War to regard the convergence of machines and biology with uneasy reverence. Computer virus. Future terror.

Arjun himself had little time for science fiction. For him it was all Romance. Pyaar. Being the hero of the Vx boards was a sterile thing in some ways, because the point of being a hero is to get the girl, and on the Vx boards there were none. Not one. Not even (as in other zones of the net) anyone pretending to be one.

Pyaar. Pyaar. Pyaar. Throughout South Asia you can't get away from it. Perhaps the rise of Love has something to do with cinema, or independence from the British, or globalization, or the furtive observation of backpacking couples by a generation of young people who suddenly realized it was possible to grope one another without the sky falling on their heads. There are those who say Love is just immorality. There are those who believe it is encouraged by amplified disco music. There are even those who claim that the decline in arranged marriage and the cultural encouragement of its replacement by free-choice pair-bonding are connected with the obsolescence of the extended family in late capitalism, but since this is tantamount to saying that Love can be reduced to Money, no one listens. In India (the most disco nation on earth) Love is a glittery madness, an obsession, broadcast like the words of a dictator from every paan stall and rickshaw stand, every transistor radio and billboard and TV tower. While Arjun tried to concentrate on public-key cryptography or the Hungarian naming convention, it kept knocking on his bedroom door like an irritating kid sister. Will you come out and play? He would have paid no attention to it (what could be vaguer and less logical?) but sickeningly all its absurd rituals and intricacies led back to something he wanted, something he had started to crave with a longing bordering on panic.

Touch.

Love was the price of touch. Love was the maze through which you had to find your way. In the May heat, when the heavy air was like a hand on his body as he lay awake at night, he could feel the need for another person as a hard ache inside, an alien presence which had formed in his chest like a tumour.

As far as it is possible to piece together, the sequence of events runs like this.

At 21.15 PST, Wednesday, *badmAsh* appears on #vxconvention, which at the time is running on a server belonging to a private internet-service provider in Indonesia. By 21.28 PST he has completed a negotiation with a regular user known as *Elrick21* to swap a copy of a packet-sniffing utility for a compressed file containing a list of around a million email addresses, the kind of list that spammers use to send people messages about penis enlargement, great investment opportunities and requests for urgent business assistance. In return for the home phone number of pro golfer Tiger Woods (which *badmAsh* had acquired as part of a batch in a previous trade, and which *Elrick21* thinks 'would be cool just to have'), he also acquires a list of a dozen or so IP addresses belonging to computers on to which, unknown to their owners, *Elrick21* has installed a piece of software known as a remote-access trojan.

Between 21.32 and 21.37 PST *badmAsh* attempts to communicate with these machines. Only one responds: a PC physically located in the *banlieue* of Paris, which its owner, a junior doctor called Patrice, has hooked up to a broadband connection so he can play Second World War flight Sim games. Patrice sometimes thinks he would rather be a fighter ace than a medic with a crummy apartment in a bad part of town. Patrice tends to leave his computer on all the time. Right now (it is early on Thursday morning in Paris) he is still at the hospital, and so is not present to watch *badmAsh* establish communication with the trojan, send a set of commands to his machine and take control of his email software.

Between 06.50 and 09.23 CEST, when Patrice returns, spots

through a haze of tiredness that something weird is happening and pulls the power plug out of the wall, his computer sends emails in a constant stream, contacting hundreds of thousands of people around the world to say:

Hi. I saw this and thought of you.

At 14.05 KST fifteen-year-old Kim Young Sam, who is cutting his English class at Seoul Science High School, comes back to his bedroom with a bowl of microwaved instant noodles and wonders why he has mail from France. He opens it and clicks on the attachment. Nothing happens. Ten minutes later, when his computer sends copies of the email to everyone in his address book, he does not notice because he has fallen asleep.

Kelly Degrassi, insomniac, mother, receptionist at the offices of the Holy Mount Zion Church in Fort Scott, Kansas, opens and clicks.

Darren Pinkney (dairy farmer, Ballarat, Australia) clicks.

Altaaf Malik (student, Leela Zahir fan, Hyderabad, India) clicks and is disappointed. No pictures.

Ten minutes after the first mail went out from Patrice's computer, forty more people have unknowingly distributed it to their friends and contacts. Half an hour later 800 have done so. By the time Patrice phones technical support at his internet-service provider to say that he thinks something might be wrong with his connection, the mail containing what will come to be known as 'first variant Leela virus', or *Leela01*, has made its way on to over 17,000 hard drives around the world.

The truth is that Leela was not one thing. She was not even a set or a group or a family. She was a swarm, a horde. At the same time as *Leela01* was being spread via email, other Leelas, other things with her face, were being uploaded to shareware sites, were tunnelling their way into webservers to be doled out as Applets, were propagating at a phenomenal rate through peer-to-peer networks. There were versions of her that broke completely with the past, that were targeted at the complex operating systems used by businesses and universities, at the stripped-down ones designed for cellphone handsets and personal organizers. So many Leelas. So many girls with the same face.

The glory of all these variants, the glamour that caught so many people unawares, lay in their power of metamorphosis. Since the first virus crept on to the first unprotected hard drive some time in the 1980s, a process of evolution had been under way, an arms race between virus writers and scanners that had thrown up new and unforeseen mutations. In the beginning all the detectors had to do was trap a viral sample and write software to look for a telltale trace or signature. So the viruses began to use encryption to hide themselves, and the scanners responded by learning to hunt for the decryption routines. Soon the viruses began to appear in multiple shapes. The scanners evolved with them, and learned to look not just for signatures but for give-away behaviour. Unexpected events could signal an intrusion. Changes in file size. Unauthorized modifications.

Leela was a step beyond all of this. She could take on new forms at will, never staying stable for long enough to be scanned and recognized. Each generation produced an entirely new Leela, her organs rearranged, mutated, hidden under a novel layer of encryption. Worst of all, from the point of view of the people tasked with finding her, she could camouflage herself within the programs she infected, inserting herself in between legitimate instructions, covering herself over by resetting all references to the changes she had made. When the scanners peered at a Leela-infected file, it looked normal. It still functioned. Nothing appeared to have been altered since the last clean sweep was made. Legitimate programs were doing legitimate things. Until they stopped. Until she took over.

Release + 3 hrs: 17,360 hosts
Release + 4 hrs: 85,598 hosts
Release + 5 hrs: 254,217 . . .

So when Arjun appeared at work the next morning, haggard and drawn from a night without sleep, despite the infection raging around the world, not one sample had come into Virugenix for analysis. Leela was in the wild, and for the moment entirely invisible.

Who clicked? Did you click? Were you curious enough to try? Packets of data streamed through the wires, through MAE-West and East, into hubs and rings in Chicago and Atlanta and Dallas and New York, out of others in London and Tokyo, through the vast SEA-ME-WE 3 cable under the Pacific and its siblings on the sea bed of the Atlantic. Data streamed up to communication satellites, or was converted into radio waves to be spat out of transmitters, passing through people and buildings, travelling away into space.

Leela found Guy Swift at 35,000 feet as he was travelling back to London from New York, and when she reached him it barely registered because he was asleep. She had been batched with other messages, compressed and trickled down from a satellite to a computer on board the Airbus A300 in whose first-class section Guy was reclining, drowsily checking emails on the airphone. He removed his laptop from its padded ripstop case, swiped his company credit card through the reader on the phone and hooked the two devices up. Then, just for a moment, he closed his eyes and drifted into a place of abstraction and warmth. A few seconds went by. The abstraction darkened, and he experienced a sudden unpleasant sensation of falling through his own interior space, *through himself*. Cast unpleasantly out into consciousness, he breathed heavily and opened his eyes to see ten new mails in his inbox. *Check it out!* Disoriented, he clicked. Nothing happened. His annoyance registered as a little spike of distaste, a momentary disturbance in the smooth sine of his working day. Hotel shower, breakfast tray, lobby, limo, lunch meeting, shopping, hotel, limo again – the grid of Manhattan streets sliding by, the silent driver easing him out towards the airport – all noiseless, perfect . . .

Time at origin: 02.14
Time at destination: 07.14
Time here: ?

What time was it up here? What time was now?

Some time later Guy watched blearily as London assembled itself around his taxi. Beside him on the seat was a bag from a lingerie boutique, a last-minute gift for Gabriella. Leaning forward, he called out directions to the driver, who was listening to a phone-in programme on the radio. Up ahead, he caught sight of the building where he lived, a mountain of blue glass looming over a pair of low-rise eighties blocks. He loved that moment, the best moment of any journey. Coming home.

Home. *In Vitro*.

As every Londoner knows, In Vitro, Sir Nigel Pelham's landmark housing complex, is a blue-glass ziggurat, twenty storeys high at its peak, curved along a shallow arc on the south side of the Thames. Each of its 324 luxury apartments has a balcony, screened in such a way as to give the illusion of complete solitude. 'The effect,' said Sir Nigel in an interview with *Archon* magazine, 'is one of absolute calm, a heavenly sense of floating free of the cares of the world.' The lifts and other services have been placed at the rear, leaving the river view uninterrupted. The lowest accommodation is four storeys above the ground, and Sir Nigel's partnership has crammed the space below with all the amenities appropriate to an international-standard residential development. At the concierge desk, a map is available showing the location of In Vitro's Olympic-sized swimming pool, its gymnasium, saunas and solaria, its float tanks, tennis courts, bowling alley, underground parking and innovative Hopi Indian meditation space, a white padded room into which hidden speakers pipe the natural sounds of the American South-west.

Guy had bought his place at the height of the late-nineties boom. As *Tomorrow** took off, he felt it appropriate that as CEO of a world-class agency, he should have a world-class pad. There were other factors which influenced his decision. He sometimes suspected, though he could never be sure, that the apartment was one of the reasons Gabriella agreed to move in with him. Sometimes he even suspected that subconsciously the main reason he bought it was to persuade Gabriella to move in with him. It was a psychological area which would not repay close scrutiny. The price of course was astronomical, but at the time it had seemed worth taking on the debt just to see the look of envy on the faces of his contacts when he invited them over for the housewarming.

Though Guy was a millionaire, it was in a rather technical sense. While his picture in *Future Business* magazine's list of the 100 Top Young Entrepreneurs of the Next Millennium was printed next to a 'personal worth' figure of £3.1 million, almost all of this was based on a valuation of *Tomorrow**, in which, after the last round of venture capital funding, Guy now held a reduced stake. His liquid assets were relatively modest. At the time he had rationalized the purchase of the apartment as a networking opportunity. Surely in the corridors of such an exclusive place, he would bump into all sorts of potential clients.

To his disappointment he found when he moved in that the complex was eerily deserted. The facilities, while beautifully maintained, were little used. Though most units were allocated before the development was even complete, many were owned by foreign nationals and remained unoccupied for much of the year. Others were company flats, or corporate lets whose occupants changed every few weeks. When Guy met residents of In Vitro in the gym, they nodded warily and tried to hide their surprise at encountering another person in this normally empty place. The sauna heated and cooled untenanted, and in the meditation space the coyotes cried unheard. Early in the morning, before the European markets opened, a few people could be found swimming laps of the pool, but they were usually strangers to one another. In the lifts, occupants fixed their gaze on the flickering digits of the LCD display. Sometimes they sneaked glances at the faces reflected in the polished steel doors. Sometimes they did not.

He paid the driver, and a concierge came out with an ice-white In Vitro umbrella, which he held over Guy's head as he made his way into the atrium. The concierge wheeled his case over the tarmac and asked if he had enjoyed his journey. Like all the front-desk staff at In Vitro, this one had an unidentifiable Eastern European accent. Guy disliked it. Eastern Europe did not say customer service to him.

Inside the atrium a pair of crew-cut men sat on swivel chairs watching a bank of video monitors. The security post was 'dramatized', as the Pelham Partnership put it, by being located inside a giant glass oval, reminiscent of an eye, suspended at mezzanine level over the front desk. The development's blanket electronic surveillance was a major selling point for its corporate clients. Landings, stairwells, gardens, riverside – everything was covered. The oval was intended to be reassuring, a symbol of safety, but lately Guy had found the bored men and their constantly shifting panoptical views were having the opposite effect. He tended to walk a little faster as he passed beneath the smoked-glass camera domes in the car park. Fitting his key into his front door, he felt furtive. Closing it behind him was a guilty relief.

He ignored the concierge's parting salute and took the lift up to the fifth floor. As usual the landing was deserted, unless you counted the quasi-human presence of the glossy yucca trees which stood sentinel by each door. Inside, No. 124 smelt unpleasantly of cigarette smoke. A trio of empty Moët bottles and a dirty ashtray stood on the Corian worktop in the kitchen. Gabriella had obviously been entertaining. Shedding his clothes on the bedroom rug, Guy stepped into the shower and stood for a full ten minutes under a transforming blast of hot water. Then he shaved, selected clean clothes from his steel-fronted wardrobe and padded barefoot back across the slate tiles into the kitchen to make coffee at his vast espresso machine, an activity which always gave him a satisfying engine-driverly buzz.

Guy had known even before he moved in that this was a living space which would require something extraordinary. Feeling both time and knowledge-challenged, he had (at the suggestion of the attractive brunette property consultant) employed an agency to help him buy furniture. That way, he reasoned, he could be certain everything about his personal environment was in the best possible taste. And so the white leather table with the cut-out airport city-code motif, the chandelier made from ceramic castings of compact discs, the vicuña pouffe, the Danish ergonomic salad servers and disposable cardboard fruit bowls, the nest of matt-black powder-lacquered steel cubes by the conversation pit, the cable-suspended Vuitton-print polyvinyl vanity unit on which he had mounted the plasma screen and electrostatic speaker-array, the knitted ornamental pods on the bedroom ceiling and the low-rise smuggled-teak patio furniture on the balcony – all of it was personalized, individual, *signature*. It was all, every sandblasted bathroom tap of it, him.

The art had been easiest to choose. At an online gallery (another suggestion from Tania the property consultant) he had clicked on several Cibachrome prints of blown-up urban detailing, manholes and rough sleepers and pigeons and so on, plus a cross-processed shot of an industrial estate in Dalston where he had once been to a launch. Enjoying himself, he had also bought a couple of wall-plaques made out of neon tubing and a sculpture consisting of two interlocking steel circles, based, said the site, on the dimensions of a particular supermodel's head.

He slid open the glass doors and sipped his doppio, looking out at the Thames. Traffic flowed over the bridges. A refuse barge went past, headed for a downriver landfill site. As usual, though he loved the view, he found himself thinking how much better it would be from higher up. On the upper storeys of In Vitro were some spectacular penthouses, and at its summit was a single two-storey glass-walled cube with a floating platform floor, an undecorated shell which the developers had yet to sell. Sometimes, catching sight of the building from a distance, Guy imagined himself up in that penthouse, raking all of London with his gaze.

A few drops of rain landed on his face. As he finished his coffee, his phone rang, playing the hook from a 1980s soft-rock tune. Like his occasional visits to greasy-spoon cafés, his collection of John Holmes videos, his current haircut and the posters of state-socialist leaders in the dining area, Guy's ringtone was ironic. The caller was Kika, his PA.

'Guy?'

'Kika, hi.'

'How did New York go?'

'They loved it, Kika. Really positive. Their communications VP was totally blown away.'

'That's great news. So we've got the account?'

'They haven't committed as yet, but they will. Believe.'

'Oh, I see.' She sounded sceptical, which annoyed him.

'Guy,' she asked, 'are you coming into the office?'

'Kika, I'm kind of wiped out. I just walked through the door a few minutes ago. Did something come up?'

'Perhaps. Maybe it's not important, but I think you should know Yves Ballard is here. And he's sort of – inspecting things.'

This was bad news. Guy looked behind him at his living area, subconsciously scanning for something to sniff or swallow to counteract it. 'Yves? What the hell is he doing in the office? I didn't even know he was in London. And what do you mean inspecting things?'

'You know – looking at stuff? He's peering over people's shoulders. Asking them what they're working on. He says he just wanted to get a feel for our culture. He seemed to know you were away.'

'That fucker. That fucking fucker. He didn't even have the decency to – oh shit – Kika, do something for me? If he goes anywhere near Paul's section, try to distract him. I don't want him looking over any financials until I'm there. I'm going to hop in a cab right now –'

'How am I supposed to do that? He's just wandering around, chatting.'

'I don't know. Be creative. Make him tea. Flash your tits.'

'Guy, that's not called for.'

'Kika, just go the extra mile, OK? I'm coming as fast as I can.'

'Great to see you, Yves,' lied Guy. 'Welcome.'

Yves reached up, shook Guy's hand and blandly lied back, something about flight connections, chance, a morning to kill. It was an awkward moment. To welcome him to *Tomorrow**, Guy had to pretend that Yves was not already ensconced on the Balzac chair in the brainstorm zone, reading through a sheaf of spreadsheets.

For a second, they stared at each other, then broke eye contact and looked out in opposite directions over the converted Shoreditch factory. *Tomorrow**, as Guy liked to remind visitors, was not so much an agency as an experiment in life–work balance. Guy's stated commitment to his staff was to provide an environment that fostered creativity and innovation, while spurring them on to excellence – an environment that made work fun and fun work. That environment was made up of three floors of open space with large windows, exposed brickwork and polished boards scarred by the installation and removal of heavy machinery, now dotted by random clusters of tables and workstations, the outcome of an unsuccessful experiment with hotdesking. In return for Guy's commitment to them, around eighty people were at that very moment balancing life and work by researching, auditing, analysing, conceptualizing, quantifying and qualifying, visualizing, editing, mixing and montaging, arranging, presenting, discussing, and all the other activities that Guy liked to group under the general heading *getting one's hands dirty at the brandface*, by which he meant convincing people to channel their emotions, relationships and sense of self through the purchase of products and services.

'Shall we go upstairs?' he asked.

'No,' said Yves. 'We sit down here. It is comfortable.' He pointed to a beanbag next to the armchair. The idea of being invited to take a seat in one's own company HQ was a new sensation for Guy, and not one he found pleasant. The offer of the beanbag was clearly a trap, but he had to make the best of it, so he dragged the bulky leatherette sack to a place where he could at least lean his back against the pinball machine. In this position his eyeline was almost level with Yves's own.

Yves nodded sagely, the nod of a man with an INSEAD MBA giving his professional approval of a meeting tactic. Guy noticed with a feeling of impotent rage that the papers in his hands were recent company expenditure records. He forced himself to smile. 'Are you sure you wouldn't rather go upstairs?'

'It is OK here.'

Guy had to do something to regain the initiative. To buy time, he pretended he had to take a call on his mobile, and, making a 'one minute' gesture to Yves, clamped the handset to his ear and took a walk in the direction of the front desk. Circling in reception, he tried to think. A surprise visit by Yves Ballard could be interpreted in a number of ways, none of them good. Yves was a partner at Transcendenta, the venture-capital firm whose investment had helped *Tomorrow*★ get off the ground. Recently a certain frostiness had appeared in Transcendenta's communications with *Tomorrow*★. There was talk of setting performance targets and realizing a near-term capital return. Guy glanced back at the Frenchman. Yves was dressed in the international business-casual uniform he always wore: chinos, penny loafers which showed a lot of argyle sock, a blue cotton button-down shirt with the logo of a conservative fashion house on the breast pocket – clothes as internationally acceptable and context-free as his forty-something face, with its pleasant yet somehow under-used features. Those features had currently composed themselves into a surface of studied placidity, a treacherous ornamental pond of a face. Yves was here to talk money, no doubt about it.

Guy flipped his phone shut and walked back towards the brainstorm zone, which was thought of by most *Tomorrow*★ staffers as the recreation area, containing as it did soft furnishings, a TV and a PlayStation. Yves was idly examining the antique industrial sewing machine, salvaged by the renovating architects from the building's previous life as a garment sweatshop. Guy liked to take new members of staff to stand by the machine. Your inspiration should come from there, he would tell them. That hunk of metal understands the true meaning of work.

'You've taken on more people,' said Yves.

Guy explained the benefits of setting up an in-house production team, and extolled the good job being done by the new researchers. He was gabbling, nervously aware of the direction Yves was taking.

'Look, if we went upstairs, we could both have a proper seat.'

He tried to make it sound like a joke, but it came out as pleading. Half of the top floor was taken up by an area designed to foster Guy's own creativity and innovation, a space with a view over the council blocks and repurposed warehouses of east London that he sometimes referred to as his brainscape. In addition to the usual office items, the room contained a daybed, a draughtsman's table, boxes of unused art and design supplies, a home-cinema set-up and a cabinet filled with a quantity of toy robots and Quentin Tarantino mementoes. It was his place, his domain. If they went up there, Yves would not be able to make him feel so exposed.

Yves paid no attention to the question. 'I hear you won a new account?'

'We're closing the deal at the moment.'

'I thought that was why you went to New York. This new product from Pharmaklyne. The SSRI.'

'Exactly. It was a very productive meeting. Our creative work impressed them. We had a cross-section of young urban professionals make video diaries about their anxiety.'

'But they didn't sign.'

Guy was angry at being cornered in this way. 'Yves, it's great to see you, but I'm surprised you didn't schedule this meeting with Kika. We're working on several pitches at the moment. It would have been easier to fit this in if I'd known you were coming.'

'Of course. But I was in London and wanted to see how things were progressing at *Tomorrow** – just informally. I'm here as a friend, Guy. I'm here to support you.'

The rain had stopped, and a watery light filtered in through the windows. Above Guy's head a trio of giant red banners, relics of a pitch for a newswire service, fluttered in the draught from an open window. On each was a single motivating word written in an exploded sans serif font:

Play

Change

Inspire

The newswire had gone with another agency, but the banners had seemed too good to waste. Today, despite their positive messages, they seemed to Guy to be part of *Tomorrow**'s problem rather than its solution. For all its organizational innovation, ethos of openness and holistic approach to brand repositioning, *Tomorrow** was somewhat short of actual clients. Transcendenta had injected several million Euros in venture capital, but what with the building, the expansion, the post-9/11 loss of confidence and his penchant for really cool business toys, Guy had more or less burned through it. The last proper project, a brand audit for a semiconductor manufacturer, had wound up two months ago. He had a sudden twinge of paranoia. Did Yves know about his expenses? He had startled even himself this past month.

'Maybe,' Guy moved tentatively, 'we should do this over lunch?'

'No,' said Yves. 'No lunch. That would make us fat.'

'I'm sorry?'

'We don't want to get fat. Fat people move slowly. Fat companies too. Things are very bad now, Guy. It is not a time for self-indulgence. I sent one of your secretaries out for sandwiches. We will eat them here and you will point out to me the parts of your business that are really necessary.'

It was worse than he could have imagined. And Leela had not even begun to do her work.

Around the world, Thursday, 12 June, was a quiet day. Bombs went off in Jakarta, Jenin and Tashkent. An elderly single-hulled tanker sank off Manila, releasing its load of crude oil into the South China Sea. In Malawi a man was diagnosed with a previously unknown retroviral infection. At London's Heathrow Airport two dead Ghanaian boys were found frozen to the undercarriage of a Boeing 747.

As Guy ate bitter sandwiches with Yves, sunrise on Friday was sweeping across the Pacific. Over the Gulf of Mexico a US Navy F16 fighter made brief contact with an unidentified flying object, and at the bottom of a ravine in Tasmania a mother of two was found trapped in her Ford Cortina, having survived for three days on melted snow and packets of Hungry Jack's barbecue sauce. Arjun was still awake in his room at Berry Acres, staring at his screen. He did not sleep and went into work early, sitting on the bus listening to the soundtrack from *Crisis Kashmir*, the one in which Leela Zahir plays a soldier's daughter caught up in a web of terrorism and international intrigue.

He spent the morning running and checking a patch written by Clay for a common macro virus, yellow dots of tiredness swimming in his vision. People left him alone. Since he had lost his job he was no longer a real person, already fading into memory. He sat at the terminal and watched the clock at the bottom of his screen, waiting for the magic hour. Leela Zahir had been born at 10.12 a.m. on 13 June. If he had managed to do anything, if his code didn't have some unforeseen bug, it would not be long before the effects were felt. He was so tired that he could barely think. Lyrics from Leela's big *Crisis Kashmir* love song circled round in his head.

O my love, O my darling
I've crossed the line of no control
I hear your gunfire in my valley
You've tripped my wire
You have my soul
I've crossed the line
The line of no control

Just before lunch, or what would have been lunch had anyone at Virugenix observed such conventions, an excited-looking group of Ghostbusters gathered in Darryl's office. After a short conversation they moved into the hot zone, and watched something on one of the screens. Arjun, meerkatting over his cubicle partition, knew at once. Someone had sent a sample in for analysis; the game had started. By mid afternoon the entire senior AV team were in the plexiglas-walled room, watching Leela Zahir dance across ten monitors, a jerky five-second loop from the holi dance in *Naughty Naughty, Lovely Lovely.*

The thrill was indescribable. Leela, widening her eyes and making a flirtatious ticking-off gesture at the viewer, London's West End briefly visible in the background. And again. And again.

It worked.

Arjun knew what was going on behind the eyes and the smile, how Leela was stealing resources from other programs, taking up disk space, making herself at home. How perhaps she was also doing other things: malicious, corrupting things. Now it was just a question of how hard the analysts would find it to counter her. When a bright-eyed Clay strode past his desk, Arjun could not resist asking what was going on.

'Man, it's the real thing, that's what's going on?' Clay's voice betrayed his eagerness, his tone rising at the end of each sentence as if this event were putting everything, the whole world, into question. 'In the last ten minutes we got five different samples from like three places in East Asia? Customer support just took a call from a guy in Auckland which is a place in New Zealand? The CTO of some insurance company? He just had to shut down his whole network, I mean like everything? He was totally freaking out?'

Clay bustled off, smacking left fist into right palm with college-sports enthusiasm. A little needle of fear made its way up through Arjun's tired brain. Shutting down a whole company. That was serious.

As 10.12 a.m. struck the Kiritimati atoll in the Pacific and an unlucky shrimpboat skipper started to swear at his laptop, Guy and Gabriella left the opening party for a film that was a remake of another film and got into a taxi. Guy had barely spoken to anyone all evening. Gabriella, on the other hand, had been the centre of an animated group, telling jokes and receiving cards and mobile numbers and offers of lunch. Guy was too preoccupied to be jealous.

The whole situation was very Old Economy.

Yves Ballard's message had been stark. Transcendenta would feel unable to complete a further round of funding unless *Tomorrow** cut overheads and generated new business. Without funding, *Tomorrow** had cash to last only a couple more months. Yves had been evasive about what might happen, but left the general impression that Transcendenta would not hesitate to pull the plug.

He drifted back into calculation. *Tomorrow** and everything associated with it now depended on three pitches. The one for the SSRI drug he had just made in New York, and two he had to make next week – to a leisure chain in the Gulf, and to PEBA, the new Pan European Border Authority, an artefact of EU integration intended to harmonize the immigration and customs regimes of all the member states. As long as one of them came off, it might be enough to persuade Transcendenta to hold fire. Although, if he were honest with himself, he would have to say the drug company people had not seemed convinced. Two pitches, then. Two chances.

Gabriella was saving someone's number into her phone. Sensing him watching her, she angled the screen away slightly.

'Sweetie, have you had any more thoughts about Thailand?'

'Not really, Guy.' She flipped the phone shut and turned to look out of the window.

She was not sure how much longer she could stand him. When she first came to London, she was in the same headlong rush that had led her sister to the exit. There was a boyfriend and a magazine and parties. Her father found her and sent money. She tried things, worked in someone's gallery, even spent a term studying law. All the time she could feel the urge to run bubbling inside and grew increasingly certain that the only way to survive would be to settle, to throw out an anchor.

Then someone offered her a job coordinating magazine press for a film. It probably worked out because she cared so little for any of it, not the aura of glamour around the industry or the empty grace of the picture itself. Instead, placing stories and chaperoning the cast of young actors as they were interviewed about gangsters and Britishness and what it was like to work with the famous female lead, she discovered if not a calling then at least a distraction. There was a calculus at the heart of a media operation, an assessment of value: *what can you do for us, what do you want in return*. It was honest. Here human relations were out in the open: you were either on the list or off it, depending on what you had to trade. She worked hard because work dispelled her sister, and the company offered her a contract.

She had been doing the job for a year, enjoying having her own money, real money instead of the inexhaustible play-money which had killed Caroline. Then she met Guy. He came up to her at a boring party and immediately started running lines, old ones: I saw you across, what a beautiful, anyone ever said, such a coincidence. What astounded her was his gall, the impression he gave that the world and all the things in it were listed for him on a menu. Unlike other men she had met with the same confidence, there was nothing mannered about Guy. He was, in that respect, innocent. Life had always obliged, always given him what he asked for.

Because he would not allow her to refuse, she agreed to be taken out and so unleashed a storm of drinks and dinner, a barrage of delivered flowers. Within a couple of weeks she was confronted with the inevitable: a sofa and a dimmer switch and no good argument against letting him undress her. He did nothing weird or offensive and seemed so happy afterwards that it made her contact-happy too; she felt wanted, chosen. Soon she was turning down other dates to stay in with him at his new apartment. They watched DVDs and ate ice-cream. About once every twenty minutes he got up to survey his river view, talking continually about the future of this or that, the latest, the next wave, the bleeding edge. He always had a stack of men's magazines and a new gadget whose manual he was struggling to decipher. He was, she decided, quite sweet in an English sort of a way.

Though he idolized rock stars and rebels, there was nothing self-destructive about Guy. He didn't want to change the world, just to be in the lead as it moved forward on its preordained path. Gaby herself had never seen much sense in rebellion (things always stayed the same whatever you did), but even she was struck by the unconsciously ruthless way he set about taking pole position in life. Without appearing to try, he always ensured he was first in line. He was the very opposite of Caroline; he seemed to feel no unease about his entitlement.

Guy drummed out a rhythm on his knees and Gaby watched him. He slid the cab window open and she sat with her arms wrapped round herself as they crossed the river. Evening news-stands were headlining the latest terrorist alert. Somewhere in Victoria they passed a street which had been blocked off by a pair of squad cars. Maybe, she thought, it wasn't her. Or even him. Maybe it was the city which had gone bad. There was a sourness about, an aftertaste of fear.

Oddly, she had moved in with him because of his parents. He seemed to find them embarrassing, and she had to wheedle her single visit with flattery and sulking. They drove through Sunday rain to an old vicarage in a Shropshire market town, a house filled with ornamental china, heavy oak furniture and the flatulent smell of a pair of elderly chocolate Labs who spent most of their time asleep in their baskets in the kitchen. Gilly and Edward seemed a little intimidated by their son, and Guy adopted an imperious air around them, self-consciously mocking his father's opinions and fidgeting over lunch as if to signal his impatience to get away. Gaby found unexpected pleasure in the dog hair and the untuned piano and the row of wellingtons by the back door. These solid homely things were helpful, even comforting. They seemed to lie behind Guy's confidence like a guarantee, and it was partly the idea of being connected to them that made her say yes when he suggested she give up her flat and move in with him.

These days Gaby was hearing that voice again, the one which told her to get out, to smash up all the emotional chairs and tables so there would be no going back, so she could tear down this version of herself and start again.

The taxi pulled up at In Vitro, and one of the concierges opened the door. They passed through the tall glass doors into the atrium. As they waited by the lift, they both looked for the hundredth time at the vitrine set into the marble cladding of the wall, containing objects found during the building's construction. There were old bottles, Roman coins, a shoe buckle, a human shin bone.

Guy liked the presentation more than the things themselves. He accepted the principle that heritage added value; even the past had a future, and though in itself this display was more or less a collection of rubbish, here it was at least contributing to the texture of a contemporary living space. Gaby straightforwardly wished it would go away. It was an unwelcome reminder that beneath her feet was an earth full of household waste and human remains, disposables that even after hundreds of years had not been disposed of. Rising up in the lift, they both felt a sense of relief, of having made a lucky escape from the mud sucking at their heels.

'I wish they would put in some flowers instead of that horrid thing,' said Gaby. You can't choose, she was thinking. You can't choose the things you keep.

'So do I,' replied Guy eagerly. It was the first conversation she had initiated in almost two hours, and he was keen for it to go further. But he could think of nothing interesting to add about flowers or archaeology. The chance fizzled out.

They made their preparations for bed in silence, circling round each other and folding clothes, their thoughts soundtracked by the insect whine of electric toothbrushes. Gaby smoked a cigarette on the balcony and Guy took a shower, during which he surreptitiously masturbated, thinking about a fantasy partner who was like Gaby but kinder, less abrasive. Then he set his bedside alarm (which checked its accuracy using a signal sent by an atomic clock in Greenwich) and switched out the light. After a few minutes Gaby slipped in beside him.

They lay for a while in the dark. Guy thought about pitches. Gaby thought about Guy, about his absurd sense of his own importance, about the way nothing bad had ever happened to him. If there was a buffet table in a room, he walked straight up and began to eat. If there was one chair, he sat down. Thailand or Mauritius or Zanzibar or Cancún or Sharm el-Sheikh or Tunisia or Bali or the Gold Coast or Papeete or Gran Cayman or Malibu. So many places for Guy. All the same.

The next morning (by which time variant 01 had infected an estimated 3.2 million individual hosts around the world) Leela started to work her glamour on the life of Guy Swift. Her subject went off to work, leaving his girlfriend in bed, pretending to be asleep. On the journey he flicked through the cab driver's *Sun*, skimming stories about paedophiles and TV presenters, a football team buyout, a 34DD publican's daughter from Surrey. He had slept badly, jerking awake several times during the night, convinced he was late for a meeting. Now he felt as if his mental activity were being filtered through a diffuse obstruction in his brain, something porridge-like in texture and consistency which was preventing key synapses from firing.

The Shoreditch street on to which the *Tomorrow** building faced was of Dickensian narrowness and squalor. At ground level, flyposters and stencil graffiti coated the walls of the high-windowed brick buildings. Someone had dumped an old sofa by the row of council bins. As the taxi grumbled round the cobbled corner and he caught sight of the *Tomorrow** banner above the sweatshop door, Guy experienced a twinge of apprehension. Most mornings, unless he was feeling fragile from the night before, the sight of his company headquarters filled him with excitement. Today he had an obscure sense that something was wrong, which was confirmed as soon as he stepped through the door.

About a dozen people were standing around in reception. Several more were playing a game of table football. They all seemed cheerful, which was probably not unconnected with the fact that none of them was working. In his rare moments of self-doubt, Guy sometimes fretted that some elements of his organization were not a hundred per cent committed to achieving

*Tomorrow**'s objectives. To counter this he had formulated a tripartite management strategy, fostering (bullet point one) a culture of goal-sharing, (point two) publicly rewarding excellence and (three) eavesdropping on email and phone conversations, hoping to find out who was against him. The need to spy took hold only occasionally, and usually turned up no conclusive evidence. He had held off altogether since the Stoli-fuelled evening when, trawling through the pictures of David Beckham in the receptionist's outbox, he found a message that referred to him in the course of three lines as 'his lordship', 'fancypants' and 'mister quiffy'. The next day, in the midst of his hangover, he had terminated the girl's contract, citing 'presentability issues' (a low-cut top he had previously rather liked) as the reason. He had confided in no one and subsequently the episode had made him uneasy; he was not altogether sure it fitted his ethical profile.

Confronted by a mob of idle employees, his latent paranoia bloomed forth. Now, of all times, when the very future of the company was at stake, the bastards were going to turn on him. He froze in the doorway, battling an irrational desire to flee.

'Guy, we've got trouble.'

It was Caedmon, the network administrator. Guy nodded nervously. 'I can see that. What the fuck are they doing?' He turned to his staff, holding out his hands in a placatory gesture. I am your king. Return to your garrets. 'What are you all standing around for? Come on, people, this isn't a game. We've got the Al-Rahman pitch due in a couple of days.'

No one made a move to sever his periwigged head with a guillotine. Instead they all started talking, gathering round to profess their fanatical eagerness to be at work and their shock and dismay that they were being prevented from slaking this desire for productive labour by the shutdown of the office computer network. One or two people were genuinely annoyed; unsaved data had been lost; important things had yet to be done. When Guy heard this, his own emotional state started to oscillate between stark horror at the news and relief that his authority was intact. To make any sense of things, he had to drag the sysop upstairs to his office and sit him down on a chair. Caedmon, a shy bespectacled young

Welshman with a number one crop and a seemingly infinite number of t-shirts bearing the logos of independent record labels, did his best to explain.

'I had to do it, Guy. The whole network. I didn't have a choice. About twenty minutes after I got in this morning it just kicked off. Every screen in the place started displaying pictures of this Indian woman.'

'Question, Caedmon. What the hell am I paying you for?'

'Guy –'

'This is so not supposed to happen.'

'I know. I'm really sorry. It's a virus –'

'Oh, Christ. Please, please, please, do not be about to tell me it's eaten everything.'

'No, it's OK. All our data is backed up on to tape. It's just a question of –'

'Spare me the details. Just tell me how long. When's it going to be up again?'

'It's going to be a while. Unless there's a patch, I think I'm going to have to clean-install everything from –'

'Caedmon.'

'Certainly the rest of the day.'

An hour or two was what Guy had in mind. That seemed an appropriate amount of time for the situation to resolve itself. Instead he was going to lose a whole day. A vital day. Was he going to have to live for the rest of his life as the man whose company was brought down by a *computer problem*? A bloody *technical hitch*? It was like something from a bad b2b ad campaign. *Don't be the manager whose department caught the virus.*

'All day? What the hell is that? All day, Caedmon, is no good. It has to be quicker.'

'I'm sorry, Guy. If I had an assistant – but it's just me –'

'Just you? We've got millions of computer people.'

'They're graphic designers, Guy.'

'Oh.'

'Look, even if some of the others muck in, it's going to be a while. It's not just *Tomorrow** who are having problems.' Caedmon mentioned the names of two rival agencies and a bank where his friend was temping. Guy allowed himself to be slightly mollified. He waved Caedmon out. 'Go on, then. Get on with it.' The gesture, he noticed, came out with a peculiar flourish. More *ancien régime* body language. Not a good sign.

By lunchtime his mood had worsened. Every time he walked somewhere he felt he was mincing. Switching on his laptop, he was confronted by a little pixelated woman and a snatch of screeching violins. He took the machine down to Caedmon, who nodded glumly and told him he would make it a priority. At two he sent most of the staff home. At three he took a call from New York.

The call confirmed that Pharmaklyne was going with another agency to brand its SSRI. Guy expressed his disappointment, thanked the product manager, and put the phone down. The first thirty seconds passed calmly. Then, shouting inarticulate obscenities, he threw the phone across the room. It felt good, so he followed it up with a promotional paperweight which somehow went off course and shattered the glass doors of the case where he kept his collection. When Kika came in to find out what was happening, she discovered him on his hands and knees among the shards of a bottle of *Reservoir Dogs* commemorative table wine. He screamed at her to get a cloth.

Kika helped him mop. Mainly Kika mopped and Guy paced up and down, trying not to mince and muttering fuckfuckfuck under his breath.

'It's a movie star, apparently,' she said, gingerly picking up glass with her fingers.

'What?'

'The woman in the picture. She's an Indian movie star called Leela Zahir. Ranjit said so.' Guy looked blank. 'Ranjit,' Kika prompted. 'Your senior copywriter?' Guy nodded vaguely. At front desk, Kika informed the remaining loiterers that Mr Quiffy was really falling to bits.

As the stress ratcheted up, Guy brooded behind the closed door of his creative space, increasingly self-conscious about the foppishness of his gestures and ever more in need of someone to blame. Caedmon was the obvious target. Hourly he appeared in a more useless and ineffectual light. A problem by definition was someone's fault, and who else's might it be? There was, now Guy came to think about it, something smug about him, with his definitive collection of fanzines and encyclopaedic knowledge of early-eighties new-wave bands. Women in the office babied him. For his birthday they clubbed together to buy him a mountain bike. But when it came to a real emergency, when *this* happened, who cared whether your geek was popular? He obviously wasn't up to the job. Guy called Kika and told her to get some computer-security specialists to quote for cleaning up the mess. Then he had a little chat with Caedmon. After that things went rapidly downhill.

Some time later he found himself standing in the middle of the brainstorm zone, screaming into his mobile phone. Little tears had formed in the corners of his eyes. Junior employees were watching like spectators at the site of a road accident. 'Do it now!' he was pleading. 'Why can't you just come and fucking do it right now?'

Disconcertingly, Caedmon had seemed unfazed at losing his job. He frowned and sauntered out of the meeting, saying he would be in the pub if Guy changed his mind. A few minutes later Kika came in to tell him that she had phoned five companies and none was available to help. 'They said perhaps in a day or two,' she explained. 'They said they had to give priority to their existing clients.' Guy told her she was useless and made some calls himself. He shouted, threatened, got nowhere. Apparently everyone had this thing. Possibly it was some kind of Muslim fundamentalist attack.

As the reasons for Caedmon's nonchalance started to dawn, sitting down no longer seemed appropriate. For a while Guy flounced around the building with his phone pressed to his ear. Then he noticed he was flouncing and made an effort to stride with masculine purpose. It made no difference. No one would listen. No one would help. Like many business people he had a quasi-theological view of computers. They were important and mysteriously beneficial, but it was the job of the priesthood to engage with them. Finding himself with no technical support was like standing naked before the judgement of God. He had no idea how to proceed, no way of even gauging the seriousness of his predicament.

At this point he realized he was vocalizing. And that his staff were staring at him.

Kika persuaded him back upstairs. She sat him down on his Eames lounger with a glass of spring water. She switched on the TV and handed him his remote. As the flow of images worked its calming magic, she gently suggested he might try to unfire Caedmon.

There was no alternative. He made the call. Caedmon didn't sound surprised to hear from him. Guy apologized. Caedmon said no sweat. He already had another job offer, and because of his notice clause (he named the section and subsection numbers) he would in effect be getting two salaries for a while. So it had worked out fine.

Guy apologized again. Then, experimentally, he begged a little.

Caedmon had the decency to keep any note of triumph out of his voice as he swiftly negotiated a bonus, an £8,000 rise and two extra weeks of paid holiday. When he announced that for the moment he was happy in the pub, and so would be unable to start again before the next morning, Guy made a superhuman effort to control his temper. He succeeded, more or less. Caedmon said he would be in the next day about nine.

Drained, Guy stared at the television. It was talking about 'widespread chaos in the City of London', about 'brownouts' and 'disruption'. There was an interview with the manager of a logistics company who didn't know where his trucks were, and with a scruffy computer journalist who said he had always thought something like this would happen. They showed a picture of the little dancing girl, who apparently was known as 'India's sweetheart'. The journalist theorized that it might be some kind of promotional stunt.

Guy switched off the TV. The office was quiet. Leeched of all energy and emotion, he set the alarm, bolted the door and went home. When the driver tried to start a conversation, he shut the partition. Even the sight of In Vitro's glass panels glowing in the city sunset failed to lift his spirits. On the kitchen worktop there was a note from Gaby. *Something has come up. Work want me to go to Scotland*. She did not know how long she would be away.

'A *virus*? My God! What are you telling me, yaar?'

Up on Pali Hill, Zee TV was hurriedly muted. The click-clack of nails on cellphone carapace, by which the maid judged the progress of her mistress's many conversations, ceased abruptly. Spotting warning signal number two (the chaat-filled palm stalled ominously between dish and mouth), the maid hitched up her sari and made a discreet exit. The explosion followed seconds later.

'Behan-chod! What kind of dirtiness are you talking? My daughter has infected who . . .'

It took some hours before Mrs Zahir could be made to understand all this business of computer diseases. Such nastiness! Such complication! Once she understood, it took several more to recover from the shock. After an interval in a darkened room, she emerged, fortified herself with paan and sweet tea, and started to take charge of the situation. Her first call was to a very dear friend, who happened to have a column on *Stardust* magazine. The second was to her astrologer. By the time she had ticked off a list of advisers (spiritual and temporal), national media outlets (print and broadcast) and was stuck into the first of the international newswires, a clear line was emerging.

'To be stolen like this,' sobbed the artiste's stricken mother, 'is too too terrible. Our feelings are shaken. My daughter is sincerely protective over her creativity. For someone to come and use it for criminal purposes is shocking, really.'

Maa Zahir then appealed to the Chief Inspector of Police, 'an old family friend', to catch the violators forthwith. We say, look out, goondas! Whether inland or phoren, Leela's mad-as-heck mummy will hunt you down! Lovely Leela herself, currently locating in romantic Scotland on the next Rocky Prasad smash, is said to have gone into seclusion . . .

Mrs Zahir had always had her daughter's financial interests uppermost in her mind. From their first audition, and her inspired idea to change the girl's Persian name to something Hindu-friendly, Leila-Leela's marvellous career had taken her on an upward path of almost unprecedented rapidity. It had also been satisfyingly free of the blemishes that attached to other Bombay starlets. True, in the early days certain people remarked on a seventeen-year-old girl being seen so often in the company of elderly film mogul K. P. Gupta. Some may even have made a connection between that and the starring role Gupta gave his unknown protégée in *N2L2*. People were dirty-minded. There was nothing you could do against that. But this! For a thing like this to mark her daughter's twenty-first birthday! It was a public-relations disaster.

Stolen. *Piracy*. The same five-second loop, repeated again and again. Five seconds from the fully copyrighted holi dance in *Naughty Naughty, Lovely Lovely*. Five seconds, one hundred per cent royalty free. Mrs Zahir could almost feel her jewellery getting lighter, each unlicensed frame shaving a little heft from the bangles on her wrists, loosening a stone from the rings on her fingers. It had to stop. It had to cease forthwith.

Hunched in his cubicle, the violator carried on counting. Pens in his Cisco Systems promotional mug. *18*. Post-it notes left on the pad. *37*. Keys on his keyboard. *105*. Bead of sweat on the delete key. *1*. He wiped it away with a fingertip. It was an effort to focus on his screen.

Hour by hour, the list of Leela-related disasters was growing longer. Clients from all over the world were contacting Virugenix, wanting to know how to remove her from their systems. The helpline staff posted updates to a page on the corporate intranet, and Arjun returned to it obsessively, to look at what he had done, the trouble he had caused for knitting-machine manufacturers and management consultants, adult magazines and university departments, for an auto-parts supplier in Austin which couldn't track its inventory, a public-relations company in São Paolo which had lost its contacts database. Late in the afternoon a router went down, shutting off most of Boston's internet traffic for almost an hour. Entry by entry, it all went up on the page. *Nature of incident. Severity. Advice given*. Mostly the advice given was to shut down the email system and wait for a fix.

A fix the AV team had yet to come up with.

Waves of nausea kept rising up into his throat. He could feel his heart beating in his chest, an amplified rattle suggesting illness, crisis. Letters in paragraph one of the text on his screen. *342*. Number of ceiling tiles visible between the partition wall and the row of recessed lights running through the centre of the office. *75*. The hot zone was full of arguing engineers, Darryl perching on a desk in a corner, swinging his legs and watching the action as Clay and the Vietnamese analyst Tran conducted a hand-waving debate, scrawling on the whiteboard and angrily crossing out each other's glyphs. Occasionally other people butted in and the argument would diffuse through the room. It did not look to Arjun as if they were making much headway.

It was time. He knew if he waited, he would lose his moment. Still, something kept him fixed to his chair. He wanted to speak to his sister. He wanted to hear the voice of someone who knew him, who cared. Chris came into his mind and he put her out of it again. He waited until most of the people had left the hot zone, then knocked on the door. Only Clay and Darryl were inside, drinking bottled smoothies from the office fridge and flicking despondently through a printout of decompiled code. Seeing Arjun outside the door, Clay pulled on his face mask and Darryl started oscillating his hands in a frenetic shooing motion.

'What are you doing?' he stuttered, as Arjun poked his head into the room. 'There are rules, Mehta. You're not authorized.'

'I need to talk to you, Darryl.'

'I – I don't care, OK? This is not good. This is not good at all. You have to leave.'

Arjun almost acquiesced, half turning to go, but he steeled himself.

'It's important.'

'This is a bad time, OK? This is like a crisis period? We are dealing with something major, so if you could just close the door and depart, Mehta, things would be a lot better. Clay, tell him. Make him go.'

'It's about the Leela virus.'

'Good name, huh?' said Clay to no one in particular. 'I think they should give all viruses chicks' names. Like ships. Or hurricanes.'

'Hurricanes often have masculine names,' snapped Darryl. 'Andrew, for example.'

'I believe that until 1979, women's names only were used,' said Arjun. 'Since then there has been an alternating list.'

'Mitch,' said Clay. 'Bob and Alice.'

'That's crypto,' said Darryl. 'Mehta, what are you still doing here?'

'I think I spotted something, sir.'

'You're right, man,' said Clay. 'Hey, Arjun, this Layla Zoo-hair is like an actress, isn't she? You ever see any of her films?'

'What do you mean, spotted something?'

'About the virus.'

'She's hot. To me a lot of Indian chicks are hot.'

'Clay. Mehta, what were you doing looking at that code?'

'I – I was curious. Interested.'

'That is totally irregular. You're not holding a sample on your machine, are you?'

Arjun didn't answer. Instead he laid out, as if it had just occurred to him, an elegant solution, a way to scan for Leela using a signature pattern of behaviour. The two analysts looked at him in frank amazement.

'That would totally work,' said Clay.

Darryl nodded thoughtfully. At that moment Tran and Brian wandered into the room, throwing quizzical glances at Arjun.

'You can go now, Mehta,' said Darryl. 'I'll bear in mind what you said.'

Arjun went back to his desk. He wasn't sure if it was enough. He had impressed them, certainly, but would it make Darryl see? Arjun Mehta, his indispensable team member. Arjun Mehta, the one who shouldn't get fired. Somehow it didn't seem like he had gotten the full effect. The moment should have had more drama. When he was planning it, he had imagined a climax. Excitement and gratitude. Backslapping. Speeches. Now behind the hot-zone glass Darryl was explaining something to the other engineers. There were high-fives. They were laughing, shaking his hand.

They were treating Darryl like a hero.

The world suddenly seemed very far away to Arjun, with himself as a spaceman, attached to it by a slender umbilicus.

'Aw, man.'

Clay hung over the rim of his cubicle. There were seventeen cowrie shells on his necklace. In the phrase *enticing guava-lime blend fortified with citrus bioflavonoids, ginseng, rosehips and spirulina* which appeared on the side of his drink bottle, there were six instances of the letter *e*. Clay looked at him darkly.

'He burned you, man. He told them it was his idea.'

Arjun nodded, mute. Clay leaned down a little closer. 'Arjun, tell me something. How did you know?'

'I'm a good employee, Clay.' He almost whispered it. He was trying not to cry, or shout out. 'I'm very dedicated.'

Clay looked over his shoulder. He felt bad about Arjun getting fucked, but big emotional scenes were not his thing. He tried to look encouraging. 'It'll work out,' he said. 'I know it will.'

'How do you know, Clay? How do you *know*?' Mehta suddenly looked violent, unpredictable. His eyes were glittering. Clay was afraid.

'Hey, figure of speech, man. Just trying to help.'

Clay backed away. The guy was being seriously uncool.

‘Yes, Ma, very well. Of course I am. Main tikh huh. You shouldn’t worry so much. Accha.’

Over there it was morning. Malini would be making tea, putting out the breakfast things.

‘Could you put Priti on the line?’

He waited, looked out of the window at the complexities of the tree.

‘Bro?’

‘Hello, Sis. Why are you still speaking in that accent?’

‘What accent? You’re very bad, Bro. You haven’t phoned for ever so long. Mummy was worried.’

‘She told me.’

‘Hey, it’s gone mad here. You wouldn’t believe – you sound funny. Is everything OK?’

‘Are you on your way to work?’

‘In a minute. Hold on. I’m taking it into the other room.’

The acoustics changed. Priti had shut herself in the smaller bedroom.

‘You’re not all right. What is it? I can hear it in your voice.’

Arjun was silent for a very long time. There was so much to say, all of it unsayable.

‘I miss you. There’s no one to talk to here.’

‘I miss you too, you bigshot. When are they going to give you some time off? Surely you deserve it. And if you’re head of the whole department, can’t you just tell them? Say you need it. Say you’ll come back for Manoj-bhai’s wedding. Everyone would love to see you.’

He wanted desperately to tell her the truth.

‘Bro? Say you’ll come. Mummy would be so happy.’

I'm afraid, Sis. Afraid.
'Bro?'
He told her he had to go, and put down the phone.

Virugenix did well with *Leela01*. They got a fix and removal instructions up on their site before their competitors. According to etiquette, they shared their information, and soon the other software houses caught up, but the speed and efficiency of their solution were enviously noted. There were caffeinated smiles in the Michelangelo Building. At around 03.20 PST on the morning of the 14th, Darryl Gant posted a JPEG to the internal departmental list. It was a rough of a new t-shirt design, a blood-splattered fist squashing an Indian dancing girl.

Arjun did not sleep at all that night. His boss was on his mind, looming over his bed in the darkness, an irritable bearded gatekeeper barring the way to happiness. No amount of soothing calculation could dispel him. Arjun imagined curves and estimated the area beneath them. He hypothesized complex shapes and distorted them according to esoteric rules of transformation. Still Darryl persisted, dressed in his Gemini Mission souvenir MAI flight jacket, shaking his head and laughing maniacally.

Denied.

At some point during the night he realized there would have to be a confrontation.

The next morning when he got into work there was a mail from the personnel division, giving him a date to vacate his apartment. It was the stimulus he needed. As the little potbellied figure shuffled in and shut itself in its den, he got up from his cubicle and knocked on the office door, his knuckles hitting the small area of laminate visible between the SETI poster and the handwritten *What part of DO NOT DISTURB do you not understand?* sign. Darryl's voice came from the other side.

'It's too early. Go away.'

He ignored him and went in.

'What the fuck?' said Darryl, retreating defensively behind his desk. He shot a little glance over Arjun's shoulder, as if looking to see who might be around to assist.

'Darryl, you must sit down and listen to me.'

'I must do nothing of the kind. This is my space, Mehta. My space. It is clearly demarcated. There is a sign.'

'I think you've treated me very unfairly.'

'You did this yesterday too, this walking in. Do you – I don't know – have a problem with boundaries? Do you maybe have a condition? This is a compulsion, right? Compulsive boundary-transgression syndrome.'

'Please, Darryl. I helped you yesterday. I don't mind you taking credit for it.'

'Whoa there. Just back up. You are being very aggressive, buddy. That's something I don't hold with.'

'I'm sorry. I apologize if I was disturbing you, but I think you should give me some kind of recognition. This is very important to me. And I was helpful. I could help more.'

'Just stay back, Mehta. I know aikido. I can break bones. Look, isn't this something you could have done on email? You don't have to come into my office with this stuff.'

'Please, Darryl.'

'Crumble bones. Literally reduce them to dust. I can concentrate all my chi in my palms.'

'Please give me my job back. That's all I'm asking.'

'Stop talking. That's an order. I don't feel comfortable.'

'Even on a trial period. I'll be the best worker you ever had. I swear it.'

'Could you – OK, I'll think about it, right? I'll think about it.'

'You will?'

'I said so, didn't I? No. No. Stay the other side of the desk. Just – OK. I'll think about it.'

Arjun left the office, and for five minutes existed in a state of minor but perceptible hope. Then a mail dropped into his inbox.

To: arjunm@virugenix.com
From: darrylg@virugenix.com
Subject: Boundaries

You are clinically ill. You cannot do this to people. There is a LAW. Also re: your request/THREAT there can be no change. What did you think? This is policy please do not discuss it further with me. THERE IS NO USE IN CRYING OVER SPILT MILK. I remind you of my EXTENSIVE security measures.

Arjun cradled his head in his hands.

The worm which became known as *Leela02*, or *LeelaServer*, was first reported on the afternoon of 13 June in the Philippines, where network traffic was slowed to a crawl as ever-proliferating copies of the organism scanned for new machines to infect. In the US the rate of spread was slower, but a series of high-profile security breaches conspired to give Leela's second public incarnation a level of media visibility which its creator had never in his worst nightmares imagined possible.

At 08.45 a.m. MST on 14 June, some hours before Arjun's attempted confrontation with Darryl, a water-treatment plant in the town of Guthrie, Oklahoma, was forced to suspend activities because the machines controlling its filtration process had crashed. In the hours after trading opened, major companies in several states, including a regional investment bank, reported trouble with database software running on public servers. At 11.10 a.m. MST an operations centre providing 911 service for three suburban police departments and fifteen fire departments in Boulder, Colorado, suffered 'catastrophic computer-systems failure'. Its operators were reduced to using pen and paper to log calls and send out response teams. The Colorado state government sent a message to Washington, asking whether it had reason to believe the country was under cyber-attack. Washington replied in the negative, but, after hurried consultations involving the FBI, the Department of Homeland Security, the National Infrastructure Protection Center and the Central Intelligence Agency, the categorical denial was rescinded, and the President's spokesman, Gavin Burger, famous for his double-breasted suits and unabashed comb-over, held a conference which described the administration's assessment of the situation as 'pending'.

During the next morning's daily briefing, Burger faced a barrage of questions. The press, who had seen the international stories on the wires about the plant closure in Montevideo and the data-traffic brownouts in the Far East, wanted to know the worst. Was it emanating from a rogue state? Some hostile underground network? Had any government departments been affected? How would he characterize the economic impact? The *New York Times* wanted to know whether the administration could confirm or deny that the country was under attack. Burger responded by reminding the assembled journalists that 'any attempt to compromise or mitigate our ability to function effectively in terms of our critical infrastructure, whether that be in the realm of telecommunications, energy, banking and finance, water facilitation, government operational activity thresholds or the smooth and unhampered running of our essential emergency services, must be viewed as taking place within a framework strongly suggestive of deliberate negativization, threat or hostile intent. We are in the process of investigating and assessing the current situation, and will move with the utmost alacrity and vigour to institute proportionate, reasonable and devastating countermeasures appropriate to the ultimate outcome of that threat assessment.'

The woman from the *Times* was not sure if this meant yes or no, but filed a story which made the situation sound very tense indeed. Across America, citizens started to look with suspicion at the computers on their desks. These machines which had always terrorized them in small ways – by crashing, hanging, demanding meaningless upgrades or simply scolding them in the persona of an annoying cartoon paperclip – were now revealed to harbour something more sinister, something with an agenda. This was it, the enemy within, a technological fifth column in the homes of ordinary Americans. By the time talk-radio got hold of it, a consensus had emerged that the attack should be avenged in blood. Calling into a nationally syndicated show, Bobby from Topeka summed it up for a lot of people.

'Torture,' he said. 'That's the only way we'll find out who's behind this.'

Torture who, asked the host.

'Hell, I don't know,' said Bobby. 'Whoever they got to, I suppose.'

At the boundaries of any complex event, unity starts to break down. Recollections differ. Fact shades irretrievably into interpretation. How many people must be involved for certainty to dissipate? The answer, according to information theorists, is two. As soon as there is a sender, a receiver, a transmission medium and a message, there is a chance for noise to corrupt the signal.

There is no doubt that legally and morally Arjun Mehta must bear responsibility for the outbreak, but actions have been ascribed to Leela, and hence to him, for which he could not possibly be responsible. There were rumours that the virus was 'attacking the water supply', and the claim circulated that the Colville plant shutdown was part of a strategy by a foreign power to contaminate drinking water with (depending on who you spoke to) cryptosporidium, *E. coli* or LSD. Alarms, mostly false, were raised in various US government offices, at power plants, dams and military bases. Lack of technical knowledge contributed to the confusion. In Honduras, Leela was suspected of blowing lightbulbs in the Ministry of the Interior. A man in Ottawa papered his bedroom in silver foil, convinced that his son's PC had started to emit harmful rays. In Bihar, police acting under orders from a regional politician conducted raids on various local markets, confiscating pirated VHS copies of Leela Zahir films which were believed to be 'spreading disease'. Back in the US, when the administrators of the website for the Houston Airport System discovered that references to *George Bush Intercontinental Airport* had been mysteriously changed to *George Bush is Incontinent Airport* they issued a press release accusing the anonymous author of Leela of perpetrating the outrage.

Conversely, other events which may be attributable to Leela have dropped through the cracks. To this day much remains invisible to the counters and chroniclers, those whose function it is to announce what happened, to come to some conclusion about how it must have been. There were market movements, jitters and shakes, reconfigurations of money and confidence and power that for the most part were not discussed or even comprehended at the time. Leela was in the system like a quintessence, a breath.

Within twenty-four hours of *Leela01* being identified and countered, variants were reported. Some were obviously the work of copycats, crude alterations to the subject line of the delivery email, superficial tweaks to the code. Others were more profound, and analysts were reluctantly forced to classify them as entirely new organisms. *Leelas03*, *04* and *05* were identified. *Leela06* (the so-called *RingtoneLeela*), which programmed cellphone handsets to play a melody from *You'll Have to Ask My Parents*, caused particular alarm. It displayed a knowledge of mobile-telephony systems which shocked the telecoms corporations, forcing them into a hasty security redesign. *Ringtone* is also one of several Leela variants which have never been conclusively linked to Arjun Mehta, a gap in the record that opens up vertiginous and troubling possibilities. Were other people out there dreaming of Leela Zahir?

In the first few days of the outbreak, various groups and individuals claimed responsibility. Maoist revolutionaries in Chiapas sent a fax to a Mexico City newspaper announcing that Leela was the latest step in their campaign to cripple the infrastructure of global capitalism. A Lithuanian hacking group called the Red Hand Gang revealed that they had concocted it to demonstrate their superiority to their rivals, the Riga-based HacktiKons. Serial confessor James Lee Gillick III was (as usual) ignored, since he had no access to computers in his Ohio penitentiary. The Shoreditch Brigade, which preoccupied the British tabloids for several days, turned out to be a student rag-week prank.

Behind the scenes, global law-enforcement agencies took action. Subpoenas were obtained for the logs of service providers. Phone records and news-group postings were examined for clues to the source of the epidemic. In China the government seriously considered shutting down internet access altogether. Gavin Burger announced to the Washington press pack that 'sources within the computer underground' were cooperating with federal investigators, and the bulletin boards confirmed that more or less anyone with a record for computer crime was being taken in for questioning, from old school superstars, the Mittnicks and Poulsens, to script kiddies who had been caught defacing corporate websites, people no one seriously believed had the knowledge or motivation to create anything on Leela's scale. Day by day the atmosphere curdled, became vengeful and uncertain.

Arjun watched the arrest of seventeen-year-old Thierry Hofmann on CNN. *Breaking news: virus suspect held.* As technicians carried plastic evidence bags containing hard drives, disks and manuals to a waiting van, the Swiss teenager was led out of the front door of his parents' Montreux home by a pair of uniformed policemen, a look of absolute incredulity on his face. It was that look which broke Arjun, shattered the screen he had erected to shield him from what was taking place. Even Hofmann's release the next day could not wipe it away, the panicked turn towards the camera as a hand pressed down on his head to ease him into the police car. Bewilderment and fear. Bewilderment and fear that rightfully belonged to him.

He curled up among the foil trays and coffee cups, the printouts and crushed corn chips on the floor of his room, and started to cry. Perhaps if he said sorry to the people he had harmed, who had lost their data? Vignettes of forgiveness (*I'll make it up to you, even if it takes a while*) spooled through his mental projector. But what about those who had lost money, or couldn't get an ambulance when they needed one? Were people being hurt by Leela? Had anyone been *killed*?

At that moment he understood. Sooner or later they would find him and then life as he knew it would be over. *All I wanted was my job back. All I wanted was to work and be happy and live a life in magic America.* None of that would count for much in court. Would there even be a court? They were calling him a terrorist, which meant that he would probably just join the ranks of the disappeared, the kneeling figures in the orange suits against whom anything was justified, to whom anything could legitimately be done. It was the revenge of the uncontrollable world. He had tried to act but instead had made himself a non-person.

The Dutch steward gabbled a paragraph of corporate communication, his wayward accent reinventing his employers as 'Europe's leading locust airline' and advising passengers of the 'streamlined chicken process' planned at UK airports. Gaby, whose own vowels (when she concentrated) had been hammered flat into near-perfect London slumming posh, smiled wryly at the boy's mistakes, distracting herself from what she always thought about during take-off and landing, which was death. The sudden eruption of light and air into the cabin, the unpeeling of the fuselage – the pictures were compulsive, almost pornographic in their specificity. Twice a flight she would imagine the cold sucking wind freighted with pillows and carry-on bags and vodka miniatures and headsets that would rush past her in the final moments of consciousness, and would feel close to the mystery, to the centre of things.

With a bump the wheels hit the tarmac. Death disappeared in the boredom of the scramble in the aisle, and by the time she walked into the arrivals hall at Inverness she had, as always, forgotten it. They had sent a runner to meet her, locally hired crew rather than Indian, a smug Glasgow film lad all distressed denim and hair gel, chewing gum *and* smoking a fag while checking himself out in the mirror at one of the concessions. He threw her case in the back of the minivan and in what was apparently his fuck-me voice told her to call him Rob D. On the way down the A82 he spoke a name-dropping monologue to her breasts, and she looked out of the window at the rock and the yellow gorse and the sparkling water of Loch Ness. As far as he was concerned, the whole production was tits-up, the Pakis didn't know scheduling from their erse and now with these reporters running round he wouldn't be at all surprised if . . . When he ran out of opinions he fell silent and played house music on the CD, and she got a chance to look at the notes they had given her.

They translated the title of the film as *Tender Tough*, which made it sound as if it was about meat. The plot concerned a disillusioned cop who becomes a gangster after the death of his family in a food-contamination scandal, then is redeemed by a young dancer who shows him the path of peace and righteousness before herself dying tragically in a bungled shoot-out. The stars were a guy called Rajiv Rana and the one who all the trouble was about, the heroine, Leela Zahir. In his publicity photo, Rana was wearing a white wife-beater and leaping through digitally enhanced flames. In hers, Leela Zahir was wearing a baby-blue sweatsuit and peeping out from behind a tree. The publicity materials gave their birth dates and star signs. Rana was in his late thirties. Leela Zahir was precisely twenty-one.

When Dan Bridgeman had phoned her about the trip, he had presented it as a bad job, a favour Gaby would be doing the company. Bridgeman & Hart made a speciality of handling PR requirements for foreign crews on location in the UK, but that usually meant Americans or French, occasionally outfits from other parts of Europe. A request from an Indian producer was a novelty. No one really knew what to do. After all, as Phoebe Hart pointed out at lunch, they had their own media, didn't they? Mainstream film people knew the basics about 'Bollywood': chorus lines and chiffon saris. They also knew that Indians functioned in their own way, had their own publicity and marketing and distribution networks, and one didn't really need to worry about them. However, the situation had been explained. An off-the-film-page story had broken about their lead star, and they were being besieged by requests from all kinds of media outlets. There was some additional unspecified complication, but on the whole it seemed to be something B & H could help with. They wanted someone to firefight. Gaby wasn't on anything important, so the firm sent her.

At eight the northern summer sun was still so bright that it felt like mid afternoon. The hills changed colour as clouds passed overhead, cycling through phases of purple and green and brown. They had reached the west coast, near the bridge connecting the mainland with Skye. A narrow road twisted its way between a sheer granite cliff faced with wire mesh and the gravelled shore of Loch Lone, whose disturbed surface looked like a huge scratched sheet of steel. As Rob D. pulled the minivan through the stone gateposts of the Clansman's Lodge Hotel, she saw her work standing around, watched by a wary local constable. A TV van and a few hire cars had pulled up on to the grass verge, and a scattering of bored journalists, news people from the drab look of them, were smoking cigarettes and making phone calls and eating sandwiches and pissing against the trunks of the conifers in the plantation which ran up to the boundary of the hotel grounds.

Rising steadily above the water, the Lodge's driveway ran for about half a mile, executing a gentle arc around the lake shore, until the building itself came into view, a stark two-storey manor house with whitewashed walls and steeply gabled grey slate roofs, set in an acre of immaculate lawn. The building was neither ugly nor beautiful, a functional place whose architecture spoke of Christian modesty and the need to insulate against winter draughts. In the driveway a group of workmen were loading folding chairs and tables into a pair of large catering trucks, buffeted by the wind. Rob D. parked in front of a glassed-in porch and, as he pulled her bag from the back of the van, told her, as if it were a valuable and possibly even classified piece of information, his room number. She suggested he had a wank. 'Bitch,' he muttered under his breath.

Though the exterior of the hotel was stark, the entrance hall (and, Gaby later discovered, the bar, the restaurant and the billiards room) was carpeted in a violent red–green tartan and crammed with a Victorian clutter of stags' heads, dirks, rusty guns, pewter, banners, cases of fishing flies and golf balls, prints of weeping swains and ruined castles, sporting trophies, sagging furniture and, by the stairs, a dubious-looking suit of armour. At front desk was a sour-faced clerk and a rack of leaflets inviting Gaby to taste authentic Scottish offal cookery, visit a woollen mill and discover the eternal mystery of the Picts. As the clerk looked up her name in a leather-bound ledger, a haggard-looking Indian man appeared and introduced himself as Rakesh, the location manager.

'Are they still outside?' he asked.

'The journalists? Yes, they are.'

'We have a situation,' he said, with the mournful expression of a diplomat telling his premier that war is inevitable. 'It is most delicate.'

'What kind of situation?' asked Gaby. Rakesh looked nervously at the clerk, who was making no effort to disguise his interest in their conversation.

'Come to Mr Prasad's room in half an hour. We'll explain everything.'

Rocky Prasad was younger than she had expected. He sat by the window looking wistfully at the sunset, his smooth round face like that of a schoolboy who has another hour of maths before break. He could not, Gaby decided, be much older than twenty-five. His neat white polo shirt and pressed jeans reduced his age still further, and she had to remind herself that this was a man who had already directed three feature films and was (or so claimed the cuttings faxed through to Bridgeman & Hart) the great hope of Indian commercial cinema. During the meeting he said almost nothing, whispering intermittently to the DP, another fresh-faced young man whose downy moustache and conspiratorial fidgeting reinforced the schoolboy impression still further.

The talking was done by the producer, Naveed Iqbal. A portly man in his fifties, he was the only one of the group gathered in Prasad's hotel room to be attired in (semi) traditional Indian dress, the long tails of his cotton kurta hanging down incongruously from beneath a lemon-yellow Pringle golf jumper. He had the look of a man who had recently been fed and would soon be again. From his Afro-like shock of wiry grey hair to the pouches of dark skin under his eyes, everything about him repelled Gaby, a feeling compounded by the frank sexual relish with which he examined her as she sat down. While he spoke he rubbed his hands together as if it was important to keep them occupied to prevent involuntary grabbing or pinching.

'Do you have midges in proper London, Miss Caro? Or is it only in your northern parts?'

'Midges? You mean the insects?'

'Yes. Biting insects. Very serious bite, Miss Caro. God knows capable of putting actress out of action for days and days.'

'No, they don't have them. At least I don't think so. I don't follow.'

'You see, we are here in Scottish Highlands to picturize an important song, the theme song to our movie. It is very romantic song such as would bring tears to your beautiful eyes, madam, if you spoke Hindi–Urdu language and hence calls for mountains and castles and so forth. It does not call for biting insects, which are also here in romantic Scottish Highlands. Two days ago when preparing to shoot the battlement sequence over at fort location our heroine Miss Zahir has been bitten. Doctor is attending and pronouncing no trouble, top bill of health, but Miss Zahir is insisting all is not well inside, and so naturally concerned we have halted schedule for one day. Yesterday when her first call comes in the morning we are told midge trouble is not yet gone away and also she is having bad case of lost voice due to the cold air and climate. And today also Miss Zahir continues to feel unwell despite the occasion of her birthday and large party planned to celebrate. Miss Zahir is a most sensitive young woman, Miss Caro.'

'I can see that. So I take it she won't be making herself available for interviews about this computer-virus story?'

'Interviews? I personally would be grateful if she would be making herself available for shooting first.'

It was unclear in which sense Mr Iqbal meant this comment, but around the room there were scowls and nods of assent. This, Gaby realized, was not a happy production.

'She does not come out of her room,' continued Iqbal. 'This morning we gave a cake. A hundred candles ordered from Harrods London and still she will not come out of the room. After we go away cake is gone from outside room. Later approximately half of cake is discovered in flowerbed underneath room window.'

'She probably scoffed the rest.' The speaker was the only other woman present: thirty-something and comprehensively beautified, her black hair tied up in a long pony-tail. Her tracksuit, bearing the logo of an American designer diffusion label, was accessorized with metallic pink tennis shoes and a lot of silver jewellery. Gaby smiled at her, and she deliberately swivelled her black-rimmed eyes away, pretending to examine her nails. The choreographer, apparently.

Iqbal looked at her, then back at Gaby. 'The last thing on our minds is this computer business. In my opinion, computer business is perhaps at the root of Miss Zahir's midge bite. For us, the important thing is to get back to work. Every hour she lies in her bed I have to pay electricians and caterers and Miss Jain's twenty-five beautiful dancers and the old Lord skinflint who owns the fort and God knows who else, so you can see, Miss Caro, it is one hundred per cent imperative to make all these newspaper fellows go away so we can carry on making a masterpiece of modern contemporary cinema.'

Gaby thought for a while. 'The quickest way to make them go away is for her to talk to them. It doesn't have to be all of them. I could arrange a schedule. One or two of the key news people, perhaps.'

Iqbal gave an exasperated shrug, indicating the impossibility of this idea.

'Well, then, a quote. If necessary I could write something. Give it to her for approval.'

This, Iqbal thought, was possible. They went through the details, and at the end of the meeting Gaby went back to her room to work on a draft statement. As she was fitting her key in the lock, she heard a cough behind her. It was Vivek, the DP.

'I heard her singing,' he said. 'In the room. She says she has lost her voice, but behind closed doors she is singing.'

Gaby sat up working on the press statement until the room's heavy rose-patterned wallpaper started to oscillate before her tired eyes. Deciding the paragraph she had written was finally usable, she shut her laptop down. Before she cleaned her teeth, she stood at the window and smoked a cigarette, looking over the lake at Dimross Castle, *Tender Tough*'s 'fort location'. Coloured spotlights had been placed strategically around its base, bathing the walls in dramatic violet and blue. By night the hills surrounding Loch Lone were no more than a denser band of darkness, and Dimross stood out against it like something supernatural, a faerie structure superimposed on the ordinary night.

She went to bed shivering a little, pulling the chintz covers up to her neck and feeling relieved to be away from London and all the clutter of her life. And Guy. Especially Guy. From the perspective of a big double bed in a mansion by a lake in Scotland, Guy Swift seemed more or less irrelevant. She went to sleep half-heartedly scripting the conversation the two of them would have to have. She hoped he would not make it too hard.

Some time later she was woken by the sound of knocking at her door. She got up to answer it, but something stopped her, something in the tone of the knock: a slyness, an insinuation. The thought came to her, surely illogically, that it was Iqbal, and once it was there the idea would not go away, so she waited, standing at the door listening to the tapping until it stopped and she heard footsteps heading off slowly down the carpeted corridor.

She felt uneasy. Without switching on the light, she pulled on a jogging top, groped for her cigarettes and went back to the window. The moon was out, and the swathe of striped lawn that led down to the water was illuminated like a stage set. The ambience was so gothic, particularly with the castle glowing eerily in the background, that it took her a moment to separate the figure in the white robe from the rest of the scene. It was as if a frame from an old horror film had come to life. Her unlit cigarette drooping from her top lip, she stared, bristling, at the thing gliding spectrally over the lawn. Then she saw an orange dot rise and fall close to its face, and realized that it too was smoking. As her eyes grew accustomed to the darkness, other details emerged. The sweater over the nightdress. The trainers. The young woman walked down to the very edge of the water and stood for a while, looking out at the loch. Then she dropped the cigarette butt, ground it into the grass with her shoe, pushed her long dark hair away from her face and headed back inside.

Miss Leela Zahir wishes to disassociate herself from the computer virus which has been causing so much destruction and confusion around the world. She wishes to emphasize that she has no connection with the person or persons responsible and hopes that they will be brought speedily to justice. Her sympathy goes out to everyone who has been affected, especially those of her fans who may have mistaken these malicious emails for an official communication from Miss Zahir, LovelyLeela Pvt or some other person or company connected with her. As an artist, she has found the whole experience distressing and disruptive. She hopes that, having made this statement, she will be left to pursue her path of thespian creativity in peace.

The flourishes were added by Iqbal, who considered Gaby's draft too formal. 'We need a little emotion here,' he said. 'Some touching sentiments.' He also altered 'Ms' to 'Miss' and ordered that the whole thing be typed in a tacky handwriting font, 'to give a personal touch'. The statement was slipped under Leela's door, but elicited no response.

Gaby ate breakfast sitting cross-legged on her bed, watching CNN. Unusually for her, she had an appetite and ate a quantity of toast and muesli, washing it down with cups of strong tea. The virus was the second lead story. According to one of the talking heads, it was a new variety. According to another, it was thought to originate in India. They alternated video of various upsets and commotions with clips of Leela Zahir singing and dancing, commenting that after a tennis player and a stripper the actress had become the latest in a line of women to be associated with this type of computer crime. Apart from the publicity stills it was Gaby's first proper sight of her. She shimmied down the middle of a London street in front of a squad of identically clad dancers, looking flirtatiously into the camera and drawing a hand over her face. On her eight-by-tens she had looked like every other production-line Indian actress, a perky black-haired Barbie, but in the midst of the song-and-dance routine Gaby thought she discerned something else, a hollowness behind the eyes which seemed at odds with the broad smile and the come-hither look those eyes had been trained to deliver.

After a mercifully short meeting with Iqbal, Gaby photocopied the completed release in the Lodge's tiny business centre and drove the minivan down the driveway to meet the press. Their numbers seemed to have increased since the previous day, and were swelled by several dozen Asian teenagers, who sat in their cars playing hip-hop and sending text messages to each other on their phones. Where they had come from (Glasgow?) she had no idea, but they were causing chaos, making obscene gestures behind the local news reporter as he tried to record a piece to camera and asking everyone, including the nervous policeman guarding the hotel gate, if they had seen 'Rajiv Baba' or 'Leela Zee'.

Gaby handed out copies of the statement, which, as she had expected, did little to satisfy any of the correspondents. They crowded round her, pushing and jostling, each trying to get in first with their requests for interviews and photos. As she tried to deal with them, her sleeve was tugged by kids with cards and soft toys and photos they wanted her to pass on to the two stars. Just one picture. All my editor wants, ten minutes, five minutes, I love him innit, I made this myself. Muscling her way to the front came a middle-aged Indian woman dressed as if she were going on an Antarctic expedition, complete with scarf, hat, Gore-Tex jacket and hiking boots. Introducing herself as chief showbiz reporter of *Film Buzz* magazine, she asked whether the 'latest rumours' were true.

'What rumours?' asked Gaby.

'That Leela has walked off the set.'

'No, absolutely not.'

'But there has been no shooting.'

'I can confirm that Miss Zahir has been slightly unwell due to an allergic reaction to an insect bite. They had to suspend shooting while she recovered, but it's nothing serious. She'll be back at work very soon.'

'It must be an unpleasant bite. Maybe from bad boy Rajiv, perhaps?'

'I understand,' Gaby improvised, 'that her arm was very swollen.'

'And this virus tamasha is all a publicity stunt, am I correct? This is Rocky Prasad drumming up interest in his picture.'

'As Miss Zahir's press statement says –'

'Well, it *would*, wouldn't it?'

'I'm from Fox News,' butted in a tall blond man with a North American accent. 'We want to talk to the girl.'

The *Sun*, *Asian Age* and most of the others wanted the same thing.

'Miss Zahir is recovering, and won't be giving interviews.'
'But I'm from *Fox*,' said Fox incredulously.
'Are you saying definitively that the producers are not responsible for the computer virus?' asked the man from the *West Highland Advertiser*, who knew a conspiracy when he saw one.
'Of course they aren't.'
'Rubbish,' said Ms *Film Buzz*. 'This kind of thing is always happening in Mumbai.' Several of the other reporters started quizzing her about the link between computer crime and Indian film marketing. The situation was heading in an uncomfortable direction. Gaby was trying to get things back on track when her voice was drowned out by the rumble of a V12 engine and a burst of high-pitched hormonal squealing. Turning round, she saw a sight so macho it was almost a period piece, a poster memory of the moneyed eighties. The Ferrari Testarossa throbbed like an engorged metal penis, its bright red paintwork glinting unironically in the sunlight. Its driver, a man in his forties, wore aviator sunglasses, a black leather biker jacket and a tight white t-shirt. His straight black hair was slicked back from his forehead with quantities of gel, a few strands artfully curling over one mirror-shaded eye. He waved and signed autographs, his empty passenger seat filling up with teddy bears and home-made greetings cards. Rajiv Rana made (no, surely not) a pistol shape with his fingers and fired it off at a couple of simpering girls, then pulled down his glasses, looked directly at Gaby and grinned. He gave her a little wave all of her own, then gunned the engine and screamed up the hotel driveway.
For reasons known only to himself, the policeman actually applauded. 'Did ye see that?' he asked. 'Did ye bloody well see that?'
That afternoon it started to rain. Gaby had a meeting with Iqbal. As his hands slithered obscenely around his lap, she emphasized again that his best chance of being left in peace was for Leela to appear for photos. He just shrugged gloomily and asked whether the press would be diverted by meeting Rajiv. She explained that most of them were news people, and had no interest in Rajiv or the production. Leela was the story. Only she would do.

At front desk the manager was swearing at his computer, which was displaying an animation of his guest. Rob D. was propping up the bar, watching the dancers play squealing argumentative hands of cards. To Gaby's surprise every one of them was blonde and English. 'This,' one of them confided, 'is brilliant. We get paid to stay here and we've had to do bugger all for days.' Gaby agreed it was a good deal. 'The actual producer wants us to go to the Gulf with him later in the year,' explained another. 'To give a *performance*.'

That evening she went down to the restaurant for dinner and was asked to join a large but subdued crew table. Avoiding the empty seat next to Iqbal, she was settling herself next to Vivek when Rajiv Rana strode in and pulled up a chair between them. His entrance sent a ripple of little glances, facial touching and adjusted clothing through the Indian crew, the involuntary self-consciousness generated by the presence of fame. Among the British the only reaction came from a couple of the dancers, who idly checked him out, as they would have any other presentable man. It was bizarre. To half the people in the room Rajiv was a superstar. To the others he was unremarkable.

'Hi,' he said, loading the syllable with meaning.

'Hello,' said Gaby.

'Rajiv,' he said.

'Gabriella Caro from Bridgeman & Hart.'

He had taken his sunglasses off, and in place of the cheesy leather jacket was wearing a plain blue Oxford cotton shirt. She was forced to admit it suited him. He was tall, conspicuously worked-out, and had the kind of clean good looks she liked. During the meal he focused almost entirely on her, and though he talked mostly about himself it was not the testosterone-testarossa monologue she was expecting. There was a sincerity in the way he told his story, which, as narrated by its principal character, was a classic rags-to-riches tale. He had grown up in a poor family in a small town in the Punjab and run away to Mumbai at the age of twelve. After working at a chai stall and a bicycle-repair shop, he had found a job fetching and carrying for one of the big studios. By watching the stars rehearse and perform he taught himself to dance, and started to attend cattle-call auditions for extras. When he began to get work he was able to afford acting and dance lessons, and eventually was cast in a small role in *The Chain*, an action movie. 'And that, Miss Caro,' he concluded, 'was how I made myself famous.' As he said it, he rolled up his shirtsleeves and fixed her with a direct look. She found herself distracted by the musculature of his forearms, their light dusting of hair.

'Call me Gaby,' she said.

In her room she looked at her phone, which was charging on the bedside table. There was a text from Guy: *miss u ring me?* Also two voicemails. He wondered where she was, sorry not to have made contact. Then he was on his way to Dubai to make a key pitch. He would see her when he got back. Guy's pitches were always key, or vital, or essential. She deleted the messages.

She took off her shoes and lay on her bed, watching a Rita Hayworth film. Some time after midnight she went to the window to smoke and watch the castle lights. At the very edge of the loch, where the lawn dipped down to the water, stood the woman in the white nightdress. Tonight there was nothing ghostly about her. She was wearing a dark-coloured coat which came down to her knees and some kind of headscarf over her hair. She looked human, mundane; an insomniac hotel guest wrapped up against the chill.

On a whim Gaby pulled on a jacket and stepped out into the corridor. From beneath one of the neighbouring doors seeped the faint sound of a television. She skirted the front desk, where the night porter was sleepily picking his nose over a paperback novel, and tiptoed through the darkened dining room, which was already laid for breakfast, elaborately folded napkins and teacups and silver cutlery formally arranged on the tables. A pair of French doors looked out on to a small terrace. They were, as she expected, unlocked. Outside, the air cut through her clothes and a wave of dampness rose up from the lawn against her face and hands. The sky over the hills was a rich purple, the not-quite-blackness of the northern summer night.

She walked over the lawn towards the loch, keeping some

distance between herself and the figure staring at the castle. Even so, she managed to startle her. As Gaby drew level, the woman gasped and took a couple of steps backwards, half turning as if to run. Gaby waved at her and spoke, her voice sounding painfully loud in the silence.

'I couldn't sleep. Sorry.'

'It's OK.' The voice was Indian accented. Soft and girlish. Gaby walked closer and found herself face to face, as she expected, with Leela Zahir. India's dreamgirl was smoking a B & H Gold, the shiny pack clutched in her free hand like a talisman. Even under the moonlight Gaby could see that she was not quite the double of the dancing girl in the film clips. This Leela's hair was unwashed, lank strands of it sticking out from beneath the shawl round her head. There were dark shadows under her eyes and what might have been a cold sore on her top lip.

'Got a light?'

Leela Zahir nodded and handed her a box of matches. As Gaby lit a cigarette, she flicked hers into the water. Then, without hesitating, she took another from the pack.

'What's your name?'

'Gabriella. You must be Leela.'

'Yes,' she said in a small voice. 'I must be.' She smoked with the cigarette pressed between middle and index fingers, which she held very straight, pursing her lips as she took a drag, like a child imitating the grown-ups.

'Happy birthday for yesterday,' said Gaby. Leela shot her a suspicious look.

'How did you know?'

'They brought me up here to work on the film.'

'Doing what?'

'Public relations. You probably know about all the journalists.'

Leela nodded and jerked her chin at the castle.

'And they want to know why I'm not over there, running up and down on the roof.'

'That's more or less it. That and the computer virus.'

Suddenly Leela reached out and clutched Gaby's wrist. Her grip was surprisingly strong.

'Are they bringing my mother here?'

'I don't know. Why? Do you want her to come?'

'No!' She half spat. 'She will, though. As soon as they tell her their precious film is in trouble, she'll come here.'

Gaby recoiled. Leela let go of her arm and looked back out across the loch. 'It must be so cold,' she said, thoughtfully. Then she picked her way forward over the rocks. Gaby thought she would stop there, but she carried on, taking several paces out into the water. Her nightdress billowed round her knees. Alarmed, Gaby started after her.

Leela laughed. '*So* cold!' She lost her balance for a moment and stretched out her arms to right herself. There was a little flash of gold in the water. 'Drat, I dropped my smokes.'

'Come back,' pleaded Gaby. She had an idea that Leela was about to go further, that she would walk out until she vanished under the surface. Instead she turned and sloshed back to the shore. When she made it back on to the spongy surface of the lawn, she suddenly danced a few steps, curling her outstretched arms in a sinuous movement as she hummed a snatch of a song.

'I learned the number,' she said. 'I did that for them, at least.'

'You must be freezing,' said Gaby. The girl's dripping nightdress was plastered to her legs. 'Maybe we should go back inside.'

'They're all bastards, you know.'

'Who are?'

Leela waved at the hotel. 'All of them. They don't give a fig about anything but their super-duper careers. They certainly don't care about me.'

Gaby did not know what to say. Leela shivered and rubbed her hands. 'Well,' she said, 'I'm going to bed now. They have MTV here. Do you like MTV?' Gaby shrugged. 'I do. You can watch other people dancing routines instead of having to do them yourself.' She gave a half-hearted little laugh, as if to underline that she was making a joke. How young she is, thought Gaby, with her awkward play-smoking and her nursery language. Drat and fig. More like twelve than twenty-one.

Leela took a few paces across the lawn, then turned back.

'Could you do a favour for me?'

'Sure.'

'Don't tell them you saw me.'

'Of course.'

Gaby watched her tramp over the grass and disappear into the building. She was left alone, cloaked in a silence that was frayed at the edges by the sound of the water lapping at her feet.

As *Leela02* died down and samples of *Leela09* started to hit the Virugenix GSP, June temperature records were broken in several places around the world. There were a few spectacular events – the suspension of the Bolsa de Valores in Lima, the Olympic ticketing fiasco – but on the whole the effect was cumulative, an accretion of frustration, a furring of the global arteries. Simple tasks took on new levels of difficulty. You wanted to book a railway ticket, but the site was down. The social-security department was unable to process your claim. Your new TV was redirected to the crackheads downstairs, but the company's records said you signed for it so, sir, you *must* have got it. Breakdowns, closures, suspensions and delays, all taking place in the sweltering heat. New York City ran out of electric fans, but whether it was simply the spike in demand or the container truck that somehow went missing on the New Jersey Turnpike, no one could say with certainty.

Over the Desert Creek Golf Course in Dubai, tall steel poles tipped with fanned arrays of nozzles sprayed a fine mist of humidity into the air. From the ground came a regular thumping sound, the chug chug of 8,000 sprinklers irrigating 200 acres of dwarf Bermuda grass, a solid mat of vivid paintbox-green like a mould on the red skin of the desert. Beneath it, veins and arteries, ran miles of plastic tubing, connecting the green mat to a site down the coast where a vast desalination plant boiled Arabian Gulf seawater to a thousand degrees centigrade, filtered it and daily pumped two and a half million gallons of it here, for the grass and the golfers.

Like all golf courses, the landscape was a ghost of Scotland, an environmental memory abstracted into universal signs. Bunker, fairway, rough. To this the poles, defoliated silver birches, added the suggestion of forest. At one side, this virtuality peeled away to reveal artful vistas of the sea. At the other, it rose up in a lip to shield itself from the wind-blown sand of the dunes.

Under his sun visor, Guy felt immensely disoriented.

Abdullah was driving the golf cart like he drove his Lexus, bouncing it across the bright green landscape with maniacal intensity. The cart's little electric engine gave off an angry whine. Guy held on tighter to his laptop.

As soon as he had landed at the airport and met Abdullah, he had known it was going to be a difficult pitch. His contact was standing beneath a Dubai development-agency billboard: *Move your company to the gateway of the globe. 1.5 billion consumers await you at your arrival. A business base with a first-world infrastructure – at a third-world cost.* He was a young fuzzy-cheeked man wearing a black-banded headdress and a white dish-dash from beneath which peeked the toes of a pair of hand-made penny loafers. Grinning under the lenses of his oil-slick Ray-Ban Wayfarers, he finished his call. Then he slipped the phone back into a voluminous pocket and told Guy he was welcome in Dubai and please to follow to the car. He did not offer to help with the bags.

As they left the terminal building, the heat hit Guy like a solid object. Sweat started to percolate up through his skin, trickling down his back under his shirt. Abdullah led him across the car park to a barn-sized black car. In a gesture of politeness, he turned up its air-con to Arctic levels and with a screech of tyres turned out on to an eight-lane blacktop highway that seemed to lead to nowhere.

'Nice weather we're having,' he said cryptically. The thermometer on the dash put the outside temperature at 41°C. Out of the window an expanse of red sand flashed past. There were almost no cars on the road, but Abdullah deliberately tailgated those there were. By the time the speedometer touched 155 k.p.h. they were a foot behind a 4 x 4 with an 'I ❤ Islam' sticker in the rear window. Abdullah punched the horn and flashed his lights until it pulled over.

'You should be a rally driver,' Guy joked nervously.

'This is already my hobby. For two years I am driving desert races. It is good, except I crash too much.'

To take his mind off this answer, Guy peered through the grey tint of the windscreen. In the distance a city skyline was approaching and soon half-built skyscrapers started to appear at the roadside, their skeletons criss-crossed by plastic lines hung with the drying dhotis of Indian labourers. Construction was taking place all over the city, and the architectural thrust appeared to be towards the creation of some kind of Islamic Las Vegas. There were huge bank towers incorporating pointed arches and minarets, thirty-storey office blocks faced in green-and-gold smoked glass like giant onyx writing sets. One building appeared to be topped with a gargantuan dimpled golf ball. Another had a portico shaped like the front of a 747. The whole insane mess rose up out of the sand like a mirage, and even once he was among it Guy had a lingering sense of disbelief. Here was the future, arriving at mouse-click velocity, CAD/CAM sketches cloaking themselves in concrete and steel before his eyes.

The hotel was a glass wave, sprawling along an artificial beach whose white sand, as Abdullah proudly pointed out, had been imported from the Caribbean. The car door was opened by a Filipino dressed in dusky pink plus fours, a pink argyle jumper and an oversized urchin cap. Pinned to his chest was a badge which identified him as *Gary*. By his side was *Carolyn*, a Singaporean woman dressed as a pink explorer, complete with rose-coloured pith helmet. Together they showed Guy and Abdullah into the lobby. Once Guy had checked in, a time-consuming process because of a fault in the hotel's reservations system, Abdullah handed him his business card and told him he would return in the morning to drive him to his meeting with Mr Al-Rahman. In the meantime, he was to make himself comfortable in his room. Abdullah's politenesses had an odd way of sounding like orders. When he read the full name on the card, Guy understood the reason for this. Abdullah bin Osman Al-Rahman was no ordinary junior driver. This was obviously a family which liked its younger members to start at the bottom.

The lift took Guy and a pink South Asian bellhop (*Bruce*) to the twentieth floor. Once he had found his room and got rid of *Bruce*, he slung his stuff on the bed and switched on the TV. Almost at once there was a knock at his door. *Doug*, a dark-skinned young man who was perhaps Indonesian, arrived with a plate of fruit. Would there be anything else? Guy didn't think so. A minute later there was a second knock. *Calvin* with a spare bathrobe. Then came *Keiran* to fluff his pillows. Always they ended with a direct look in the eyes and the same question: 'Is there anything *else* I can do for you?' Guy told himself he was imagining things. After the fourth time he stopped answering the door.

The phone went and a voice asked whether his accommodation was to his satisfaction. For a moment he thought it was another room-service rent-boy, until the voice identified itself as Abdullah and asked his shoe size. He told him. It was only after he put the receiver down that he thought to wonder why.

With a choice of seventeen restaurants (Lebanese, Argentinian, the Viennese Café, the Dhow and Anchor British Pub . . .) he somehow ended up eating at the Main Street USA Bar and Grill, where it was New Orleans week. The space was hung with bunting, and in the centre of the room was a two-thirds scale model of a Mississippi riverboat. He sat down at a little table and *Carey-Ann*, who was maybe Chinese and was dressed as a pink Norman Rockwell soda jerk, gave him a menu. He chose the gumbo and looked around. A group of elderly men in Hawaiian shirts were crammed with their instruments on to a corner stage, playing light jazz funk. Above them a sign read *Retail This Way*, which for a brief moment he mistook for the name of the band.

Around him was a landscape of small round tables, each occupied by a shirtsleeved businessman. In front of each businessman was a cellphone, a menu and a tall glass of juice topped with a cocktail umbrella and a pair of jaunty straws. Guy ate his gumbo and watched the row of Caribbean palms outside the window. Afterwards, in his brightly lit bathroom, he took twenty milligrams of a prescription sedative and got an early night, falling unconscious to the jabber of a rolling news channel on the TV.

The next morning he was woken by a knock on his door. He put on his bathrobe and let in *Burt*, who had brought him a wrapped rectangular box 'courtesy of Mr Al-Rahman'. Yawning, Guy opened it to find a pair of golf shoes and a leaflet drawing his attention to certain of their technical features, which included a temperature-responsive waterproof membrane and a visible-heel air-sole unit. The sight of the shoes sent his guts into immediate spasm, and he took Abdullah's morning call from a doubled-up position on the toilet.

'But you don't seem to understand. I have visuals. There's a PowerPoint presentation. For God's sake, there are hand-outs. How am I supposed to do hand-outs on a golf course?'

Abdullah said that his uncle was a man who loved golf above all things, and pointed out that the choice of venue was appropriate to the nature of the conversation. There was no way Guy could object.

Bouncing around in the cart, he reflected that at the end of the day, all factors being taken into consideration, this was Yves Ballard's fault. When setting up *Tomorrow** Guy had felt inclined to stick to what he knew: to pitch for British youth-sector business and maybe reach out occasionally into alternative demographics. Instead, Ballard and the other Transcendenta partners had pushed him in a different direction. There had been a reception in Barcelona, with canapés in the shapes of dotcom logos and waiters dressed as Antonio Gaudí. He had stood at a poolside bar, and they had asked him to imagine a truly globalized branding agency, concentrating on the local needs of transnational clients. If *Tomorrow** placed itself at this node, it would potentiate the synergetic emergence of something, thus maximizing feedback in something else and placing everyone at the apex of a place they all wanted to be. They stood, they told him, on the crest of the latest Kondratiev Wave. Transcendenta, nine months old, was already valued in the hundreds of millions. Who was Guy to argue? So instead of being wedged in a West End toilet cubicle with a couple of nightclub PRs, he now found himself on the other side of the world, being driven around in an unstable electrical vehicle by a rich kid with a death wish. About to play golf.

Two men were waiting for them at the first tee, both dressed in immaculate Prince of Wales checks. As the cart skidded to a halt, Guy was almost blinded by a glint from the elder one's wrist, which resolved itself on closer inspection into a diamond-encrusted

Rolex Oyster watch. Muammar bin Ali Al-Rahman, a heavy-set man in his sixties, shook Guy's hand and introduced him to Mr Shahid, his VP of marketing. Mr Shahid smiled briefly.

'Welcome, welcome,' said Al-Rahman. 'How do you like my place?' he asked, making a sweeping gesture which took in the course, the clubhouse and quite a lot of sea.

Guy nodded vigorously. 'It's beautiful, Mr Al-Rahman. Very impressive. And may I say what a lovely day it is today. I can see why you would rather be here than stuck in the office.' The two men laughed, displaying expensive orthodontic work beneath their flourishing moustaches.

Abdullah produced a bag of clubs from the back of the cart and stood respectfully to one side. Guy declined the invitation to tee off first. He knew he would not be saved for long, but at that moment any delay seemed like a good thing. If he were honest (a condition he had hoped to avoid for the duration of his stay in Dubai), golf had never been his thing. It was not a sport he had ever actually *played*, as such. Or even watched on TV. This blindspot in his recreational prowess had never previously been an issue, and probably would not matter now were Mr Al-Rahman not the owner of a leisure group which specialized in golf resorts, which in fact owned twenty-four scattered across the world from Osaka to British Columbia. The resorts for whose business he was here to pitch. And putt.

Al-Rahman lofted his ball down the middle of the fairway. Shahid did the same, his drive diplomatically landing a few feet behind that of his boss. They looked expectantly at Guy, who realized that he was facing one of those moments in which you can either go forward in bad faith or trust in honesty to carry you through.

He decided to blag it.

His first attempt at a drive hacked a large divot in the ground. On the second he sliced the ball hard to the right, sending it off in the direction of the water. He laughed self-consciously.

'Bad luck,' said Mr Shahid in a slightly stunned tone.

'Bad luck,' said Mr Al-Rahman.

It took him nine strokes to reach the first green.

'Perhaps,' said Mr Al-Rahman, watching him line up his third putt, 'you should tell me what you feel you can do for my company.'

Guy considered retrieving his laptop from the cart. His creatives had spent hundreds of hours preparing audio, video and still imagery to accompany this pitch. But the sun was beating down, and even if Al-Rahman were receptive to visual stimuli, it was doubtful he'd be able to see the screen. So he swallowed hard and began. 'What I do,' he told them, 'is take a business and transform it from being an abstract thing into an entity that consumers can feel emotional towards.'

'Bad luck, Mr Swift,' said Mr Al-Rahman.

'I didn't make a shot yet.'

'Oh, my apologies. Perhaps you are fatigued by the game. You would maybe prefer just to walk and talk?'

'Yes, absolutely. Great. Yes.'

'You were saying?'

'Um, right. You see, there's a virtuous circle. Perhaps later I could show you a picture of it.'

'Of the circle?'

'Yes. You see a happy brand is a learning brand. A brand should make you feel good, because if it knows what makes you feel good, then it can position itself correctly and help you to make your choice. And if once you've made your choice the brand nurtures and protects you like a caring parent – and here I'd really like you to imagine some emotional imagery of a baby – then you feel good about the choice you've made and the brand learns from your good feelings.'

'And the circle?'

'Exactly, it's a circle.'

'I'm afraid I don't see what you mean.'

'Oh, OK. Well, this would probably be easier with the graphic, but in essence what I am proposing to do is to help Al-Rahman Resorts get a GPS reading on its location in the heart-and-mind topography of the consumer. The method *Tomorrow** uses, which is a proprietary process, is called TBM. This stands for Total Brand Mutability, and like I say it's our thing. No one else will be able to do TBM analysis for you, or will provide Brand Mutation Vector Maps, which are the tool we use to help our clients achieve their full Brand Evolution Potential. *Tomorrow** will generate a full ongoing set of vector maps – in fact, I've got a sample on the computer if you'd like to see it?'

Mr Al-Rahman was practising his tee shot. He shook a finger at Guy. Guy made the thumbs up.

'OK. Well, maybe I'll show you the vector maps in a bit. But um –' He watched Al-Rahman drive his ball down the fairway. Shahid and Abdullah congratulated him on the shot. Guy was embarking on an explanation of the increasing importance of brand definition in an uncertain leisure climate when without warning Al-Rahman leaped into his cart and sped off in the direction of the next green.

They followed, with Abdullah at the wheel, his dish-dash ballooning up as they flew over the bumps, exposing a pair of long black knee socks. 'You are not a golfer,' he said accusingly to Guy. Guy admitted that this was true, technically speaking. Abdullah snorted.

'Please,' said Mr Al-Rahman, when they finally caught up with him, 'explain to me clearly what you can do for my business.'

'Right,' said Guy, trying to concentrate. 'A question for you, sir. Do you think your employees are living the Al-Rahman brand in a holistic way? What does Al-Rahman actually stand for?'

'We are a very old family, Mr Swift.'

'Sure, sure. But you know, at the moment Al-Rahman stands for – well, for *golf*. And that's it. Golf is great, don't get me wrong. But is it really something your people can get behind? At *Tomorrow**, my team came up with a kind of banner heading about where we feel your company is at now. We think of you as "the faithful". We have this great animation for the concept. You see this guy hitting a hole in one and it says in like, your traditional Arabic calligraphy style, "There is no game but golf and Al-Rahman is its prophet."'

There was a silence. Guy tried to fill it.

'You have to go under the surface and think about why people play golf. Golf means freedom. Golf means, um, style. The way *Tomorrow** sees it, the Al-Rahman "faithful" should become the Al-Rahman "rangers". Rangers, that's our heading, right? For being able to get out there and do your thing. Anyhow – the basic thrust of our plan is to take Al-Rahman beyond golf and into the realm of total leisure experience. That way your employees, golfers or not, will have feelings of greater identification and inclusivity about the Al-Rahman brand. Your consumers too.'

Mr Al-Rahman looked at Guy, then called Shahid aside and whispered something in his ear. Shahid nodded and whispered something to Abdullah, who made a phone call.

'Mr Swift,' said Al-Rahman, shaking Guy's hand, 'I am very grateful to you for taking the trouble to come out here and share with us the benefit of your experience.'

'Thanks very much. No problem. I just hope that later on I can show you the creative work we've done.'

'That won't be necessary,' said Shahid. Al-Rahman walked away and started to settle himself in his cart.

Guy opened his mouth, and closed it again. Al-Rahman steered the cart in a wide arc, drawing up next to Guy. Shahid put his bag of clubs in the back and got in beside his boss. Al-Rahman, for the first time during the meeting, removed his thick black sunglasses to reveal a pair of weary heavy-lidded eyes.

'Mr Swift,' he said, 'the green fees on this course are the highest in the Middle East. We have a driving range which can accommodate up to 200 people at once. We have a swing-analysis lab which utilizes software developed by our own experts. It is a question of respect, Mr Swift. I like to do business with people who respect the things I do. You, I suppose, respect other things, such as your circles and maps. So I say to you, go and do business with men who like circles and maps. In the meantime please accept the hospitality of the beach resort. Abdullah will be pleased to dine with you and perhaps share with you the appreciation of some of our world-famous nightlife. I wish you a safe flight home.'

With that, he drove away.

Sometimes there is fear ahead of the curve. Sometimes in a hotel bathroom you may visualize an immense white-capped wave bearing down on you. Then there is nothing for it but the minibar, the crawl towards the red dot of the television, the dissected room-service tray silhouetted by the open refrigerator door. Guy poured vodka miniatures over ice and sat on the end of the bed, trying to work out what to do. He was fucked. That was all there was to it. Yves had phoned, asking for confirmation that Al-Rahman and PEBA were the only two pitches they were working on. 'I really hope they happen for you,' he had said. That was clear enough.

Next door there was a party. Through the wall he could hear music and the sound of laughter. There were people out on the balcony. He took his drink to the window and furtively looked out. They were women, five, maybe six of them, all beautiful; European and Asian women in evening dresses. Thigh and cleavage. High heels. A short middle-aged man was among them, a cellphone in one hand, the other kneading the breast of a tall blonde in a silver sheath dress. She looked down at him indulgently. The others seemed either not to notice or not to care. The man's white dress shirt was unbuttoned almost to the waist, showing a brown expanse of hairy chest and belly. As Guy watched, he took the blonde's wrist and pulled her inside.

The vodka ran out and he started on the gin. A repetitive bass thud came through the wall, like an amplified racing heart. His life appeared to him as a web or a suspension bridge, each tensed element related to the next. Remove *Tomorrow** and what would be left? Downstairs the lobby opened out on to an atrium which reached a giddy twenty storeys up towards the little box in which he sat, finishing the gin and moving on to the whisky. A structure wrapped around a vast emptiness. It all seemed part of the same improbable joke, the atrium, the rows of balconies, the restaurants; 2,000 rooms full of people like himself breathing freeze-dried artificial air and watching cubes of desalinated water melt in their glasses. And beneath their feet, somewhere under the foundations, the red shifting desert.

The bass line thudded. And another sound, high pitched and intermittent. A human sound. Either sex or pain.

He needed to speak to Gabriella. He could tell her how things were, how important she was now everything else was going to hell. Maybe she would be kind. It was a risk letting her hear him like this, but then again she was his girlfriend. She was supposed to make things better. He dialled her number on the hotel phone, drunk enough not to worry about the cost. It diverted to voice-mail, so he tried international directory inquiries, which was down. Finally he got the concierge to look up the number of her hotel and patch him through.

A Scottish-accented voice confirmed that Miss Caro was in 106.

The phone rang eight times. Just as he was about to give up, she answered. Her hello was breathy, distracted. Mixed in with it was some artefact of the telephone system, a strange electronic rushing noise. It sounded like splintering information, communication space.

'Hello? Hello?'

'Yes?'

'Gaby, it's me.'

'Oh, God. Guy.'

The voice at the other end was muffled, and for a moment he was left alone with the interstellar howl. He had an idea she had placed a hand over the receiver.

'Gaby. Hello?'

'Guy – I'm –'

'Is this not a good time?'

'No. No. Yes, of course it is. What do you mean?' She sounded agitated. Gaby was usually so calm. 'I thought you were in Dubai.'

'I am, sweetie. I just wanted to hear your voice.'

'Why are you calling? I mean, it's very late, you know.'

'Not that late, surely. I looked. It's ten o'clock where you are.'

'Right,' she said. 'Right.'

'What's wrong?'

'There's nothing wrong. Christ, Guy, why are you always like this? What's wrong. Nothing's wrong, OK?'

The volume of the electronic interference increased. Part of it detached to become a feedback whine, a tone rising and falling through the shards of her voice.

'Hello?'

'Hello?'

'Gaby, I just wanted to talk to you. Things aren't so good here.' There was no response. 'Gaby? Hello?'

'I hope you didn't call just to talk to me about your work.

Because, you know, I'm just not going to be able to do that right now. I have my own world, Guy. I'm working here too, remember?'

The rushing reached a crescendo and fell away again. Through the bedroom wall the boom of the party seemed to grow louder. Weirdly the party sounds seemed to be coming out of the receiver as well. He felt he could not be sure of the source of anything he was hearing. Then the muffling descended, but too late to block out the sound of a man's voice. Was someone there with her?

'Who is that, Gaby?'

Silence.

'Gaby? Gaby, can you hear me?'

'Guy, I can't talk now. We need to talk, but this is not the right time, OK?'

A little stone formed in the pit of his stomach. 'Gaby? What are you talking about?'

'I can't do this now. Not over the phone.'

'What's wrong? What do you mean not over the phone?'

'Call me when you get back. Call me when you get to the airport.'

'Gaby? Hello?'

Abruptly the noise ceased.

The first Chris knew of it was when the cops phoned. It was very early in the morning and the formal tone of the voice freaked her out. 'Are you Ms Christine Rebecca Schnorr?' Chris never dealt well with authority, especially on a hangover. Nic was sacked out beside her in the bed, one arm thrown over her chest. She pushed it off and sat up, rubbing her face.

'Yes, this is she.'

'This is Deputy Janine Foster, calling from Snohomish County Sheriff's Office. Are you the owner of a white Honda Civic licence plate 141-JPC?'

'Yeah. I mean yes, I am.'

'Are you aware of the location of your vehicle?'

'Pardon me?'

'Are you aware of the location of your vehicle at this time?'

'Far as I know it's parked outside.'

'I see. When did you last utilize the vehicle?'

'Yesterday evening. I got in around eleven.'

'So you say you drove the vehicle home around eleven.'

'Uh, yes. What's this regarding?'

Nic had woken up and was propped on one elbow, listening groggily as the cop told her what had happened. It seemed that some time after they got back from the Brewhouse, somebody stole her car from the driveway, drove it north on I-5 and then just before four in the morning ran it off an exit ramp near a place called Smokey Point, about twenty-five miles away. A tree branch had gone through the radiator and it wasn't drivable, but apart from a few dents and a smashed windshield, it was OK. Whoever did it must have walked away, but it looked as if they had been hurt in the crash, since the highway patrol had found blood on the dash and the upholstery.

'How much blood?' asked Chris. 'Like, a lot?' A new radiator and windshield would probably already come to more than the battered twelve-year-old Honda was worth. With mystery car-thief bloodstains thrown in, she was not entirely sure she wanted the old rice-cooker back. She promised the cop that she'd call later to arrange for the car to be picked up and went into the kitchen to make coffee. Two minutes later she was back.

'Nic, where did I put the car keys last night?'

'What? I don't know. Where you usually put them?'

'In the bowl. I always put them in the bowl. But did you actually see me put them there last night?'

'Come on, Chris. How should I remember?'

'Nic.'

'I don't know, Chris. Sorry.'

'Well, they're not there now.'

Nic looked at her sceptically. Then he swung his legs out of bed and started to look for the keys. The two of them hunted for over an hour. Chris had to call a taxi to get to work, and she left him still opening cabinets and pulling out appliances to squint behind them. He emailed her mid morning. The keys were definitely gone. There was only one possible explanation: whoever stole the car had come into their house and taken them. The thought made Chris feel sick. Someone creeping around their kitchen while she was asleep upstairs. She and Nic had gotten out of the habit of locking the door. It was a safe neighbourhood. Nothing ever happened. She left a message for Deputy Foster, and that night slept with her softball bat by the bed. The next morning she called a salvage yard about the car, and sat all day at her desk imagining the same thing over and over again, the unknown person coming up the steps, opening the screen door, slipping into the darkened house . . . Beyond the basic spookiness of it, there was something uncanny about the intrusion, something just beyond her comprehension. It came into focus only on the third morning, when her boss at Virugenix called her into a meeting and she found to her astonishment that the FBI was there to interview her.

*

'What is the nature of your relationship with Arjun Mehta?'

The agent looked blandly over the desk, successfully performing that cop trick of inducing feelings of guilt without doing anything obvious with his face or eyes. He had a bushy brown cop moustache, square metal-framed glasses, and the kind of chunky bracelet watch which works eight miles under water and tells you the time on Venus. He probably divided his leisure time between mending his boat and looking at coprophiliac pictures of cheerleaders.

'He's a friend.'

'What kind of friend?'

'You know, like a *friend*? You have those, right?'

'I don't appreciate your attitude, Miss Schnorr. I say again, what kind of friend? Did you, for example, go on dates with Mr Mehta?'

'No. Well, yes. We went to the movies. Mostly I gave him driving lessons.'

'In your white Honda Civic.'

'That's right.'

'Did you ever allow him to drive the vehicle when you weren't present?'

'No.'

'Did he often visit at the house you share with your – your boyfriend, Nicolai Peet – Pit –'

'Petkanov.'

'Nicolai Petkanov.'

'Once or twice.'

'Did you on any of these occasions have sexual intercourse with Arjun Mehta?'

'What? What kind of question is that? Look, Dragnet, that is none of your damn business.'

'I'll thank you not to use profanity, Miss Schnorr.'

'Profanity? Christ, where did you grow up? Sesame Street?'

'Or to take the Lord's name in vain. And as an agent of the Federal Bureau of Investigation it is entirely my business. Did you or did you not have sexual intercourse with Arjun Mehta?'

'No.'

'Are you sure about that?'

'I said so, didn't I?'

'Did you or Mr Petkanov conspire with Mr Mehta to intentionally damage information systems by writing and spreading a computer virus?'

'*What?*'

The worst of it was how it looked. As she realized what they were inching towards, Chris started to feel faint. At the beginning of the interview she had experienced equal parts confidence and irritation, angry at the way her boss had sprung this 'informal chat' on her but satisfied that whatever the Bureau wanted, she had done nothing wrong. Now she was not so sure. It seemed Arjun had failed to appear for work since the day her car went missing. Someone from the Virugenix personnel department had gone over to his apartment to talk to him about vacating it, and discovered the door unlocked and most of his computer equipment smashed up. The police were called and initially recorded him as a missing person. After they searched the place they changed their minds. Now they were treating him as a fugitive.

The problem was Nic. Nowadays he was just another engineer, setting up and maintaining data-storage systems, but once upon a time, back in the prehistoric days of computing before the worldwide web and dotcoms and all the rest of it, he had been a very bad Eastern bloc boy indeed. As a high-school student in Bulgaria he had learned to use a machine called a Pravetz 82, mass produced by the state computer company from shamelessly reverse-engineered Apple IIe components. He and his friends from the National Mathematics High School in Sofia had fooled around, doing a lot of stuff they weren't supposed to, and when his parents brought him to the US he had carried on, eventually earning himself a minor place in American criminal history as one of the first kids to be prosecuted for breaking into computer systems. That was all a long time ago, but you could see the way these people's minds were working. Whatever Arjun had been cooking up in his apartment, they thought she and Nic had had a hand in it.

'Miss Schnorr, your car wasn't stolen at all, was it? You gave it to Mehta so he could escape justice.'

'That's not true. If it was Arjun who took the car, he did it without my knowledge. And besides, Nic has never even met him.'

'We'll find that out from Mr Petkanov. Now, to return to these so-called driving lessons . . .'

His head ached and he felt very tired. Sometimes he thought he would vomit. He was not sure how long he had been walking. He just knew it was important to go on.

Headlights came screaming up the highway, making him squint and throw up a hand to shield his eyes. Once a car slowed down, but the driver took a look at him and changed his mind about stopping. He had a brief vision of the man's face, the mouth a black O of shock. The car spat gravel, sped away.

The sticky stuff was blood.

His mouth was dry. The bag was heavy. He could not remember what was in it, could not to be honest remember why he was dragging it down the gritty margin of this road. They were coming for him. They were coming for him and he had to get home. Where home was he could not have said precisely. Up ahead somewhere. At the end of the road.

For a while he lay in a drainage ditch and closed his eyes. When he opened them again, the sky was light and the invisible nighttime world had retreated behind parched yellow grass and a line of scrubby conifers. He tried to sit up and felt as if his head would crack. He was sitting in a litter of food wrappers and beer cans. His face was caked with dried blood.

He carried on.

Things came back. The car, the slow-motion lurch off the curve. Canada had been the point of it. Leave the country before they found out. The taxi had dropped him on the corner, and he had stood and listened to the sounds of the suburban night, trying to think of reasons not to follow through with his plan. What alternative did he have? There was nothing left for him in

America. Every day he stayed would bring the pursuers closer, and if they found him they would never let him go.

He had thought about leaving her a note. *Sorry. So sorry.* Another in his list of apologies. Then he decided it would be better to write to her from Canada. He imagined himself sitting at a table outside a log cabin, describing the parking lot where he had left the little Honda, nicely washed and valeted, maybe with a present in the glove compartment. Flowers would perish. Perhaps chocolates. With a card. On the map it had looked like a short drive. A lot further than he had ever driven before and the first time he had driven at night. But possible.

dear chris there was no other way to do it the only way was by car and the only car i can drive is yours i hope you are not having too much inconvenience from this – arjunm

He had not counted on needing gas. But there it was, the needle in the red, the warning light flickering. She always forgot to fill it up. So three times lost, twenty-five miles north of the city, two narrowly avoided rear ends and one almost ex-passing motorcyclist later, he was peering nervously into the blackness, looking for a gas station. He spotted the sign too late, nearly missed the exit, tried to make the turn anyway, pulled the wheel too hard . . .

And now he was on foot. He counted his paces in hundreds, tried to concentrate on the discrete, the knowable, instead of spiralling out into the dark. Off among the trees there was water. He left the road and picked his way towards it: a pond, half evaporated, muddy and brackish, clogged with blue plastic and rusting iron siding. He took off his shirt, dipped it in the dirty water and used it to clean his face and hands. Then he bunched it up and threw it out into the middle, where it spread out its arms as if imploring him not to abandon it in such a place.

Three thousand two hundred.
Three thousand three hundred
Three thousand four hundred . . .

There was an exit. Near the off-ramp was a gas station, located in the middle of a little retail strip between a fast-food franchise and a place selling wooden patio furniture. As casually as he could he walked across the parking lot into the store, where he bought a bag of chips, a bottle of Sprite and some Band-Aids, and asked the clerk for the key to the bathroom. No gas? He shook his head. She looked uneasily at him, then out of the window for his car. Finally she gave him the key, sliding the enormous wooden fob over the counter very slowly, as if he might steal it or use it to assault her.

He changed clothes, brushed his teeth and cleaned himself up properly, removing streaks of mud from his face and pulling a comb through his hair, careful to avoid the big gash on his crown. There was nothing he could do about the bruise on his cheek, or the cuts above his left eye. Feeling dizzy he sat down on the toilet, leaning his head against the dirty plaster wall. He must have fallen asleep because the next thing he knew the clerk was banging on the door. Hurriedly he zipped up his bag and made his escape. As he walked purposefully out on to the highway, he was all too aware of the scowling woman watching him through the window, clutching the key in her hand.

Then he was in the passenger seat of a battered pick-up. He was not sure how he came to be there. The driver was a stone-faced man dressed in work clothes, overalls and a checked shirt. They passed between tall trees, the sunlight falling in irregular bright strips across their faces. By the roadside giant billboards advertised a reservation casino. *Blackjack. Roulette. Fortune Pai Gow Poker. Keno. 21.* Then the trees gave way to strip malls and rows of single-storey houses. The man said nothing, and Arjun could think of nothing to say back to him that was not muddled by the pain in his head. Where are. Who are. Why is. Though the road surface was smooth, the vibration was enough to make him feel nauseous. He closed his eyes.

'There you go,' said the driver. They were in a town, parked on a main street of plate-glass storefronts and parading traffic.

'Is this Canada?' asked Arjun. The man looked at him strangely, then reached across him to open the passenger door.

'Bus-station's right there,' he said. 'You take care now. You don't look so hot.'

The man in the pick-up pulled away into the traffic and left him swaying there beside his bag in this town whose name he did not know. He crossed the road to the Greyhound Station, where there was a bus about to depart, and he stood in line with the other passengers until he reached the door and the driver asked where his ticket was. He stood in line again at the booking office, his head throbbing. At the counter there was more confusion. The woman rolled her eyes and clattered her long fingernails on the rim of her keyboard, and he pleaded with her just to give him a ticket for the bus, but she kept saying which bus which bus, and he said the one outside, and finally she sold it to him, making a face at her monitor as if to confide in it that this was the craziest yet in all the day's long line of crazies.

He took a seat at the back near the rest room. Felt the roar deep in his body as the driver started the engine, then drifted away to an air-conditioned place which became gradually colder, until it seemed to him that he was pierced by slivers of ice, slender arrows which became a forest and eluded every solution except the physical one of shivering them off, which he did, a cascade of ice-needles falling around him like a shedding Christmas tree.

He opened his eyes into stark country, bare prehistoric hills whose yellow backs were cracked open in places by dark ravines. Giant pylons walked away to the horizon, the only human sign in the bleakness. Sitting beside him was an elderly man in a white shirt buttoned up to the neck. He was reading a religious tract, scrutinizing the pamphlet with great care through a pair of wire-rimmed spectacles.

'Where are we?' Arjun asked.

'Almost there,' said the man.

Then the ice-forest of his dream was replaced by a real one, trees pressing in towards the road like a green mob coming down from the hills. Above them stood a mountain with a smear of snow on its peak, and the road ran on towards it, and the engine roared, and the old man said, 'Even in these last days it is not too late to dedicate your life to the Lord.'

'What time is it?' asked Arjun.

'The time of apostasy, young man. The Tribulation is on its way. You may be nothing but a hell-bound sinner, but if you dedicate your life to Jesus Christ and get born again, even now it is not too late.'

'This must be Canada,' said Arjun, and the old man became an abstraction of an old man, a landscape graph of energies and potentials which could be flattened into silence. Then it was evening and there were lights and behind him someone had a transistor playing country music and the old man had turned into a fat black woman in pink stretch pants who spoke to him in a language he did not understand. The streetlights slowed down and finally came to a halt. As the hydraulic brakes gave a last gasp and the bus settled, she stared at him with an evil stare, then pushed past him into the aisle.

'You asshole,' she muttered. 'What *is* your problem?'

He saw that his bag was open and started to panic about money, about all the cash he had withdrawn from his checking account since you have to have cash because they can trace you with a card. But it was still there and the driver told him to get off the bus now and he walked down the steps to find himself in Bend, Oregon. He had gone the wrong way.

In London, Leela had taken away the power. She corrupted data at the New Cross and Littlebrook substations, seducing the control software, whispering you are overloaded, trip the circuit-breakers, shut down the lines. Across the city trains slowed to a halt, traffic lights dimmed, and household appliances failed to respond to their angry owners. As night fell, the street lighting did not come on. Opportunities were seized. Bricks went through windows. Padlocks were forced and back fences climbed. From the highest penthouse of the In Vitro building, the West End looked like a chessboard, alternating squares of light and dark. The estate agent and her client looked out from the balcony and were afraid.

They checked their messages. When they turned to go, they found the lifts were dead. Reluctantly they began the twenty-flight walk downstairs, feeling their way by holding on to the banisters. After four flights the estate agent took off her shoes. After seven the client called out to her, asking was she still there, could they stop for a while to rest. Somewhere below their feet, firemen in reflective clothing led dehydrated commuters through a darkened underground tunnel, towards the orange glow of platform emergency lighting.

Eddies ran through the national grid, echoes of Leela's voice. In parts of East Anglia, Wales and western Scotland, there were momentary breaks in transmission. For a second, no more, the Clansman's Lodge went dark. Then the power came back. Digital timers started to flash. A burglar alarm began to ring in the office. Gaby glanced at the bedside lamp and lay back on the bed, watching Rajiv Rana's naked back. While she was talking to Guy, someone had called Rajiv too, and now he was speaking rapid Hindi into his mobile, one hand fiercely scrunching up a pair of her knickers.

He stood up and went into the bathroom, slamming the door

behind him. She could hear him raising his voice, arguing with the person at the other end. She slid a hand between her legs and turned on to her stomach, trying to decide what she felt. There were red fingermarks on her arms where he had held her down. She smelled of spermicide and aftershave.

It had been inevitable, she supposed. That morning the crew had appeared tired and agitated, muttering about the bland food, the rain. There had been a lot of activity in the corridors during the night, and at breakfast people were saying that one of the dancers was on a train home to Birmingham, upset at something that had happened. Rob D. had an unexplained black eye, the waiting staff were rattling the plates and on her way back up to her room she noticed a handyman taking a bedroom door off its hinges. Someone had kicked a hole through one of its lower panels.

Leela was still claiming illness, and the doctor had again been summoned to pronounce that he could find nothing physically wrong. At the morning production meeting Iqbal announced that Mrs Zahir was flying out from Mumbai but had been held up by an air-traffic control shutdown. When the mother arrived, he said darkly, she would soon settle the girl's problems. Rocky Prasad and the unit were told to make the best of the break in the weather and drive out to shoot scenery.

Prasad, in the first display of directorial personality Gaby had witnessed from him, shouted that he had had enough. 'Are you going to let her do this to me? One call to your friends in Karachi, one call and you could make it stop!' Iqbal slammed his fist down on the table. There was an ugly silence. He turned to Gaby and gestured for her to leave the room.

She wondered how she was supposed to work. More journalists than ever were camped at the gate. The local police had arrested several 'rowdy Asian youths', and one or two of the tabloids had picked up the story of Leela's illness, running reclusive-star stories on the inside pages as part of their coverage of the global cyber-terror alert.

Threat level was up. Markets were down. Rajiv Rana rang her room to ask if she would like to have lunch with him on Skye.

She agreed, on condition he first came with her to meet the press. When the Testarossa roared down the drive, there was a minor commotion, and she realized uncomfortably that, at least for the Indian media, she had just committed the cardinal public-relations sin of making herself part of the story. Rajiv charmed people and signed autographs. She dodged cameras and struggled to maintain the pretence that there were no production problems. Again and again journalists tried to make a link between the virus and the girl. Could Gaby categorically confirm that it wasn't a publicity stunt gone wrong? Were they really expected to believe that Ms Zahir and her backers were in no way connected with the dissemination of her image around the globe?

She promised more later and told Rajiv that lunch was off. With things as they were, she would need to spend the afternoon on the phone. Would he drive her back up to the Lodge? Sure, he said. She got into the Ferrari's passenger seat. He grinned, gunned the engine, screeched through the crowd and turned on to the main road.

She told him to turn the car around. He reached across her into the glove compartment and put on his shades. She shouted at him, called him irresponsible. He switched on Simply Red and sang along. She insulted his music taste in English, Italian and Parisian *verlan*, and then, having run out of options, sulked. Above them the wind rolled balls of cumulus cloud across the sky, rotating light and shadow over the water around the Skye Bridge. The wind whipped at her hair and soon she was smiling through her irritation, enjoying the sights: black-faced sheep grazing on the island's rough moorland, shaggy incurious cattle penned at the side of double-glazed stone cottages.

They cut away from the main road and walked across a field strewn with plastic bottles and pieces of fishing net to look at the view from a line of sea cliffs. He took hold of her hand and shot her a smouldering look. 'You're not at work now,' she told him. He laughed and said he was just practising. Then he drove her across the island to a restaurant in an old croft where all the tables were full of people with English accents and apart from the sky and the hills outside the window she could have been in London.

He talked constantly, and, though he was preening and self-obsessed, it was refreshing to be with him. He made her feel far away from herself, from the mud dragging at her heels.

He drove her back in time for dinner at the hotel, and the crew pretended not to watch as India's former number-one action hero followed the foreign woman up to her room.

Sex funnelled up between them with sudden violence. He ground his face against hers, his stubble raking her lips and cheeks as they struggled towards the bed. She sank her nails into his neck, and he tugged her skirt up around her waist, digging between her legs with a hand. Every action was forceful, angry. As he threw her down she caught sight of his face and she could tell he wanted to hit her; and at that moment part of her wanted him to do it too, to confirm her insubstantiality, her potential for vanishing. She came almost immediately. Five minutes later Guy phoned.

'Sweetie?'

For Rajiv Rana, sex these days was primarily about relieving tension. If you are famous for your calm under pressure (when being attacked by a gang of lathi-wielding thugs, for example, or hanging from your fingernails beneath a collapsing suspension bridge), it may be important for your public persona to mirror your on-screen one. The emotional vocabulary of the action hero is limited. No tantrums. No weeping. You must face adversity with a witty one-liner and a left hook.

INSPECTOR KHANNA
(smiling ironically)
You know you shouldn't smoke . . . It's bad for the health.

ZEBISCO's car explodes in a ball of fire.

For almost fifteen years Rajiv Rana had played himself to the hilt, at parties and shows, at openings and premières and charity auctions and political rallies. He was a professional. He was smooth. He was pent-up.

He was scared.

A crowd shouting his catch-phrase.

You . . . shouldn't . . . smoke! . . .

His voice echoing in a hotel bathroom, cornered and hollow.

'Baba, how good to hear you. All the way from Dubai. I am honoured. And your health?'

Film heroics mean nothing here. Speak to Baby Aziz on the phone and your mouth goes dry. It's partly the stories from the old days, the Mumbai street days. A garland of severed fingers. A broken-limbed tycoon left to crawl along the sea wall of Marine Drive. The shootings, the faces burned with acid – all that belongs to the past now. It must be a long time since the man at the other end of the line did anything more physical than lift his portly frame on to a sun-lounger. But memories underwrite the present, guarantee that in these hands-off times of hawala couriers carrying money from the Far East, fixed cricket matches in Durban, apartment complexes in the Gulf and RDX caches in Azad Kashmir, you will hear his wheezy beedi-smoker's voice and remember that you too, despite your money and your millions of fans, lie within his sphere of influence.

'So a party. Your parties are famous. How many ladies at this one, eh?'

Aziz laughed a thin perfunctory laugh and, although this was not the question he had been asked, dropped the names of several famous men who were at that moment enjoying his hospitality. A fast bowler. The head of a soft-drinks company. In the next room, getting his cock sucked, was a member of one of the Emirates' ruling houses. Aziz was pleased. *The next room. I could hold the receiver up, eh?* This was the kind of thing he enjoyed. He was remarkably indiscreet.

'Speak up,' he told Rajiv. 'There's a strange noise on the line.'

Then he got down to business.

Baby Aziz had not always owned Rajiv Rana. A film star can exert muscle of his own when dealing with the underworld. Producers are used to extortion attempts, and, though sometimes it is better to pay a little protection money for a shoot to go smoothly, there are ways of staying clear of Mumbai's dark side. It is difficult, but possible. At least until you do something wrong. Until you accept a favour.

Rajiv's descent began with a little customs trouble, a matter of some undeclared currency and an overzealous commissioner who didn't have time to go to the movies. With a possible court case looming, Rajiv was looking at a big fine instead of a new jeep, a state of affairs which left him sulky and prone to tetchiness on the set of *Hit Man Hindustani*. He complained loudly enough to be heard by a certain Mr Qureishi. His business card described him as a lawyer, but he spent most of his days at a corner table in a Bandra restaurant taking bets on sports fixtures. Qureishi saw a way round Rajiv's problem, and, sure enough, in return for a donation to a charity helping destitute slum girls, the commissioner's zeal faded and the star was able to drive around town with the wind in his hair.

Rajiv was grateful, and more than happy to lend a little glitter to Qureishi's daughter's wedding. There he was treated royally and had his picture taken with some other people who turned out to be just as helpful as Qureishi himself. Whether it was accurate stock-market predictions, cheap imported Scotch or introductions to Alitalia stewardesses keen to get to know the real Mumbai, Qureishi's friends seemed to be able to make Rajiv's life better in small but meaningful ways. They loved having him around because he was Rajiv Rana, and he accepted that as his due.

Though it was common knowledge Qureishi was involved with Baby Aziz, Rajiv was unconcerned. Aziz himself had lived in the Gulf since the murder of a policeman in the mid 1980s, and as the city changed in the following years, with Hindu nationalist political gangs, the Pakistani secret service and old-fashioned financially motivated thugs all vying for power, he had made his presence felt indirectly, manipulating events from a distance. He was in some ways a mythical figure, not-quite-real, a bogeyman.

The next year Rajiv went out to Dubai as one of a group of stars playing 'The Multimega Millennium Concert', re-creating great screen moments for a stadium of excited fans. He was invited to a lavish after-party in one of the city's new luxury hotels. There a rotund man with dead eyes and a smoker's cough made a gesture of adaab and begged him to do him the favour of taking the microphone and leading the party-goers in a rendition of 'Pull my trigger, Rant', the wildly popular love song from his recent hit *Big Gun Number One*. Rajiv obliged, and Baby Aziz spent much of the evening slapping him on the back and introducing him to industry contacts. Later he provided personal entertainments of a kind even Rajiv, accustomed to pleasure, found exotic and surprising.

That year Rajiv Rana was hot-hot. He impersonated moody

loners, maverick police inspectors, ordinary joes turned have-a-go heroes and gym-toned loverboys in a series of hits that made him India's favourite tough guy, the idol of the chai stall and the schoolyard. He started an affair with the only woman who seemed worthy, a former Miss World turned movie heroine who had skin like butter and a figure which inspired in him unprecedented feelings of jealousy and possessiveness. He asked her to marry him, and when she turned him down he asked her again, arriving at her apartment late at night with a full wedding orchestra, causing irate neighbours to phone the police. He showered her with gifts (she was indifferent), covertly threatened her co-stars (she was angry), had her name tattooed on his left buttock (she laughed), then made a terrible mistake which drove her away and turned him into Baby Aziz's puppet.

She was modelling bridal wear in a show at the Oberoi Hotel, a favour to the friend who had designed her Miss World gown. A group of young men started wolf-whistling when she came down the runway, their leader calling out that he loved her, asking when was coming the garam swimwear section. Rajiv was furious at the insult but equally concerned not to make a public scene. Having discovered the identity of the boy (the son of a wealthy tyre manufacturer), he allowed himself to be escorted from the building by his companions. Later, drunk and brooding, he made a series of phone calls, sounding off to anyone who would listen about disgraceful behaviour, lack of respect, reputation, punishment.

The next morning, in the midst of a blinding hangover, he took a call from a whispering male voice. 'Baba asks. Baba is looked after,' it said, then hung up. That evening the television news reported that Rahul Subramanian, heir to the S.B. Radials fortune, had been found burned to death in his car in a slum area of the city.

Rajiv went into his bathroom and vomited into his hand-carved marble sink.

He did not leave the house for several days, during which time rumours about Subramanian's death flew around Mumbai society, rumours which thankfully did not touch him. He went to see Qureishi, who claimed not to know what he was talking about, but suggested it might be helpful if he took a holiday, at least until he felt a little calmer. 'You need relaxation,' said the bookmaker. 'You are our hero. We want what's best for you.'

The next few months were terrible. He considered confessing. But to whom? And to what? He hadn't wanted the boy killed. He hadn't asked anybody to do anything specific. At night he dreamed of flames and melting faces. He could not concentrate on work, walking out of *Abs*, a project produced by the team responsible for his greatest box-office successes. Miss World, bored by his increasingly erratic behaviour, was seen out on the town with a rising young model-turned-actor. When she stopped returning his calls, Rajiv arrived on the set of her latest romantic comedy and caused a scene. The movie magazines had a field day. Miss World gave *Stardust* an 'everything is over between Rajiv and Me' exclusive. Then Baby Aziz started calling in favours.

It began gradually. Rajiv made personal appearances at functions organized by Aziz's friends. He signed on for *Look Out . . . Love Alert!* A box-office bomb that it was 'suggested' would be useful for his career. If he questioned things or got angry, a call would come from the Gulf. 'When we think of you,' the wheezing voice would croon, 'our hearts are filled with emotion. We would never want to reveal anything harmful to your public self.'

The demands got heavier. He lent money without real hope of return. He agreed to store some crates (of machine parts, they told him) at one of his country properties. People in the industry began to whisper. When he complained that the rumours were damaging his image, Aziz was unsympathetic.

'People always talk,' he said. 'You must learn to ignore it.'

Rajiv Rana, accustomed to giving orders, got used to taking them. He had little choice about the restaurants and office parks he opened, the products he endorsed, the tinpot little weddings at which he had to sing. Aziz's people were renting him out to the highest bidder like any other asset, a car or a woman. He endured the humiliation quietly until they told him to turn down *Heroes of Kargil*. It was too much. A wave of patriotic fervour was sweeping the country. The director was talented. The songs were great. There was even a completed script. The film was a sure-fire hit.

He refused.

When Aziz called, he told him he didn't understand the movie business. 'I wouldn't lecture you on how to run your affairs, so leave choice of roles to me.' Aziz said he thought the treatment was biased. There was Shiv Sena money in the picture. 'Bhai,' he whispered, 'you wouldn't wish to inflame communal passions at such a time.' Rajiv (*Filmfare* headline: *I'm not political, I'm an entertainer*) hung up on him.

The next day Karim, his driver, was delivered to his front door in a sack. He was alive, but his ears and nose had been cut off. Rajiv had several lakhs of rupees couriered to the man's hysterical wife, and when Aziz called again he listened, trying to hold the receiver steady in his shaking hand. The message was blunt. 'You will not do this Kargil rubbish. Instead you will make yourself available for a new film. To be called *Tender Tough*. Like me. You will clear all dates completely. As a favour I will allow you to take one third of your standard fee. This, you understand, is my gift, my friendship token. Do not worry yourself about artistic standards. *Tender Tough* will be a hit movie. You will be given best director, large budget. You will even have choice of co-star. Now you may thank me.'

Rajiv mumbled something and left the house on a three-day bender, after which he had to pay money to a bar owner, a hotelier and a model whose facial bruises would prevent her from working for several weeks. A version of it made the gossip columns: *Has Raju become Big Fist Number One?*

He turned down *Kargil* and saw the role go to his rival Salman Khan. His image was trashed. Having been a hero for so long, he had developed the habit of referring to himself in the third person, shortening himself to his initials, a fan's affectionate nickname. But was 'R. R.' now to be the villain? Slumped in front of the giant plasma screen at his Juhu bungalow, he found relief in a sequence from *High School Hearts*, a film he had ignored when it was released the previous year. As the heroine learned her boyfriend had been killed in a traffic accident, her stricken face filled the frame. It seemed to radiate vulnerability, trust, a need to be protected. He groped for the remote, replaying the sequence again and again.

The girl's face turning, her eyes sparkling with glycerine-drop tears . . . He found himself in tears too, crying for innocence and purity, everything that had vanished from his own life. Everything this girl would surely be able to replace.

He told Aziz that the actress he wanted for *Tender Tough* was Leela Zahir.

The bathroom had an echo, but there was something else, electronic interference on the line, fragments of voices.

'Isn't this a matter for Iqbal?' he asked, trying to concentrate on Aziz's murmuring, which seemed to fade in and out of the interference.

'This is your film, Rajiv-bhai. I have promoted it for you, out of consideration for your interests. If it collapses because of this silly girl you chose as your heroine, I think it's obvious who should take the consequences.'

'I know she's being difficult, but what can I do? It's out of my control.'

'You must persuade her. She was your choice. The mother is coming. The two of you will have to work together.'

'She won't listen to anyone.'

'If you feel you can absorb these costs, then so be it.'

'Absorb – what do you mean?'

'If this film does not happen, you must bear the burden. Iqbal will be able to give you an estimate.'

'You can't be serious.'

Down the line came a stabbing sound which might have been laughter. Rajiv balled his fists, looking for something in the hard-surfaced bathroom to punch.

'So you will persuade the girl.'

'Yes, of course I will. I'll make sure. Yes.'

There was a logic to Arjun's decision, if only the kind produced by vending-machine coffee, bacon-flavoured corn snacks and the hard 3 a.m. strip lights of bus-terminal waiting areas. It went like this: *They think you'll be going north.* So what if he'd made a mistake? Instead of retracing his steps, he would carry on. Instead of north, south. Instead of Canada, Mexico. Log cabin goes to adobe hacienda. Find and replace.

It was the kind of tactic that had worked for Rajiv Rana in *Run from Injustice*. In Bend he bought a ticket for the next southbound bus, and, as night turned to day and then faded towards night again, he watched the strip of America by the side of the interstate change from green to brown and back to green, until the sky closed down to a misty grey and drops of moisture streaked the safety glass and suddenly there were whitecaps on open water and they were driving across the Golden Gate into San Francisco. In that city he ate a microwaved quesadilla which wilted its plastic plate and purchased a newspaper which concentrated on sports and freak weather occurrences, making no mention of either Leela or him.

He stood in a long line at the ticket office, where harassed clerks were issuing tickets by hand, then boarded a bus headed for San Diego. Hour by hour California lost its trees and flattened itself into a dusty plain lined with strip malls and fields of bright green lettuces through which Latino pickers moved in ragged gangs. In some places the crops were grown under glass or covered with plastic sheeting that glared in the sunlight, passing the window in blinding flashes which persisted until the sun went down and the disposable settlements and tentative landscapes vanished, leaving only illuminated franchise signs and a constant stream of headlights, as if the rest, the physical, was supplementary to the reality of still and moving light.

He never knew the name of the place where they made the rest-stop. It looked like every other bus terminal in America. It was long after midnight. The concessions were shuttered up, and the Traveler's Aid booth unattended. In one corner a video-game arcade chirped and growled. Rows of plastic contour chairs faced bays into which the arriving buses pushed their noses; above each was a monitor displaying arrival and departure times. Some of the chairs had coin-op TVs bolted to the armrests, and here and there people were feeding them money, receiving tiny black-and-white flickers in return. Arjun's eye for American class distinctions had sharpened. Many of the waiting people were obese, the paradoxical sign of poverty in this paradoxical place. Others, dirty and ill cared for, slept with their arms wrapped tightly round plastic sacks of clothing. A man with a beard and a cap saying 'Mustache Rides 5c' called out hey baby hey at every woman who went by. Another jogged his legs up and down, his bird-like head darting nervously from left to right as if searching for an attacker.

Arjun picked up his bag and went to the rest room, where he washed his face and changed his shirt. There were ten minutes before the bus was due to leave again. He went to the bank of telephones on the wall and was about to dial his calling-card number when he realized it was early afternoon in India and Priti would still be at work. He dialled anyway. Malini picked up, sounding excited to hear from him. Then someone else took the receiver away from her.

'Bro? Sweet as! Where have you been? I've been calling and calling.'

'I – I've been away. I'm not at home now.'

'I've got so much to tell you. Hey, everything is totally chaotic at work. All our systems went down. The entire place. It was madness! My manager would have been tearing his hair out if the old baldie still had any. I told you about him, right? The baldie? You must be working hard hard with all this virus business. But guess what – I'm not! Are you jealous? They had to give us the day off.' She lowered her voice conspiratorially. 'I spent most of it with Ramu. Oh, Arjun, so much has happened. I haven't even told you about Ramu. I will but you have to promise not to say anything to Ma and especially not to Pa.'

It was all too much, the happiness in her voice, the excitement. He held the receiver away from his face so she would not hear him crying.

'Wait a minute,' she said, and he heard the sounds of her shutting herself in a bedroom.

'Ramu is – you know he's not like anyone else. He's intelligent and he's kind, and he's not an idiot like most of the other guys at work. He's so funny. I know you'd like him. And his brother is in Australia. Actually in Australia. He lives in Bondi, next to the beach. What do you think of that? If we went, we could go surfing. Arjun? Are you there?'

He tried to control his ragged breathing. 'Yes, I'm here.'

'Arjun, I think I love him. We want to get married.'

'What?'

'He's spoken to his father and they're going to come and talk to Ma and Pa.'

'Married?'

'What do you say, Bro? Are you happy for me? Arjun?'

'Where's he from?'

'Kolkota. They're Chaudhuris. Arjun, don't talk like Ma. Aren't you even a little happy for me?'

'Sure.'

'Well, you could sound more like it. When we get married, Ramu wants us to move to Australia. Actually to go and live there.'

'What about our parents?'

'Is that all you can say? I tell you I find the man of my life and you say what about our parents?'

'It's very bad, Priti. Things have gone badly.'

'You're so selfish sometimes. Why does everything have to be about you?'

There was a long silence. He realized she could hear his ragged breathing. She knew something was wrong.

'Arjun? What's happened?'

'It's complicated. And it means I might not be around in the future, so – so, well, Australia is out, OK? You have to promise me you'll stay and look after Ma and Pa.'

Now it was her turn to be quiet.

'Sis?'

Her shouting distorted the signal. 'Oh my God. Why are you saying this? This is so typical. You get to go away and be a bigshot in America. Just because I'm a girl I have to stay and play nursemaid? You're – you're a drongo. A sexist drongo. Why shouldn't you look after them when they get old, eh? Why not you? You're as bad as Papa.'

'Priti, please. I'm scared.'

'What?'

'I've done something. I screwed up. And it means I might not be coming back.'

'Arjun?'

'What will happen to them if both of us aren't there?'

'What are you talking about?'

'Sis.'

'Oh, Arjun, I knew something was wrong. You've been so strange.'

'I made a mistake, OK. A big mistake. And there's no way to put it right.'

'I don't understand. What are you saying?'

'You'll find out. They may come and ask you questions, so it's better that you don't know anything. I love you, OK? And you must tell Ma and Pa that I love them too.'

'But what's it about?'

Arjun could not answer. He held the phone loosely in one hand, his mouth hanging open like a fish's as he watched his face appear on screens all around the bus terminal. Madness or a bad dream. Trapped on the other side of the glass. A news report. *Cyberterror suspect: FBI releases picture.*

Slowly he put the pay-phone handset back in the cradle and turned to face the wall.

In the picture he was smiling, wearing a striped shirt and making the thumbs-up sign. It had been cropped from a snapshot taken at Jimmy's Brewhouse in Redmond. Taken with Chris's camera. Which meant they had been talking to Chris.

Sorry, Chris.

He risked a glance back at the TV, which had exchanged his face for images of long lines at an airport check-in. After that there was a comment from a scowling Republican congressman in a striped tie, and then *her*, Leela Zahir, dancing on a desk in *High School Hearts*. Not her best film, or even (bobbed hair and a lemon-yellow jumpsuit) her best look, but she still brought his heart into his mouth. Ten seconds of yearning and then over to sports, body-armoured gorillas piling up on the goal line, a seven-foot teenager jumping for a hoop.

What now?

'You all done there, buddy?' Pointing at the phone was an elderly African-American wearing a t-shirt advertising a community regeneration programme. *Make a difference for Dinwood*. For a moment Arjun did not understand. *You done for buddy. You down there*. He spoke again. 'You going to use that?' Arjun shook his head and stepped away. The short walk to the nearest vacant seat was agonizing. Surely around the hall a hundred visual cortices were processing the configuration of his face, subconsciously linking shapes and colours to the mugshot on the news bulletin. Any second now would come the tap on his shoulder, the stern voice telling him to keep his hands in plain view. He hunched up, lowering his head into his jacket, not daring to look up in case he caught someone's eye.

By the time his bus was announced, the world around him had become both painfully close and infinitely distant. Noises were amplified, every rustling magazine and crying child a potential police siren. At the same time he was cut off from all the other waiting people, the homeless woman in the shower cap, the buzz-cut young army sergeant and the lady with the perm and the puzzle book, as if by a plexiglas panel.

He boarded the bus and sat down in his seat, his guts vibrating as the driver started the engine. He felt faint and realized he was unconsciously holding his breath. He had to concentrate, let it in, out again. Around him people were settling down, a tattooed Hispanic man wadding a jacket behind his head for a pillow, a mother feeding corn chips to her baby daughter. No one was paying any attention to him. It was like magic, a status quo as fragile as a soap-bubble. One move and they would be on him in a pack.

It could not last long now. How many hours of freedom did he have?

When the bus arrived in San Diego, it was getting dark. He knew from films like *Inspector 2000* and *Run Arundhati Run* that speed is of the essence for a fugitive, but something fatalistic had kicked in, some religious aspect of his nature which whispered that whatever would be would be, that his chances were so small he might as well take the opportunity to sleep for an hour or two before he faced the future.

He walked away from the bus-station as quickly as he could, putting two or three blocks between himself and the bustle before turning randomly on to a side street with a convenience store on the corner. He had a momentary glimpse of the interior, the Sikh proprietor bagging up groceries for a customer. Behind him on the wall was a calendar and an American flag and a garlanded portrait of Guru Nanak. In that store and the apartment above it would be rice and paan parag and tapes of Lata Mangeshkar and paper-wrapped cones of incense and steel dishes and Star TV on cable and pairs of worn leather chappals and soaking chickpeas and a family talking a language close to his own, words to go with the faraway smells of ghee and dust and petrol and cooking fires. His heart felt empty, a deflated paper bag.

There was a motel at the end of the block, its tall sign flashing intermittently. *Lucky's Motor Lodge: Color Cable TV Direct Dial Phone Aircon Parking Guests Only.* A bored Chinese woman took his money and gave him a lecture in the same unpunctuated monotone as the sign, check-out at noon ice-machine under stairs you break you pay no parties. The room smelled of cigarette smoke and pine disinfectant. He went to the bathroom and broke the heat-sealed wrapper on a plastic cup, filled it with water. It tasted terrible. He considered going back to the convenience store to buy a soda, but suddenly felt so tired it was all he could do to lay himself down on the padded nylon bedspread and close his eyes.

He tried to picture the border, but could see it only as an abstraction, a thick black line across the earth.

When he woke he was disoriented but not scared. At least not at first. The distant traffic noise was soothing and the sound of a TV filtering through the thin partition behind his head was comfortingly familiar, reminding him of his studio at Berry Acres. He sank back against the pillow. Then there was a loud crash outside his door. Instantly he sat upright, every muscle tensed in expectation of the Kevlar-armoured stormtroopers about to burst in. But the crash was followed by laughter, two women holding a joky argument as they kneeled down on the walkway to pick up whatever they had dropped.

The truth of his situation returned, dropping down over him like a bell jar. He swung his legs on to the floor and rubbed his eyes. Having no idea of the time, he took a peek through the curtains. The sky above the roofline of the motel court was grey and overcast. Dawn or dusk. It didn't really seem to matter which.

Struck by a sudden urgency, he pulled his laptop from his bag and dug around among socks and undershorts for a little golf-ball camera whose flex he untangled with shaking fingers. He plugged it in and, while he waited for the computer to boot up, placed an upturned waste-paper basket on the bedside table and set the camera on top of it, angling it to capture his image as he sat in a chair in the corner. It was time to explain himself, to face the public.

An hour later he left the motel, a handwritten map in his hand giving directions to a gamer's café called Boba Fett's, which looked, according to the *Yellow Pages*, like the nearest place with a fast public internet connection. Going out on to the street was risky, but the files he had created were large; from the motel they would take too long to upload. It was, he had discovered, early evening. A lurid petrochemical sunset was subsiding into darkness. The air was still warm, and, as he followed his map through the grid of downtown streets, bass lines pulsed out of open car windows and knots of people stood on corners. Happy, relaxed people. Citizens. Consumers. He hurried past.

Outside Boba Fett's it was all about the sportswear. Also the gold chains, the steroid cream and the hair gel. A huge group of teenage boys were clustered around a double line of cars, smoking cigarettes and conducting arguments in a variety of South-East Asian languages. They kneeled down to check out wheel rims, played with pagers and cellphones, opened doors and trunks to display throbbing sound systems, struck gangsta poses and checked out Arjun suspiciously. They were blocking the sidewalk, and, as he shouldered through them to get to the café, he was stared at, coldly appraised. He realized nervously that he had blundered on to well-marked territory.

As he opened the door, wistful memories of Aamir and Gabbar Singh's Internet Shack were blown away. He was hit by a wall of electronic sound, a terrifying amalgam of soundtrack music, gunfire and simulated v8 engines. Boys, Vietnamese and Korean for the most part, were engaged in combat with rail guns and lasers and flails and alien pulse weapons. They were decapitating one another, forcing each other off the road, razing their enemy's cities with balls of flame and devastating his crack divisions with tactical nuclear weaponry. Some wore headphones, lost in solo trance. Others were the centre of knots of excited spectators. At the far end of the room a counter served bubble tea and snack-foods, the twenty-something manager going about his work wearing a pair of yellow foam earplugs. Apart from the board displaying drinks prices and hourly terminal rates, Boba Fett's was undecorated, a grey cinderblock box with a silvered plate-glass front and an air-conditioning unit bolted to the back wall. Life here took place on screen.

Arjun rented a free terminal and sat down with a beaker of chocolate-flavoured tea. On either side, kids were playing the same first-person shooter game, charging through a complex maze as they twitch-fired at one another, their screens filling with static as their avatars took hits, fading to white when they died. Arjun uploaded his home-made videos to his secret space on the NOIT server, then created an account on a free email service and used it to send messages containing the location to the people he wanted to watch them: Priti, Chris, the FBI and Leela Zahir. Not having an address for Leela, he posted to several newsgroups and discussion forums, and for good measure copied Aamir.

so sis i don't know where to begin

dear federal bureau is that the correct form of address?

chris i was going to return it but

this is for you leela zahir as a way of saying sorry for all that has happened i have always loved you would never do anything to hurt you but you see I was desperate

When he was finished, he took his disk and left, not looking behind him. He did not spot the pair of boys, perhaps thirteen or fourteen years old, who detached themselves from the crowd outside the café. As he headed back to the motel, they walked up the street after him, keeping their distance yet careful not to fall too far behind.

We don't lose.

That was the first principle, the only one that mattered. Whether it was university entrance or getting on to the guest list, *people like us don't lose*. In private, his father would have linked it to breeding or something equally dogs-and-horses sounding. In public, unless someone had given him spirits (drink made him belligerent), Mr Swift would consent to put it down to grit or manners or some other factor unique to English upper-middle-class-occasional-churchgoers resident outside London. As far as Guy was concerned, his parents' parochialism, their belief in the virtue of moderation, their suspicion of pleasure and their obsessive thrift were all so much self-denying rubbish. As if holidaying in Devon and driving a battered Rover made them morally superior! Luckily all the horrible fifties austerity which had produced them, all that dullness still hanging around when he was growing up, had been wiped away. There was money now. Money and balsamic vinegar and Design. Yet despite his subsitution of the future for the past, long boom for stiff upper lip, he still secretly agreed with that basic handed-down premise: We are better than other people. We don't lose.

Guy's 'we' was different from his father's, though it would be hard to specify who other than himself was included. He had been through a phase of reading popular-science paperbacks and thought of his success as the outcome of a process of natural selection. *We* were on top because we were better adapted to the environment of the global city. We took chances and made opportunities for ourselves. We knew how to network, how to manipulate the flows of money and information to produce Results.

Sitting in the plane on the way back from Dubai, he found

strength and comfort in this idea. His meal untouched on its tray in front of him, he fidgeted and thought about adversity. So what if he was looking financial ruin in the face? So what if Gabriella might be about to leave him? It was just a question of digging deeper, finding his hidden reserves. When the stewardess took away his tray, he opened up his laptop and began to type, pressing down keys with slow rigid forefingers. This was what you did when things went wrong. You pushed harder. It was another of his father's traits. If the world is not doing what *we* want, we have to bend it to our will. Ignoring the tiny figures drifting around on the armrest TV, he typed a new mission statement, a plan of action for his next twenty-four hours. He worked and reworked it until it had been whittled down first to short paragraphs, then sentences, then bullet-pointed phrases and finally four single words. Extreme concision. Total summary:

- Jamal
- Gift
- Office
- Eurobastard

JGOE. Jay-go. He started putting it into operation as soon as he landed at Heathrow.

Jamal was an elegant young man who, growing up on the Stonebridge Park Estate in Harlesden, started out in life with fewer options than Guy when it came to demonstrating fitness for survival in a global city. The decision to sell powder rather than rock brought him into contact with an upmarket clientele, and this access, combined with his unthreatening manner and natural business acumen, had allowed him to develop a thriving retail operation catering to the media, advertising, music industry and legal sectors. These days Jamal lived in a windswept gated development in the Docklands, wore Prada and Armani and drove a silver Audi TT. Guy took a taxi from the airport and kept it waiting while he made a short trip up to Jamal's place, where he found him relaxing with a few friends around a coffee table on which was scattered perhaps £10,000 in cash. After concluding his transaction and saying goodbye to Jamal's friends (most of whom appeared to be Austrian aircrew), Guy told the driver to take him home.

The cabby droned on about the power cut, traffic jams, Leela Zahir and Chelsea Football Club, folding in his own theories about cybercrime and 'the al-Qaidas'. Guy leaned forward and closed the glass partition. As usual the sight of the sun glinting on In Vitro's curved glass façade was hopeful and affirming. He paid off the cab, acknowledged the salute of the moon-faced Eastern European concierge, made his way across the lobby into the lift and after a short vertical interlude (during which he imagined himself travelling all the way up to the still-untenanted penthouse at the top of the building) strode into his flat, ready to get to work. After a few minutes in the kitchen with Jamal's coke, he felt he had rediscovered the positive self-image drained away by the previous few days. Once again he had the will to win.

Gift. It had to be impressive. Impressive was the only way. Subconsciously Guy tended to think of Gabriella as less a partner than a situation to be managed. Often when he was with her he felt like a pilot steering a ship through a narrow channel, or a policeman facing an angry sports crowd. Though he found her emotions opaque, he had gradually turned that into a virtue, imagining her privately as 'elemental' or 'inscrutable', words with an erotic ring. He once tried to explain this to her, drunkenly kissing her and telling her she was 'kind of Japanese'. Instead of confirming it, she gave him one of her looks. Management tools which worked on Gabriella were hard to come by. Pleading, for example, was not wise. Temporarily lacking imagination (though surging with confidence), he reverted to his default setting, which was to throw money at the problem. Money, he reasoned, was something she understood. If she was thinking of breaking up with him, perhaps a display of economic confidence stood a chance of changing her mind.

He paced up and down thinking of the possibilities, and when he found he was concentrating on the pacing rather than the thinking, went to the computer for inspiration and typed 'expensive gift' into a search engine. After a period examining Dom Pérignon presentation baskets, mother-of-pearl inlaid humidors, monogrammed desk sets and space vacation packages, he pushed the mouse away in disgust. None of it seemed appropriate. One company would deliver a top-of-the-range jet ski to her door. Interesting. But wrong. He returned to the kitchen, did another line, drank some mineral water, switched on MTV.

There it was. Bling bling. Shaking it in his face.

And so to Bond Street. More taxis. Sometimes, he mused, life was just a string of taxis. Hop out of one and into another, like a sequence from a Beatles movie. Maybe if there were four Guys, all identical, getting into a taxi one after the other, it would look cool, visually. As he paid the driver, he wondered whether he should make a note of this idea. He was feeling creative today. It would be a shame to lose anything.

Bond Street sounded like the coming of autumn, the susurrus of shopping bags filling the air as expensively remodelled matrons made their way between boutiques with terrifying speed and efficiency, like customs dogs searching a cargo hold. Guy spotted a young couple hesitating outside one retail bunker, intimidated by its whiteness, the three pairs of shoes on display in the window. They took a step forward, then bustled away as if signalling to the world that they had never really been tempted to go inside.

At the entrance to the jeweller's stood a uniformed doorman wearing an earpiece. Guy focused (it was important to retain focus) and dived past him into the theatrical gloom of the shop. Narrow spotlights illuminated glass-covered trays of gems, leaving their human attendants veiled in mystic darkness.

'Impressive,' he affirmed, from between clenched teeth.

The staff seemed taken aback by the forcefulness of his purchasing style. A young assistant in a cheongsam showed him some loose stones. He kept repeating *impressive* to her, until she vanished and the manager took over. Together they looked at diamond necklaces and bracelets and studs. There was a great deal of technical detail to do with weights and settings. Guy tried to get the manager to dispense with this. Couldn't the man see he was pressed for time?

The manager obviously conceptualized his role as a cross between door picker and guardian of a very exclusive religious shrine. *This*, he intoned in a High Church voice, is a very important decision. Guy raised his eyes to the ceiling. Too right it was important. The bitch was going to leave him if it didn't work. Impressive, he reminded him, exasperated. *Really* impressive. Dripping disapproval, the manager shot his cuffs, suggesting that perhaps Guy would like to give the matter some thought. It was, after all, a major purchase. With poorly concealed impatience, Guy explained that no one had a clearer idea of what was at stake than him.

It was like wading through treacle, but eventually he left with what he wanted, a ruinously expensive collar that maxed out his credit card and nestled in a tiny leather case in his jacket pocket. The manager appeared reluctant to let the item go. Guy almost had to snatch it out of his hands.

Office. He entered the *Tomorrow** building feeling deflated. The battle for the collar had drained him, and he was apprehensive that fresh troubles might be waiting at work. People would want to know about Dubai. There was a risk of negatively impacting morale. Putting on his best CEO face (breezy, competent), he accelerated purposefully as he walked into reception, greeting the girl at front desk with a big smile.

'Hi, Nicky. Holding the fort OK?'

'Charlotte.'

'Are you new?'

'No. You have messages.'

'Later.' He held up a hand and turned towards the stairs. Unfortunately he had been spotted. People were already converging on him with documents and questioning expressions. For all his study of management theory, Guy had never quite got the hang of delegation. Since *Tomorrow** was supposed (according to its mission statement) to be a 'seamless extension of his personal creativity', he felt justified in taking an intuitive approach to the day-to-day running of the company. His staff were used to meetings where goals were suddenly redefined, new work magically created, and old work made irrelevant. As a result, they tended to check with him at least twice before embarking on anything time-consuming. He had not been in touch since he left for the Gulf. There was a backlog.

Brushing off the questioners, he locked himself in his creative space and did some more coke. His life–work balance restored, he called in Kika and told her to organize a Village Council meeting for later in the afternoon. The whole office. Attendance mandatory.

'Does that mean you've got some good news?' Kika asked.

'Have you done something to your hair?'

'Jesus, Guy. The pitch. Did we get the work?'

'It wasn't right for us. They weren't ready for what we were offering. You've done a kind of – what have you done to it?'

'Oh, hell.' She looked crestfallen.

'Don't worry,' he said brightly, 'it's under control.' He took the collar out of his pocket. 'Could you get this couriered to Gabriella? She's in Scotland. I'll forward you a mail with the address.'

Kika looked at the name of the firm engraved on the box.

'Just this?'

'Yes. And it has to get there ASAP. By tonight if at all possible. Assuming their service isn't fucked, like everything else.'

'I mean – don't you want to put a note in with it?'

'Oh,' he sniffed uncertainly. 'A note. Right. A note.'

What to say to Gaby? *Please don't leave me. I have medium-term plans for us up to and including marriage and babies*? He wasn't even certain that was what was on her mind, but, having spent several hours on the plane turning over the details of their phone conversation, there seemed to be no other possibility. That phrase. *We need to talk*. No one used it in any other context. She would have to choose now, when he had so much else on. The PEBA pitch was tomorrow morning. He had to fly to Brussels tonight. There was simply no time to *do* relationships right now.

It was an eloquent necklace. It was intended to speak for itself. But Kika was right – there should also be words. He took a compliments slip from a drawer and wrote in large marker-pen letters:

Impressed? xG

It seemed to have the right tone. Attention grabbing. Challenging, if there was another man in the picture. Why did she have to have a job where she met actors? They were such bastards.

Kika looked at the note. She looked back at Guy.

'Julia's resigned,' she said. 'The letter's on your desk. I think there's one from Yuri too. Oh, and Yves Ballard called.'

'Fine,' said Guy. 'No problem. No prob*lemo*.'

An hour later he came down, newly fortified, to address the Village Council. The workplace-as-rural-community paradigm had always appealed to him, and, though these office meetings were naturally weighted towards his own role as Headman (he spoke, his employees listened), he felt they gave a democratic flavour to *Tomorrow** which was surely good for cohesion.

The workforce had assembled promptly in the brainstorm zone. Guy scanned the rows of young faces, the bodies whose fashionably casual clothing shaded into informal businesswear as one passed from creative to financial personnel. He felt proud, elevated. There were people from several ethnic minorities. There was, if you counted Carrie's leg, a disabled person. It was a microcosm of society. His society.

'Hi, everybody. Settle down please. So, I know there's been a certain amount of uncertainty lately. We've all been putting our shoulders to the wheel, and we're just moving into the time-frame when we're really going to start seeing some results. I've just come back from what I feel is a really defining meeting in Dubai, where, in a way, I saw everything that traditional old-economy businesses are doing wrong. Total linear thinking, no perspective on the time–energy landscape whatsoever. But although we won't be working with Al-Rahman' – here there were audible groans – 'I'd like everyone to give themselves a big round of applause. We've all worked very hard, so come on, give yourselves a hand.'

Looking at each other glumly, the employees of *Tomorrow** clapped.

'Well done. That's right. You know, guys, I've come back from

Dubai feeling more certain of our goals than ever. The meeting there, and this very backward herd-mentality company's failure to mesh with our philosophy, was a total vindication of what we're doing. Like I always say, we're not a company, we're a visionary network, and with that in mind I'd like to take this opportunity to announce a new programme. As you know, what we do best is imagineer the future for our clients, but it's time for us to turn our skills inward and look at our *own* future. Call it the tomorrow of *Tomorrow**. We've been very outer-directed and now it's time for us to cherish our in-house experience. So as of today we're going to clear the decks and embark on the project of creatively visualizing our own hopes and dreams. We're making ourselves the client, if you will. I'd like each of you to ask yourself what do I want to be tomorrow? How about in a year's time? How about five years? And *where* will we be? That's an important one. Should *Tomorrow** retain its physical location in east London, or is it time perhaps to take off in a metaphorical spacecraft? Should we, for example, build temporary architectural structures for each project? Or scatter in survival podules around the world? How do we become more *like* ourselves? Can we learn to shoot our creative essence further and with greater force? These are all questions we need to address, and now is the time to address them. As some of you know, I'm going to fly to Brussels tonight to make the PEBA pitch. I think the work we've all put in on that one speaks for itself. So I'll be doing PEBA and while I'm away I want you to think about the tomorrow of *Tomorrow**. In two days' time I'll facilitate a meeting in which we'll assign working groups to the best of the ideas that arise from this process. OK, thanks everyone, that's all.'

It was, in many ways, a brilliant speech. A re-energizing speech. He felt he had hit them right between the eyes, turning employee doubt into new opportunity. There were a good number of responses, though not all as positive as he would have liked. Paul, the finance director, wanted to know if he was certain he wanted to direct all company resources towards the tomorrow of tomorrow project. The new senior designer asked whether it meant they had no client work. This was of course true, but Guy told him sternly that prioritizing creativity had always been company policy, and if he wanted to work for an outfit which didn't value blue-sky thinking, he should look elsewhere. That shut him up.

With things back on track at the office, it was time for the hardest part of his plan. He went back up to his creative space and set the phone directly in front of him on the desk.

Eurobastard. It wasn't big or clever, but it was the only nickname he had ever found for Yves. Guy had become very involved with Europe, both as an idea and as the place where his funding came from. Transcendenta had its offices in Amsterdam, in a seventeenth-century townhouse overlooking the Herrengracht. Guy had visited frequently since they agreed to back him, and he was, if he was honest, a little in awe of Yves and his partners, a Dutchman, a Belgian and a very beautiful Spanish woman called Inés who always seemed to be away when he came to town. There was an air of calm about them as they moved through their world of blond wood and oriental rugs, a calm stemming from proficiency in several languages, control over the disbursement of large sums of money and trust in the social importance of their work. At first, during the period when they left him more or less alone to run *Tomorrow**, Guy viewed this calm as a sign of wisdom and consequently bracketed 'Europe' with 'Japan' as a geographical subdivision of the future, an exciting land of the imagination where tomorrow was happening today. Lately, as the climate had soured and some of his plans (the newswire, the relationship with the German car manufacturer) failed to materialize, Transcendenta had shown an increasing tendency to interfere. Their own finances were, the rumour went, far from secure. Calm had turned to coldness. He had been dodging Yves's phone calls for months.

Now it was vital to mollify him. After Al-Rahman it would not be an easy call.

On the plane home from Dubai, Guy had finally accepted that perhaps he could do without the in-house video production team. The coolhunters could probably go too – they just seemed to spend all their time in Brick Lane photographing people's haircuts. But even with radical surgery there was a possibility that Transcendenta might not wish to continue funding. There had been a board meeting in Amsterdam. Yves claimed to have faced stiff opposition when arguing *Tomorrow**'s case.

Against all this there was PEBA. The contract was potentially huge. It offered the opportunity to brand the entire combined European customs and immigration regime. Logos, uniforms, the presentation of a whole continent's border police. If he secured that business, everything else – Al-Rahman, Pharmaklyne – would instantly go away.

Just as long as they didn't cut the credit line.

He was gearing himself up to face Yves when the phone in front of him rang. He put down his credit card, moved the framed Mr Pink photograph to one side and answered. It was Kika. Yves was on the other line.

'You must be psychic,' said Guy, trying to inject his voice with warmth and enthusiasm. 'I was about to call you.'

'Really?' said Yves.

'I just wanted to talk to you about PEBA. We're feeling really psyched up about it here.'

'That's great, Guy. I'd expect nothing less. I wanted to talk to you about that too. I have good news.'

'What?' He thought he might have misheard. 'Really?'

'Yes, really. I'm going to come to Brussels. I've pulled a few strings and organized a dinner tonight. Just a small thing, but I think it will help our case.'

Our case, thought Guy. *Our* case?

'The two of us, plus Director Becker, the Director-Designate of PEBA and the Chair of the SIS Liaison Committee. Everyone very much likes what they hear, and these people want to meet you before the formal pitch tomorrow.'

Guy was genuinely shaken. 'Yves, that's amazing. That's – that's wonderful! So they're really on side, then?'

'On side? Oh, yes, on side. They are very enthusiastic, yes. Monika Becker the most, I think. She is very big on presentation issues.'

Yves gave him the details of the meeting and warned him to leave plenty of time for the journey. There were travel disruptions all across Europe. Guy, still not quite believing the turn the conversation had taken, told him with genuine feeling that he was looking forward to seeing him. He put the phone down and punched the air.

Gabriella lay on her stomach on the bed, listening to Rajiv Rana dressing. As he pulled up his trousers, he muttered to himself in Hindi, his belt buckle clattering as he fastened it. She did not turn over to watch him. At the door he stopped and said, in the tone of someone leaving a business meeting, 'No doubt I will see you in the morning.' She did not reply.

She lay still for a long time. Then, feeling cold, she crawled under the covers. She must have slept because when she next opened her eyes the alarm clock read 1:08 a.m., and the noise from the bar had stopped. She switched off the bedside light and rolled on to her side. Out in the corridor there was a muffled thump and the sound of people arguing. She could not hear what they were saying, but had the idea one of them was Rajiv.

Under her window a woman laughed. She thought about Rajiv and Guy and other men, things they had said or given to her, things they had wanted her to do. So many exchanges. Such complexity. Tomorrow she would ring her office and tell them she was coming back. It would be a waste of time for her to stay.

In the morning she cleared her things off the bathroom shelf, packed her case and went down to the dining room, where she took a table on her own by the window. She was sawing at a segment of grapefruit when she heard the sound of a car pulling up outside the hotel. A minute or two later Vivek rushed in and asked whether anyone had seen Iqbal. Soon crew members were rushing around, making phone calls to each other and generally behaving as if the sky were about to fall on their heads. Leela's mother had arrived.

Gaby pushed the grapefruit aside and went to reception to take a look at the woman who could cause such panic. The small curio-cluttered space was crowded with people, so the first thing she saw was the luggage, a six-foot Vuitton pyramid whose base was an enormous steamer trunk and pinnacle a tiny vanity case. Its owner was in her fifties, quite tall, and had probably once been beautiful, but surgery had pulled her face into a taut mask, accessorized with tattooed eyebrows and an incongruous retroussé nose. Her long black hair was streaked with red, and she was dressed, as far as Gaby could see, as a teenage drag queen, in shiny snakeskin-effect jeans and a tiny t-shirt with the word *Angel* picked out in sequins across the front. As she received Iqbal's fulsome salaams, she smiled theatrically. The effect was vampiric, debauched.

To everyone's astonishment, just as Iqbal was embarking on a pompous speech of welcome, Leela Zahir came scampering down the stairs.

'Ma!'

It was a great entrance. Dressed in an electric-blue salwar-kameez, she was virtually unrecognizable as the despondent chain-smoker whom Gaby had seen wandering by the lake. This morning she looked like a film star, all hair and chiffon and perfect understated beauty. At first the crew appeared stunned, uncertain, but, as their heroine rushed into her mother's arms, they erupted into spontaneous applause. They would be able to start work again! The film would be completed!

Gaby watched the two women perform their reunion for the crowd, Iqbal rubbing his hands, Rocky Prasad and his DP hugging like schoolboys whose team just scored the winning run. Leela was clinging to her mother's neck, nuzzling her like a child.

'Ma, you look so tired. Was it a dreadful journey?'

'Beti, I can't even tell you.' Mrs Zahir raised her voice a little, so everyone was included. She stroked Leela's cheek, her unnaturally smooth face registering a certain strained intensity which might have been the remains of a tender expression. 'Things are terrible. Even in first class it is terrible. Arré! When you make a complaint all they will say is so sorry this is *down*, that and the other is *down*. Shocking how we all rely on these computers. Really.'

'Oh, Mummy.'

'But you have been ill. They have been phoning me with tales about biting insects, losing voice, all sorts.'

'I was feeling so sick, Mummy. But when I heard you were coming I got much better. I will be able to shoot now you are here.'

'I am glad to hear it.'

'Madam, I too am rejoicing,' said Iqbal, rolling his eyes and holding up his palms to the heavens.

'Iqbal-saab, could you do something about these bags?'

'Of course, of course.'

Rajiv Rana sauntered downstairs, wearing tight jeans and a denim shirt, unbuttoned to display his depilated chest.

'Ah, didi! You are a healer! It's miraculous what an effect your presence has on the young.'

He embraced Mrs Zahir like an old friend, making no eye contact with Gaby, who watched with distaste as the other woman simpered, brushing his collar with her fingers. It occurred to her that perhaps they had been lovers. The idea disgusted her.

'Rajiv-bhai,' purred Mrs Zahir, 'you look as good as ever.'

He laughed expansively. 'Now that you are here, Faiza, we will be able to work.'

'That's excellent news for all concerned. Now perhaps someone will show me to my room?'

Mrs Zahir decided she was displeased by the hotel. Its location was remote. The bellboys who were making faces at one another as they struggled upstairs with her cases were neither handsome nor well groomed. Even the clutter of memorabilia failed to charm her, but then old-fashioned things rarely did.

Her room, with its uneven boards and floral wallpaper, was barely habitable. There was a large wooden-framed bed and old pictures of men in skirts and hairy cows and such like on the walls. More dusty nonsense. A friend had recently recommended a Vastu practitioner to her, a good-looking Hindu boy who also worked as an astrologer. He was American-educated, bang up to date, and had recently been matching her biorhythms to the rhythms of the universe, one by one. It was very soothing. She decided to phone him for advice. Perhaps the room should be cleared for the duration of her stay. Perhaps even painted.

Annoyingly, Mr Vastu was not answering his phone. So Mrs Zahir changed out of her travel clothes and ordered some tea. Outside, engines were revving as cars and vans ferried the crew round the loch to the castle. Some flunkey knocked on her door to tell her that her daughter was ready to go to the set. She sent a message that she would follow on later. She needed to lie down and compose herself. She needed to think.

The little bitch was up to something, she was sure of it.

The journey had been gruelling. Air-traffic control at Mumbai had melted down and the backlog of flights trying to leave had caused immense delays, even after the airport reopened. Amazing to think all of it was because of Leela. At first this whole computer tamasha had looked like a disaster, but the more she found out about it, the more she came to see it as an opportunity. Leela had been a household name in India for some years. Now her face would be known all over the world. Mrs Zahir had always harboured ambitions of cross-over. Her daughter had pale skin, a skinny body. No desi bignose or ghee-fed fatness to the girl. It was an international look. This virus business could turn out to be the perfect springboard.

Then Iqbal had phoned saying she was ill. And after Iqbal, Rajiv. For Rajiv to call! Faiza knew the situation must be serious. On the phone he had sounded worried. He said he did not believe there was anything wrong, just that for whatever reason she did not want to work. When Faiza spoke to her, she had sounded ill enough, telling stories of cold draughts and stomach aches. Faiza decided to be soothing. No sense in pressurizing her without knowing the cause. She was, after all, the key to everything. Only when Leela started to work seriously was Faiza able to sever ties with Zahir. The ape knew his only hold on them was his money. Without it the two of them had no other income but Leela's acting. It was a situation that needed to be handled with care.

When Rajiv phoned back, Faiza counselled caution, but she agreed that this was not the time for the girl to be making trouble. When Baby Aziz had money in a picture, the time for trouble was never. Waiting for her travel agent to call back with fares, Faiza regretted letting Leela go away alone. It was an experiment she would not be repeating.

At the start of Leela's career, Faiza had never left her side. Though she had given up her own ambitions to marry Zahir, she had kept in touch with the industry. She was not, she told the magazines, the kind of mother to live vicariously through her daughter. It was simply that, having been in the business herself, she was aware of the opportunities. Leela had talent just bursting to get out. To stunt its growth would be criminal. So she had overseen every photo shoot and interview, had chosen Leela's clothes, her activities and her friends, spending day after day on baking-hot sets and night after night at parties and launches, showing her around, pestering producers and directors to give her a break.

Of course the child did not appreciate her work. In private she would cry, ask why she had to do the things her mother told her. She did not want to talk to all these old men. She did not want to wear such tight blouses, such filmy saris. It was an uphill struggle. What other daughter cried at being taken away from her schoolbooks to go to a party?

In film circles, Faiza Zahir earned herself a reputation as a doting parent, a reputation she carefully nurtured through sentimental articles and mother–daughter magazine portraits. Seventeen-year-old Leela was often quoted on the subject of their mutual adoration. *My maa is my best friend. I can't bear to spend a day without seeing her*. The absence of Mr Z. was occasionally the subject of malicious gossip, but on the whole the writers (and the millions of fans whose opinions they moulded) were awed by Leela's beauty, the grace of her dancing, the way she had of conveying a sense that behind her perfect features and flawless skin was a well of emotion, an understanding of pain and tragedy.

Sometimes, Faiza found herself unnerved by her daughter's increasing fame. She seemed to be floating free of all control. The money was flowing, they had extricated themselves from Zahir and his tedious steel factory, but at home Leela was withdrawn and Faiza jealous. The arguments became fierce, protracted.

'I feel like I don't even have a name! I'm not a person, just Leela Zahir's mother!'

'Well, I never wanted this!'

'At least you could show me some gratitude!'

And so on, round and round. Sometimes one of them would smash something. Once the silly child swallowed some pills. Faiza had a discreet doctor and nothing ever came out in the press, but slumped on a waiting-room chair she did regret some of the things which had been necessary. That wizened old bag Gupta, for example. It must have been hard for a young girl. But she too had done difficult things. In this life, the sooner one ditched one's silly notions about romance the better.

She took a shower in the poky little bathroom, then swung open the trunk and looked through her wardrobe for an appropriate on-set-in-Scotland outfit. When she had changed, she rang front desk to tell them to bring a car round.

It was one of those highland days when the sun filters down through the clouds in soft yellow threads and the world takes on a spiritual quality; when the moisture in the air refracts every beam of light, deviates every eyeline, opens up a gap in which things can exist unobserved.

Gaby had forgotten all about leaving. Shielding her eyes with a folder of production notes, she stood by a scaffolding tower, watching Leela Zahir dance her way along the battlements of Dimross Castle. Leela was dressed in emerald-green and carried a huge square of silk which billowed out behind her like a sail. She was followed by a squad of dancers in contrasting lilac, mirroring her moves as she pirouetted and swayed along the narrow walkway.

Loudspeakers had been rigged up at the base of the castle walls. Giant reflectors and thousand-watt lamps were trained at the battlements. The cracked asphalt of the castle car park was almost invisible beneath ranks of five-ton trucks and trailers and generators and catering vans, drawn up to besiege the girl in the green sari; an onslaught of sound and light. Rocky and Vivek were perched behind a camera on a hydraulic crane. Each time Rocky called action, the tiny platform reared towards the girl, who turned to face it and flung her arms wide in a gesture of ecstasy. Between takes the lights were dimmed, and figures appeared from behind turrets and crenellations to adjust clothing and make-up, to bring Miss Zahir a drink of water and a folding chair. Then the whole process was repeated, the amplified violins and high-pitched female voice, the blast of light, the moment of abandon.

It was extraordinary. Gaby had been on many film sets, but even from a distance she could feel Leela's power over the camera. It was as if she had drawn this aggregate of people and equipment to her by force of will. The crew, like all crews bored and cynical as a matter of professional principle, seemed hypnotized.

This shot completed, they moved on to the next, positioning the camera to capture close-ups of Leela at the head of her troupe of dancers. Gaby skirted gingerly around a huddle of electricians wrestling lengths of cable into a distribution box, trying to spot Iqbal. If Leela was suddenly feeling her film-star self again, she might also be able to do a few interviews. In front of the visitor's centre, an L-shaped wooden building which housed a ticket booth, the Scotch Mist Souvenir Shop and the Jac-o'-Bite Snackbar, there was a crowd of spectators, about equally divided between locals, press and Asian fans. A length of plastic tape separated them from the crew, but several of the photographers were wandering around the perimeter, taking telephoto shots of Leela and crouching down in front of laptops to wire them back to their agencies. They had varying degrees of success. As she watched, one stood up and skimmed his machine into the loch. It disappeared with a dull splash.

She found the producer with a red-faced man in a Barbour jacket, who stood leaning raffishly on a walking stick that was almost as tall as himself. The man's brown corduroy trousers were tucked ostentatiously into a pair of thick socks, which in turn disappeared into a pair of stout brown leather boots. Iqbal was at his most insinuating, unctuously pointing out aspects of the production and describing the context of the scene in progress. 'Very emotional song, My Lord,' he was saying. 'Heart strings will be tugged and guts wrenched, no doubt about it.'

This was, Gaby supposed, the Laird of wherever they were, the owner of Dimross Castle. As she approached, Iqbal waved to Rajiv Rana, who came sauntering up to be introduced. He was in costume, sporting an outfit of what could only be described as disco tweed, a riot of marshy-greens and acid-yellows topped with a deerstalker hat. There was an awkward moment as he caught sight of her and hesitated. The bastard was actually looking around for an escape route. Gaby was stunned. Who did he think he was? *She* had been doing *him* the favour, not the other way round. She controlled her anger and waited while Rajiv was introduced to the red-faced man.

'This is the Lord of Dimross. My Lord, this is our hero, Mr Rajiv Rana.'

'Lord,' said Rajiv. 'It's an honour to meet you. What a cool place you have.'

'Um, thank you.' Dimross turned rapidly to Gabriella. Beneath his fogeyish exterior he was probably in his early forties. He looked pleased to see her.

'And who might this charming lady be?'

Iqbal made a vague gesture with his hands. 'Our publicity girl, Camilla – Jamila- ah –'

'Gabriella Caro. How do you do.'

Dimross shook her hand vigorously. 'Dimross. How do you do. Call me Kenny. Are you part of this outfit, then?'

'I work for a public-relations company in London. You're very lucky to live in such a beautiful place.'

'Thank you, my dear. Of course there was nothing there at all eighty years ago. Just a pile of rubble.'

'I'm sorry?'

'Oh, yes. Absolutely true. Once upon a time there was some kind of fortification on the rocks over there, but it all collapsed. Or was it razed? I can never remember. My grandfather was something of a romantic. Sword in the stone and all that. Made a lot of money in coal and got it into his head that he ought to have a family seat. So he bought the title and most of the land hereabouts and built the place from the ground up. Rather successfully, if one does say so oneself.'

Gabriella was disappointed. 'I thought it was medieval.'

Dimross looked perversely pleased by this. 'Shows what an eye the old man had. It's far more picturesque than any of the real ones, and the tourists certainly don't know the difference. British heritage at its best, I'd say.'

Rajiv and Iqbal seemed annoyed that they were being ignored. Rajiv put an arm around Dimross's shoulders and asked him if he hunted. Dimross gingerly removed it before he replied.

'Well, depends what you mean. I own a grouse moor. And occasionally one shoots rabbits, that kind of thing.'

Rajiv promised him that if he were ever in India they would go hunting together. As a celebrity he could, he hinted, get government permits for certain species which were normally off limits. When he launched into a description of a shotgun he coveted, Gabriella had an opportunity to speak to Iqbal.

'You'll have to ask the mother,' he said. 'Everything goes through her now.'

She found Mrs Zahir enthroned on a folding chair, her face almost hidden behind a vast pair of dark glasses. One of the runners hovered nervously as she held a conversation with a man who was plainly a reporter. She peered at Gaby, who realized that her appearance was being assessed. A sour whiff of hostility rose up from the chair. Mrs Zahir finished the interview, shooed the man away, and snapped open her phone.

'What pretty shoes,' she said.

'Thank you. What a pretty top.'

The atmosphere of malice was complete.

Gabriella waited while Mrs Zahir had a conversation with some kind of astrologer about the placement of her chair in relation to a nearby spotlight. She was concerned that the radiation was disrupting her connection to the healing energies of the universe. Ought she to move? The answer appeared to be yes, and the runner was duly instructed to shift the chair. Safely repositioned two metres to the left, she turned her attention to Gaby, who explained what she wanted. After a ritual raising of difficulties, a phone call was eventually put through to Leela on the battlements. Yes, she was willing to talk to the press. Yes, in a group. Photos. All fine. Gaby set off to spread the good news.

She looked into the souvenir shop, tightly packed with kilted teddybears, tins of shortbread and books of soft-focus pictures.

There were Glencoe Massacre board games and kits from which you could build a small cardboard croft. There was a cuddly midge. The best location for a press conference would clearly be the snackbar. She borrowed one of the runners, told him to set out a table and went off to procure a microphone.

An hour later things had got completely out of hand.

One by one the vehicles had turned into the car park, ten, fifteen, twenty of them – outside-broadcast vans, taxis shared by squabbling newspaper people. They were from Taipei and Moscow and Frankfurt and LA. They had been told to get here as quickly as they could. The press pack, more or less manageable before, now numbered nearly 200. Backed into a corner by a jostling crowd who all had questions, special requirements and reasons for demanding priority over the others, Gaby found herself simultaneously trying to move the conference to the hotel and call her office for support. Finally she grabbed a particularly irritating tabloid reporter by the lapels and asked her what the hell they were all doing there.

'Yes, that's right,' she told Dan Bridgeman a few minutes later. 'There's a tape. Of the terrorist. No, I don't know what he's saying, but apparently it's a message to her.'

By this time filming was impossible. Leela had fled inside the castle. Rocky was throwing a fit, screaming at anyone who came into range to clear his set. Gaby found that if she retreated behind the snackbar counter it was at least possible to limit the number of people who could get at her. Unhelpfully, Iqbal forced his way through and started to berate her for losing control of the situation. She did her best to be polite. Outside, the production manager failed to stop a pair of photographers rushing the bridge on to the island, and a brief fistfight took place between some riggers and a Portuguese news crew who had moved a reflector.

Standing at the counter facing the mêlée, Gaby felt like she was working the Saturday-night shift at the bar in hell. Miss *Film Buzz* was trying to attract her attention, waving and smiling ingratiatingly. From somewhere the woman had acquired a tam-o'-shanter hat, which perched in her hair like a Black Watch bird's-nest. Through the window Gaby caught a momentary glimpse of Rajiv

Rana, surrounded by a group of Asian teens. They seemed to be trying to remove his shirt.

Finally she made a break for it, telling anyone who caught on to her clothing that the press conference would now take place at the Clansman's Lodge Hotel. She found Rob D. and growled at him to turn round one of the production vans, ready for a getaway. They managed to bundle Leela inside before being spotted, but Rob still had to inch his way on to the main road through a crowd of people holding cameras up to the windows and tapping on the glass.

Flash and shutterwhine. Leela sinking down in her seat. Her mother grinning and making clipped little royal waves at the lenses.

At the hotel, the manager bolted the doors. On the front lawn a line of TV reporters set up for pieces to camera, using the lake as a backdrop. Gaby took phone calls and tried to get a copy of the terrorist's tape.

'We need to see it before we can do anything . . . No, I'm not going to promise you that, but it's in your interests because nothing's going to happen until we see it . . . yes . . . yes . . .'

Eventually one of the cameramen took pity on her and posted a VHS through the letterbox. The production team crowded into Iqbal's suite and closed the door. With the curtains closed and twenty people inside, the heat was stifling. At first Leela did not want to watch. 'I've seen it,' she said. Then she gave in and sat down cross-legged at the end of the bed, holding her mother's hand. Vivek put the tape into the machine and pressed play.

A gaunt Indian face appeared on the screen. A hand reached forward to adjust the frame. The quality of the image was low, but Gaby could see he wore glasses and was quite young, in his early twenties perhaps. He was hunched in his seat, knees drawn up towards his chest. It was impossible to tell where he was located. Interior. An apartment?

He didn't look much like an international terrorist.

'This is personally for Miss Leela Zahir,' he began. His voice was thin and uncertain. 'Anyone else watching this who is fortunate enough to know her, please would you pass it on? It is important. So, um, thank you, Miss Zahir, for your attention. I hope it reaches you because something might happen to prevent me explaining in person and I want you to know how sorry I am. Of course I don't claim responsibility for everything bad in the – sorry, forget that. I know I have associated your good name with – oh, I should say first that my own name is Arjun Mehta. I grew up in New Delhi but I am presently NRI in America. Sorry. I am doing all this in the wrong order. I want to say first, before everything, ever since your first movie I have been such a big fan of yours. I saw *Naughty Naughty, Lovely Lovely* eight times and of course I saw all the others also, most of them more than three but less than seven times. You are my heroine. You are the kind of girl I would like to – in my dreams only of course – I'm not – I'm only – I mean, all this must sound strange, well – crazy really, to you. I'm not crazy. My online poll scores indicate not. And I'm not a terrorist. Oh, this is going badly. I'm sorry. That's what I want to say. I'm so sorry. I never wanted to hurt you, because you mean everything to me. But I was going to lose my job. I made a bad decision. Virugenix is a top international company, and all I wanted was a chance to show my capabilities and instead they told me I would lose my job and Darryl Gant, who is head of Ghostbusters and if you ask me a very difficult man, an angry man, Darryl Gant wouldn't listen. How could I tell him? If I lose this job, I have to go back to my parents in disgrace. Although of course I'm a much bigger disgrace now. What will happen to them? And my sister also, who is going to marry this fool of a Bengali and run off to Australia. I tried to tell him. I offered to work for nothing. But they still said I have to go because of first in and first out and being foreign national and all. I meant to cause a little disruption, just a small problem, because then I could step in and solve it and be the hero. But instead I am here and they are calling me terrorist and FBI most wanted and I'm scared, Miss Zahir. I feel I can tell you this. You're an understanding person. It shows in your eyes, especially in *Home of the Heart*. You know what I'm talking about because you are sensitive and also beautiful, this I can tell from your performance. I used your pictures and your songs without permission because they are irresistible and – and I'm sorry. That's all really.'

He reached forward and switched off the camera. The screen

went blank, then started showing old news footage, material the journalist had dubbed over when copying the tape. Everyone in the room started talking at once. He was damaging the film industry, this sisterfucker, besmirching the image of India. The maniac. The *pervert*. To Gaby the speech seemed sad, pathetic even. The boy had the haunted face of someone who knows his link to the world is extremely tenuous.

The only person who had said nothing was Leela Zahir. She was still staring at the screen, watching tanks move through a Middle Eastern town. She looked as if she were about to cry. Feeling someone watching her, she glanced up and managed a forced little smile. Gaby found it hard to know what was more depressing, the boy on the tape or this girl, this famous movie star who was so love-starved that some weird fan's devotion could touch her like this. Suddenly her situation was obvious. What kind of a life did she have, shackled to that bitch of a mother, shoved around by this team of idiots?

'He looks quite sweet,' she said tentatively.

Gaby shrugged and pretended to do something with her phone.

As the arguments progressed, Leela announced that she was feeling overcome, and asked her mother if she could go to her room. As she scuttled out, hiding behind her hair, she briefly took Gaby's hand and squeezed it. Gaby felt a sinking sensation in her stomach, the sensation she always felt when someone made an emotional demand on her. Oh, God, the girl wasn't going to drag her into her mess, was she?

Iqbal ordered most of the crew out of the room. Gaby sat down on the bed but took no part in the discussion, which was mostly conducted in Hindi. Through it all, Rajiv Rana, still in the torn remains of his costume, paced up and down by the window, murmuring, 'Shit, oh shit.' 'Salim-bhai,' he burst out at one point, 'you must tell Baba none of this is my fault, OK?' At the end Iqbal told her what had been decided. 'We will,' he said, 'be releasing immediate press statement. Leela Zahir pleads with the terrorist to give up to proper authorities forthwith and if he is her true fan to stop using her pictures to damage international commerce. He is copyright infringer and criminal and must be giving up right now.'

'With respect,' said Gaby, 'you've employed me as a press officer, which means that perhaps my opinion on this would be of some use?'

'Please, this is no time for insubordination. Mrs Zahir will write the words and you will read it out – unless girl is willing, for once. Go and tell them outside we will have the statement in one hour and afterwards they will please to disperse.'

Gaby was too astonished by the way the man was treating her to be properly angry. Without a word she left the room, went back to her own and locked the door. Then for the first time in as long as she could remember she started to cry. She allowed herself five minutes, then took a series of deep breaths and went into the bathroom to repair her make-up.

Some time later Mrs Zahir caught up with her in the bar and handed her a piece of hotel stationery. She had changed and was now wearing an understated late-afternoon ensemble incorporating patent-leather boots and a top with an appliqué elephant picked out in gold on the front. Her eyes were unnaturally bright, her face grim. There was a red mark on her cheek, as if someone had slapped her.

'Leela is too fatigued to speak to her public,' she snapped. 'However, I think this captures the tone.'

Written on the paper in large faltering loops of purple biro was a press statement. At least that's what Gaby supposed it was. The grammar and spelling were appalling. It made very little sense.

'You don't seriously intend to release this to the media, do you?'

'What did you say?' smiled Mrs Zahir sweetly. 'You have such a strong accent, my dear. It is sometimes hard to understand you.'

'*I* have a strong accent?'

Mrs Zahir was peeping through the curtains at the mayhem on the front lawn. 'What? Yes, you sound foreign. Now if you give me the paper back, I will go and speak to the international press.' She put an emphasis on the first syllable of 'international', drawing it out so far that the mob of reporters waiting outside seemed to take on the luxurious allure of a bubble bath or a box of chocolates.

'You?' spluttered Gaby.

'Darling,' said Mrs Zahir, with the weary finality of a matador dispatching a sickly bull, 'though I'm not saying you couldn't be pretty if you made an effort, you don't have the necessary *presence* for this kind of public appearance. You should really think about brightening yourself up a little. It would probably help you in your work.'

Gaby found herself spitting swear words at the woman's departing back. Mrs Zahir strode through reception, batting a hand at a set of mounted stag's antlers which got mixed up in her hair. She drew the bolt on the main door, swung it open and announced herself to the world outside.

'Listen to me,' she instructed it in a ringing tone. 'I am Faiza Zahir. The mother.'

There was a pause, then the flashguns started firing, bathing her in epileptic sparkle. Absurdly she started to wave. Gaby stamped upstairs to her room and slammed the door. To hell with this, she thought. To hell with their film and to hell with Scotland. She was going back to London.

But first she was going to bed. She shut the curtains, dumped her clothes in a puddle on the floor and crawled under the covers. After a while she switched on the TV and spent a desultory hour channel-hopping between episodes of *Friends* and the local news, which seemed to consist entirely of arguments about fish. Finally she took an airline mask and a pair of earplugs from her bag and determined to shut out the world for as long as possible. Certain she had some Valium somewhere, she got up again and squatted on the bathroom floor with the contents of her upturned washbag in front of her. She was in luck. Thirty milligrams later she returned to bed and stretched out.

The next thing she knew it was dark, her mouth was parched, and there was an insistent buzzing sound in her right ear. The sound resolved itself into a ringing telephone, which cut off as she groped for it, leaving her in a state of semi-conscious confusion. She had just retreated back into sleep when someone knocked on her door, calling out her name.

'Who is it?' she croaked.

'It's Davey from front desk, Miss Caro.'

'Go away.'

'Could you open the door?'
'I said go away.'
'Miss Caro?'
Finally, she wrapped a kimono round herself and asked the embarrassed night clerk what he wanted. There was a package for her. No, he couldn't have kept it until morning because the courier needed her signature. He was sorry to wake her. She shut the door in his face.
Looking at her alarm clock, she saw it was 1 a.m. She had slept for about five hours. Grumpily she padded downstairs in her bare feet, signed for the package, came back and threw herself down on her bed. When she saw Guy's address on the waybill, her mood worsened. She tore off the wrapping and opened the box.
The collar was beautiful. Beautiful and tacky and slightly sad. For a moment she almost felt affection for Guy, for his absurd conviction that money could make everything all right. Then she saw the note.

Impressed? xG

And that put the awfulness of her life into perspective. She had spent three years with this man. He had nothing to say to her.
The old feeling came surging back, the need to break and run. She would leave here tomorrow. Then she would leave London and leave Guy. Start again. She was thinking about planes and packing when there was another knock on her door. She ignored it, but the person on the other side carried on hammering.
She swung it open and found Rajiv Rana. He looked dishevelled.
'You? Don't think for a moment you're coming in. You can go to hell, you arrogant bastard.'
'Is she with you?'
'What are you talking about? Go and pick on one of the dancers if you're feeling horny.'
'She's gone,' he said. 'Is she with you?'
'Who's gone?'
'Her. Leela. There's no one in her room.'

'She's probably out taking a walk. She goes to smoke by the lake. Why are you bothering me with this?'

She slammed the door. But all the same she went to the window. There was the castle, floating like a mirage over the lake. There was the mournful plantation of pine trees. The lawn stretched away into the darkness.

In the EU quarter of Brussels, like all areas devoted to government and administration, the physical has been ruthlessly subordinated to the immaterial, to the exigencies of language. It is a zone of discreet office spaces and muted parks, of affluence without ostentation, expenditure without visible waste. Diplomats from 160 embassies mingle with representatives of 120 governmental organizations and 1,400 different NGOs, all seeking to perfect the most modern of European arts: the exercise of control without the display of power.

Accordingly there is no hint of fascist grandiosity in the EU quarter, though a trace of unhappy classicism remains in its architecture and oddly also in the marmoreal atmosphere which pervades life here at the heart of the new Europe. The restrained anonymity of the built environment is the outward manifestation of something deeper, which has its origin in the Union's noble but somehow sinister aim of a final consensus, a termination to the Continent's brutal Dionysiac history.

Regulations, statistics, directives and action plans; in the EU quarter language is order and with order comes violence, coded into the harsh planes of the Berlaymont Building, the uniforms of the bored police on security detail outside parliament. It is a violence that has been coated in language, incrementally surrounded and domesticated by it, until it has taken on the soft hue and low light of the rest of the European project. Discreet violence, like surveilled privacy and humanitarian war. Typically European paradoxes.

Guy was driven at speed down the Rue de la Loi. The passenger seat of Yves's Porsche smelled of leather and the admiration of his peers. 'I am *so* stoked,' said Yves, and at the wheel of his yellow car with the streetlights shining on his face he looked like the future in human form. Guy wondered when he had first learned this American phrase, during what teen movie or holiday to Florida he had heard it and filed it away for use in conversation.

'Me too,' Guy said. He meant it. He had taken all the rest of the coke before he got on the plane. His heart felt like it was about to punch through his chest wall.

They parked the car on the street and made their way into the hall of a nineteenth-century townhouse which had been turned into a boutique hotel. The redesign, Yves announced, was the work of a revolutionary. Guy was not sure if this meant the designer was political or just very good at designing things. The lobby was certainly extreme, in an understated way. The walls seemed to glow with a soft internal luminescence, and the staff wore long white tunics, like representatives of a benevolent higher civilization in a science-fiction movie.

The restaurant, Séraphim, was set under a glass canopy on the roof. The maître d' greeted them beside a bust of a heavily bearded man. Guy looked at King Leopold II. King Leopold looked back at Guy, who checked his tie to see if it was straight. He was sweating.

Elegant waiters floated between tables occupied by groups of quietly conversing people. The patrons, men and women, wore the charcoal-greys and navy-blues of trust and probity, a visual field of sober business clothing broken very occasionally by a patterned tie or piece of silver jewellery. A more astute observer than Guy might have noticed the indecipherable quality of these small personal touches, as if instead of being the products of genuine quirks of taste or outlook their function was merely ritual, gestures of support for the idea of individuality rather than examples of its practice.

They were shown to a table by the window. Director Becker and Signor Bocca were already waiting. Introductions were made, and the Director, a trim blonde woman in her early forties, broke the news that Gunnar Nilsson would not be able to make the dinner. Guy breathed hard and flashed smiles at Becker and the gaunt-faced Italian beside her. He tried not to view Nilsson's absence as a setback. This thing was just as much her baby, really. She would, she said, be chairing the pitch meeting. Which was something, at least. He tried to will himself to stop sweating. His shirt was plastered to his back.

Yves started to make small talk about a production of *Aida* he and the Director had both attended in Verona. In deference to Guy he spoke English, constructing elaborate sentences which the Director matched, clause for clause, the two of them performing a kind of second-language fencing match. Bocca, whom the topic was obviously intended to draw in, stared silently at his hands. He had placed them palms down on the white tablecloth and was assiduously examining his long fingers, as if deciding which of them to sever first.

'Tell me about your work,' Guy asked him.

'Informatics,' said Bocca, without looking up.

'Really,' said Guy, feeling the quest for connection was already hopeless. Bocca shot him a sardonic look.

'The informatic dimension is central to the whole harmonization project,' offered Director Becker, reaching forward and smiling at Guy, who smiled gratefully back. He found himself wondering what it would be like to go to bed with her.

'The question of the border is a question of information,' remarked Bocca. Guy was not certain what he meant. It sounded like a quote.

'Naturally,' said Yves.

'Naturally,' agreed Guy, following his lead. He was taken aback when Bocca looked up from his hands. 'You feel this also?' he asked.

'Very strongly,' said Guy, trying not to grind his teeth. The waiter arrived to take a drinks order and left again, as Bocca, with the sudden intensity of a man who feels he may finally have found a friend in the world, fixed Guy and Yves with a hopeful gaze and began to discourse on the centrality of information technology to a modern customs and immigration regime.

'I believe,' he said with subdued passion, 'it is the most important tool we have. A common European border authority must have common information collection and retrieval. This much is obvious. Otherwise you find some terrorist or economic migrant in one country and lose him again when he crosses into another. Any proposal for the presentation of our border police must incorporate the information dimension.' He tapped the table to make his point. The waiter returned with a bottle of wine, which Bocca tasted, staring into his glass as if it were a *clandestino* trying to get work in his mouth.

Guy gulped his wine, making positive noises as Bocca described the enormous value of the Community's Schengen Information System in the control of illegal migration. 'The problem with these people is they lie, they destroy their papers. You have no way of knowing who they are. They say they're from a war zone but actually all they want is to take a job from a citizen. But if you combine the database with biometrics, you can cut through everything. No more lies.' He illustrated his point with a slicing clap of the hands, sitting back in his chair with an air of finality.

'You are so right,' said Guy, pouring himself a second glass. 'And we've picked up on that aspect of PEBA's role with the creative work we've done at *Tomorrow**.'

'Really?' said Becker.

She was smiling at him again. How old was she? Fifty? Forty-five? He took another swig of wine. 'Really. What my team has come to realize is that in the twenty-first century the border is not just a line on the earth any more. It's so much more than that. It's about status. It's about opportunity. Sure, you're either inside or outside, but you can be on the inside and still be outside, right? Or on the outside looking in. Anyway, like we say in one of our slides, "The border is everywhere." "The border", and this is key, "is in your mind." Obviously from a marketing point of view a mental border is a plus, because a mental border is a value and a value is something we can promote.'

'I'm glad you see things in this light,' said Director Becker, who looked (it occurred to Guy) like a woman who made good use of her gym membership. 'This youth perspective I like very much. We have a difficult time teaching citizenship to the young.'

'Oh, certainly,' agreed Guy. 'Citizenship is about being one of the gang, or as we like to say at *Tomorrow**, "in with the in crowd".

As everyone knows, being in the in crowd is a question of attitude and at *Tomorrow**, that's our bread and butter.'

The conversation was going his way.

Director Becker started on a convoluted explanation of the genesis of PEBA, which unit of which directorate had supplied personnel for which working group, which interested parties had sent observers, which blocs within parliament had lobbied for which changes in the legislative framework. Guy, who had no appetite, poked a fork into his carpaccio of tuna and tried to keep his mind on what she was saying. It was not easy. The fish glistened suggestively, and all at once, like football fans crowding on to a tube train, a series of graphic images flooded his head. Every one of them (for reasons he knew he ought to be ashamed of) involved Director Becker in the kind of sensibly cut blue swimming costume once worn by girls from his sister school in Gloucestershire. He had spent a lot of time examining those costumes during joint sports days. They would turn from navy-blue to black when they got wet.

He had to get a grip.

'. . . towards the establishment of a common border authority, which, while allowing initially for member states to diverge in certain details of their individual policies . . .'

'That's right,' he said. 'Yeah.'

'I beg your pardon?'

'Sorry, Monika. Carry on.'

'OK. Well, so far progress has been good, and we're actually at the stage of implementing joint actions under the PEBA banner, so of course the incentive is now there to move towards a common look and feel to overlay the policy harmonization.'

'Which is where we come in,' remarked Yves. Guy gave up on the tuna. He put his knife and fork down on his plate and poured himself more wine.

'I must tell you a secret,' said Bocca conspiratorially. 'Monika is being coy about the PEBA implementation. You know why Gunnar couldn't make it? Officially he's in Helsinki for the expansion conference' – here he paused and looked about with exaggerated caution – 'but in reality it's even more exciting than that. Today is the launch of Operation Atomium. He's in Paris, watching it from the police control centre.' He slapped the table triumphantly, like a debater who had just made a telling point.

Guy blocked out thoughts of towel-flicking and backstroke and framed his face into an expression of interest. Whatever Bocca was on about, it certainly made him happy, and if it made him happy it was important to the pitch.

'Operation – ?'

'Atomium.' Director Becker laughed, tossing her hair girlishly. 'It's just one of those silly boy's names policemen give their projects. Though it is an important development, this is true. And tonight is an important night. Since Signor Bocca –'

'Please Monika, Gianni.'

'Since Gianni has let the cats out of the sack, I think I can tell you.' She wagged a finger severely at Yves and Guy. 'You will not talk to the press?'

They put on grave expressions, to demonstrate that such a thing would be unthinkable.

'Well,' she carried on, 'this is actually the name of the first coordinated PEBA action, which is taking place right now in eight capital cities.'

'What kind of action?'

Bocca pushed his chair back from the table and crossed one leg over the other. He was unrecognizable as the dour man who had sat looking so glumly at the table. He was relaxed, animated. Guy noticed he was wearing pink and blue argyle socks. 'A sweep,' he said, reinforcing the image with his hands. 'A coordinated sweep, aimed at taking 5,000 *sans papiers* off the streets by tomorrow morning. Identify them, process them, and return as high a percentage as possible to their countries of origin within seventy-two hours. All based on common information handling, and taking place under the flag of PEBA. What do you think of that?'

'Wow,' said Guy. It seemed to be the right response.

'It is an emotional moment for Gianni, as you see,' said Becker. 'And for me too. We've tried so hard to make PEBA a reality. And now it is real, a working institution. Not paper any more.'

'We should make a toast,' suggested Yves. He and Becker and Guy and Bocca raised their glasses, and it seemed to Guy that there was a moment of perfect communication between them under the glass dome of the Séraphim, an instant when all channels were miraculously clear.

The main course came, food arranged like cuneiform characters on oversized white plates. Guy found he had ordered more fish. Bocca started to dismember some kind of small bird, a quail perhaps, teasing out tiny gobbets of flesh with the tines of his fork and inserting them one by one into his mouth. His eating had something remorseless about it, something mechanical. Guy had to look away. He spent a period pushing fish and leaves through a squiggle of yellow sauce, then waved the empty wine bottle at a waiter, who floated over and replaced it with a full one. Monika and Yves had moved on to the subject of America.

'We need to take a lesson from them,' she was saying. 'They sell themselves so well through their media. Everything American is the biggest and the best. They tell us this and we believe it, even when it is rubbish, like the cars.'

'Or the food,' added Bocca, crunching a fragile bone between his teeth.

Yves nodded agreement. 'Even the bad things in America are always the worst. Their cities are the biggest, the most polluted, the most dangerous. You tell them how Paris is, they don't believe you. They can't hear it, you know? It is like a religious faith.'

'Or Rome,' said Bocca.

'Or the coffee,' said Guy, who had only been half listening.

'But this is the economic power of Hollywood! It is imperative we compete! Europe needs its own factory for dreaming! Not for vanity. For economic reasons. I have said this to Commissioner Papadopoulos many times. We must have a programme to fund the promotion of positive images of Europe through all media. The cinema, television, *bandes dessinées*, everything. At the moment it is like the Cold War and we are not even fighting.'

'But,' said Bocca, 'there is already good work in these areas.'

'Certainly, but please, Gianni, I don't think classical music and television dramas about the Romans are enough. The promotion of heritage is one thing. We have won this argument. We are the oldest, no contest. It is the youth we must persuade. Hip-hop gangster rappers must drive European cars. They must fire European guns!'

'They do, sometimes,' pointed out Guy.

'This is Guy's area of competence,' Yves reminded her.

'Of course,' she beamed. 'And I'm sure you would have many ideas for this. I recently circulated a document urging the creation and promotion of a Community hero. They have Captain America and Colonel Sanders and so on. What have we? But really, I am going off the point. Culture is of course not my directorate. This is more a hobby. What we came to hear are your ideas for PEBA and instead I am talking so much about these other things. I am very excited by what Yves has told me so far, but it is not so much. I was thinking, can you give us a taste?'

'I'd be delighted,' said Guy, sitting up in his chair. It was the moment he had hoped for. His heart had slowed down to a sustainable level. He was prepared. Under the table was his laptop case, and a folder of samples and hand-outs. Yves looked on encouragingly.

'I think the two things are linked,' he started. 'The idea of promoting Europe, making it seem like a hip place, was a central focus of our thinking at the agency.' He handed out four outline maps of Europe. Across the top was written *Tomorrow*'s continent as well as yesterday's*. 'And of course people's first contact with Europe is usually through its border police.'

'Exactly!' Bocca slammed his hand down on the table, making the glassware jingle like a peal of little bells. One or two people looked up from nearby conversations.

'Gianni,' admonished Monika. 'Please, Guy, continue.'

'Well, we have to promote Europe as somewhere you want to go, but somewhere that's not for everyone. A continent that wants people, but only the best. An exclusive continent. An *upscale* continent. And our big idea is to use the metaphorics of leisure to underscore that message. Here's what I mean.'

He reached into his folder and brought out some keycard blanks. Each had EU blue and gold on one side and the words *Platinum Member* embossed on the other. Becker and Bocca turned them over in their hands.

'Ladies and gentlemen,' Guy announced, with a verbal flourish he had been practising on the plane, 'welcome to Club Europa – the world's VIP room.'

Director Becker was visibly charmed.

'Of course you're familiar with club culture, so you know that being on the right side of the velvet rope makes all the difference to young opinion formers both within the EU and outside. It's a concept they're familiar with. It's one they respect, and we feel it speaks both to the citizen and to the prospective European. It's a question of conveying the message that you should only try to get past our doormen if you're wearing the right kind of clothes, so to speak. We've made a short film to support our pitch.'

'Guy,' said Yves, 'why don't you show them?'

'Now? You want to watch it now? I have it on my hard drive.'

'That would be fabulous,' said Becker. Bocca nodded and made a carry-on gesture.

Guy took his laptop out of its case and laid it on the tablecloth, carefully clearing crumbs and glasses out of the way to make a space. He switched it on, and while they waited for it to start up he passed round his team's sketches for PEBA insignia and uniforms. The border authority's acronym was shown as a blue neon sign, as a pattern of sparkling bulbs, and printed in a variety of seventies disco lettering styles. Shaven-headed male and female immigration officers were depicted wearing headsets and mirror shades, their futuristic black bomber jackets embroidered on the back with a PEBA portcullis logo.

'Very striking,' said Becker. Bocca pointed out that perhaps black shirts were a controversial look.

'We're not wedded to black,' Guy reassured him. 'Blue and gold is another obvious possibility.'

By this time the laptop had started up. It sat on the tablecloth, humming and displaying a whirling Windows screensaver.

'OK,' said Guy. 'I'll just find the file. We call the film *Europe: No Jeans, No Trainers*.' He clicked on the icon. Nothing happened. He clicked again and the screen went blank. Instead of the 'DV odyssey through European clubland' put together by his creative team after a punishing transcontinental bender, there was the stuttering sound of a troubled hard drive, a tinny blast of Indian music and a depressingly familiar little dancing figure.

'Shit,' said Guy. 'Please, not now. Oh shit.'

'What's wrong?' asked Monika. She peered across at the screen.

'You have a problem,' noted Bocca.

'Yeah, thanks for pointing that out.'

'Guy,' warned Yves.

'I hope it is not the destructive variant,' said Bocca.

Guy could feel himself slipping into panic. This was supposed to have been sorted. This was supposed to be over. 'Shit,' he said, stabbing the power switch with his finger. 'Shit.'

'Did you see in the news?' Monika asked Yves. 'The man has gone on television. He is some kind of stalker for this actress.'

'Calm down, Guy,' said Yves. 'You have other copies of this data, yes?'

Guy tried to regain some control over himself. This should not have been happening. Not when things were going so well. 'Yes,' he croaked.

'So, you can phone your office.'

'This bloody machine. I swear it's a conspiracy.'

'Maybe we should get some coffee,' suggested Yves.

Monika looked sympathetic. 'Guy, don't worry. The meeting is not until two tomorrow. You can get this film by then.'

Guy looked from one face to the next. They were all smiling, sympathetic. They wanted him to succeed. He felt like a cable that had been stretched too far. He wanted to shout at them, tell them how everything depended on this pitch. His business, his home, his relationship – everything. He wanted to cry. Instead he muttered an excuse and went to the toilet, where he splashed water on his face and locked himself in a cubicle. He sat there for a few minutes, trying to regain some kind of command over himself. Why didn't he have any more coke? That would have helped. Fuck it. Fuck it. Fuck. It.

He punched the cubicle door, as hard as he could.

The pain was excruciating. He thought he might have broken something. Clamping his throbbing hand with his armpit, he swore repeatedly under his breath. When it had receded to the point where he could concentrate on the outside world, he pushed his way out of the cubicle and ran cold water over the injury.

When he got back to the table, Yves caught his eye and made the thumbs-up sign. Someone had powered down the computer and put it away.

'Signor Swift,' Bocca told him, with expansive courtliness, 'please don't worry. These technical things are not important. It is the quality of the ideas that interests us.'

'We have both been most impressed by your presentation,' added Becker. 'You communicate very clearly.'

'Thank you.'

'Of course,' added Bocca, 'it still has to go through a formal procedure, but informally I can say that we have seen several presentations and the quality has been, ah – variable. In my opinion you do not have serious competition.'

'You mean –'

Yves grinned.

'We mean nothing,' said Director Becker. 'This was an informal conversation, and these are private opinions. You should not think a promise has been made.'

'But I loved the keys,' put in Bocca.

'And the logo is super-good.' Becker gave Guy an unambiguous look. 'You are a cool fellow, Mr Guy Swift. Here is my card, if you have any questions before the meeting.'

'Shall we get some coffee?' asked Yves.

'Yeah,' said Guy, surreptitiously massaging his knuckles. 'Coffee. Great.'

Half an hour later they were saying their goodbyes on the street outside the Séraphim. Bocca slapped Guy on the back and promised to lend him a document on the workings of the SIS which he was sure to find fascinating. Director Becker let him know that if there was anything he needed in the short term, she would be up for a few more hours working on some papers.

Feeling drained, he fell into the passenger seat of Yves's car.

'My friend,' said Yves, running a comb through his hair in the rear-view mirror, 'we need a drink.'

Guy looked over at him uncertainly. 'I don't know, Yves. I think I should try to sleep.'

Yves pantomimed incomprehension. 'Don't be stupid. The meeting is not until the afternoon, and the contract is already in your hand. Come on, Guy. Don't be so serious. I know these people. They have to pretend to be cautious, but they love you. That woman wanted you to go with her, I don't know, into a cupboard. Anywhere. She would do whatever you say.'

Guy managed a wan smile. Yves playfully punched him on the shoulder. 'You need to relax. If you feel so tired, look in the glove box. There is something to help.'

'Really?' Guy opened the car's glove compartment. Inside was a small leather-bound case, which unzipped to reveal an antique men's grooming kit and a screwtop phial of white powder. Attached to the cap was a tiny silver spoon. He found himself reappraising Yves.

Ten minutes later the idea of going on for a drink seemed like the best possible idea, the only feasible response to such an outstanding business success. Yves, who had done some reappraising of his own, was of the opinion that an ordinary drink would not suffice for men as world-beating as they. The future rulers of the earth needed a real drink. He gunned the engine and lurched out into the traffic, accelerating past a taxi and heading in the direction of the city centre.

'Relax,' he told Guy again, once they were under way. 'I know a good place.'

The good place was called the New Morning, a club with a frontage of discreet Ionic columns and a red plush entrance hall where they paid a cover charge to enter a large gloomy room with a brightly lit stage at the centre. They took seats at a sunken oval bar which put them at eye level with the crotch of a young dancer, naked but for a pair of shiny PVC boots and a garter into which was tucked a number of neatly folded banknotes. Yves ordered a bottle of vodka which they drank over ice, watching the girl perform an athletic routine, hanging upside down from a pole, sliding on her back across the floor and scissoring her legs in the air.

Yves talked in a constant stream. The business opportunities stemming from the PEBA deal could, he maintained, be enormous. 'Guy,' he urged, 'think about it. The Community has so many activities, so many things that need good presentation. The whole look and feel of immigration, customs, border police – all these things are so old-fashioned at the moment. The uniforms! My God, it's like some twentieth-century bad dream. If you could make it more – more *funky*, instantly it would be so much better, more acceptable to modern people. All the protest they get, all the negativity, most of it is about the *feel* of these things. People don't give a shit about power, not really, not if it looks cool.'

Guy was only half listening. He felt ethereal, light-headed, drugs and alcohol and stress and lack of sleep prising him loose from his body and the place where it sat, propped up on its elbows in front of a glass. A new stripper had come on. She was jerking her body about like a whip, an elevated, almost manic smile on her face. She twirled round the pole in a kind of spastic dance, then threw off her leather jacket and bra to reveal a small but perfect pair of breasts. Her body glowed blue-white under the lights, and he thought, fuck Gabriella. Fuck that bitch. This is a woman. The real thing.

The dancer noticed the way he was looking at her and dipped low, crawling towards him on all fours. Yves laughed, urging him to give her some money. He fumbled in his wallet and pulled out a banknote, which he tucked into the top of one of her boots. In response she kicked her legs and ground her hips and licked her tongue round her mouth like a cat. Guy watched the crease of skin where her thighs met her buttocks, the outline of her ribs as she put her arms over her head. At last she unclipped her knickers and he held his breath at the sight of the little vee of pale skin that framed her cunt.

'Come on.' Yves was tugging at him. 'Time for more.' Guy half fell off the stool and followed him in the direction of the toilets. A doorman barged after them into the Gents', but Yves palmed him €500 and instead of throwing them out he stood guard while they wedged themselves into a cubicle and did hits of Yves's coke.

Yves was unrecognizable as the suave venture capitalist of daytime meetings at Transcendenta. His hair had fallen over his face. His shirt collar was undone, and his silk tie hung in a bedraggled noose round his neck. He looked wasted. He looked almost *British*. 'You,' Guy told him, 'are fucking amazing. You are the man.'

'No, *you* are amazing. This is so great, you know. You're going to get so much work from those people. The way that Becker was looking at you, I thought she would jump over the table.'

'You know what? I thought she was all right.'

'All right?'

'You know. Fit. Sexy.'

First Yves started to snigger, then Guy. The two of them clung on to each other, laughing so hard they almost tipped the drugs into the toilet bowl. Physical closeness put Guy into a confessional mood.

'You know, Yves, if this hadn't worked I'd be fucked. I mean really fucked. As it is, I don't know if my fucking girlfriend has left me, or what the fuck is going on. But at least now I know you're on my side. I've been thinking you were going to pull the plug.'

Yves looked at him and cracked a woozy smile. 'That's funny. You want to know a secret? I need this deal to work as badly as you. This fucking market is so down, I can't tell you. All these technology companies we funded? They turned to shit. Every one. And if we don't make some money soon I'm going to be fucked too. What do you think of that?'

'Really?'

'Really. Why do you think I'm here? Your fucking company *has* to work. My ass is on the line, the same as yours.'

They looked at each other and started to laugh again. Guy thought he might be sick. The doorman banged impatiently on the cubicle door.

'Time to go, I think,' drawled Yves.

They stumbled back out into the club. Guy slumped on to his stool. He looked at his watch. It was past two. Yves put an arm round his shoulder, leaning on him heavily.

'It's too fucking bad about your girlfriend.'

'Sure.'

'But you're with Yves Ballard and your company is going to be a lean machine and you got a new client and you're the tomorrow man, right?'

'Right.'

'So now you got another girlfriend.' Yves jerked a thumb behind him. Two of the dancers were hovering in the shadows, smoking cigarettes and whispering to each other.

'Take whichever you like.'

'But –'

'Don't worry. It's all fixed. They all do a little work, you know, on the side. The manager takes a cut. It's that kind of place.'

'It's late, Yves.'

'Don't be a pussy. You English, you're all such fucking pussies. Come on. You don't have to spend the night with her. Just let her show you a good time for an hour, then kick her out the door. Come on, I already paid.'

'You did?'

'Sure. Don't tell me I don't look after my investments.'

Guy looked at the two women. There she was, the one he'd stared at, her long permed hair tied up, dressed now in a short white dress and high-heeled sandals. Even with her clothes on she was exciting. The prospect of going home with her was a little daunting.

'What's your name?' he asked.

'Irina,' she said in a flat Eastern European accent. He felt a twinge of misgiving. Not a customer-service voice. But sexy, potentially.

'So, all settled?' asked Yves. 'I see you tomorrow at the hotel.' He shook Guy's hand and left the club, leaning on the other girl for support. Guy realized Yves was even more wasted than he was. He wondered if he was going to get into his car.

Irina asked where they were going. Guy had a vision of trying to sneak her through the lobby of his hotel. He wasn't sure it was a sensible idea.

'Um, I'm not sure. Do you know somewhere?'

'Sure,' she said. 'Come.'

Outside they found a taxi. Irina gave an address and they started off, the driver examining them in the rear-view mirror. They drove away from the city centre and the girl let a hand fall casually into

Guy's lap, squeezing experimentally. It was more an appraisal than a caress, the gesture of a housewife at a fruit stall. He couldn't feel anything. His head was bubbling with pornographic fantasies, but they were all somehow disconnected from his body. He felt anaesthetized, worn out. A hard-on would require an effort of will.

Relax, Guy, he told himself. Yves was right. It was a bit of fun. But he looked out of the window at a street of darkened houses and wondered uneasily where they were going. It was three in the morning. They were heading out into the suburbs.

The border between the United States and Mexico is one of the most tightly controlled in the world. From Brownsville, Texas, to the California coast it runs for 2,000 miles, monitored by armed patrols equipped with thermal-imaging cameras and remote-movement sensors, portable X-ray devices, GPS optics, satellite maps and other technologies intended to prevent (or at least minimize) the unauthorized crossing of goods, vehicles and people. At San Ysidro, just south of San Diego, twenty-four lanes of traffic funnel into an artful system of concrete barriers designed to prevent vehicles turning or reversing as their details are checked against databases and trained dogs are encouraged by their handlers to sniff their wheel arches.

On the north side of the border is an outlet mall, where, under red-tiled roofs with fake adobe façades, piles of discount jeans and sports shoes are sold by sleepy staff who look out all day over the parking lot, hoping and dreaming about whatever you hope and dream about if you are administrating the disposal of surplus clothing and footwear at the very edge of America.

Arjun arrived on the morning shoppers' shuttle, which made the journey from downtown San Diego in twenty minutes. It felt too quick. He needed more time to prepare. He stood for a while on a road bridge over the freeway, watching the vehicles inch forward towards the barriers, then meandered back into the mall, stopping to look in the window of a shoe store. Was it safe just to stroll out of America? That's what all the other people were doing. They were just walking into Mexico. Surely that was too easy. Shouldn't he take precautions?

He decided on a disguise. The unit next to the shoe store sold sunglasses, so he bought a pair and put them on. A few minutes later, catching sight of himself in the plate glass of Laura Ashley, he stopped to bite off the tag. Then he carried on, aimlessly wandering from Nautica to Levis to Banana Republic.

His first sight of Mexico had scared him. Beyond the parking lots and freight yards on the US side was a wide concrete river channel. Beyond that was a range of low hills clustered with flat-roofed cinderblock buildings. The air was hazy, scented with oil fumes and sewage. Over the sullen-looking city on the far side of the river, a giant Mexican flag hung limply on a tall pole. When Arjun saw the flag, the forlorn droop of it against the yellow-grey sky, he found he no longer knew which frightened him more: the possibility that he would be captured or the possibility he would not. For days the border had acted as the outer limit of his imagination. Beyond it were abstractions: Escape, Freedom, The Future. Now the future had a landscape, a mess of flat roofs strung with telephone and electrical wires, the store signs and billboards written in a language he did not understand. What kind of a life could he have over there?

The place on the other side of the river had a hopeless quality, not at all like the Mexico portrayed in cowboy movies. Where were the cacti, the white-clad peasants with the big hats? He browsed neurotically through racks of souvenir t-shirts. Their humorous slogans (*one tequila, two tequila, three tequila, floor!*) passed through his mind without leaving a trace. As he picked up snow globes and methodically sorted through postcards he had no intention of buying, his body started to send out contradictory signals, most of them related in some way to physical distress. He felt hot and cold simultaneously. Under the arms of his pink polo shirt (the one he had been wearing for the previous seventy-two hours) there were large circles of sweat. He decided to drink coffee. Coffee, in his experience, was a drink with negentropic properties.

Slang terms for coffee: java, a cup of joe. In his first weeks in America, he had said these words to the mirror. Later he had carried his plastic beaker to work like a runner with the Olympic torch. He wished he still had that cup. As he stood outside Starbucks, a paper cup heating his hand, he conjured up a soothing image of a darkened room and a TV set. A TV not tuned to a news channel.

A TV showing an easy-to-follow narrative fiction in which he was not the central character. Preferably with romance and songs. And a happy ending.

A block behind the San Ysidro Factory Outlet Center was the Riverside Motel. Carrying his coffee in one hand and his bag in the other, Arjun crossed the road and checked in, taking a room on the second floor with a south-facing balcony. The two teenage boys who had followed him all the way from San Diego watched from the parking lot as he briefly walked out on to it to look at the view. He took a sip of coffee, then went back inside, closed the curtains and stepped into legend.

Noise

'We want to abolish the unknown,' writes one Leela researcher. It is a common enough desire. As humans, we want to know what is lurking outside our perimeter, beyond our flickering circle of firelight. We have built lenses and Geiger counters and mass spectrometers and solar probes and listening stations on remote Antarctic islands. We have drenched the world in information in the hope that the unknown will finally and definitively go away. But information is not the same as knowledge. To extract one from the other, you must, as the word suggests, inform. You must transmit. Perfect information is sometimes defined as a signal transmitted from a sender to a receiver without loss, without the introduction of the smallest uncertainty or confusion.

In the real world, however, there is always noise.

Since 1965 the Russian Academy of Sciences has published a journal called *Problems of Information Transmission*. It is, insofar as it is possible for a scientific publication (even a Russian one) to convey an emotional tone, a melancholy read. Threaded through recondite papers on Markov Chains and Hamming Spaces and binary Goppa codes and multivariate Poisson flow is a vocabulary of imperfection, of error correction and density estimation, of signals with unknown appearance and disappearance times, of indefinite knowledge and losses due to entropy. Sparse vectors are glimpsed through a haze of Gaussian white noise. Certainty backslides into probability. Information transmission, it emerges, is about doing the best you can.

In media dissections of the impact of the Leela variant viruses, the period when there was most noise in the global system has come to be known as Greyday. Greyday certainly lasted more than a day and was only grey in the most inexact and metaphorical sense, which means the person who invented the term was probably not an engineer. Nevertheless, the name captures a certain cybernetic gloom that hung about the time, the communal depression of network administrators yearning for perfection while faced with appalling losses, drop-outs, crashes and absences of every kind.

Greyday was an informational disaster, a holocaust of bits. A number of major networks went down simultaneously, dealing with such things as mobile telephony, airline reservations, transatlantic email traffic and automated-teller machines. The details of those events are in the public domain. Other systems were undoubtedly affected, but their military, corporate or governmental owners have been unwilling to discuss in public what may or may not have happened. As for the number of smaller cases, the problem becomes one of counting. Home computers? Individuals? Do you know anyone whom Leela did not touch in some way?

Leela's noise passed effortlessly out of the networks into the world of things. Objects got lost: a van carrying armaments from a depot in Belgrade; a newly authenticated Rembrandt. Money in all sorts of physical forms dropped out of sight, but also money in its essence, which is to say that on Greyday a certain amount of money simply *ceased to exist*. This is a complicated claim. Money tends to virtuality. It hovers about in the form of promises and conditionalities, lying latent in the minds of market technicians until actualized through confidence, central bank fiat or a particularly long lunch. It is hard, in the end, to judge whether some of the money which did not exist after Greyday actually existed before it. Had Greyday not happened, perhaps a certain amount of unborn money might have come into the world. We cannot be certain. We do know that money disappeared, but how much and where it went are questions to which the market makers don't really want an answer. Better, they say, to forget about it. Better to move on, dream up more.

So Greyday names a moment of maximal uncertainty, a time of peaking doubt. We have records of events which may not have taken place. Other events took place but left no record. All that can be said with honesty is that afterwards there were absences, gaps which have never been filled.

Empty hotel rooms, for example. Three rooms whose occupants are no longer there. When a person disappears, the objects they leave behind can be almost unbearable in their muteness. The more personal they are, the more they seem to underline the absence of their owner. The chambermaid at the four-star Hotel Ascension in Brussels turns down the bed, leaves on the pillow a chocolate and a voucher for a complimentary shoe-shine. On the dressing table is a litter of British coins, taxi receipts and other small items. Walkman headphones. An electrical adaptor. She hangs the suit-carrier in the cupboard and moves the washbag from the top of the television into the bathroom. The passport on the bedside table she does not touch. The maid working the morning shift receives no response to her knock. She enters to find everything exactly as her colleague left it. The bed has not been slept in. The toothbrush is dry. At lunchtime, the management take a call from a business associate of the occupier. He has failed to keep an appointment. Ten minutes later he calls again. At two, the hotel bills the absent businessman for an extra night. The police are not called until the following morning, by which time it is clear that something untoward has happened to Guy Swift.

A room upstairs at the Clansman's Lodge Hotel in Scotland. One of the better ones, with a view over the garden and the loch. A mess of chintz and lace and rose-patterned wallpaper. A bowl of pot-pourri on the nightstand and a white plastic drinks-maker on the dresser, next to a little basket containing filters, creamer and vacuum-packed sachets of coffee. Most of her things are there, the expensive Banarsi saris, the make-up bags, the rows of spray cans and bottles in the bathroom. She has left a little portable DVD player and a stack of unwatched discs, still in a duty-free bag. She has left the giant stuffed monkey someone bought her as a get-well present. Under the bed is an empty cigarette packet and a torn-up copy of the shooting script, but Leela Zahir herself is not there. Her mother, sedated and incoherent, manages to communicate that she thinks some clothes have gone. Also her daughter's laptop. Iqbal is holding Leela's passport, but it is possible she has another. The police are reassuring. In rural Scotland, an Indian girl will not be able to travel far without attracting attention.

Events at the Riverside Motel in San Ysidro are more violent. Acting on information provided by a member of the public, the FBI has traced a man on their most-wanted list to a room on one of the upper floors. Though the suspect is not believed to be armed, he has known militant connections and the team assembled at the FBI field office in San Diego includes staff from the Joint Terrorism Task Force. Written orders have been received confirming the authorization of maximum force. Weapons specialists from the police, the FBI and the Bureau of Alcohol, Tobacco and Firearms draw equipment from stores and under the direction of a senior officer from the San Diego Police the team proceeds at speed to the named location. A command post is established in a nearby parking lot, and a discreet perimeter is set up around the motel, a priority being not to cause panic among shoppers at the outlet mall. Staff are evacuated from the area before the team moves in.

Access to Room 206 is swift and brutal. The door gives way immediately under the impact of a 35-pound close-quarter battle ram. Agents shout a warning to the occupant, who does not respond. Shots are fired. The occupant goes down. An ambulance is called and arrives quickly, but the victim is pronounced dead at the scene. Later the corpse is transferred to a morgue in San Diego. Unfortunately for the arresting team, when examined it turns out to be not Arjun Mehta, suspected terrorist and subject of a federal warrant, but an unidentified South-East Asian teenager. The dead boy is found to be carrying a cheap .22 handgun.

Within minutes local news media is on the scene. The officer who fired is taken back to the field office for debriefing and psychological assessment, while the Riverside Motel is cordoned off and a series of photographs of the room are taken, photographs which will rapidly leak out on to the internet and spawn detailed speculation about (among other things) the brands of packaging in the waste-paper basket, the crumpled Oakland Raiders shirt in the bathroom. Some information trickles out to the media. The boy's name was Kim Sun Hong, a high-school student from San

Diego. The gun was of a type sold for $7.98 in certain out-of-state gun stores. What he was doing in Arjun Mehta's room remains, for the moment, a mystery.

Though dramatic, the disappearances of Guy Swift, Arjun Mehta and Leela Zahir are not unique. They form part of a much larger pattern of virus-related disturbance: on Greyday there was heavy traffic across the border between known and unknown. The easiest story to resolve, or at least tell, is Guy Swift's, for the simple reason that he came back. His foray into the zone lasted just under a month, during which time an intensive (if under-resourced) search was conducted across the UK and northern Europe. Police followed up sightings in Bremen, Malmö, Le Havre, Portsmouth. The media circulated the theory of underworld involvement, and at one point police announced that they believed the 'runaway UK businessman' had orchestrated his own disappearance to avoid financial problems.

After his return to the UK, Swift went to ground. The initial wave of media attention focused on the possibility of legal action. Everyone confidently expected a damages claim, a claim he surely would have won given the extraordinary treatment he had received, but it quickly became apparent that all he really wanted was to slip out of sight. The supposedly flamboyant marketeer turned out to be a poor interviewee. His few press statements were unrevealing, almost monosyllabic. After a while, the media lost interest.

Today anyone wanting to speak to the 'London highflyer' discovered 'washed up on holiday beach' has to find him first. Following *Tomorrow**'s collapse, its Shoreditch offices were sold and the old sweatshop now houses a direct-mail company. Its former CEO is no longer resident at his old riverside address and does not appear on the electoral register elsewhere in London. Research confirms that a Battersea estate agency handled the sale of the In Vitro apartment on behalf of *Tomorrow**'s creditors, but they will say only that the new owner is a US-based financial institution which uses the place as accommodation for senior staff visiting London. Swift's former CFO and creative director, both now working at the Geist Agency, claim to have had no contact with him since his ill-fated Brussels trip. Interestingly both hint that it was Swift's changed personality and lack of interest in *Tomorrow**, rather than its ongoing liquidity problems, which ultimately caused its demise. Speaking on the phone from LA, where she is working as a lifestyle manager, his former assistant Kika Willis puts it simply: 'He wasn't Guy any more. It turned him into a freak.'

Determined digging will finally lead up a long rutted farm track which runs off a winding b-road in the North Pennines. At its end, sheltering under a lowering granite escarpment, is a single-storey stone cottage with deep-set windows and a slate roof, a squat little structure designed to withstand battering by the Northumbrian wind and rain. The bleak landscape around it has changed very little in hundreds of years. Sheep graze moorlands marked by dry-stone boundary walls. Down in the valley a river cuts a channel through rich pasturage that is waterlogged in spring and frozen hard in winter. The nearest village is five miles away. From a distance the house appears disused. Rusting agricultural equipment sits outside, and on a rainy day the only hint of colour is the red paintwork of the elderly Ford Fiesta parked by the door. The plume of smoke rising up from the chimney comes as a shock, a sign of human presence where none was expected.

The man who opens the door does not look much like the press photos which circulated at the time of his disappearance. He wears a full beard, which hides much of his face and gives him a severe and patriarchal look. He is dressed in shapeless cord trousers and a thick cableknit sweater with a hole in the sleeve. It would be hard to imagine someone who looks less like a London media-agency boss.

As Guy leans over an elderly gas stove to boil water for tea, the visitor seated at the kitchen table can surreptitiously look at his or her surroundings. The oak table is scarred and pitted by years of use. A set of windchimes hangs by the window, and on the sill by the sink there is a row of odd misshapen pots holding garden herbs. The impression is of neatness, domesticity. As he brings the tea, served in big blue and white enamel mugs, you might notice his hands. They are calloused, the nails cracked and dirty.

Guy likes to talk about the earth. It is, he claims, the source of life. 'Before,' he recalls, 'I lived under a great deal of geopathic stress.' He subscribes to the theory that London (and to a lesser extent other cities) causes an immense distortion of the earth's natural energy field, a distortion which inflicts physical and psychological suffering on the people forced to live inside it. 'It took,' he says, shaking his head, 'a total life change to get me well again.' Moving to this remote spot was the only solution. 'Otherwise things would have run away from me completely.'

The earth is also behind Guy's post life-change career choice. The pots on the windowsill are his. One room of the cottage has been converted into a workshop, complete with a wheel and a small electric kiln. At the drop of a hat he will demonstrate his throwing technique, or offer to share the secrets of a favourite blue glaze. Despite his enthusiasm, he is not the most talented potter, but, though they may be lumpy and erratic, his pieces have a certain charm. They are sincere pots. The new Guy Swift is a sincere man.

Ragdale Scar, the escarpment behind the cottage, plays an iconic role in Guy's life. It is the source, he says, of his healing power. Somehow it seems best to skirt the question of his having a healing power in the first place. He has had little success in selling his ceramics, and, though he put up a notice in a nearby village pub, no one has yet come to him to be geopathically realigned, despite the conditional refund offer. Recently he has started to supplement his dole money by helping a crew of local men repair field walls.

His most treasured possession is a small bottle of sand. It comes from the beach in Puglia where he was found by *carabinieri* in what the British Consul in Naples drily terms 'a state of distress', having been dumped from a dinghy into the sea some distance from shore by a crew of Albanian people-smugglers. The story he told the police was barely credible, and when it was confirmed caused ripples throughout the European Union, not least in the offices of the nascent Pan European Border Authority, which was later held directly accountable.

He was, he thinks, partly to blame. Blind drunk and heinously misaligned, he allowed himself to be taken to an unknown suburb of a strange city by a woman of easy virtue. He describes himself now, with a certain prim disgust, as a 'drinker and substance abuser', though these traits were, he accepts, evidence of the distorted geomagnetism of his living and working environment. He has no distinct memory of what happened to him between leaving the lapdancing club with the woman he knew as Irina and waking up some time later, lying on a bed in a small room with green bamboo-patterned wallpaper. Black plastic had been taped over the window. Apart from the bed and a chipped melamine dresser, the room was empty.

His head ached and he was naked apart from his tie, which was tied round his head like a Japanese headband. He was still wearing his watch, which told him it was 5.10 a.m., news that threw him into a panic because of the pitch meeting later that day. He found his clothes under the bed and stumbled out of the door to find himself looking down the stairwell of some kind of apartment building. The door on the other side of the landing was open and through it he could see a bedroom full of Chinese men, sitting two or three to a bunk, smoking and playing cards beneath lines of drying washing. He wondered if he was in some kind of hostel.

A bell rang. Someone must have opened the front door, because the next thing he heard was the sound of shouting, and heavy boots coming up the stairs. Half awake and hung over, he reacted slowly. All around him chaos was erupting. Chinese men were running by, clutching trousers and cigarette cartons and pairs of trainers. A pair of young East African women, one carrying a baby in a sling, ran on to the landing, then turned round and fled back inside. Guy decided to return to his room. Whatever was happening had nothing to do with him. A moment later he was gripped in a headlock by a man dressed in a dark blue Belgian police uniform.

'All right,' he remembers calling out in English. 'Christ. Take it easy.'

The policeman forced him to the ground and kneeled on his neck. 'English,' Guy gurgled. 'I'm fucking *English*.' By that time he had worked out what was happening. He was in the middle of an immigration raid.

He did not make the connection with Operation Atomium until he was already in the police van. He had been squeezed in with the East African women, several Chinese still in their underwear and a shaven-headed gendarme who looked blankly at him when he tried to talk to him in English. Going through his pockets, he realized his wallet and phone were missing. He supposed Irina had stolen them. At least she had left his watch. It was a good watch. It was water resistant to 200 metres.

As the van made its way through the streets of Brussels, the Chinese men started to smoke and talk in low unconcerned voices, as if this were just another confined space, just the latest in a series. The police van filled up with a blue tobacco haze, and Guy tried to work out the quickest way of extricating himself. With no ID it would, he supposed, take an hour or two to establish his identity. He would be short of sleep, but he should still make the meeting. He might get time to have an hour's nap. There was even a potential upside to what was happening. In a certain light, being picked up in PEBA's first coordinated sweep could be viewed as a work-related activity. He was seeing the system in operation. His misadventure was actually *research*. Mentally he started to script a new section of his presentation. *At Tomorrow* we believe in getting our hands dirty. We believe in first-hand knowledge of the brand in action* . . . He settled down on the metal bench and smiled at the people opposite him. All he needed was Nurofen and access to a phone. Everything was going to be fine.

A temporary processing centre had been set up by Belgian immigration in a hangar at Zaventem Airport. The van parked at a side entrance and, still smiling, Guy was given a number and led into a holding area. Sitting on plastic seats were tall Somalis and tiny Latinos, Nigerians and Byelorussians, Filipinos and Kazakhs. Groups of young men conferred in huddles. Parents comforted crying babies. There were more illegals than Guy had expected. It looked as if they had turned the city upside down and shaken it. An impressive operation.

After a few minutes of relatively interesting observational research, his good mood began to fray. His chair was uncomfortable, and the elderly Arab next to him kept falling asleep on his shoulder. Though he tried to attract the attention of the guards, none seemed interested in talking to him. He spoke loudly and clearly. *I am EU cit-i-zen. I need ta-xi to my ho-tel.* As the minutes lengthened, his serenity waned to irritation.

He tried to snatch some sleep, but was kept awake by the noise and the brightness of the hangar's halogen lights. One by one the detainees were being interrogated in a row of roofless cubicles at the far end of the hangar. Afterwards, most were returned to the holding area. At 7.45 a.m. his number was finally called. He went in shouting, giving full vent to several hours' worth of indignation. Leaning across her ugly little desk, he berated the immigration officer, demanding instant access to the British Consul and throwing around phrases like 'wrongful arrest' and 'unlawful detention' with all the righteous anger of a man whose free passing has been subject to both let and hindrance, and who reckons that local standards of assistance and protection have fallen well below what Her Britannic Majesty would expect.

Though factually he was probably justified in most of the points he made, his approach was unhelpful. The officer appeared unruffled, addressing him first in French and then (when he screamed at her that she was a stupid deaf bitch who would lose her job in two minutes if she didn't fucking call him a cab) switching to English to ask in a flat monotone, 'What is your name?'

He told her his name. She asked his real name. He told her his name again, and then told her to fuck off.

'You speak very good English,' she said. 'What is your first language?'

'*English*, you idiotic tart.'

Banging the table was a bad idea. She must have pressed some kind of panic button, because two policemen ran into the room, threw him to the floor and sat on his back, cracking his head against the concrete a couple of times to make sure he got the point. Only when they judged that he was calm did they let him sit back down on the chair. Each time he spoke he was told to be silent. The third time he opened his mouth one of the policemen casually slapped him round the face. He was too stunned to be angry.

The immigration officer had no further questions for him. He made conciliatory faces at her, increasingly desperate faces intended to convey strong European fellow feeling. She supervised as the policemen took his fingerprints and would not meet his eye as he was frogmarched out of the room towards a part of the hangar he supposed was the secure area, a screened-off wire-mesh enclosure patrolled by policemen carrying semi-automatic weapons.

The enclosure held about a dozen men, who eyed him suspiciously. He looked at his watch. It was just after 8 a.m. At 8.30 a.m. he finally gave in to the crushing realization that none of his fellow prisoners had a mobile. He had repeated the world *telephone* in various accents, spreading out the fingers of one hand and making circling motions with the other. He was stuck. He decided to try to get some sleep.

At 9.15 a.m. two Afghans tried to steal his watch. They were prevented by the guards. After that he tried to stay awake.

At 10.20 a.m. he was called into a second interview room. Two men sat behind a desk. There were no other chairs. His police escorts stayed at his side. As one man addressed him in bursts of rapid French, the second translated into a strange, guttural language full of *z*'s and *j*'s. Guy kept asking them to speak English, repeating that he did not understand, that there had been a mistake, until the interviewer threw up his hands in an expression of mock-despair and said something which made everyone else in the room burst out laughing. A formal declaration of some kind was read out, in which he was addressed as Monsieur Georges something or other. 'Please,' he told them, 'je ne comprends. I'm not that person. I'm British. Moi Guy Swift, citeezahn Breeteesh.'

The immigration officer smiled. 'Of course, *Mr Swift*,' he said sarcastically. The policemen led him out of the room.

It was the man's smug expression that made Guy panic. Certainty in a job well done, *good riddance to bad rubbish*. He started to scream that he needed a lawyer, was being kidnapped, had to get to an important meeting. A policeman winded him with a swift blow to the stomach, which stopped him struggling long enough to be handcuffed and thrown back into the wire-mesh pen. He shook the wire, shouting for help and banging the fence posts with the heel of his shoe in the vain hope that someone else in the room, some British police observer perhaps, would hear his accent and come to his rescue. He made so much trouble that he was taken across the tarmac on to the specially chartered plane with his hands and legs cuffed to a wheelchair. Tape was stuck over his mouth to stop him shouting, and a motorcycle helmet was shoved down over his head to prevent him biting his escorts or knocking himself out, both of which he had been seriously considering as options. At 2 p.m., when he was supposed to be sitting down with Director Becker and the other members of the PEBA public presentation working group, he was at 35,000 feet, flying deportation class en route to Tiranë, Albania.

How Guy Swift, young marketeer, British national and vocal speaker of English came to be identified as Gjergj Ruli, Albanian national, suspected pyramid fraudster and failed asylum seeker in Germany was one of the more bizarre stories to result from the infection of the Schengen Information System by what is now known as Variant Eight Leela, the so-called transpositional worm. The 'shuffling' action of *Leela08*, which randomly reassociates database attributes, was responsible for the destruction of a huge number of EU immigration records before it was finally spotted and the system closed down some thirty-six hours after Guy Swift's deportation. The same infection in machines hosting the Eurodac fingerprint database produced a number of false positives, identifying innocent people as known criminals, failed asylum seekers or persons being monitored by European intelligence services. Combinations of the two types of infection led (at a conservative estimate) to some thirty mistaken deportations. Since Operation Atomium relied almost entirely on two bullet-pointed strengths – [slide 1] *the fast identification of deportation candidates through Eurodac and the SIS*; and [slide 2] *special powers to accelerate processing of deportation candidates* – it led to a situation in which (among other abuses) people were plucked from their homes at night and deposited in some of the world's more troubled places without so much as a change of clothes, let alone money or a way of contacting home. Ukrainian brothers Pyotr and Yuri Kozak made contact with members of a Russian oil-exploration team who spotted them begging outside a bar in Port Harcourt, Nigeria. A Pakistani grandmother, 71-year-old Noor Begum, who had been visiting her family in Bradford, was repatriated from the Yemen via a religious charity.

Asked to describe Tiranë, Guy Swift just shakes his head. 'I won't talk about that place,' he mutters. On his return, doctors described him as being 'in poor physical condition'. The nature of the twenty-six days he spent in Tiranë can only be guessed at from the testimony of Albanians who saw a man fitting his description foraging for scraps behind restaurants in the city centre.

The only aspect of his time in Albania that Guy is prepared to discuss is the kindness shown to him by someone called Rudolph, a seventeen-year-old Liberian he met near the ferry dock at the port of Durrës. It was Rudolph who helped him sell his watch, which he had miraculously managed to keep safe, in return for a berth on one of the regular powerboat runs which took would-be Europeans to the Italian coast.

The boat was a small inflatable dinghy, carrying two crewmen and four other passengers, a Bangladeshi couple and their two children. The sea was choppy and visibility was poor. When the lights of a customs launch were spotted in the distance, the two traffickers immediately pitched all five of them into the sea. As Guy fell overboard, he remembers his absolute sense of certainty that he would drown. Asked what passed through his mind, he refuses to answer. It was, he says, 'just luck' that he swam in the right direction. He was washed ashore just before dawn on a tourist beach south of Bari. At first light he was found, semi-conscious, muttering incoherently and clutching handfuls of European sand. He has, he says, no idea what happened to the Bangladeshis.

Guy Swift dominated the media for two or three days after his return. Arjun Mehta, the 'evil scientist' (*New York Post*) whose 'twisted genius' (London *Evening Standard*) threatened the world with 'techno meltdown' (Sydney *Daily Telegraph*), has rarely been out of the headlines since the last confirmed sighting of him at the Riverside Motel in San Ysidro. Despite an immense investment of police time and resources, Mehta, whose image is now one of the most widely circulated in the world, has never been apprehended. The FBI believes he is no longer alive, a position they recently reaffirmed despite the negative outcome of DNA matches performed on a corpse, thought to be his, dredged out of the LA river.

The San Ysidro Factory Outlet Center has become a favourite pilgrimage site for conspiracy theorists, who take notes and photographs, speak into dictaphones and measure distances with pocket ultrasonic devices. Like the Zapruder footage or the Watergate Tapes, the mall's surveillance record of Arjun Mehta's seemingly aimless amble from the Timberland Store to Starbucks has been pored over, debated and scrutinized for signs of tampering by the police and security services. As Leela researchers try to forge connections, reaching into ever more recondite areas of speculation, the other people on the tapes, the 'pony-tailed man', the 'loving couple' and the slight figures of Kim Sun Hong and Jordan Lee have all been the subject of intense research. So far the results are inconclusive. As time passes and the volume of secondary material increases, the true meaning of the Leela occlusions is becoming, if anything, more obscure.

Attention has focused on the $8.99 yellow-rimmed 'Freebird' plastic sunglasses purchased by Mehta during the so-called 'coffee-walk'. Their conspicuousness invites speculation that they were some kind of signal, a position reaffirmed (or according to other Mehtologists, refuted) by the ethnicity of the clerk. Sunglasses manufactured in South Korea. Bought from a clerk of Vietnamese origin. On various Leela websites a photograph of the Seoul plant where model 206-y was manufactured is presented as evidence. Beside the company name is the Cho-Sun Plastics logo: a dancing female figure.

From Mehta's behaviour on the tapes, it appears he was unaware that he was being followed. As he walked into Starbucks, he was picked up by the in-store camera, which recorded him putting down his bag, conspicuously polishing his new Freebird model 206-y's and fishing in his pocket for money. Some weeks after the coffee-walk a tape surfaced, purportedly made by a student sitting at a table near the cash register who was conducting an interview for a graduate history project. In the background of a conversation about the Little Landers, a utopian agrarian community which existed in San Ysidro in the early years of the twentieth century, two voices can be heard. Spectrographic analysis has confirmed that they belong to Arjun Mehta and Ramona Luisa Velasquez, whose biography on the LeelaTruth site alleges that soon after the conversation she was fired, ostensibly for joining a union. It should be noted that even LeelaTruth's floridly paranoid webmaster has failed to connect this to the main thrust of his Mehta-disappearance theory, which unites the Rosicrucians, CNN and the opening of the global pineal eye.

A transcript of the so-called Little Lander tape:

VOICE 1 [Arjun Mehta]: Latte to go please.

VOICE 2 [Ramona Velasquez]: Regular or tall?

AM: Tall.

[inaudible]

RV: There you go / That'll be two thirty-five / Sugar and lids are over there.

AM: Thanks.

RV: No problem / [inaudible: *on a ten*?] / Have a nice day.

AM: [inaudible]

There is very little, short of cabbalistic letter substitution, that can be done to extract hidden meaning from this exchange. This has not stopped prominent Leela researchers from claiming variously that (a) Velasquez passed some kind of tool or document to Mehta in the coffee cup; (b) she was in the pay of a governmental agency (probably the Bureau of Alcohol, Tobacco and Firearms); or (c) the drop-outs on the tape were caused by the high-frequency electronic data bursts which the Old Ones use in place of human speech.

Despite being labelled a terrorist by governments and media agencies around the world, Arjun Mehta has admirers. According to Julia Schaffer of the Symantec Corporation, who has written extensively on Mehta's programming techniques, the viruses he unleashed represent 'a revolution in code'. The range of the innovations in the Leela variant viruses is, she says, 'simply breathtaking'. Her research group has developed several applications based on Mehta polymorphic engines. 'He was a black hat,' she admits, 'and that's kind of a shame.' Pinned to the corkboard by her desk she has Mehta's picture, next to that of Claude Shannon.

The figures of the outlaw and the unrecognized genius are dear to many in the computer underground, and Mehta (combining both) has become a hero to a younger generation of disaffected hackers who feel their contributions are undervalued by the corporations and misunderstood by an ignorant and hostile public. Judging by the hagiographic tone of postings and zine articles, there is certainly no shortage of people who would be willing to assist the fugitive if he arrived on their doorstep. The supernatural perfection of his vanishing act has only added to his mystique. A series of autonomist tracts written in Italian and signed with his name caused a huge stir in left-wing European political circles. The hope that the genius hacker might also be a revolutionary was so strong in certain quarters that it has survived the revelation that the Leela papers were the creation of a group of Bologna-based radicals, who had appropriated Mehta's name as a gesture and invited anyone else who wished to use it to do the same. In recent times 'Arjun Mehta' has authored statements on the food industry and the World Trade Organization. His Virugenix employee ID photo, the same one Julia Schaffer has by her desk, has been screen-printed on to t-shirts with humorous anti-capitalist slogans. Arjun Mehta, Gap loyalty-card holder and habitué of Seattle Niketown, is rapidly changing shape.

For a long time the police could not explain Kim Sun Hong's presence in Arjun Mehta's hotel room. The boy was from a conservative middle-class Korean family, a good student whose main interest was in computer gaming. Nothing in his previous behaviour suggested any propensity for violence, let alone terrorist connections. Questions abounded. Had Mehta met the boy in a chatroom? Was there a paedophile link? Had Hong been coerced into assisting Mehta in his 'campaign to undermine America' (Fox News)? Civil-rights groups accused the police of covering up their reckless use of firearms. Korean-Americans demonstrated outside San Diego City Hall. The claim that the teenager had 'levelled his weapon' at Officer Corey Studebaker was widely disbelieved.

A breakthrough in the police investigation came only when analysis of mall surveillance tapes recorded images of Hong and another boy following Mehta at a distance. Jordan Lee, a classmate, was identified as Hong's companion and rapidly broke down under interrogation. The story he told police was so fantastic that for some days they refused to believe it. Could he and Hong, aged respectively thirteen and fourteen, really have been acting as bounty hunters?

The Criminal Investigation Bureau of the Korean National Police Agency substantiated the background to Lee's tale. Logs subpoenaed from the Boba Fett Game Café did the rest. It seemed that five days before the Riverside raid, a computer centre in Seoul was hit by variant 04 (*rhizomatic*) Leela, not one of the more destructive strains but difficult and time-consuming to eradicate. The incident would barely have registered had the centre not housed the servers for ElderQuest, an online role-playing game vastly popular in Korea.

ElderQuest is set in a fantasy world with the usual furniture of dragons, wizardry, castles and large-breasted barbarian women. Players, of whom there are four million in Korea alone (almost one in twelve of the entire population), join adventuring groups, trying to gain the power and experience points which will allow them to move up in the social hierarchy of the cod-medieval land of Yerba. When not battling an array of monsters, players spend time in various kinds of social interaction. Marriages are contracted. Political factions are formed and dissolved. There is even a legal system, set up to curb the actions of those who abuse ElderQuest's complicated barter system. Economists have written papers about the evolution and management of the game's markets. Korean social scientists are starting to look seriously at so-called Virtual World Syndrome, whose sufferers appear conflicted about the value of their real and game-world experiences.

The Leela infection meant that the ElderQuest servers had to be shut down and reset from backups, an operation which took two days and involved some loss of data. Effectively, all the characters operating within the game-world found themselves back where they had been two days previously, minus all experience and attributes picked up in the interim.

This was annoying for many people but disastrous for the Honour Friend Sword Clan. The day before the shutdown their surprise attack had decimated the superior forces of Lord Farfhrd's

Power Blood Pledge Society, gaining them control of Castle Obsidian and a huge quantity of treasure. Now safely in possession of the Axe of Maldoror, S'tha the Muscular had attained the forty-fifth level in Swordsmanship and would henceforth receive tithes from all the lands around the castle and the nearby free city of Bigburgh. It was the greatest victory in the clan's history. After the reboot the Power Blood Pledge, who now had foreknowledge of the attack, descended on S'tha's camp under the protection of an Adamantine Shield spell and killed sixteen characters, including S'tha himself, who was reincarnated in Freetown as a first-level apprentice with three gold pieces, a knife and a small leather buckler. S'tha and the Honour Friend Sword were understandably angry.

S'tha (in real life 26-year-old Li Kwan Young, well known to Seoul police) had not simply lost imaginary status and treasure. So popular is ElderQuest that its potions, scrolls, weapons and armour have real-world value: the going rate on eBay for a good-quality summoning spell is over $80. Young, who had amassed an enormous magical armoury (allegedly through extortion of other players), had lost a genuine fortune.

Young wrote several outraged emails to the game administrators. He was told there was nothing they could do. In desperation he and several other players from Honour Friend Sword turned up at the offices of NambiSoft, the game's owners, to demand the reinstatement of their victory. When security tried to remove them from the building, a scuffle broke out in the lobby and the police had to be called.

By any standards, the following day's posting to the ElderQuest message scrolls was an escalation. Honour Friend Sword offered fireballs, invisibility lotions, the Stay Wand of Ha-Shek and other game goods to the value of 30,000 gold pieces to anyone prepared to 'undertake a RL quest' to 'disincarnate' the person who caused the server reset. Mehta's picture was being widely circulated by the FBI. The amount of the bounty was huge. To the amazement of the police investigators, it appeared Jordan Lee was telling the truth. Every reality-challenged role player in the world had been out looking for Arjun Mehta. He and Hong were just the ones who got lucky. They had skipped school and tailed him to San Ysidro, checking his face against the FBI mugshot. To get the gun, they had traded Tiger Woods's home phone number with a Thai kid who came into Boba Fett's to play Starcraft. At the Riverside Motel, Jordan had got scared, and after a whispered argument Hong (who in the previous month had logged 210 hours connected to the ElderQuest servers as Peenar the Stealthy, an eighteenth-level footpad) had climbed through the window alone. At the critical moment Jordan was waiting on a street corner two blocks away. He did not see Mehta at any point after he came out on to the balcony.

Jordan Lee was never charged with anything, although Boba Fett's computing equipment was confiscated, and it eventually lost its licence. As the only person to have spent time observing Mehta in the hours before his disappearance, Lee rapidly acquired celebrity status. He underwent hypnosis on television, testified before the Homeland Security Select Committee of the House of Representatives and now makes regular public appearances at gaming and paranormal conventions around the US.

A major area of disagreement among Mehtologists is how Arjun made his escape from the Riverside Motel. Various methods have been proposed, ranging from the theory that he impersonated Consuelo Guttierez, an off-duty chambermaid inexplicably sighted at work that morning, to the possibility he spent several hours wedged above a ceiling panel in the bathroom. However he managed it, his trail went completely cold in San Ysidro, and most people believe he crossed the border, probably in disguise. There was no further activity on his bank account. He did not, despite careful surveillance, appear to make contact with family or known acquaintances. How is it possible, in a world of electronic trails, log files, biometrics and physical traces of every kind to slip so completely away? Researchers have tried to prove connections with the criminal underworld, or the various international terrorist organizations to which, in the first hysterical days of the manhunt, he was linked. So far, nothing convincing has emerged. Were there friends who might have provided assistance? One possible accomplice was the 'pony-tailed man' caught on camera at the outlet mall, whom many people have identified as Nicolai Petkanov, the boyfriend of the woman whose car Mehta stole when fleeing Redmond. A convicted virus writer, Petkanov denies ever having met Mehta, but confirms that it was a trace placed on a landline at the address he shared with Christine Rebecca Schnorr which led the FBI to the Riverside Motel. Schnorr has admitted a romantic relationship with Mehta, a relationship of which Petkanov was apparently aware. Whether this makes his cooperation in a plot to assist Mehta more or less likely is hard to know. Schnorr, confusingly, denies that she had any kind of conversation with Mehta after he left Redmond. She and Petkanov have both recently relocated to Mexico, where they intend to set up a body-modification parlour in Oaxaca.

Journalists researching Mehta's background have focused on his use of the North Okhla Institute of Technology server as a test-bed and distribution node for his viruses. When they became established in new host machines, certain Leela variants even downloaded plug-ins from this site. The lack of security was universally condemned, and admissions for NOIT's information-science courses have boomed. Unfortunately Mehta seems to have formed no strong personal bonds with anyone from his course, and interviews with former teachers and classmates have yielded few clues.

Aamir Khan, manager of Gabbar Singh's Internet Shack and Mehta's only known close friend, is considered the most likely source of help. Sought by police in connection with various offences under the Indian Penal Code relating to the distribution of pornography, Khan has not been seen since soon after Mehta's identification as the originator of the Leela viruses. Did he organize fake papers for his friend, then fly him to a clinic in Shanghai for facial reconstruction? Did he send him through a network of mujahedin safehouses to an underground madrassa in Kandahar? Gabbar Singh's is now a fancy-goods shop, much to the disappointment of the stream of teenage boys who turn up to hang around outside the door. The manager, disregarding the entrepreneurial opportunity staring him in the face, has hired a chowkidar to drive them away.

Mehta's family no longer live in Noida. The media attention, not to mention the grief and worry about their son, led them to flee India for Australia, where they now stay close to their daughter and son-in-law in the Sydney suburb of Fairfield. Mr Mehta, who has retired from the world of business, refuses all interviews. Priti Chaudhuri and her husband Ramesh released a statement through their lawyer to the effect that they have not had contact with Arjun since he fled Redmond and do not believe in the 'wilder accusations' made against him.

Like Arjun Mehta, Leela Zahir has never reappeared. Despite the evidence that she had planned her exit, India went into hysterical mourning on hearing the news, as if their star were dead instead of missing. One fan announced that he would walk backwards from Bangalore to Madurai to propitiate God to bring her back. There were unconfirmed reports of people setting themselves on fire.

Tender Tough looked doomed, but, with a certain amount of coaxing from his backers, Rocky Prasad managed to swallow his artistic scruples about completing the film with another actress. The version which made it to the screen includes scenes in which the young dancer Shanti is seen only from behind, and throughout the film the character's voice has been dubbed, yet it contains several moments which possess an extraordinary retrospective poignancy. The song 'Now You See Me, Now You Don't', including the legendary battlements sequence, can still, after all this time, be heard blaring from every tea stall in the country. Frame by frame, people have searched it for some clue about Leela Zahir's state of mind. Her Scottish 'illness' and her history of personal problems soon came into the public domain, providing weeks of fodder for the film magazines, but as the camera lunges towards the tiny figure dancing on top of the castle, it reveals no sign of sadness or disaffection. Quite the opposite: in no other performance does Leela look so completely, joyously engaged with the world. She is so alive that her imminent absence appears obscene, proof of a terrible and oppressive power over human life.

The film, it goes without saying, was a huge hit. Prasad, Iqbal and Rana were photographed drinking virgin coladas at the lavish première, held in a Mumbai hotel banqueting suite decorated to look like a Pacific Island. After ritual expressions of sorrow at Leela's absence and a few minutes of vague embarrassment, things more or less proceeded as normal. Deals were struck, catty remarks were made behind glamorous backs, and everyone looked over each other's shoulders as they chatted, in case something scandalous was occurring on the other side of the room. The film world knew they had lost something in Leela Zahir. They just didn't know what they ought to feel about it.

A more honest reaction came from Leela's people, the faithful cinema fans who had projected their desires on to her towering luminous face. Eighteen months after its release, *Tender Tough* was still showing daily at one Mumbai cinema. People had already started to refer to the missing actress as Leeladevi, and among the cinema-goers, Hindu and Muslim alike, her simplicity, her beauty and above all her supernatural absence had come to seem like holy qualities. Little votive pictures appeared on market stalls. In a village in Bihar, a boy was reported to have been miraculously cured of blindness while a pirated VHS of the film was being shown on the headman's television.

How the film star vanished from the Clansman's Lodge Hotel came to light only after the tragic death of the wife of media mogul Brent Haydon. During the eighteen months of her marriage, Gabriella Haydon-Caro had been a fixture on the European and American social circuits. She and her husband, who at fifty-five was gradually stepping down from the day-to-day running of his various interests, had described a glittering eastward path across the globe, from their Bel Air home to their ski lodge in Aspen, through the Grenadines, the Hamptons, Barcelona, San Tropez and finally Mykonos, where they chartered a yacht to take a group of friends on a three-week cruise around the Greek islands. Their progress was fawningly documented by European paparazzi, and several photographers witnessed the third Mrs Haydon's death from Elia Beach, the nearest public vantage point to the *Paloma*'s mooring. It seemed impossible that she had not seen the jet ski skimming across the water. Indeed pictures appear to show her looking in its direction seconds before she dived from the deck of the yacht. She was killed instantly.

A few days after the body was flown to Firenze for cremation, a French lawyer stunned the world by announcing that two weeks previously Mrs Haydon had deposited with him a computer disk, with instructions that in the event of her death it be passed on to newspapers in the US and Europe. The disk turned out to contain a single document, an erratic and rambling narrative which is part autobiography, part diary of the first year of her marriage. She describes an unhappy early life, alienated from her father and unable to make friends because of her mother's peripatetic lifestyle. Repeatedly she returns to her sister's suicide. In one undated line, she writes, '*Chaque jour plus vite: Caroline, moi.*' She appears to have married on a whim, meeting her husband when he came to view a penthouse in the building where she lived with her former boyfriend. 'I just wanted to go somewhere,' she writes. 'I didn't really care where.'

Though affecting, most of the material is only of personal interest. The important passages concern the period just before she met her husband, when she was working as a film publicist and became involved in the Leela Zahir disappearance. The Indian media had developed a particular fascination for her because of a rumoured entanglement with Rajiv Rana. The document appears, in part, to be a statement to them, in which she confesses to helping Leela leave Scotland.

Mrs Haydon's testament appears to show that Zahir's disappearance was not abduction (as her mother claimed) or suicide, but a well-planned bid to 'escape prison'. 'Why would she stay?' she writes. 'She had nothing. It was a kind of prostitution.' The idea that Leela Zahir, idol to the nation, was actually the 'slave of her brothel-keeper mother' shocked India profoundly. Leela's suffering augmented her holiness, and angry mobs gathered outside several houses owned by members of the film community, burning Faiza Zahir's Pali Hill residence to the ground in a night of rioting that spread across Mumbai and left several people dead. Faiza Zahir was abroad at the time, and now occasionally rings journalists from her new home in Dubai to denounce the 'Caro bitch' as a liar.

Gabriella Haydon writes that she was looking out of her window at the Clansman's Lodge Hotel, when a face appeared at it looking 'like Cathy in *Wuthering Heights*'. Since she was on an upstairs floor, this was quite frightening. As she stared in horror, she realized it was Leela Zahir, who had somehow climbed up on to the roof and then down a drainpipe to tap on her window. She let the girl in and found that she was warmly dressed, and carrying a small backpack. To her surprise Leela 'hugged me and said I was her only friend. We sat on the bed and she told me about her life and the things her mother made her do. I was horrified.'

Gabriella claims Leela had a well-thought-out plan of escape, but needed help. 'I was sympathetic to her,' she writes, 'and I hated all the people involved in that film. So I said I would hide her in my room and drive her to Inverness Airport the next morning.' She did not ask where she was heading after that, but 'she said she had a friend. A boyfriend, she said, and then corrected herself. He was not a boyfriend, but she'd talked to him on the internet and they were going to meet each other. She did not say any more.'

The next morning, while police were beginning an intensive search that would eventually involve helicopters and teams of divers searching Loch Lone, Gabriella made good on her promise. 'We said almost nothing to each other during the journey. Then she took her bag and walked into departures. I thought of asking to go with her.'

By the early autumn, the various Leela-variant viruses had been brought under control. Shaken sysops were able to go into work without a sense of dread, and computer-security specialists started to count their money. Of course blame had to be apportioned somewhere, and by general consensus it fell on the Virugenix corporation. With its reputation shredded and its share price locked into a downward spiral, the company's senior management was forced to resign en masse. Even this was not enough to turn things round, and within a year the Virugenix brand had disappeared from the world's screens, its assets absorbed by its rivals. From a secret address in Montana, former Ghostbuster Darryl Gant now runs Mehtascourge.org, one of the more extreme Leela research sites, which focuses on hunting down the man he sees behind many of the world's ills, from his own redundancy to the scaling down of the American space programme.

Gant has his work cut out. There are sightings of Arjun Mehta and Leela Zahir around the world, sometimes alone, sometimes in company. She is seen begging in the streets of Jakarta and talking on the phone in the back of New York cabs. He is spotted one day at an anti-globalization demo in Paris and the next coming on to the pitch in a hockey match in rural Gujarat. He has got enormously fat. She has been surgically altered to look like a European. One persistent report, mostly from Pacific Rim countries, has a young man fitting Mehta's description accompanied by a South Asian woman of a similar age, 'tomboyishly' or 'punkily' dressed. They are sometimes seen kissing or holding hands. According to conspiracy theorists, there is only one possible explanation, only one pattern that makes sense.

Acknowledgements

Thanks to Dan O'Brien of NTK, Fred Cohen, Natasha Staley, Sarah Gordon and Carey Nachemberg for technical advice. Thanks to my father for other kinds of advice. Thanks also to Simon Prosser, Jonny Geller, Donna Poppy and many others at Curtis Brown and Hamish Hamilton.